UNSEEN HORROR

Dick Britton peered into the waves of rising heat to see the distorted image of a horse and rider pounding toward him as though pursued by an unseen horror. He realized that the rider was David Davis. Why wasn't Shannon with him? They'd ridden off together less than half an hour earlier.

"What the hell happened, Dave?" Britton shouted.

Davis's eyes flooded with the terror of a stalked animal. His jersey top was stained with thick blotches of rich, fresh blood. Later, when he'd had time to think about it some, Britton would recall, with astonishment, the amount of blood that covered Davis's shirt. You could butcher a full-grown hog and not get that much blood on your clothing.

"Dick, you've got to help me," Davis gasped, his eyes wild and filled with fear. "There's been an accident, Shannon's hurt. . . ."

ROBERT HEMMING is a veteran journalist with over twenty years' experience with such papers as *The Detroit News* and *The Detroit Free Press,* as well as the author of two books.

MURDEROUS MINDS

☐ **THE SLEEPING LADY:** *The Trailside Murders Above the Golden Gate* by **Robert Graysmith.** The law finally caught David Carpenter, whose thick glasses and shy stammer concealed an insatiable sexual appetite and a murderous anger. This is the detailed story of the hideous crimes, the gripping manhunt, the sensational series of trials, and the secret self of the killer who *almost* got away with it. (402553—$5.99)

☐ **DEATH SENTENCE:** *The Murderous Odyssey of John List* by **Joe Sharkey.** The riveting story of mass-murderer John List, who savagely killed his mother, his wife and three children—then "got away with it" for eighteen years! One of the most chilling true crimes of the century.
(169476—$4.95)

☐ **THE SEARCH FOR THE GREEN RIVER KILLER by Carlton Smith and Tomas Guillen.** In this book you will meet the young women who died hideously. You will meet the men hunting for their killer. But there is one person you will not meet. The Green River Killer himself. Like London's Jack the Ripper, this one is an unsolved serial murder case.
(402391—$4.99)

☐ **FATAL VISION by Joe McGinniss.** The nationwide bestseller that tells the electrifying story of Dr. Jeffrey McDonald, the Princeton-educated Green Beret convicted of slaying his wife and children "A haunting story told in compelling detail."—*Newsweek* (165667—$5.95)

WITH MURDEROUS INTENT

ROBERT HEMMING

AN ONYX BOOK

ONYX
Published by the Penguin Group
Penguin Books USA Inc., 375 Hudson Street,
New York, New York 10014, U.S.A.
Penguin Books Ltd, 27 Wrights Lane,
London W8 5TZ, England
Penguin Books Australia Ltd, Ringwood,
Victoria, Australia
Penguin Books Canada Ltd, 2801 John Street,
Markham, Ontario, Canada L3R 1B4
Penguin Books (N.Z.) Ltd, 182–190 Wairau Road,
Auckland 10, New Zealand

Penguin Books Ltd, Registered Offices:
Harmondsworth, Middlesex, England

First published by Onyx, an imprint of New American Library,
a division of Penguin Books USA Inc.

First Printing, June, 1991
10 9 8 7 6 5 4 3 2 1

BOOKS ARE AVAILABLE AT QUANTITY DISCOUNTS WHEN USED TO PROMOTE PROD-
UCTS OR SERVICES. FOR INFORMATION PLEASE WRITE TO PREMIUM MARKETING
DIVISION, PENGUIN BOOKS USA INC., 375 HUDSON STREET, NEW YORK, NEW
YORK 10014.

In loving memory of
Albert 'Doc' Schneider, M.D.
A man of many dimensions.
I miss him.

Author's Note

Several participants in the drama to follow have requested that their true names not be used in the narrative. The requests were made for varied reasons. To secure the greatest possible cooperation from those who possess the best and most thorough information, and because I believed the requests to be reasonable, I have acceded to them. In several other instances names have been changed, physical characteristics have been altered, and geographical locations have been disguised. These changes will be apparent and understandable to the reader.

In all cases, however, I have maintained the factual integrity of the events described herein, with one important caveat. While activities and incidents surrounding the death of Shannon Mohr Davis are incontrovertible and subject to verification, the conversations recorded herein are based largely on the recollections of those who participated or were witness to them. Unfortunately, the human memory is, at best, a frail, fallible thing. Unlike a tape recording, it cannot be replayed with absolute, unquestioned accuracy; bits and pieces are sometimes distorted and become altered after several repetitions. Then, too, the passage of time causes some memory decay. Not only exact wording of conversations but their precise time and even the exact location can become blurred.

To insure that the dialogue reported here is as accurate as I can make it, I have sought to locate and interview as many actual witnesses to the events described as possible and to obtain, wherever I could, as many versions as possible of every conversation recorded in these pages, and to have the participants read those portions of this manuscript to verify their honesty and accuracy.

*I pray that love may never
come to me with murderous intent.*

—HIPPOLYTUS
428 B.C.

Prologue

A dreadful sadness hangs over the farm on Lickley Road. The small house, even on bright and sunny days, seems cloaked in dreary shadow, its coarse rural design lending a pervasive chill to the structure. Behind the house, beyond a slight rise in the cleared fields and out of sight from the road, is a small patch of woods segmented with narrow lanes and pathways, used by previous owners as a shortcut to other points on the farm and by at least one as a bridle path for horseback riding. It is here, in this dark and clammy grove, that the melancholy is most tangible. The visitor feels a cloying apprehension that death has been here, that in this place murder may have been done.

PART ONE

The Tragedy

1

The night had not gone well for Ceil; she had found sleep difficult and transitory. The oppressive heat and the sodden air of a Michigan July had kept her damp and uncomfortable. The curtains in the open windows hung flaccid, unstirred by even the gentlest breeze. She had awakened a half-dozen times, squinting through narrowed eyes, peering in vain for the signs of an approaching dawn that would reassure her that soon she could leave her bed. Being able to move about would be decidedly preferable to lying there in the choking heat and humidity. But Shannon and David were still asleep in the next room and Lucille did not want to disturb them.

She had come to the farm, reluctantly, to house-sit while her daughter and son-in-law took a short vacation trip to Florida. She didn't relish staying there while they were away; Ceil hated the place. She had hated it from the first moment she'd seen it. She thought it dingy, dirty, and depressing—there was "chicken shit from one end of the place to the other"—and it was much too isolated for someone who had been born and raised in an urban setting with shopping malls and supermarkets and restaurants and bright lights and people around. This shabby hovel, with a cow farm on one side and a pig farm on the other, wasn't a fit place for her Shannon to live.

Shannon had always been super-special to Bob and Lucille Mohr. Not that their son Bobby and daughter

Teresa weren't. But Shannon was the last child—the baby. Ceil had lost her second-born through complications in childbirth that required future deliveries to be by caesarean section. After Shannon's birth, Ceil's doctor strongly advised her not to have any more children; Shannon would be her last. As a result, mother and daughter were extremely close.

To Bob, Shannon was his vulnerable "little girl" who, even when she was grown and considered an adult by everyone's standards, still needed protection from the ills and perils the outside world threatened; there were men out there—immoral, unscrupulous men—who might try to do her harm. And, by God, anyone who tried to get funny with his beloved Shannon would answer to Bob Mohr.

Family was of paramount importance to Bob; his children were the essence of his life. He had lost his father, Raymond, when he was eight; he understood at an early age that a close familial bond was essential to survival. The years were hard for Elenore, Raymond's wife, and her three sons, Raymond, Jr., Robert, and Alton. Everyone had to pitch in, to work together to keep the family united.

In spite of the hardship, Elenore insisted that her sons acquire as much education as possible under their restricted financial situation. Bob, although strong and healthy—he eventually topped six feet in height and two hundred pounds in weight—and a lover of sports, found it necessary to forego high school athletics in favor of holding down a job.

Working his way through high school provided one small luxury for Bob: With careful management, he was able to save enough money to buy a used car. In the early forties few Toledo high school students could boast their own automobile. Bob's best friend, Ray Schneider, didn't own one. But Ray did have a favorite aunt and uncle, Lucille and Glen Abrams, whom he enjoyed visiting. He began prevailing on his car-owning buddy to transport him out to Point Place to call on his relatives. During these frequent social excursions, Bob became quite friendly with the Abramses, particularly with their pretty seventeen-year-old daughter, Lucille.

Soon after his graduation from Toledo's Central Catholic High School in 1944, Bob enlisted in the U.S. Merchant Marines, spending the next two years sailing the Atlantic in huge convoys transporting troops and material to the Mediterranean war zone. During this time he maintained a correspondence with Lucille.

Shortly after his separation from the service in 1946, Bob and Lucille were married and, as quietly impassioned Roman Catholics, set out to be fruitful and multiply. However, it was not until 1949 that their firstborn, Robert—named after his father—arrived.

In 1952, following one failed pregnancy, their second child, Teresa, was born, and two years later Shannon arrived. Their family now complete, Bob and Lucille settled in to be the best parents they could possibly be. By most measurements they succeeded admirably: The small family grew increasingly close, loving, and loyal. Robert and Lucille Mohr had every reason to be smug and contented with what they had accomplished in their marriage.

While to Ceil the 112-acre Davis farm was singularly unimpressive, it was, in fact, not unusual among the small predominantly family-owned properties in Hillsdale County. Located approximately 100 miles southwest of Detroit, abutting the Ohio border, the county consisted almost entirely of small farms that, for the most part, produced soybeans, corn, and a few other cash crops. The raising of pigs and cattle rounded out the use of the fertile, gently rolling land within the county.

The largest city, Hillsdale—the county seat—with a population of less than seventy-five hundred permanent residents, plays host for nine months each year to another thousand or so students attending Hillsdale

College, a straitlaced, conservative institution administered by the United Methodist Church.

While a number of small subcontract factories and shops have been established in both the city and the county of Hillsdale, for the most part, major manufacturing entrepreneurs found the area too far removed from rail, water, and freeway transportation to warrant locating there.

The residents are largely Protestant by faith, Republican by philosophy, suspicious by nature, and introverted by choice. "It ain't that we don't like strangers; we just naturally wonder why they would want to come here." Still, there is a polite hospitality there. Perhaps it's a Christian benevolence among those of the county that make newcomers feel warm and welcome.

The first white men to come to the area arrived in the eighteenth century. They were mostly French fur trappers and a few Catholic missionaries come to convert the heathen Potawatomi, Miami and Wyandot Indians.

Later, settlers heading for Chicago and points west passed through. What they found was bountiful wild game, fresh water, and rich soil, only slightly disturbed by the natives who had cleared the heavy timber and cultivated the virgin land to grow corn and beans and pumpkin.

The French commandant, Sier Antoine de la Mothe Cadillac, the founder of *La Ville d'Etroit* (Detroit) had, in a 1701 report to the king's ministers, described the area as: "so temperate, so fertile and so beautiful that it may justly be called the earthly paradise of North America." Far from a paradise, the cruel winters, the frequent spring floods, the occasional uprisings of the Indian tribes, and the isolation made life for those who settled there a brutal hand-to-mouth existence. It was a hard and unforgiving place, where malaria and cholera appeared in frequent and costly epidemics. But cheap land was readily available and homesteaders were welcomed and encouraged to cast their lot in the Northwest Territory of the 1700s.

Many of the residents of present-day Hillsdale County have sprung from these hearty settlers who arrived fresh from western Europe, looking for the freedom and opportunity that was denied them in the old country.

Life has never been easy for those who choose to live there. Economic recessions and depressions seem to strike quicker and deeper; drought and flood, heat and cold are felt more acutely where there is little margin between feast and famine, and where the best years have often been measured by the number of residents who have survived compared with the number who have been forced to sell out and move on.

In today's Hillsdale County, many of the farms are operated only part time, with the owners commuting to full-time jobs in Jackson or Ann Arbor or Ypsilanti. A few make the long daily trek to Detroit or to Toledo. Shannon Mohr Davis was one of these commuters, driving the fifty-plus miles to her job in Ohio.

Shannon, city born and bred, loved living in the country. A registered nurse employed by Flower Memorial Hospital in Sylvania, a suburb of Toledo, she enjoyed the tranquility found in this rural setting, a welcome alternative to the frenetic churning of the medical center.

With a good figure on a one hundred thirty-six-pound, five-foot-five frame, an oval face, and dark brown eyes that sparkled with good humor, Shannon would not have been described as gorgeous—at least not in the Hollywood sense. And yet there was a delicate quality to her countenance, an alabaster essence like an elegant cameo that allowed a beauty to radiate through an affectionate, sensitive personality. But she also owned a pixy's impishness that quickly put people at ease and made them feel that here was a very warm and special person, someone who genuinely cared, whose affection was real and offered freely.

A methodic, serious student at St. John's parochial elementary school in Toledo, Shannon, like many eight-year-old girls of that era, decided in the third grade that when she grew up she would become a nurse. But unlike most, she never wavered in her career goals. She enrolled in the Flower Hospital student nurse's program immediately upon graduation from Toledo's Central Catholic High School. In 1975, she graduated as president of her nursing school class.

Other than nursing, Shannon's great passion in life had always been a happy-go-lucky, red-headed Irish kid named Rich Duffey.

She met Rich when she was sixteen and he twenty, and they had gone steady throughout her four years in high school. By the time Shannon entered nurse's training, Rich was a Toledo fireman. He had been the only boyfriend she had ever had, and those who knew the couple best never doubted that one day they would marry.

"They had gotten engaged a couple of times," Lucille remembers, "never formally. He never actually gave her a ring but everyone just assumed that they would get married."

"They were just great together," Sheryl Miller South, a friend from nursing school, would recall. "I always thought they'd end up together. Rich was such an important part of Shannon's life."

Rich himself had assumed that, at the proper time, they would marry. But he still had many horizons to reach before scuffing the road dust from his boots.

"She wanted to get married early. I just wasn't ready . . . I couldn't see it just then."

Shannon had always dreamed that someday she would be married and have a family just like the one she had grown up in. Having completed her education and spent several years in her career, she felt it was fast becoming time when she should be concentrating on being married and having children. If Rich didn't want her, she would find someone who did.

Unfortunately, what Shannon found was a man who wanted more than he deserved, either in fairness or under the law.

She met and began dating a young man of decided charm but not much common sense. Apparently he had never come to terms with the concept of monogamy. He proposed to Shannon a few months after they began dating without advising her that he was already married and had no plans to alter that contract. He and Shannon got as far as sending out wedding invitations when his current wife found, in the trash, a stack of the invitations he had been supplied to send to his side of the family. She immediately contacted a stunned, humiliated, and deeply hurt Shannon Mohr. The wedding was canceled and Shannon never saw the young man again.

Soon Shannon and Rich were dating again, and soon they began to argue as frequently as before—petty disagreements that erupted suddenly for seemingly no reason and often ended with a mutual vow not to see each other again. But after a week or so, Rich would call Shannon, or Shannon would call Rich, and everything would be smoothed over and the couple would act as if nothing had happened.

In the summer of 1979, they separated after one of their tempestuous arguments, neither realizing then that this was to be their final estrangement. Asked later what had caused the split, Rich responded sadly, "I can't even remember why we fought the last time."

At about the same time, Regina, Shannon's close friend and nursing colleague, invited Shannon to her wedding. But Shannon was so depressed over her frustrated romance with Rich Duffey and the debasing affair with a would-be bigamist that at first she didn't think she would go.

While she was fighting indecision about attending the impending nuptials, Tom Davis, Regina's husband-to-be, was extending an invitation to one of his friends, David Richard Davis. Tom and Dave—no relation—

had met several months earlier and had become fast friends when they discovered they shared a mutual love of hunting, fishing, and other outdoor activities.

"Will there be any single women there?" David had asked Regina after announcing that he planned to attend the wedding.

"I decided to make it a point to introduce him to Shannon," Regina remembers.

"Shannon didn't want to go," Lucille recalls, "but I urged her to go anyway. 'Maybe you'll meet somebody,' I told her."

Shannon went to the wedding and did indeed meet someone. A handsome, six-foot-two, one hundred ninety pound, athletic-looking thirty-four-year-old with blonde hair, deep, piercing blue eyes, and an engaging smile. At the wedding reception, he monopolized her evening, dancing almost every dance with her. "It was almost as if he'd come to the wedding hoping to find someone like Shannon," a friend would later observe.

Within a couple of days he had called, asking her for a date, and Shannon, who was captivated by the charming, articulate young man, quickly accepted.

"His name is David Davis, he's a Vietnam veteran, he was a major in the Marines, and he's a graduate of the University of Michigan, and he played football, and he's *rich!*" Shannon gushed, describing to her mother the man who had literally swept her off her feet.

For the twenty-four-year-old woman whose greatest romantic interest had been a reluctant childhood sweetheart, David Davis thundered into her life like Prince Charming on a powerful white stallion, to carry her out of a humdrum, frustrating existence and away to a bright and sparkling world she had only imagined in secret, adolescent dreams.

Near the end of September 1979, Shannon heard again from Rich Duffey. Unaware that a new man had entered her life, Rich called to invite her on a weekend trip to northern Michigan.

"I'm sorry, Rich, I can't; I'm leaving tomorrow for Las Vegas. I'm getting married."

They talked for a long while—a tense, embarrassed conversation during which Shannon spoke glowingly of David and insisted that she had carefully thought through her decision to accept David's impetuous marriage proposal. She wanted Rich to meet David, she said. She hoped she and Rich could continue their friendship; she assured the young man that he would always have a permanent place in her heart. It was a sensitive and tender attempt to let him down easy, and he knew it. But he felt that continuing their friendship simply wasn't practical, that it wasn't going to happen.

"I didn't see her much after that," Rich recalls. "But I still thought about her. Now, I wish I could do things over."

The sudden marriage came as a surprise and a shock to Shannon's family, who had always assumed that she would have a full church ceremony with bridesmaids and flowers and a flowing white wedding gown—the kind of wedding a proper Catholic girl should have. But this was a far too momentous event in her life to darken with questions and with statements of disappointment. Ceil and Bob buried their burning regret and attempted to approach the union with optimism and good cheer.

"We were all somewhat disappointed that Shannon and David had not been married in Toledo," Cheryl Hogan Nicolaidis, a cousin and very close friend, says. "It wasn't so much that she married outside the Church; it was just that the family wasn't able to see her get married."

Shannon hadn't been thrilled about the arrangements, either. But David had said that his ideal wedding ceremony would be held in one of "those picturesque little chapels in Las Vegas." Shannon figured if that's what he really wanted, she would go along with it.

The couple made the trip west in David's pickup truck, stopping in Utah to buy, and have shipped to Michigan, an ultralight aircraft that David planned to assemble and fly. On September 24, 1979, just seven weeks and two days after having met, they were married in one of the gaudy wedding chapels scattered around the garish gambling strip.

After a brief honeymoon, the newlyweds moved into David's Hillsdale farmhouse.

When she first saw the farm, Lucille was appalled at the nonbaronial surroundings into which their new son-in-law had brought their beloved daughter.

"But, you told us David was a millionaire," Ceil said, looking in disbelief at the weed-infested yard and the dilapidated farmhouse. Shannon insisted that David was very wealthy, that he owned farms throughout the United States and in several foreign countries.

"If he's got so much money, why did he bring you to a dump like this?"

Shannon explained defensively that David's money was largely tied up in his investments, that the money would come as he sold them off. In the meantime they planned to live here because it was about midway between Lansing, where his mother and stepfather lived, and Bob and Ceil's home in Toledo. Lucille was unimpressed but said nothing further.

Yet, if she detested the rustic surroundings in which her youngest child was compelled to live, she was unstinting in her enthusiasm for the man who had brought her there.

"If you let this one get away from you, you're nuts!" she had told Shannon the first time David had come to visit.

Bob, however, was naturally suspicious of men who showed an inordinate interest in his "little girl"— especially those ten years her senior. After less than two months of dating Shannon, David presented himself, looking like an awkward high school sophomore come to pick up his first prom date, and announced to a stunned Bob Mohr that he loved Shannon and wanted to marry her. He realized, he said, that this was sudden but explained that he was terribly busy at his Hillsdale farm, and making the long trip to Toledo to see Shannon was difficult and impractical. Since they loved each other, he continued, the sensible thing to do was to get married. Bob turned a flaming red and shouted, "Don't tell me you love my daughter; you may be infatuated with her, but you haven't known her long enough to be in love. It takes time to be in love!"

David did not argue the point but it was obvious to Lucille that he was furious. Shannon, mortified at her father's uncharacteristic outburst, threw herself in her mother's arms and sobbed.

Lucille hugged her daughter close and whispered, "Don't pay attention to Daddy. We didn't know each other very long before we got married, and look how long it's lasted."

In spite of his initial apprehensions, Bob was rapidly and thoroughly charmed by the affable, intensely brilliant young man who Bob considered a "man's man," a lover of the outdoors, and someone possessing incredible physical strength.

"I've seen him pick up a huge tractor wheel and tire and lift it into place on the axle, which is no easy thing to do. Once I saw him punch one of his horses in the nose so hard it drew blood. That's not something I would want to try."

Once the marriage was a fait accompli, the family fully accepted Davis. But then how could they not? Here was a remarkable person who had lost his father in World War II, had been raised by French-speaking nuns in a Texas orphanage, spoke several foreign languages, had served heroically in Vietnam, suffered several serious wounds, yet managed to become a successful businessman.

David was not shy about his accomplishments, often

regaling friends and family with stories of his war experiences.

"He showed us scars on his back that he'd gotten after stepping on a land mine," Bob remembers. "He was hit by an overhead rocket burst that left him blind for a year in a veterans' hospital. He didn't know if he would ever see again."

To Jack Abrams, Ceil's brother, Davis once confided that the rocket had killed everyone in his platoon.

Good friend Tom Davis, a Toledo social studies teacher, invited Davis to speak to his class when they were studying the war in Vietnam.

"I know what it's like to be in combat and hold men in your arms and watch them die," he told the class. Then he broke down and wept.

To the sports fans in the family, David was a welcome addition to the clan; he loved hunting and fishing, was an excellent shot with rifle or bow and arrow, was a superb horseman, and could be an entertaining companion who had a seemingly endless collection of stories and anecdotes about his experiences.

Jack Abrams recalls that David took great pride in the fact that he had been recruited to play football at the University of Michigan by U of M's legendary coach Bo Schembechler.

"He once described what it was like to play across the line from the Michigan State All-American, Bubba Smith; he said the man was pure energy in action."

Shannon, thrilled with her family's approval, was equally ecstatic with her new husband, sometimes embarrassing Bob and Ceil—and David—by jumping on his lap and cooing, "Isn't he the most wonderful man you've ever seen?"

David was looked upon by the Mohrs as an exceptional man, a very complex, brilliant person who required patient understanding—and some tolerance. Like many highly intelligent people, Ceil insisted, he had certain idiosyncrasies, at least one of which bordered on the bizarre. He ate raw meat—not just rare or underdone but *raw*—a penchant that proved somewhat embarrassing when dining out. He also had a passion for chocolate-covered mints, which, thankfully, posed no social problem.

Lucille was not unduly troubled with her son-in-law's odd tastes. As a matter of fact, she frequently brought a pound or two of raw ground round when she came out to the farm, presenting it to David as one might offer a box of fine chocolates. "He would sprinkle the meat with garlic salt," she recalls, "and devour it like it was a juicy, sizzling steak."

Yet what he seemed to lack in some of the more acceptable graces, he more than made up for in charm and congeniality. He had always been warm and affectionate with Lucille and Bob, going out of his way to welcome them when they came to visit—which was often every week for the entire weekend. Rather than tiring of the frequency of his in-law's visits, he gave every indication of being delighted when they arrived and went out of his way to encourage them to come to the farm as often as they wished. On one occasion he had gone so far as to suggest that they move into the old farmhouse on the land he owned across the road so they might be closer. Both Bob and Lucille uttered a collective sigh of relief when, less than a week later, the antiquated building burned to the ground.

David frequently voiced his affection for her parents to Shannon, telling her that he loved them as much as if they were his own.

But on this latest visit, Ceil sensed a change in him; he'd acted annoyed at her being there, and he complained about Brian, her eight-year-old grandson—Shannon's nephew—whom Ceil had brought to the farm with her. Davis had been abrupt and churlish with Ceil and the boy throughout the three days they had spent there.

Brian had been to the farm a number of times and had always been cordially received by David, who spent a great deal of time with him, permitting him a degree of freedom his parents did not allow, letting him crawl over the machinery and climb around the barn. The boy loved his visits and was overtly fond of David. This time, however, Davis had been less than thrilled when Ceil, Brian, and Bob had arrived.

He was in the yard working on a new van he had recently purchased when they drove up. He briefly glanced up and, rather than coming to the car to greet them as had been his habit, he immediately went back to work, offering no more than an unpleasant grunt as welcome.

Ceil went into the house searching for Shannon. When her daughter saw her, she burst into tears, sobbing, ''I'm so glad you're here.'' Ceil had asked what the trouble was, but before Shannon could reply David had entered the kitchen and Shannon quickly dried her eyes and changed the subject. Ceil assumed that the couple, after ten months of relative bliss, had experienced their first spat and that perhaps Shannon would bring up whatever had been bothering her later, but she never did.

Ceil hadn't planned to stay at the farm on this trip. She'd had Bob drive her there to bring some clothes and other articles she would need later. She was intending to go back to Toledo with Bob to attend a ceramics class, leaving Brian until she returned later in the week just prior to Shannon and David's departure for Florida. But as they were preparing to leave later that afternoon, Brian suddenly threw his arms around Ceil's legs and pleaded that she not leave him.

''You go ahead,'' David had insisted. ''Go, he'll be all right. You go ahead.'' Ceil glanced over David's shoulder at Shannon, who was standing behind and out of her husband's view. Her eyes wide, a pained look on her face, Shannon was shaking her head, silently beseeching Ceil to not leave.

''Go on back to Toledo,'' she told Bob. ''I'm going to stay.''

* * *

Most pleasant evenings that summer, Shannon and David, on the two saddle horses he kept on the farm, had gone for a half-hour ride. The couple's two English setters always accompanied them, and when she was visiting, Ceil would walk alongside Shannon's black mare to provide some small measure of security for her daughter who, while she loved horses—as she did all animals—was somewhat intimidated by their size and power. She would never allow her Tennessee walking horse to do more than slowly plod through the open fields.

On the evening of July 23, as they prepared for their ride, David insisted that Ceil lock the dogs up and stay at the house with them. Feeling slightly offended, she stood in the yard as the couple rode out. Nubbins, the younger of the dogs and the one most fond of Shannon, broke loose and ran to catch up to the riders. David stopped and shouted to Ceil to retrieve the animal and lock him up again.

Expecting Bob to come to the farm after work in Toledo that day, Ceil stayed out in the yard, sat in the shade of a tree, and watched as the pair moved slowly out of the farmyard and onto Lickley Road, heading north. Shannon turned in the saddle once, looking back at Ceil, and smiled. And then they were gone.

On his own farm, a short distance to the northwest, Richard Britton, thirty-nine, was returning from the fields aboard his farm tractor, an inoperative disc harrow in tow.

He had fussed over the implement where it had broken down, finally deciding that he would have to take it back to the barn, where there were tools and other equipment, to properly make the repair.

As he turned into the yard, Britton saw his neighbors, David and Shannon Davis. Dave was helping Britton's wife Ann move a large four-wheeled fertilizer tank back to make room for Britton's tractor. Shannon was standing nearby, holding the horses.

Though he was a tall man, Britton's sturdy frame was amply padded with years of robust country cooking that ballooned the midriff of his bib-overalls and gave him the appearance of being shorter than his near-six feet. His sun-weathered face was accented by a pair of moist blue eyes that danced and gleamed when he smiled, which was often and intensely. Dick Britton looked exactly like what he was—a farmer.

"If you saw Dick walking down Broadway in New York, or Michigan Avenue in Chicago," a longtime friend once remarked, "no matter how fancy he was dressed, you would say to yourself, 'There goes a farmer.' "

Mild of manner and soft-spoken, with the rural penchant for "minding his own business" he didn't warm up to strangers quickly.

He had spent almost his entire lifetime living within a tiny one-mile square of Wright Township in rural Hillsdale County.

At the age of two months, he had been sent to live with Kenneth and Ola Hyslop, a deeply loving couple who would raise him as their own. Dick's natural parents refused to allow the Hyslop's to adopt him, but Dick grew to look on his foster parents as his true mother and father, continuing to refer to them long after their deaths as "my mom and dad."

In June 1958, Dick married Anna Mae Figgins, a diminutive brown-haired girl from West Unity, Ohio, who had been adopted as an infant. The couple moved into a small house on Lickley Road purchased by Kenneth Hyslop on property adjacent to his own farm.

In 1959, following the pattern of their own lives, Ann and Dick adopted a little girl, Jean Ann, as their first child. It would not be until 1976 that another child would join the family—this time a boy, Norman, a foster child.

Kenneth died in 1968 and Ola followed him four years later, leaving to Dick the 120-acre farm on which he had lived all his life.

Britton put the Lickley Road home and sixty-four adjoining acres on the market. He and Ann moved into the Prattville Road home, on the balance of the Hyslop farm.

"The place had been up for sale a month or so and we only had a couple of calls about it when this young fella shows up and says he's interested in it," Britton remembers. "He wasn't from around here; I never seen him before. But he seemed nice enough."

The "young fella" was David Richard Davis.

A deal was struck, a down payment of $8,000 was made and Davis moved onto the farm with a wife, two daughters, and a $31,500 mortgage.

The couple seemed to Britton to be cordial and polite, and soon the Davises and the Brittons were exchanging visits to play cards and chat.

"They had moved in during the spring of 1973," Dick recalls, "too late to farm that season. So I farmed the land. Dave's wife Phyllis would bring sandwiches out to me in the field at lunchtime."

But Davis didn't particularly impress the locals as being terribly sociable and was left pretty much alone by everyone in the area.

The young couple began having problems and in 1976 David and Phyllis, high school sweethearts, found themselves consumed in a bitter, messy divorce, during which charges of physical cruelty and mental anguish were made.

"We weren't real surprised," Dick admits. "But I figured, if that's what they want, who am I to stick my nose in?"

Such was the creed of the countrified: Don't meddle in other people's affairs.

Phyllis and the girls moved out, leaving Davis sour and alone. He then began spending a great deal of time at the Britton's place. His visits became so frequent that it was not unusual for him to walk in unannounced at dinnertime and for Ann Britton to set another plate without a word.

The two men grew close as the months passed. Dick loaned his neighbor equipment and tried to help him in any way he could, and in return Davis was quick to do favors for his benefactor and friend.

"Anytime I needed help, he was right there. He was a good neighbor and a good friend," Britton says. "He would come over and run the tractor or the combine or do anything I needed doing. I would offer to pay him but he would say, 'I'm not doing this for money.' I really enjoyed working with him."

In April 1979, David, with a $15,000 down payment, acquired 40 acres and an old house directly across Lickley Road from his farm. His holdings now totaled 102 acres, two homes, several outbuildings and pieces of farm equipment and machinery.

During the long, quiet months of winter, when the winds blew cold and biting, the friends spent many hours seated around the table in the Britton's kitchen, drinking coffee and chatting. It was during these times that Davis began talking about his life—a colorful, thrilling, and dramatic past.

"He told me that his father had been killed in World War II, that he had grown up in Texas, where he'd lived with his grandpa; he said they used to shoot ducks while flying in his grandpa's biplane," Britton recalls. "And he told how he had been a captain in the Marines and served in Vietnam."

Dick Britton was captivated with the adventurous tales Davis spun. One thrilling experience involved Davis parachuting into the jungle and being caught in a tree. When a North Vietnamese spotted him hanging by his chute harness, he put a bullet in Dave's knee—with a French rifle.

"What did you do?" Britton asked, awestruck.

"I used my .45 and shot him between the eyes," Davis replied matter of factly.

To men like Dick Britton and neighbors Herbert Frank and Bob Godfrey and Howard Sensabaugh, who had never lived the horrors of military combat, who had never been where men were killing each other with guns and bombs and napalm, with pistols and bayonets and even with their bare hands, David's exploits offered a vicarious thrill that took them away from their largely benign, frequently monotonous lives.

In the years to come, Britton would shake his head in wonder as he recalled the evenings seated in rapture at his kitchen table, listening to stories that brought a tingle to his scalp and left his mouth agape.

Dick was vaguely aware that David was considering a second marriage; he had observed a steady stream of young, attractive women coming and going at the Davis farm. David frequently brought the women to the Brittons, apparently seeking their approval, but he hadn't expressed a preference for any one of them as far as Dick knew.

Suddenly, in September 1979, David showed up at the Brittons with a perky brunette named Shannon Mohr.

"He told us she was a nurse and lived in Toledo," Dick remembers. "We liked her right away. She was lovely, she had a beautiful personality and her appearance was immaculate; not a hair out of place. When they drove away, I said to Ann, 'There goes Miss Neat!' "

Several weeks later, Davis informed Dick that he and Shannon were leaving for Las Vegas to get married.

When the couple returned in early October from their honeymoon, the Brittons hosted a party in their honor. All but a few of the immediate neighbors attended. Shannon, a warm, bubbly young woman, was radiant and obviously pleased to be accepted into this rural society, expressing to each of the guests her gratitude for their kindness and her determination to be worthy of the honor they had bestowed on her. "If I can be of any help to you, please don't hesitate to call," she told them. "I hope you'll come visit us in our home . . . Feel free to stop by anytime."

Ann and Dick were delighted. They immediately took the vivacious young woman to their hearts and the couple soon became regular guests at the Britton home.

"I thought she was real neat. I liked her right away," Ann says. "I used to kid her, asking her, 'When are we going to hear the pitter-patter of little Davis feet?' And I told her, since her mother was way down in Toledo, I would be her mother at the farm. She would laugh and say, 'That sounds like a good idea to me.' "

Dave and Shannon became frequent visitors at the Brittons', coming over almost weekly to play cards, just as Dave and Phyllis had done. The Brittons, too, called regularly at the house on Lickley Road.

The newlyweds were, from all outward appearances, living an extended honeymoon, enthralled with each other, barely conscious of the existence of a world outside their own private Eden.

"Sometimes I'd be at their place when Shannon came home from work in Toledo," Dick recounts. "Shannon would rush up on the porch where Dave and I would be sitting, and jump in his lap and kiss him. She was so happy to be back with him."

Whenever Shannon asked David about the women in his life before he met her, his response was, "My life began the day I met you."

And the couple seemed to be doing well financially: They owned two convertibles—one was a brand-new MGB—a pickup truck, a van, and a new two-ton Chevrolet farm truck.

Shannon now felt that she was well launched on her plan to have the kind of life she had always dreamed of—a wonderful husband whom she loved deeply, a comfortable, pleasant home, and warm, friendly neighbors who had accepted her into their group. All that was wanting now was a bunch of children to cherish just as she and her siblings had been cherished by their parents.

* * *

"What's the trouble, Dick?" Davis asked when Britton had pulled the tractor and harrow up to the barn.

"Bad bearing," Britton replied with characteristic brevity.

Without further discussion, David pitched in to help his neighbor and his friend.

After about twenty minutes, the repair job unfinished, David suddenly excused himself, stating that he and Shannon were going back to their place and that on the way they would ride through the woods bordering the two farms. Shannon, who had been holding the horses and chatting with Ann, approached and asked Dick if Norman could go back with them and spend the night. Britton was about to give his consent when David interrupted.

"No! You can come by and get him tomorrow," he snapped at Shannon, who looked shocked and surprised. Ann and Dick were also at a loss to explain David's outburst. He had never refused to take Norman back to his place for the night.

David asked about a shortcut to the woods bordering their farms and Dick directed him to a spot where he had installed an electrified fence to keep his livestock from wandering.

"There's no charge on the wire, so you can just take it down and go on through," Dick told David.

"Naw, you know how horses are, once there's been a wire there they never will pass through. We'll go around at the eastern corner instead," David replied, opting for a slightly longer trip that would put them at the eastern edge of the grove.

The couple rode out of the yard at the slow walk that Shannon, who was not an accomplished rider, required, leaving the Brittons standing there, still somewhat surprised by David's unusual ire.

* * *

At the Davis place, Lucille remained seated in the shade of a tree, gazing across the rolling fields toward the grove of trees at the back of the farm.

At fifty-three, Lucille Mohr was a vision of the demure, gentle, and unassertive middle-aged wife and mother. Slight at five-foot-two and weighing barely a hundred pounds, she did not leave an impression of being tough and uncompromising. But those who knew her well were quick to disabuse that notion. She was as hard as nails. She had learned in her childhood that because she was small in stature she could never allow the belief that she was also weak, which meant that she couldn't *be* weak.

The toughness she developed, although purely a defense mechanism, turned out also to be a double-edged sword in her younger years. It caused her to have basically two types of acquaintances—those who were truly loyal and genuinely loved her, and those who misunderstood and never felt close to her.

Her friends called her Ceil and found that most of the time she was a stimulating, exciting, and fun person to be near. She had an explosive, irreverent sense of humor that exposed itself at unexpected and, occasionally, inappropriate times. And she could cuss with the best of them. But even those who admired and appreciated her knew that there was a darker, more severe side of tiny Ceil that projected itself, when she had been brought to anger, in a granitelike jaw that, when it tensed, caused her mouth to stretch into a razor-sharp line. A transformation would occur, too, in the deep pools of her eyes. Normally they twinkled and bubbled with mirth but, when she was provoked, her eyes could erupt with flash and fire, giving the impression of a cat ready to spring.

"She's a feisty gal, a *real* feisty gal," a close friend of thirty years declares. "She's a hell of a scrapper."

In her adolescent years she was frequently viewed as a battler who would fight with the zeal of a mother grizzly protecting her cubs to get her way. She tended to be inordinately suspicious of anyone she didn't know well and even unreasonably skeptical of many she did. At the same time, once her trust had been earned it was steadfast and unshakable.

She was the third of six children born to Glen and Lucille Abrams. The eldest, Albert "Bud" Abrams, was killed in World War II.

"Ceil was a real fighter as a kid," her brother Glen, two years her junior, remembers. "She didn't take nothing from nobody. When we were younger she would take care of me; the guys couldn't pick on me. She was my bodyguard. She would fight just like a man. I saw her whip a lot of guys."

When Glen, as a young man, took an interest in amateur boxing, Ceil was his sparring partner. "She could hit," Glen recalls.

As the years accumulated and began wearing away the rough edges, Lucille mellowed much. While there was still that hard steel just beneath the surface of her personality, it didn't explode as volcanically as it once did, except where her family was concerned.

Lucille and Bob were as unlikely a pair as their friends had ever seen. Bob was a quiet mountain of a man, as placid as Ceil was mercurical, as soft and gentle as she was hard and combative. And yet because of their differences, they were a remarkable blend—Bob was understanding, dependable, ever the pacifist; Lucille was solid, cautious, coiled to strike. And both were unyielding in their love and devotion for the three children their union produced.

An inborn mistrust caused Ceil to be especially protective of her brood of chicks, making it difficult for anyone outside the family to get close to them.

"Ceil wouldn't trust anybody with the kids," Glen says. "I don't think she ever had a babysitter."

While her toughness softened somewhat over the years, her competitive nature never waned. When the children were in their teens, powerful young men would frequent the Mohr home. Tiny Ceil delighted in arm-wrestling the youths.

"She used to pin them all," Glen recalls with delight. "She'd wrestle anybody and beat 'em. They couldn't believe it. They'd all try her."

On Wednesday, July 23, 1980, Bob Mohr was, for the second time that week, making the hot, tiring trip from Toledo to Hillsdale County.

Bob had been puzzled by his grandson's behavior earlier that week when he had begged Ceil to stay with him at the farm. Brian had always adored his Aunt Shannon and had quickly become unusually fond of his new uncle. During the child's visits that summer, David had taken the boy swimming several times at a nearby rock quarry and on numerous short errands into the neighboring towns and villages. Brian, who was fighting a lonely and continuing battle with the fear and uncertainty of a broken home, had been delighted with the constancy and stability that life on Uncle Dave's farm seemed to offer.

Because Brian had seemingly found a haven from his unhappiness, it was difficult to imagine what had caused him to mysteriously exhibit concern with his grandmother's departure. But, Bob thought, there's no accounting for the capricious nature of an adolescent . . . or, for that matter, of a fifty-three-year-old grandmother who doted on her grandchildren. Bob felt that Ceil had acted foolishly in not insisting that Brian remain at the farm while she returned for her ceramics class as she had originally planned.

Much later, when Brian was more closely questioned about his sudden, unexplained reluctance to stay at the farm without his grandmother, his answer then would have a special significance.

Just as Dick Britton completed work on the disc harrow, his attention was drawn toward the woods a quarter-mile away at the southern edge of his farm.

Peering into the waves of rising heat undulating from the soybean field immediately behind the house and farmyard, he saw the distorted image of horse and rider pounding toward him as though pursued by an unseen horror. He realized that the rider was David Davis. Britton was both annoyed and bewildered. Davis, returning alone and at horse-punishing speed, was running his horse through the soybeans—which he should have known Dick would not appreciate. Why wasn't Shannon with him? They'd ridden off together less than half an hour earlier.

"What the hell happened, Dave?" Britton shouted as Davis thundered into the yard, reined in his horse, and half-jumped, half-fell from the winded mount.

Davis's face bore a thin film of dust that was being washed by a torrent of perspiration; his eyes flooded with the terror of a stalked animal, his jersey top was open and the T-shirt beneath was stained with thick blotches of rich, fresh blood.

Later, when he'd had time to think about it some, Dick would recall, with astonishment, the amount of blood—fetid and gummy—that covered David's T-shirt. Having spent his life on the farm, gore was not something to which he was unaccustomed. But you could butcher a full-grown hog and not get that much blood on your clothing.

"Dick, you've got to help me," Davis gasped, his eyes wild and filled with fear. "There's been an accident. Shannon's hurt."

2

The sun was hanging low to the western horizon as Davis and Britton leaped into Dick's 1968 four-door Impala and roared out of the yard to Prattville Road and turned east onto Lickley. From there Britton turned right for about a quarter mile, where there was a narrow access road that led back into the hayfield where Davis indicated he had left Shannon to get help. As they sped across the field, Britton asked Davis, "What happened, Dave?"

"We were riding through the woods and she fell off her horse and hit her head. I drug her out of the woods and then came for you. I shouldn't have left her, I shouldn't have left her."

"You couldn't help that, Dave. You had to go get some help."

"I told her I didn't want to leave, but she said, 'I'm okay, go get help, I'm okay.' "

Britton was watching carefully as the car bumped over the rutted ground. He worried that Shannon might be hidden in the tall weeds and that he could run over her before she was spotted.

As they neared the edge of the woods, Dick spotted Shannon's black mare, standing quietly, eating the tall grass growing at the edge of the field. At the same moment, Dave pointed out Shannon's motionless form, lying in the weeds near the feeding animal. Britton noted that Shannon was on her back, her arms straight at her sides, her eyes closed. He would later describe the appearance as being "like someone laid out in a coffin."

He pulled the car in close, positioning it so the right side was next to the unconscious woman. The two men jumped from Britton's car, Dave immediately dropping to his knees and leaning over his wife. He pressed his fingers against her neck, feeling for a pulse.

"She has a pulse. It's weak, but she has a pulse," he said as Britton rounded the front of his car. Looking down at Shannon's still form, he gasped and stopped short.

"It took my breath away," he remembers. "She had a bluish-gray color. Her feet were bare and her blouse was fully unbuttoned; her breasts were exposed and I watched her chest to see if it was moving up and down; it didn't move, there was no movement at all. I'm a farmer and we have hogs die, I know what death looks like. I thought then that there was nothing really that we could do."

Dick now regretted not allowing Ann to call the emergency squad in Waldron. She had asked three times if she should call them, and Dick agreed with her suggestion.

"We gotta get an ambulance, Dave."

"No, we haven't got time. We've got to go back and get her and take her to the hospital."

Britton was uncertain.

"Dave, if she's hurt that bad, we have to call an ambulance."

"We don't have time!" Davis shouted.

Davis had once told Dick that he had spent two and a half years in medical school.

"It was his wife; it was his decision to make. I figured he knew what was best."

They gingerly raised Shannon's body and placed it in the backseat of the car, lying it on the cushions.

"You drive and I'll give her mouth-to-mouth," Davis said. "We'll take her to Hudson."

Hudson was the closest town, but Thorn Hospital was a small facility with a small staff.

"Dave, you're running a chance there might not be a doctor at Hudson. Let's take her to Hillsdale; there's sure to be a doctor on duty."

"What she needs most of all right now is assistance with her breathing. They have a respirator at Thorn."

Climbing in the back with Shannon, David had to fold her legs to shut the door.

Britton drove the eleven miles to Hudson, Michigan "as fast as the car would go; ninety-five miles an hour with the lights flashing and the horn blowing."

He heard no sound from the backseat and didn't dare take his eyes from the road to glance in the rearview mirror. Once he called back to Davis, "How's she doin', Dave?"

"She's okay," came the reply.

Britton was dubious; the memory of the still form with the ghastly pallor of death haunted him. Still, he clung to one flimsy hope—maybe she isn't dead, maybe she'll make it . . .

Kenneth Arnold, a twenty-six-year-old physician's assistant, had just left work at Thorn Hospital and was proceeding south on U.S. Highway 127 leading out of town when he observed a red sedan moving north at a dangerously high rate of speed. Arnold realized immediately that someone was in a desperate rush to get to the hospital. As the speeding auto flashed passed him, Arnold made a quick U-turn and headed back to Thorn.

Britton was traveling too fast to make the turn onto the street, which led to the hospital, and had to race through a motel parking lot to retrace his route. As he swung into the entrance to Thorn Hospital and headed toward the emergency room entrance at the rear, he laid on the horn, hoping to alert the staff.

Inside, near the front of the small, single-story facility, the charge nurse, twenty-three-year-old Mary

Emma Merillat, heard the horn and saw the auto speed by.

"When a car comes in that fast and blowing the horn, it's almost always an emergency."

Nurse Merillat rushed toward the back of the hospital, arriving at the emergency room door just as a flushed and perspiring Dick Britton ran inside.

"We need a doctor, we got a girl hurt real bad, we need a doctor right now," Britton gushed.

The nurse pushed past him, through the double doors and out into the parking lot. She could see a man in the backseat bent forward, his head and shoulders bobbing methodically. Her first thought was that it was the man who was injured or ill. But when the door was opened, a small, shoeless foot toppled out and Nurse Merillat saw, resting on the man's lap, the still form of a young woman.

Davis looked up, his eyes large. "You've got to help her, she's hurt bad." Then, as if to impress her and perhaps get more immediate service, he added, "She's a nurse at Flower Hospital; you got to help her."

He scrambled out and the nurse replaced him inside. She first pushed back one eyelid and then the other. The pupils were fixed and dilated, the face a bluish-gray, the skin cooling. Next she placed the fingertips of her right hand against the side of Shannon's throat, feeling for a carotid pulse; there was none. Placing her stethoscope on the woman's chest, Merillat listened for a heartbeat; there was none. The nurse then cupped her hand behind Shannon's head, tilting it back and raising the chin to establish an airway through which she could administer mouth-to-mouth respiration, the first step to initiating cardiopulmonary resuscitation, or CPR. But when she blew into Shannon's mouth the puff of air met instant and total resistance. The young nurse sat back. It's hopeless, she thought. Without an adequate airway to provide oxygen to the patient, CPR was ineffective.

By this time other staff members had arrived: Kenneth Arnold and nurses Joy Earl and Melanie Wheeler.

"We got her out of the car, you couldn't do CPR effectively because the cushions are too soft," Nurse Earl would later recall. "The woman's husband said he had been doing CPR on the run from the farm. But I don't see how he could."

Nurse Wheeler remembers that an "ambubag" was used to try and pump air into Shannon's lungs as she was being wheeled inside, and that CPR was attempted.

In the emergency room, physician's assistant Arnold began a hurried examination while one of the nurses rushed to the telephone to notify Dr. Harry Dickman, the physician on call. A heart monitor was placed on Shannon's chest. "We got a flat line," Melanie Wheeler recalls. Shannon Mohr Davis, twenty-five years old, was dead. But it would not be official, it could not be announced, until Dr. Dickman arrived and pronounced her medically, legally, officially, and unmistakably dead. In the meantime, her distraught husband stood in the middle of the emergency room, his blood-soaked clothes kept moist by the niagara of sweat that continued pouring from his body. Medical personnel did their best to ignore him in the hope that he would not pester them with difficult questions.

"You'd probably be more comfortable up front; there's a larger waiting room there," someone suggested, and Davis and Dick Britton moved down the corridor.

"Let me call Shannon's mother," Dick offered. But David, his head hanging down, seemed not to hear him.

"They should be here, this girl's hurt real bad," Dick pleaded, to no avail. Four times he issued the plea but Davis simply stood, sobbing loudly. "Can I call Shannon's mother, Dave? Give me their telephone number and I'll call Toledo for you."

Finally, Davis replied in a soft, almost unintelligible voice, "Ceil's at the farm."

Britton was stunned. All this time, she'd been there waiting for them to come back; all this time, wondering what had happened to Shannon and David.

He dashed off to find a public telephone, uncertain exactly how he would break the news.

In the emergency room, Kenneth Arnold and the nursing team proceeded with the ritual they were required to perform, even in hopeless cases.

A blood pressure cuff was attached to Shannon's left arm and inflated. Arnold placed his stethoscope on the brachial artery of the arm; there was no detectable blood pressure or pulse. He next checked the chest for a heartbeat while rechecking the pupils for reaction to light—they were fixed, dilated, and unresponsive. Slipping a hand behind her head and feeling for a wound, he found no palpable skull depression, although that was not proof that a fracture did not indeed exist.

At about this time Dr. Dickman arrived and took over the examination of the body of Shannon Davis.

"I was impressed with how loosely the head moved about when the shoulders were lifted from the table, leading me to believe that a fracture of the neck had occurred."

Turning the body over and examining the back of the head, Dr. Dickman and Arnold observed a deep laceration in the scalp approximately eight and one half centimeters in length and just to the left of the external occipital protruberance in the lamboid suture at the back of the head, producing quantities of bloody exude. There was, Dr. Dickman reasoned, probably intracranial damage to the dura—the tough membrane covering the brain—and to the brain itself.

A hemotoma—a blackened swelling—on the cheek below the woman's left eye was noted. Her clothing was not removed, thus any additional injuries could not have been observed. There was no reason to ex-

amine the body closely at this time; an autopsy would
be performed within a day or two. They had been told
that the woman had fallen from her horse, and indeed
there was the wound in the back of the head. Postmortem X-rays were taken of the head and neck but,
other than that, nothing extraordinary could be accomplished. The patient was DOA; no IVs were started,
no medication or drugs were administered. Shannon
Davis was wheeled to a holding room to await disposition of her remains. The "official time of death" was
arbitrarily fixed at 8:45 P.M., approximately thirty
minutes before arrival at Thorn Hospital.

Dr. Dickman and his assistant walked out of the
emergency room and down the corridor to the lounge
area to advise the woman's husband that his wife had
"expired." They had instructed one of the nurses to
alert the Hillsdale sheriff's department that the death
had occurred in their jurisdiction.

"I'm terribly sorry, Dave, but there was nothing we
could do to save her; it was simply too late," Kenneth
Arnold said softly, kneeling in front of David, looking
up into his face.

"She can't be dead, she can't be. She talked to me,"
Davis screamed, huge tears coursing down his face.

Dr. Dickman, standing behind Arnold blurted out,
"That girl never talked to you."

He didn't explain his sharp statement, and David
lowered his head, saying nothing. Later, Dickman
would remember that Davis's "grief was so loud that
I got disgusted and walked away."

David was unquestionably public in his emotional
distress. All who observed him that evening recall how
profuse were his tears.

"He kept on crying the whole time," Dick Britton
says.

The nurses on duty were aware of the devastation
Davis had experienced and tried to avoid him as much
as possible.

* * *

At 9:39 P.M., Hillsdale County deputy sheriff Charles Gutowski, manning the dispatch desk in Hillsdale, logged in a call from Thorn Hospital in Hudson stating that they had a DOA from Hillsdale County, a twenty-five-year-old female who died from an apparent injury to the head resulting, according to the deceased's husband, from a fall from a horse. The husband was at the hospital and would be available for questioning if the sheriff's department wanted to send someone around. Deputy Gutowski dispatched deputies Roger Boardman, a thirteen-year veteran of the sheriff's department, and his partner Tino Gimenez, with instructions to proceed to Hudson to take a preliminary statement from the dead woman's husband and to collect and return with any evidence that might be available. The deputies drove first to Hillsdale Hospital, where they obtained a blood sample kit; then they drove the nineteen miles to Hudson, arriving at 10:17 P.M.

While Gimenez interviewed Davis, Boardman consulted with Dr. Dickman. The doctor told Boardman that there were some suspicious indications on the X-rays that appeared to be one or possibly two fractures of the neck.

Boardman requested that Dr. Dickman draw a blood sample that would be sent to Lansing for analysis to determine if alcohol had contributed to the woman's sudden death.

Using a twenty-gauge needle, inserted near the center of the chest to the left of the sternum directly into Shannon's heart, Dickman withdrew fifteen milliliters of blood into a syringe, which was then sealed and deposited in an evidence bag and given to the deputy.

In the lounge, Deputy Gimenez continued his interrogation.

"We were going down a small trail in the woods," Davis said, recounting the events of earlier that evening, "and it's very brushy and thick. I heard Shannon scream, and I turned around and she was upside down under her horse, and her horse had bolted or jumped, and I got my horse under control and dismounted. When I got on the ground, Shannon was laying on the ground, and I ran back to her, and when I picked her up, I noticed there was some blood.

"I've had a good deal of first-aid training. I examined the wound and found it was not—I didn't think it was too serious. She was breathing well. She had a strong pulse.

"I carried her to the edge of the woods where we had just ridden in and laid her down in the grass, made sure she was breathing properly. She was conscious by this time but couldn't get up. She told me to go for help. I didn't feel that I should leave her there, but she said she'd be all right.

"I went back into the woods, boarded my horse, and rode as quickly as I could back to the neighbors."

Sometime during the questioning, Dick Britton remembers, the deputy asked a question that the police officer would later fail to recall. "Did you have insurance on your wife's life, Mr. Davis?"

Britton also remembers Davis's response: "No, I didn't have insurance on her."

The questioning over, Dick walked out into the parking lot, waiting for the Mohrs to arrive yet dreading their appearance and the time when they would learn that their daughter had died as the result of a crazy twist of fate.

Dr. Dickman was anxious to be out of the hospital. Short, with white hair that was receding and a bushy moustache that gave a distinguished, elder-statesman look to his otherwise unimpressive appearance, Harry Dickman, with more than thirty years' medical practice behind him, tended to be abrupt and sometimes cranky, having little patience for anyone other than those he was directly responsible to treat. The fellow with the attack of histrionics over his young wife's tragic death was a good example. Another was the impossible bureaucracy with which he was forced to deal.

Dickman recalled that at some point during the evening he received a call at the hospital from the Lenawee County medical examiner, Dr. Robert Harrison from his offices in Adrian, Michigan.

While the incident had occurred in Hillsdale County, the pronouncement of death had taken place in Lenawee and the official, signed certificate of death would come from this jurisdiction.

"Is there anything suspicious about the cause of death?" Dr. Harrison asked.

"Well, I'm not sure," Dickman waffled. "The head injury seems consistent with a fall such as the husband claimed . . . But the X-rays show what looks like a suspicious-looking crack in the second cervical."

"If everything looks on the up and up, sign the death certificate," Dickman was instructed.

Dickman also received a call from Dr. Philip Fleming, the Hillsdale County assistant medical examiner, who wanted the body taken to one of the county's VanHorn-Eagle funeral homes for an autopsy.

Dr. David Acus, the Hillsdale County medical examiner, would later state that both he and Fleming had been telephoned sometime that night either from the sheriff's department or Thorn Hospital. Acus, told that X-rays had been taken, asked to have them brought to Hillsdale Community Health Center for a reading. Acus also wanted an autopsy done.

"We have autopsies done in cases where there's not a real good indication of the cause of death. It's not a personal thing," Dr. Acus explained.

He remembered that there had not been a death attributed to a fall from a horse during his tenure as medical examiner in the county.

The formal report issued later by Dr. F. Burns, M.D., a radiologist, concerning "X-Ray # 53290 (7-23-80), Ap and Lat. C. Spine Views" of the deceased Shannon Mohr Davis would state that other than a slight scoliosis of the cervical spine and a minor congenital defect in the fourth and fifth cervical vertebra, "no evidence of gross displacement of the cervical vertebra is noted at this time. However, [spinal] cord damage could not be ruled out from a displaced vertebra which is now appearing in position."

Harrison and Acus spoke that same evening. Harrison said he was claiming jurisdiction over the body, which would not be transferred to Hillsdale County for an autopsy.

"I don't do autopsies routinely," Harrison would later insist. "It's too hard on the family, for one thing."

Dr. Dickman left the death certificate unsigned. "I didn't want to get in the middle." His responsibilities to the patient having been completed, the good doctor simply walked out of the hospital, assuming that an autopsy would be done. Any suspicions he may have harbored about the cause of the young woman's demise set aside, he had done all he could. It was now in the laps of the bureaucrats; let them fight their turf wars without him. Why should a simple country doctor make waves?

The following day, the X-rays were picked up by Hillsdale County sheriff's deputies and taken to the Hillsdale Community Health Center, where they were examined by Dr. Arthur Stein, the hospital's radiologist. After viewing the plates, Dr. Stein concluded that there was a "congenital anomoly; two vertabrae that had been fused together in a single block since birth."

The radiologist determined that Shannon definitely did not have a broken neck. "Why she died is not demonstrated by the X-rays," he stated. "It had nothing to do with the injury."

Bob Mohr and his niece Tori Abrams, who had driven to the farm with him, arrived just as the sun was setting. Bob began unloading items he'd brought for Ceil while Tori dashed inside to see her aunt. Almost immediately, she was back on the front porch.

"Uncle Bob. There's a telephone call for you."

It was such a lovely sunset. Through the years that followed, Ceil would recall with mechanical precision every detail of that evening, and among the clearest recollections was that of the most magnificent sunset she had ever seen. The sky directly overhead, studded with brilliant pinpoints of pulsating white, had been a deep navy blue, blending as it moved toward the horizon first to a vivid cobalt, then to a delicate periwinkle, a soft powder blue that lightened until it was fringed with aquamarine, and then a vibrant medley of yellows and reds. It was such a lovely sunset.

3

The call from Dick Britton had been all the more agonizing for what wasn't said. "Bob, Shannon fell off her horse, she's been hurt; we had to bring her up here to the hospital in Hudson. You'd better get here right away."

What had happened? The question hammered at Ceil and Bob as they sped toward Hudson.

You'd better get here right away. The words were ominous, foretelling the worst. And at this moment neither could cope with the worst, the unthinkable.

"My God . . . My God," Bob kept repeating to no one. He'd said it so many times that Ceil finally rebelled at the phrase.

"Bob, shut up! Don't do this to me right now."

She wanted his strength at that moment, while they were still uncertain and prey to panic. She knew that if their sickening suspicions proved true he would be strong, he would be a rock. But just now, he was crumbling, succumbing to his own fears, allowing the darkest terror to control him. Mindless of what Ceil was suffering, he needed instead to prepare himself so that he could be steellike when Ceil would need his strength the most.

As they drove into the wide lot at the rear of the hospital they saw Dick Britton standing outside the emergency room door. A sheriff's deputy stood next to him. Dick saw the Mohrs' car approach, and as it drew to a stop a few yards away his eyes locked on Ceil's.

She jumped from the car, hysteria burning in her stomach, shouting, "Is she all right?"

Bob rushed toward Britton. "Tell me she's alive, Dick. Just tell me she's alive."

Dick slowly shook his head. "I can't do that."

Bob and Ceil knew. They knew.

David stood at the far end of the corridor—Ceil could see him through the glass doors leading into the emergency room—his head slightly bowed, his shoulders stooped. As she moved inside, still watching him, Ceil was suddenly swept by cold shudders, a terrible sensation that was accompanied by an unimaginable thought that had her saying to herself, *David, did you hurt my daughter?*

As she and Bob approached him, David turned and faced them, looking deep in Ceil's eyes. She moved to a spot directly in front of him, studying his face, looking for an explanation to help her comprehend their mutual tragedy. She saw tears but found no other sign, his face was vacant, there seemed to be no emotion there.

He put his arms, still stained with Shannon's blood, around her. He was perspiring profusely, keeping the blood damp and causing it to transfer to her blouse. It confused her. *Why is he sweating so?* she wondered. The air conditioning was laboring—she felt uncomfortably cold because of it—and yet David was standing there, the water literally pouring from him.

He ran a hand under her chin and up the side of her face. As he did so, Ceil looked at his thumb. Both of them were malformed—a condition, genetically passed down from his grandfather, known as "hammerhead thumbs"—flat and broad, splayed to almost twice the normal width, they always had been a source of curiosity for her, and she frequently had to force herself not to stare at them. But tonight, at this terrible time, the deformity held no attraction. Instead, her gaze was drawn to a deep scratch that stretched from the base of the thumb to the wrist of his right hand. She noted another series of scratches on his face, near the chin, that looked like claw marks.

They embraced, a hard hug, patting each other's backs.

Bob had questions he wanted answered, an almost endless litany of questions that gushed from him as if the answers could miraculously wipe away the pain that had seared in him when he heard his son-in-law softly announce, "She's gone."

Ceil sat on one of the lounge couches. Dick Britton stood quietly off to one side of the room, obviously distressed, seeming not to know just what to say, afraid he could not control his own feelings, worried that any attempt he might make to console these people would go badly and he would be embarrassed and ashamed. Next to Britton, also feeling uncomfortable and out of place, stood Deputy Gimenez, waiting for his partner to complete his meeting with Dr. Dickman. David and Bob stood in the center of the room as Bob continued his questions.

When Ceil and Bob tried to recall the scene later, it came back to them as though they had been in a separate dimension, totally apart from everyone else. People walked in and out of the room like ghostly apparitions, not members of their world. Only when someone approached and disturbed the drama they were playing out did they become involved in what was occurring.

For Ceil, the full force of the last few minutes was only now beginning to sink in; her precious Shannon was dead, snatched from her and Bob, so young, so soon. She had not had time to accomplish all she could have in a full life, had not time to enjoy all the joys and pleasures of having and raising a family. She had loved children so and had wanted her own, had wanted to have a warm, loving, caring family.

Ceil's concentration on what might have been, what now was never to be, was interrupted by loud voices; they belonged to Bob and David.

"Cremated? You're going to have my daughter cremated?"

"I told you, it's what she wanted."

Ceil shrieked.

"My God, no!" Bob shouted.

"Shannon and I talked about it several times and she said when she died she wanted to be cremated."

"She would never have said that, David," Ceil argued. "She would never have wanted that."

The thought that Shannon would have asked to be cremated was preposterous; aside from her devotion to the Catholic Church which, even after extreme liberalization, continued to frown on the practice, Bob and Ceil were well aware of their daughter's personal commitment to her fellow man. As a nurse she had become extremely sensitive to the need for organ donors to help save the living.

"She had said many times how, when she died, she wanted her eyes, heart, and kidneys donated to those who needed them," Bob recalls. "She thought everyone should donate their organs when they died. I decided that if he was going to insist on cremation, I would go and find a judge to get a restraining order to stop him."

David was unyielding; Bob was just as intractable. They faced each other, barely inches apart, their eyes flashing, their voices rising as the disagreement became more heated.

Deputy Gimenez, fearing that physical violence was imminent, pushed himself between the two men, causing them to back away.

Dick Britton could no longer keep his silence.

"Dave, give her back to her parents, let them take her back to Toledo to bury. You've had her only ten months; let her go."

Davis was silent, and Ceil was certain that he would remain intransigent, that he would not allow them to take their daughter home.

Bob asked, "Did you have any life insurance on Shannon?"

Davis, his eyes cast downward, shook his head. "There may be a small policy, the one the hospital gave her. But I think you're the beneficiary on that one."

"Don't worry about that, I'll sign it over to you. Is that all there is?"

Davis nodded. "I don't have a cent's worth of insurance on her," he replied.

"We'll help pay for the funeral and the plot, if money is the problem. We'll pay for it all," Bob offered.

Ceil stiffened. Shannon's voice, from months earlier, echoed in Ceil's memory, played back like a cerebral tape recording. A casual statement made during a dinner party the Mohrs had thrown for the newlyweds, an offhand comment that Ceil had quickly forgotten until now. *David took out a big insurance policy on me.*

"Please, David, let us take her back home." Bob's voice had softened, pleading.

"All right," Davis said, finally. "You can have her for one day, and it'll have to be a closed casket."

Nurse Merillat entered the lounge and asked to speak with David. She explained that Shannon's body would be moved to a local mortician and that an autopsy would probably be performed the next day. Davis indicated that Bob would make further arrangements for the body's removal later.

The young and pretty nurse, uncomfortable and slightly flushed, as she always was when finances were to be discussed, explained the hospital charges: Thirty dollars emergency room fee; forty-five dollars monitor costs, and a twenty-five dollar doctor's fee: The total cost of having a once-splendid, dynamic woman declared dead was an even one hundred dollars.

"Okay," Davis replied, and the nurse backed away, nodding. She turned to Ceil, bent down, and asked:

"Was your daughter's maiden name Shannon Mohr?" When told that it was, Merillat said, "I remember her from nursing school; I was one or two years behind her."

Ceil was fast approaching the limit of her endurance, her nerves were raw and frayed; she felt confused and bewildered. She had always prided herself on her toughness, but tonight, in the face of the horror with which she had been confronted, she thought that she was about to collapse.

"Cry, Mrs. Mohr," Nurse Merillat told her. "Let it go, it'll be better."

But there were no more tears for now. Something more urgent than grief was building inside her. Shannon's body lay in a darkened room nearby, growing cold. Ceil had not asked to see her, not yet. She didn't want to look upon the lifeless corpse of her youngest child, did not want to see the blood-matted hair, the ashen face that had always been so florid, so fresh and full of life. At this moment her concentration was pulled to something else, a gnawing at her nerves that would not be stilled. David had lied and Ceil was at a loss to explain why.

She sat, speechless, listening, trying to fathom the disturbing imponderables that swirled and eddied around her. She suddenly stiffened. "Bob," she almost shouted, "I want to go home. I want to go home right now."

In soft, muted tones they made the arrangements to have Shannon's body picked up at Hudson's Eagle Funeral Home when the autopsy they assumed would be performed had been completed. From there it would be taken to the David R. Jasin Funeral Home in Toledo. These details completed, the couple, with their arms around each other's shoulders, slowly walked out of the hospital, leaving Shannon behind. Nurses, standing at the emergency room desk, watched them leave and then averted their eyes, bowing their heads slightly, feeling the suffering that spread from the dazed and stricken couple. *Lord, let this never happen to me.*

In the parking lot, Ceil grasped Bob's arm hard enough that he could feel her fingernails digging into his flesh.

"Something's wrong, Bob," she said. "David lied to you when he said there's no insurance. He lied!"

Bob said nothing and Ceil assumed that he was ignoring her. Actually, he was simply so numbed by what had happened this day that he heard nothing of what Ceil was saying. What Bob Mohr was hearing at that moment were the sounds of the past—the laughter, the music, the gentle voice cooing in his ear.

Ceil, living her own agonies just then, didn't pursue the matter of the blatant falsehood her son-in-law had uttered. It would all be sorted out later, she reasoned, when they had a firm grip on themselves, when the horror of tonight had been sedated.

Deputies Boardman and Gimenez, having completed the necessary paperwork and collected the blood sample, left the hospital. It was a few minutes before midnight; their shift was over. But there should be an examination of the scene of the fatality.

"It was late and dark," Boardman would recall later. "We decided to wait until the next day, when we came back on duty."

They were not scheduled back until four o'clock in the afternoon, about twenty hours after Shannon's death. In the meantime, the scene would remain unattended, unsecured.

"We had some reason to believe that criminal activity may have taken place," Boardman would admit. Still, they made no attempt to suggest to their superiors that an investigative team be sent out to the grove early the following morning, when any potential evidence might yet remain. "We didn't think of it."

There were those in Hillsdale County who looked upon local law enforcement as seriously lacking in competence and dedication. There had been cases of sudden, unexplained deaths that critics found suspicious in nature that many whispered might have been murders. There had been only two homicides charged in the county in the past ten years. This brooding suspicion gave rise to a persistent adage circulating throughout the county that held "If you want to get away with murder, do it in Hillsdale County."

Bob and Ceil drove back to the farm, collected Brian and Tori, and then began the long, melancholy trek south in miserable silence, each lost in his own private thoughts.

They killed a dog on their drive back to Toledo; a large German shepherd dashed into the road in front of them. Bob didn't have a chance to avoid the animal and there was no question in his mind that the dog had not survived the accident. They didn't stop.

Joseph Eagle drove the three short blocks from his family-owned establishment to Thorn Hospital, collected the earthly remains of Shannon Davis, and returned to the mortuary.

The body was removed from the funeral van and placed on a stainless steel "preparation table," where the clothing was removed in anticipation of an early-morning autopsy.

However, the bureaucratic process was catching up with Shannon. It was a process that would create a multitude of problems for those she had left behind and would result in disturbing her eternal rest not once but on two frightful occasions.

Shortly before two in the morning, Dr. Robert Harrison, the Lenawee County medical examiner, called the Eagle Funeral Home and announced that the body of Shannon Mohr Davis could be released immediately; there would be no autopsy. "It isn't necessary," he said.

He would come to the hospital later that morning and sign the death certificate. Over his signature, in the box headed "Cause of Death," were inscribed the words "Accident. Multiple cranial and cervical spine injuries." Below that Harrison scrawled, "Thrown from horse."

The body was placed in a "transportation container" for shipment to Toledo. The jeans and a loose-fitting blouse the deceased had been wearing were, according to Eagle's best recollection later, placed in the container with the body. The two articles of attire removed from the container by personnel in Toledo turned out, years later, not to have belonged to Shannon. The clothing she had been wearing at the time of her death, which might have contained important evidence, was never located.

In Hudson, when David's tears had finally stopped, when all the paperwork attending the "admission, treatment, and release of the patient" had been completed, he and Dick Britton, who had faithfully remained at his side, prepared to leave.

Bob Mohr, before he left the hospital with Ceil, asked Dave if he would like to come back to Toledo with them rather than return to the empty farmhouse. David declined the invitation.

"You don't want to go back to your place tonight, Dave," Britton insisted as they walked to his car. "You come home with me, stay at my place tonight."

Davis offered no objection and the two men, like the Mohrs, rode home in silence. They had been at the hospital for more than three hours. Neither had eaten, neither had had the opportunity to relax. Yet Dick knew that sleep would not come easily to him and he doubted that his dear friend would fare any better. He felt certain David's thoughts would churn with the vision of his young wife, of the ghastly way she looked in her last moments, of how radiant and vibrant she had been as they had ridden into the woods on a lovely summer evening. As for himself, there would be a mixture of memories he would struggle with before numbing sleep would come. And there were puzzles with which he would have to wrestle in the days ahead, disturbing notions that were now beginning to form in his troubled thoughts, questions that may not have answers, uncertainties that he dared not confront in the state of mental, physical, and emotional exhaustion he was now experiencing.

Ann, red-eyed and ashen, greeted them at the kitchen door. Dick had called her from the hospital immediately after reaching Bob.

"She didn't make it," he said simply, in a soft, trembling voice. Ann had walked out to the back porch, stood there in the silent summer night air and cried.

David refused anything to eat and went almost immediately to the spare bedroom and closed the door. Dick and Ann sat in the kitchen talking softly late into the night. They had telephoned a few neighbors, giving them the hurtful news.

In Toledo, as word spread, brothers and sisters, sons and daughters, cousins, nieces and nephews rushed to Point Place to gather around Bob and Ceil to spend the long, cruel night with the stricken couple. Phone calls were going out, painful, shocking calls to Shannon's friends and relatives, bringing the anguished news of her sudden, unexpected death. There was no easy way to deliver the hated message, no gentle method to prepare the way for what had to be told—and so it was just blurted out.

Rich Duffey had worked a house fire that evening. It had been a bad one; a nineteen-year-old boy had died in the blaze.

"Fatal fires always bother you. But this one . . . well I couldn't sleep all night. I was exhausted, but for some reason I couldn't get the kid off my mind."

He was, at last, drifting off at seven in the morning when the telephone rang. It was Shannon's sister Terri.

"Something terrible has happened . . ."

4

She had appeared in the early hours of the morning, just as the first light of dawn was tinting the eastern sky. He had awakened suddenly, not the slow sliding back and forth between sleep and wakefulness, but a sharp, abrupt jump from fitful slumber to sober consciousness. In the darkness her form emerged at the foot of his bed, standing there, a wispy yet solid presence. She spoke and her voice was distant yet clear and compelling. "Help me, Dick." It was Shannon.

The apparition vanished, leaving Dick Britton trembling and unable to return to sleep. Shannon's death had affected him profoundly; he had never found it easy to accept unexpected human death; the finality of it, the sudden transition from animation to eternal immobility was unsettling, even to a lifelong farmer to whom the slaughtering of animals was a common necessity for the success of agricultural enterprise. But, the sudden and senseless death of a lovely, healthy young woman seemed out of place, and the memory of her lying in the weeds, her face that awful bluish-gray was, to Dick, somehow obscene.

Two hours later, his morning farm chores completed, Dick sat at the kitchen table having a light, unenthusiastic breakfast. Looking up, he saw David enter. He looked clear eyed and rested; there was no residue of the uncontrolled weeping of the previous night.

"It looked to me like he slept real well," Britton recalled years later.

Davis sat across from Dick, a cup of coffee in front of him, staring blankly out the window. When he spoke at last his words sent shock waves through Dick Britton.

"Do you know if Ralph Wise still wants to sell his farm?"

Dick gasped at the unanticipated insensitivity of David's question.

"What? For God's sake, Dave, your wife was killed yesterday; do you think this is the proper time to be thinking about acquiring real estate?"

Davis looked back at him—a vacant expression that made it seem almost, Dick thought, as if he didn't understand what Britton was talking about, as if the words he'd uttered which so upset Dick had never been spoken.

"Never mind," Davis said simply and returned his gaze to the farm fields.

Less than an hour later he said he would have to leave; he had to go to Toledo to make the funeral arrangements.

Dick drove him back to his house and then made a circuit through the area, stopping at farms, informing the residents of the shocking tragedy of the day before, and taking up a collection for funeral flowers.

When Robert VanHorn, a licensed embalmer, arrived at the David R. Jasin Funeral Home that morning, he discovered that a body had been brought down from Hudson, Michigan, during the night.

Dennis Cowell, and an assistant, had returned with it at half-past three in the morning, put it on a preparation table in a room just off the garage, and left.

VanHorn learned that the deceased was a young woman killed in an accident, and that she was somehow related to Roberta Scherting, daughter of the funeral home's owner.

He noted that there had been no surgical procedures performed on the deceased, prior or subsequent to her death; the body bore several bruises and discolorations on the face, chest, and shoulder, and there was evidence on the back of postmortem lividity—the blackening of the skin caused by stagnant blood settling to the lowest point on a dead body. The corpse had not been cleaned; the feet were particularly dirtied, especially around the toes.

VanHorn also noticed that there appeared to be some dried blood under the fingernails of her right hand. This discovery made little impression on him; the blood, quite possibly, was the woman's own; perhaps she had placed her hand on the wound he found at the back of her head. In any event, as part of preparing the body, it would be washed and the fingernails cleaned.

Ceil sat looking at the bloodstained blouse she had worn the previous day; the blood was Shannon's, transferred from David's shirt. The stains were beginning to turn brown and she knew that if she were to salvage the blouse, it would have to be laundered immediately. Yet, washing away her daughter's blood was not something she found easy; it was as if she had the opportunity to retain something tangible, that by cleansing the blood away, she would be washing away a part of her daughter.

There was something disturbing about the presence last night of the still-damp blood that had bothered her. Was it some sign, a message from Shannon, a signal that what had happened in the woods was not as David had described it, that there was something far more arcane about the death of her precious little girl? She realized that her feelings were probably foolish and nothing more than a reaction to the dreadful catastrophe they had suffered. Still, there was a nagging deep inside her that insisted that she not discount the possibility that there was more to this than a silly riding accident.

Ceil decided on a test: She would wash the blouse;

if the blood came out, she would forget these stupid suspicions, face up to her loss, and get on with her life. But after repeated washings the blood stains remained as before.

Ceil made no further mention to Bob of David's apparent lie about insurance, believing that he had heard her comment the night before but had discounted it as being too preposterous.

"But I was becoming all the more convinced," Ceil remembers.

Later in the morning, David arrived carrying a small bag. The funeral home had asked him to bring clothing in which to dress Shannon.

Ceil glanced inside the bag. She was horrified to see a blue dress that she recognized as one Shannon had had for some time. Shannon was always so meticulous about her clothes, Ceil thought. She'd never pick an old thing like that to be buried in.

David and Ceil drove the short distance to Jasin's, mostly in silence; she found it increasingly difficult to carry on even the most insignificant conversation with the man she was becoming ever more certain had butchered her daughter.

At the mortuary, Ceil managed to pull Roberta Scherting off to one side, away from David.

"When they bring Shannon's body here, I want you to check under her fingernails," she said in hushed tones. "See if there's any evidence of Shannon having scratched or clawed someone."

"It's too late, Ceil, the body's already here; it's been embalmed and cleaned."

"They finished the autopsy this soon?"

"There was no autopsy."

Ceil was speechless; as horrible as the thought of having her daughter dissected was to her, she realized that without an autopsy there was little hope that anyone would know for certain what had caused Shannon's death. She would forever be haunted by the suspicion that her son-in-law had been responsible.

Still furious at the thought of Shannon going to her grave in the ragged old dress David had brought down with him, Ceil made up her mind that it wasn't going to be his way.

Later, she went shopping, choosing a dark green nightgown and negligee.

"I wanted to buy her a last birthday present."

She'd asked her son Bobby to deliver the articles to Jasin's and to insist that they dress Shannon in them.

"We don't give a damn what he wants," Bobby replied when told that David had wanted her dressed in the clothing he'd supplied. "We want her in something nice."

Ceil and Bob returned to the funeral home in the late afternoon to complete the details for services and burial on Saturday. They were asked if they wished to view Shannon's body. Bob turned slightly ashen—no, he couldn't, he didn't want to remember his daughter in death. While she felt much the same way, Ceil also realized that she had no choice in the matter. She must look one more time upon the face of her beloved child; she had to see what David had done to her. It was essential in order that she might have the strength later to insure that he was made to pay for what he'd done.

"I'd like to see her now," she said finally.

Roberta ushered her into a side room where, in the center on a cart, stood the highly polished dark wooden casket their son Bobby had selected earlier that morning. Inside, now embalmed and washed, lay Shannon's lifeless body, dressed in the dark green nightgown and negligee Ceil had selected.

Shannon's neck was grotesquely swollen, her chest bloated, a large bruise between her breasts, and another below one eye. Ceil gasped. Her beautiful, beautiful daughter had been reduced to this.

She tried to get a look at the fingernails but a flap of the casket covered Shannon's hands.

In Sylvania, Ohio, Tom Davis sat, shaking his head in disbelief. Regina had called from the hospital to tell him that Shannon had been killed the day before in a riding accident on the farm.

"Everyone here is just devastated," she said, barely able to control her voice. "The nurses are all crying, the doctors on her service are shocked."

Tom, too, was upset. He had been the one to suggest that David select a Tennessee walking horse because Shannon was not an experienced rider; that particular breed was very docile. And when David had gone out and purchased the animal, Tom checked the horse and found that it behaved just as a good Tennessee walker should. The thought that this horse would bolt, causing Shannon to fall, was unimaginable. That she would be killed in such a fall was unthinkable.

"A person might suffer some injury from a fall like that, maybe break an arm or a leg, but nobody, but *nobody* is killed falling off a slow walking horse."

Just before five in the afternoon, Hillsdale County deputy sheriff Roger Boardman, accompanied by deputy Charles Gutowski, arrived at the Britton farm and asked Dick to take them back to the spot where he and David had picked up Shannon's body the day before.

Following the same route, Britton and the two police officers proceeded back to the location where Davis had left his wife to go for help.

The trio moved from the hayfield into the adjoining woods, along a narrow trail. Approximately twenty-five yards inside they found, in a wide clearing, a half-buried round rock, about the size of a medium grapefruit. It was the only stone that large in the immediate area and its upper surface was coated with what looked to be blood stains. Six or seven feet from the rock, back along the trail, the men discovered a white tennis shoe and about the same distance from the first they found a second shoe. The laces of both were untied. The low weeds in a wide circle around the rock were trampled and, near one edge of the circle, two piles of fresh horse manure were spotted. Deputy Boardman took between six and ten photos of the scene. Later, he could not recall exactly how many pictures were taken because "none of them came out well" and they later disappeared. Other than looking casually about the scene, Boardman made no attempt to gather evidence; the bloodied rock was left half-buried in the ground, no scrapings were made of the stains to determine if they were of human blood and whose, no careful search of the area was undertaken and, when Britton pointed to the shoes and asked the officers if they were going to take them, Boardman replied, "Naw, you can have them."

As for his part, Deputy Gutowski did nothing. "I just kind of stood around," he said later. "Boardman was in charge."

Dick Britton was appalled at the police officers' seeming lack of diligence in conducting an investigation of the place where a twenty-five-year-old woman had died.

"They didn't seem at all interested in the rock with all the blood on it," he told Ann later. "They didn't even kneel down. They just stood there and looked at it."

If the two deputy sheriffs were not particularly intrigued, Dick Britton was sufficiently curious about what he had observed to make a second trip into the woods within minutes of the police officers' departure, taking Ann and his own camera with him.

In a longer and more detailed examination of the scene, Dick noted that the trampled weeds in a ten- to fifteen-foot circle around the bloody rock seemed to have been caused by considerable activity at that location. A struggle, perhaps? He also discovered that the low, thin branches on two nearby trees bore impressions that he interpreted as the marks of leather bridle straps left after two horses had been tied there. The pair of manure piles were located close to where it appeared the horses had been tethered. Dick found this puzzling since David had never mentioned tieing their mounts. Dick had even observed one of them—Shannon's black mare—out of the woods, standing near her body, munching on the tall grass.

Britton took a number of photos of his own, but like those of Deputy Boardman, none were clear enough to be of any value. "I guess it was too dark in the woods."

Before leaving the grove, Britton retrieved the shoes left there and brought them back to his house. Later, he took them to David's, feeling that he should have them. He was startled on entering the kitchen of the Lickley Road home. Seated at the table was Martha Brandon, David's mother. The previous night, after having called the Mohrs to come to the hospital, Dick had suggested that perhaps David's mother should also be told.

"She's on a motorhome trip to North Carolina," Davis replied. "I have no idea how to reach her."

Now, less than twenty hours later, here she sat.

"David must have gotten lucky to be able to get in touch with you so soon," Dick said, surprise evident in his voice.

"Yes, he did," she answered. "I was watering our lawn and came in for a drink when the phone rang."

The evening was clear and warm and Regina and Tom Davis decided to sit on their front porch swing. Sometime between five and seven P.M., the couple saw a vehicle approach the house, turn into their driveway, and then back out.

"That's Dave's van," Tom said. "Why is he backing away?"

Puzzled at their friend's strange action, Tom dashed out to his own car, calling over his shoulder as he went, "I'm going after him."

A few blocks away, he caught up to the van, signaled it to stop, and dashed up to the driver's side.

"Dave, why didn't you come in the house?"

Davis shrugged and mumbled something unintelligible, continuing to stare straight ahead.

"Come back with me; you shouldn't be alone tonight."

Davis consented, after a long pause, and followed Tom back.

Regina insisted he sit on the swing between her and Tom. Seated to his left, she noticed marks on the side of his face.

After expressing their condolences and exchanging reminiscences of Shannon, conversation grew difficult and there were frequent, uncomfortable pauses. During one of the prolonged silences, Regina asked, "How did you hurt your face, Dave?"

His hand shot to his cheek as though he were surprised she had noticed the marks.

"Oh, I scratched my face on some branches."

Before he left, Davis promised to come to dinner the following week.

Later, when she remembered the marks on David's face, Regina recalled that she had been riding a week earlier and had scratched her own face on some tree branches.

"Mine were jagged and irregular; his were straight and even. They looked more like claw marks," she told Tom.

In Hudson, Michigan, tall, willowy, twenty-six-year-old Barbara Matthews sat rereading the brief newspaper story that had caught her eye earlier that day. It was the report of the death in a horseback riding accident the day before of a Hillsdale County woman.

She was jolted out of her deep thought by the harsh ringing of her telephone. Laying the newspaper aside, she answered the phone. When an exchange of greetings had been accomplished, Barbara asked:

"Is the business over, David?"

"Yes," came the reply. "It's over."

5

Philip Rick had sold insurance for most of his adult life, the last sixteen as a representative for Prudential Insurance Company of America. But he didn't like to think of himself as a salesman. His philosophy had always been that his job was to provide a degree of security and protection for the public he served while representing the interests of his employers. Many of his customers had, years earlier, bought their first insurance from the soft-spoken Phil Rick, and they continued to think of him not only as their insurance man, but as a good and decent friend as well. To many others Phil was almost a part of their families. He liked that.

On Friday, July 25, Rick sat at home leisurely scanning the morning *Detroit Free Press*. His eye caught a small news item recounting the accidental death of a twenty-five-year-old Hillsdale County woman who had suffered fatal injuries in a fall from her horse. Rick recognized the woman's name as holder of an accidental death policy he had written the previous year. He shook his head in disbelief; such an attractive young woman, so alive and so much to live for. She and her handsome young husband were such a nice couple, their whole lives still ahead of them. What a tragedy, he thought as he made a mental note to send a sympathy card to the woman's husband and to follow it up later with a phone call advising him of the procedures, as named beneficiary, for filing a claim against the policy. This month's claim totals would soar. Philip

winced as he recalled that the insurance on the woman
was for $110,000, with a double indemnity rider for
accidental death.

It was cool and quiet in the viewing parlor at Jasin's
Funeral Home on Summit Street in Point Place. They
had been there throughout the day, Bob and Lucille.
Their oldest daughter Terri and son Bob sat with them
on a wide couch near the coffin, which was surrounded
with a mountain of floral tributes to Shannon. The casket was closed—a demand of David's that the Mohrs
had acceded to in order to prevent cremation and to
have her body brought back to Toledo. A thick dark
drape hung behind the coffin and standing lamps at
each end reflected a soft, subdued light upward.

There would be just this one day of visitations before the funeral on Saturday—another demand made
by their son-in-law. Consequently a heavy and steady
stream of mourners came throughout the day and into
the evening. Callers entered the large room, signed the
visitors book on a stand near the rear, and glanced
around until they recognized Bob and Ceil. Then they
approached the Mohrs to express their condolences, to
embrace each in turn, and to utter the cumbersome
phrases visitors to funeral homes feel compelled to
make. They felt all the more uncomfortable because
the coffin was closed. Inhabitants of this part of the
Midwest were accustomed to having a body on display, an object on which they could spend some time
focusing their grief. A closed casket to these people
usually meant that the body had been so terribly dis-
figured that the art of the embalmer and cosmetician
had been taxed beyond their limits. But the understanding of those coming to pay their respects was that
Shannon had suffered a nonmutilating head injury.
Why then keep the lid closed? It was difficult for many
to understand, having been raised in a culture where
the practice of ''laying out'' a body for loved ones to
view as part of the grieving process was as old as

history. They needed a glimpse of the deceased, displayed in front of them, as a form of proof that the terrible tragedy they had heard of had truly occurred.

David was there, throughout the day and evening, accepting the tearful regrets of family and friends who spoke to him in hushed and reverent tones. He did little to make them feel even slightly at ease. He sobbed uncontrollably, once burying his head in a woman's lap, his body quaking, his cries echoing throughout the crowded room.

"It was pathetic," Shirley Abrams, Lucille's sister-in-law, recalls. "Everyone else started crying, we felt so sorry for him."

During the long painful hours, David never once sat with the Mohrs, never appearing to want to share their company, to offer any comfort he might be able to extend, never seeming to want their sorrow. Instead, he avoided them, consciously remaining at the rear of the large room, seeming to prefer the attention he was receiving from the mourners coming through the doors. It was just as well as far as Ceil was concerned; she experienced her own discomfort in having him around.

Several women, in the face of the serious and solemn occasion which brought them to Jasin's, found themselves uncontrollably bemused noting that poor Shannon's husband was wearing *facial makeup*. Jane Schenck, a close friend of Ceil's, later recalled that when she greeted Davis that day, giving him a hug and pressing her cheek against his, she came away with a heavy smudge of pancake. "At first I thought it was mine, but then I could see it was the wrong shade." Another woman later remarked to a friend, "I thought it was awful weird for a farmer to be wearing makeup."

Saturday, July 26, 1980 dawned bright, clear, and warm in Toledo, Ohio. Along 116th Street and the adjoining neighborhood of the Point Place district, peo-

ple were quietly dressing in dark, somber suits and
dresses rather than the bright, colorful attire that would
be the norm on such a pleasant summer day. Instead
of heading for the boat launching facilities along the
Maumee River, frequented by the many sport fishermen who resided in this area so close to the river and
Lake Erie, they would be going to bury Shannon Mohr
Davis, to say farewell to the bright and bubbly young
woman many had watched grow from an intense and
active child to a loving, vibrant woman. Many a warm
and wonderful memory of Shannon would be interred
with her this day.

Under the impression that because Shannon had
married outside the Church, a requiem mass could not
be said for her at St. John the Baptist Catholic Church,
where she'd been baptized, received her First Holy
Communion, attended school, and been confirmed,
Bob and Lucille arranged to have Father Carl Recker,
assistant pastor at St. John's, conduct services at Jasin's and at the cemetery.

Davis sat in the front row of the jammed room during the services, his head buried in his hands. As the
mourners began filing past the closed casket topped
with a large color photograph of Shannon in her nurse's
uniform and cap, David suddenly jumped to his feet
and dashed out a side door. "He was just totally over-
come with grief," one of the mourners related later.

More than one hundred people in thirty-five cars
drove slowly through the busy Saturday morning Toledo traffic headed for Calvary Cemetery seven miles
away.

Bob, accompanied by his son Robert, had purchased
a large plot in the cemetery, selecting Calvary because
it was old and slightly rolling and the trees were tall
and majestic and the roadways were wide and winding. He chose three combined burial sites on the side
of a slight rise near the large arched wrought-iron gate
that led to Parkside, a wide, pleasant boulevard winding along an attractive neighborhood of large, older

homes. Shannon would occupy the center plot; Bob and Lucille would have the ones on either side of her when their time came.

In the cool shade, with just a whisper of a breeze and the sound of birds singing high in the trees, those who had come to bid farewell to her became submerged in their own memories of Shannon. Memories were all they had left.

Bob Mohr, standing straight and tall, refusing to allow his grief to bend his strong shoulders, remembered how deeply Shannon was attached to her family, how she proudly announced that she was a "daddy's girl," and how easy and natural she had found it to climb into his lap for heart-to-heart talks, even after her marriage. He recalled how her birthday had become a special event over the years that had him taking her out for dinner at a first-class restaurant.

Lucille, committing her daughter to the earth, was consumed in visions from the past, of the exceptionally close relationship they had shared; they were buddies who "goofed around and kidded each other all the time." Shannon called Ceil, "Goose," and would display her displeasure at something Ceil did with a chiding, drawn out, "M-O-T-H-E-R!" The sound of her voice echoed in Ceil's thoughts and the tears flowed hot and bitter. The day was an especially poignant one for her: July 26, the day she was burying her daughter, was the birthday of the late Glen Abrams, Sr.—her father.

Shannon's sister Terri remembered their quiet talks about boys and romance and life and their dreams for the future. She remembered their rare disagreements as youngsters and how Shannon could not remain angry for more than a few minutes. "She loved everyone."

Bobby, too, remembered. The years drifting back in the past with the shadowy image of Shannon as a baby, then as a five-year-old off to her first day at school, a high school senior dressed in cap and gown and a broad happy smile, a graduating nurse in her crisp, white uniform and finally, as he'd seen her for the last time at a Fourth of July picnic she and David had hosted on their farm, dressed in blue jeans and bright-colored blouse, happy with her new husband and new life. Like his father, Bobby had been unable to view her lifeless body.

And Jean Polcyn Navarro remembered. It was in the third grade that they had begun a friendship that continued uninterrupted for more than a dozen years.

"In high school, when we both had boyfriends, we saw each other less, but we always remained friends. If we didn't talk for six months, Shannon would call and we'd talk like we'd talked only the day before. No strain ever. We could gab for hours and hours. She always knew what to say."

Sheryl Miller South, Shannon's roommate in nursing school, remembered. "Shannon was a petite, pretty woman with naturally curly hair. She was meticulous in her appearance and always demanded that her nurse's uniform be spotless. But she had an impish side, too."

Sheryl remembered a time when they were in a laboratory studying for an anatomy test and, although they'd been cautioned not to touch the skeleton hanging in the corner, they allowed their curiosity to get the better of them. The result was that one of the skeleton's hands snapped off. They ran to the dorm in a panic and quickly chewed piece after piece of bubble gum and then crept back to the lab and used the gum to stick the hand back on. It worked. They would occasionally wait after class until everyone had left and then check on the hand; the bubble gum was still there, silently doing the job they had assigned it.

After passing her state licensing board exams, Shannon had gone to work at Flower Memorial Hospital on the general medical-surgical floor.

"She was an immediate hit with all the patients," Sheryl remembered. "She could win over the crankiest of them all and have them eating out of her hand in no time. She was so likeable, I honestly don't know anyone who didn't adore her.''

And Regina Davis remembered with warm, comforting pleasure the special, wonderful relationship Shannon had with David—a relationship Regina had long dreamed her dear friend would have when she had found that special person with whom she would happily spend the rest of her life. After observing how radiant Shannon had been in the months following her marriage to Davis, Regina was thrilled that it seemed to have happened in just the way those who loved her so much had prayed it would.

"Everything was beautiful. They never had any problems. She kept waiting for the bubble to burst because things were so good. She couldn't believe it. She was very, very happy."

Kathy Bocik, a close friend from high school, remembered. "We were all aware of her intense feeling about marriage and children. And it was taken for granted that when the time came she would marry Rich."

And, certainly, Rich Duffey remembered. "I watched her grow from a sixteen-year-old girl into a twenty-five-year-old woman. She was always mature for her age, ready earlier than some to settle down and start a family. I guess I wasn't ready to accept responsibility. I had to get some breathing room."

Rich thought of Shannon as vulnerable. Not naive, but not streetwise, which made her easy prey for someone who might want to hurt her.

"I wish I could do it over."

He couldn't, of course, and he knew it. He would have to live with it.

At the short graveside ceremony, Ceil stood across the casket from David. "I watched him carefully. He kept his head bowed most of the time, but I could see that there were no tears, no sorrow. Sometimes he would glance around, like he was bored with it all.''

Others noticed David's actions. Dick Britton remembered looking out of the corner of his eye and seeing Davis staring at him. ''It kind of made me feel funny.''

From the cemetery the mourners returned to Point Place; neighbors of the Mohrs, Dick and Phyllis Horner, had graciously offered their home as a place for friends and family to gather for refreshments. The weather being warm and sunny, most congregated in the backyard, seated on folding chairs. Ceil chose not to attend: ''I didn't feel that I could be anywhere near David at that time.''

One couple present were largely unknown to many who were there that day. They introduced themselves as Martha and James Brandon, David's mother and stepfather.

Jerry and Thelma Foley, longtime friends of the Mohrs, sat with the Brandons, hoping to make them feel welcome and at ease.

Attempting to make friendly conversation, Thelma commented, ''We all feel just terrible about what's happened. This on top of all David has suffered, it's just tragic.''

Martha nodded and thanked Thelma.

''After all he went through in Vietnam,'' Thelma continued.

''In Vietnam?'' Martha asked, a questioning look coming over her face.

''Yes, you know, with the injuries he received while in the Marines.''

Martha shook her head. ''There must be some mistake. David was never in Vietnam or the Marines. He wasn't in the military at all.''

6

David left the luncheon early, driving to Grass Lake, Michigan, near Jackson where he looked up a friend, Dr. Robert A. Burns, Jr., a dentist. Davis suggested that they go fishing. Burns, unaware of Shannon's death, asked why he had not brought her with him as he normally had. David replied coldly, "She died; I buried her a couple of days ago."

Burns was astonished. David had not called him to tell of his personal misfortune, he had not informed him so that he might have at least attended the funeral. Was David so devastated that he could not bring himself to talk about his sorrow? After all, Burns was not a complete stranger to personal calamity. Certainly David knew that Bob had lost his first wife shortly after their marriage in a terrible boating accident. Why should David feel reluctant to bring his own grief to his close friend?

Burns had met Davis in 1969 when the pair worked at the University of Michigan Hospital blood bank, drawing, typing, and cross-matching blood. Burns was in his second year of dental school and had taken the job, part time during the school year and full time during summer recess, to supplement his income. David was a part-time employee.

To begin with, Davis was to Burns "just a fellow who worked on down the bench." But when Burns discovered that Davis and he shared an interest in hunting and fishing, "we became what I would consider good friends."

Both men had an enthusiasm for bow-and-arrow hunting. On one occasion early in their friendship, Davis made a casual reference to ''hunting with a nerve-paralyzing drug or tranquilizing drug'' that was apparently legal to use on arrows in some southern states.

Burns later stated that he believed that the knowledge of the tranquilizing drug available for hunting came from David's brother-in-law, who was a veterinarian.

''We had a discussion that if either one of us or Doc, his veterinarian friend, ever had reason to be in a state where it was legal, we would investigate the purchase of it.''

Burns, because of his close friendship with Davis, had known his wife, Phyllis, well, and was aware of the marital problems the couple suffered before their divorce. He was, therefore not surprised when the marriage crumbled and fell apart.

''David had begun dating a girl I knew, a woman named Kay Kendall. David had relationships with several women, both before his divorce from Phyllis and after. The most noteworthy was Kay because she meant the most to him, I do believe. And it was also the longest.''

Burns recalled that David had asked Kay to marry him and the relationship had progressed to the point where they had actually purchased wedding rings. But at the last moment Kay backed out.

''David never told me that he had asked Kay to marry him or that she had eventually broken off their relationship. But it was pretty obvious that it had happened and David was terribly depressed about it.''

Davis took up with several other women before his marriage to Shannon.

''Our friendship cooled off just before he married Shannon and I didn't see too much of him after that. I believe he came around with Shannon just twice. On one occasion she and my wife went horseback riding. She was a lousy rider.''

The next evening, David drove out to the Sylvania home of Tom and Regina Davis to accept their invitation to dinner.

Regina, feeling deep compassion for their newly widowed friend, slipped away and called another friend, Cheryl Hogan, asking her to come over. Regina had a dual reason for choosing the lovely twenty-year-old bachelorette. Cheryl was a first cousin of Shannon's and her dear friend; she and Shannon had spent a great deal of time together over the years.

''We lived just three blocks from Uncle Bob and Aunt Ceil,'' Cheryl recalls. ''They had a big in-ground swimming pool, and I would go there often during the summer. Shannon was five years older than I was, but we became very close friends.''

Shannon's death had affected Cheryl deeply. In addition, Cheryl, Regina had learned, had just lost her job and was suffering a double dose of emotional agony. Regina felt that a quiet evening would be beneficial to both David and Cheryl, who she knew were well acquainted.

When Cheryl arrived she found Tom and David in a private, almost hushed conversation, which, she gathered, had to do with some financial problems David was experiencing.

''What's going on, David?'' Cheryl asked after a few minutes.

''I'm going to lose everything,'' he replied, pain etching his face. ''I don't want you to tell your family about this, but I don't have enough money to cover the funeral expenses. I'm going to lose my farm and everything because of inheritance taxes.''

''David, my family wouldn't want you to lose anything; they would help you.''

''No,'' he insisted. ''I don't want them to know about this.''

He's lying, she thought. Shannon had told her about the large life insurance policies he had taken out on both their lives. Cheryl knew he had insurance on Shannon. She knew he was lying, but *why* was he lying?

"Let's go out to dinner," David suggested suddenly. "Let's go to the Loma Linda."

The others were somewhat startled; the Loma Linda was a Mexican restaurant in Toledo that was a favorite of young adults.

Cheryl objected to the restaurant as inappropriate but Regina, taking her aside, told her that she felt Davis needed reassurance and the support of Shannon's family. Regina said that it would help Cheryl cheer up as well. Later, however, Regina would admit, "I thought it was out of place to be at Loma Linda's at all. It's a big bar. It's a party place."

The four drove there in three separate cars, and once inside, Davis ordered margaritas and nachos at the bar while waiting for a table.

"When we were seated," Cheryl recalls, "the first thing David did was toast his 'loving wife who is now smiling down on me.' He said it so sarcastically, I started crying."

Regina recalled that David's toast had included the comment, "I wouldn't change a thing, but I wish she could have cooked better."

Cheryl became so upset by what she felt was a heartless and tasteless statement that she excused herself and rushed to the parking lot. Davis followed her out of the restaurant and caught her just as she reached her car.

"I started crying again and he put his arms around me as if to comfort me and I rested my forehead on his chest."

"You're now the most beautiful woman in my life and we've got to stay in touch," Davis said, sliding his hands down her back until they rested securely on her buttocks.

Cheryl was horrified. *Oh, my God. What is he doing?* she wondered. "But then," she says, "I realized exactly what he was doing."

She tore herself away from him, hurriedly entered her car, and quickly drove away. She continually checked her car's rearview mirror throughout the terrifying drive to her apartment. Inside, she locked the door and, without turning on the lights, telephoned Aunt Ceil and Uncle Bob.

"Wait right there, Uncle Bob will come and get you," Ceil told her when Cheryl described the incident at the restaurant. "Don't open the door to anyone."

Still trembling in uncontrolled fear, Cheryl stayed on the line with Ceil until Bob arrived to pick her up.

Once inside his car, Cheryl turned to Bob and said cooly: "He killed her, didn't he?"

Bob's head pivoted to look at her.

"Why did you say that?"

She explained the circumstances of the restaurant confrontation and her knowledge that David was lying when he claimed to have no insurance and no money. As well, there were several other unconnected but troublesome incidents. At the Fourth of July picnic at the farm just three weeks earlier, Shannon had taken Cheryl up to the bedroom for a private talk and urged her, "Before you make any commitment to anyone, be sure to ask a lot of questions; don't be gun-shy, ask about extramarital affairs, ask who is going to be the breadwinner, ask about previous wives, ask everything."

She recalled how upset David had been on that occasion to have Cheryl and Shannon talking quietly in the bedroom where he couldn't hear and how he had shouted through the door for Shannon to get back down with the others. The memory of these troubling incidents flooded back now, ultimately leading the twenty-year-old to the belief that Shannon's death had not occurred in the manner Davis was claiming.

Bob began to cry, his huge body shaking in spasms. Finally, he was able to whisper: ''We do have some suspicions.''

PART TWO

The Revelation

7

Sunday, the day after the funeral, had been difficult for Ceil and Bob. They were bordering on total exhaustion; getting through the past four days had been an exercise in raw courage for them.

After Mass at St. John's that morning, a number of parishioners and friends had approached them to renew the condolences they had extended earlier. Father Raymond Etzel, St. John's pastor, embraced Ceil as she left the church and whispered words of comfort to her and Bob.

Bobby stopped by in the afternoon, followed by Terri and Brian later in the day.

During the hours when they were alone, left to grieve in private, they tried to fill the time with some kind of activity, anything to avoid sitting and reliving the horrors of the last one hundred hours. Bob puttered around the house, his mind numbed to what he was doing, moving aimlessly as if in a trance. Ceil sorted through the stack of sympathy cards that had poured into the small home on 116th Street.

Over the last ten months they had spent almost every weekend at David and Shannon's farm. Now there was no reason to make the long trip to Hillsdale County, there would be no phone calls during the week to chat for a few minutes, to laugh and kid with Shannon. The sounds of Shannon's laughter would never again ring happily in her parents' ears, and the firm but tender and loving hugs she had so liberally given were now denied them forever. Their visits with her from now on would be in the quiet, tree-shaded cemetery where she would lie through eternity.

There was a hollowness in their lives now which they knew could never be filled as they moved through the years stretching out before them. Their life could never be as it had been just a few days ago; all tomorrows would dawn with a stabbing pain in the heart, an agony they would suffer every bleak and friendless day.

Well-meaning friends had told them that, in time, the pain would pass. But they knew that was nonsense. The pain might ease over a long period, but it would never disappear. Losing someone very dear was not like suffering a toothache. You didn't just get over it; the hurt continued, first as an unspeakable anguish, eventually subsiding to a steady, never-ending throb.

On Monday, July 28, Davis appeared at the home of Philip Rick, the Prudential insurance agent, where he initiated the claim form on the insurance policy he held on the life of his deceased wife Shannon. Rick offered to contact the Jasin Funeral Home for him and request that a copy of Shannon's death certificate be sent to Davis at his farm. He explained that the document would be necessary before he could forward the claim to the home office for processing.

"He seemed shaken up and distraught," Rick remembers.

Back at his farm, David filled several suitcases with personal belongings. He then drove over to see Dick Britton.

"I'm going out of town for a while," he told Britton. "Would you pick up my mail? I'll send an address where you can forward it. I'm expecting a letter from Jasin's Funeral Home that I'm especially interested in getting as soon as possible."

Britton promised to take care of it.

Tuesday morning David showed up at Bob and Ceil's, bringing with him several pillows Ceil had left at the farm.

Entering the house, he approached her with his arms outstretched to embrace her as he had so many times before. She pulled away from him.

He looked puzzled and hurt.

"Why?" he asked.

"I've had a bad day, David. I think you know why."

He didn't pursue the matter. He told them that he was leaving for awhile, that he had to get away.

"Where are you going?" Bob inquired.

"Oh, I don't know. I'm just going to start driving west until I get to the desert."

Neither Bob nor Ceil mentioned the incident in the Loma Linda parking lot a few nights earlier, which Cheryl had described. After less than five minutes, Davis left.

Lucille stood, looking up the street as the yellow van disappeared. How strange, she thought. She had always been so delighted with her son-in-law, so pleased to see how happy Shannon had been, so confident that her baby daughter had married well. She had been so happy for her. But now everything had changed. The young man she had given her daughter to turned out to be none of the things they had thought he was; the dramatic and honorable life he'd claimed to have led was a sham, a monumental falsehood. He was none of the things he claimed to be; the image he had projected had dissolved like a wisp of smoke. Ceil was left with only the fond memories of a talented, loving girl who offered the promise of giving her parents many delightful years watching her with a family of her own, being able to share a portion of the great bounty of love she had stored and nurtured since her childhood. For the devastated Lucille Mohr, among the ruin of her illusions there was little remaining but the memory of the bruised and battered body of her cherished daughter.

"I thought Shannon's marriage had been made in heaven," Ceil says. Now, just having David near sent cold chills through her, making it impossible to tolerate being touched by him, by the hands she was certain had taken Shannon's life.

On Sunday, while Terri and Brian were at the house, the subject of Brian's reluctance to stay at the farm without Ceil came up.

"I was scared because Aunt Shannon and Uncle Dave were having a big fight."

Ceil was shocked; she had been there the whole day and witnessed no argument between them.

"You were out in the yard pulling weeds. They stopped before you came in the house."

Brian explained that David had acted so "scary" during the argument that he was afraid to stay at the farm without Lucille being there.

Additional bits of information concerning their son-in-law were beginning to filter in from other sources—disturbing, frightening, incredible information.

Roberta Scherting, in a phone conversation with Ceil on Monday, mentioned the scratches she'd observed on David's face and his attempt to conceal them with makeup. Several friends, obviously disturbed, reported statements made by David's mother that dramatically disputed his oft-repeated claim to having served with the U.S. Marines in Vietnam. The scars on his back, his mother insisted, were surgical scars from a herniated disk operation he'd undergone several years earlier. Though Davis asserted he'd been wounded in the foot by a land mine and had plastic bones inserted to replace those blown away in the explosion, his mother denied this, saying that the only foot injury he'd ever suffered was a broken bone when he had gotten drunk on the night of his high school graduation and had jumped or fallen from a second-floor window.

And there was the matter of his previous marriage. Before giving their blessing to Shannon and David's marriage, the Mohrs had specifically asked him if he'd been married before. He had assured them that he had not. Now they discovered that not only had he had a previous marriage but he had fathered two children and had divorced his first wife.

What kind of man is this? Ceil wondered in amazement and horror. *How could he have expected to continue to live a lie and not be discovered and disgraced?*

When Davis left the Mohrs, he drove to the Franklin Park Mall, a large shopping complex on Toledo's west side, where he picked up Barbara Matthews. He had dropped her off there on his way to visit the Mohrs, telling her to "do some shopping while I attend to some business."

From the mall, they drove to a nearby entrance ramp leading to Interstate-75, pointed the new van not west toward the desert but south toward Florida.

8

Things were moving too fast!

Roberta Scherting sat looking at the letter she'd just opened. It was from Philip Rick, a Prudential insurance agent in Hillsdale. In his letter he requested that a "copy of the certified death certificate for one Shannon Davis" be sent to David Richard Davis in order that Rick might process the insurance claim filed in connection with Shannon's death.

Roberta readily recalled the conversation she'd had with Davis the night before the funeral, during which he commented that he would probably have to sell some of his farm equipment to pay back the Mohrs for the funeral expenses. Too, she was well aware that Bob and Ceil had mentioned that David had told them that he had no insurance on Shannon and that Lucille was suspicious of this claim because of something Shannon had told her shortly after she and David were married. Roberta's mind reeled. It was July 30, exactly one week since Shannon's death, and now an insurance company was preparing to make payment on a policy that, according to David, didn't exist. Things were moving too fast.

She put down the letter, picked up the telephone, and dialed Bob and Ceil's number.

"I was right!" Ceil all but shouted after her brief conversation with Roberta. "That son-of-a-bitch did have a life insurance policy on Shannon."

They sat at the kitchen table, Ceil chain smoking, her hands trembling whenever she lit another cigarette, while Bob, his palms flat on the table, shook his head back and forth in disbelief.

Never in their lives had they had any connection with a murder, known anyone who had committed a homicide, or been acquainted with a person who had been murdered. Now Bob was sitting there, finally having to face the real possibility that he not only knew a murderer but that the murderer was his son-in-law. Not only was he acquainted with someone who was the victim of a homicide, but the victim was his own daughter.

They had to decide what to do with this new information, now that there was no longer any real doubt in the mind of either of them that Shannon had been deliberately killed for the insurance money. After some discussion they decided that the following morning they would go to Hillsdale and lay what they knew before the county sheriff.

"Maybe we should call Dick Britton and have him come with us," Bob suggested. "He heard David tell the deputy that he had no insurance at all on Shannon."

"No!" Ceil stated firmly. "He's David's best friend. I don't think we should trust him just now; he might tell David what we're doing."

Dick Britton strolled alone into the woods behind his farm, moving almost reverently to the spot where the blood-stained rock projected out of the moist earth. He had been here several times in the past week, drawn almost hypnotically to the place where Shannon had died.

It had been a difficult seven days for Dick and Ann; they had been haunted by the spectre of a lovely, innocent young woman, her head bloodied, her skin a ghastly tint, her vivid, happy personality lost to them forever.

Les Sizemore, a neighbor, had come to the Britton's the morning after Shannon's death, announcing in no uncertain terms what he believed had happened the previous day.

"He killed her. The minute my wife told me last night that Shannon had been thrown off a horse that day and killed, the first words out of my mouth were, 'Bullshit! He killed her.' "

Sizemore, a man whose intellect far exceeded his educational experience—he'd had a year or two of college—had never joined the coterie of Davis admirers who had accepted, root and branch, his claims of valor and daring.

"I'd always had severe doubts about the man's honesty and integrity," Sizemore says. "Being good friends with Dick, I always felt ill at ease around Davis because I didn't really care for the man. Dick seemed to put him up on a pedestal, was quite enthralled with him and I really didn't want to say too much. But I always felt he was a liar and a cheater. My father spent twenty years in the military; I grew up around fighter pilots and men who were in actual combat units. And I'd observed that men who were in combat didn't like to talk about it unless they were around other men who had been in combat, too. It's like a very exclusive club. Davis, on the other hand, seemed to go out of his way to talk about being shot through the knee as he hung from a tree in a parachute. Yet in the summer, when he wore shorts, I noticed there was no disfigurement, no scars. He was a liar, a bullshitter, a phoney."

Dick was having his own doubts about the man he'd thought of as almost a brother. Still, it was incomprehensible to accept the possibility that Davis would cold-bloodedly murder his wife.

"Why would he do it?" he asked Sizemore.

"There are three reasons why he might have killed her. One is in sheer anger, someone will accidently kill someone, hit them too hard or something like that; that's an accident. The other two are always deliberate; that's love and money."

"Well, as far as I know he loved her."

"Yes, but did he have another girlfriend he was in love with, or does he have any life insurance?"

"No, I heard him tell the sheriff's deputy that he had no insurance on her."

"That's what he *said*," Sizemore replied.

Now, standing in the wooded grove, Britton looked down at the stained rock and saw a pair of blood-red toadstools growing from the damp earth on the very spot where Shannon had died.

As they drove into Hillsdale, Ceil suddenly told Bob that she wanted to stop at the county prosecutor's office before going to the sheriff.

"Why?" Bob asked, assuming that presenting their suspicions to the sheriff would be sufficient.

"I don't know why; I just want to talk to him as well."

County prosecutor Ronald C. Zellar listened attentively, nodding occasionally and making notes on a legal pad in front of him, as Bob and Ceil presented their fears and suspicions in a quiet, controlled fashion. When they had concluded, Zellar rose from his chair, extended his hand, and recommended that they go down the street to the sheriff's office.

"I'll call and let them know you're coming," Zellar promised. "And I'll be in touch with you."

Sheriff Edward O. Webb was not available when Bob and Ceil arrived and they were directed to the office of Detective Al Schindler, a hard-nosed police officer with a skeptical nature and a tendency to view most everyone with a jaded eye.

It was now his turn to listen politely to the Mohrs, which he did without showing emotion or making comments; only once did he raise an eyebrow, when told that Davis had left town after having filed a claim for payment on an insurance policy he had denied having. He looked quizzical when the meeting was interrupted by a phone call from Toledo. It was for Bob from Terri, who informed him that Roberta Scherting had just called the house. There were more requests for death certificates coming in from several other insurance companies.

"Thank you for coming in, Mr. and Mrs. Mohr," Schindler said when they had completed their presentation. "I'll look into this and get back to you."

Bob and Ceil left, driving back to Toledo feeling strangely uncertain about what had occurred that day. Would anyone really do anything about this? Did they really care at all?

The following day, Dick Britton, now consumed with his own uncertainty, with an emotion that had begun to gnaw at him like a raw acid in his gut, made the decision that he would have to "talk to somebody about this." He didn't want to mention his suspicions to Bob and Ceil because he was afraid they might tell Dave. After the funeral on Saturday, he had considered approaching Bob to try to determine whether he and Ceil had any suspicions about Shannon's "accident." He had gone after Bob, following him into the house on one occasion only to have David suddenly appear in the kitchen.

One of Dick's good friends was a policeman in Hudson; he decided to seek his advice. But the friend was out of town and Dick returned home more troubled than ever.

He couldn't wait until he was able to contact his friend; he had to get the ache in his belly out. He phoned his sister Joy, telling her of his concern.

"If you feel there's something wrong, then go see the sheriff," Joy advised him.

He told Ann he was going to Hillsdale. He was going to talk to the sheriff.

Al Schindler had been busy since the Mohr's visit the previous day. His first move was to contact the insurance agents who had requested death certificates to determine exactly how many insurance policies were in effect and what the total payoff would be. He was interrupted in this inquiry when the desk sergeant stuck his head in the office door to tell him that a citizen wanted to speak with him about the Shannon Davis death.

"David Davis's wife died and I think he killed her," Dick began haltingly, struggling to find the right words. "I don't know why; they seemed to have a good marriage, he's a nice person. But there's just too many things here that don't make sense."

Schindler sat quietly, letting Britton do all the talking. When Dick finished, the detective thanked him for coming in and promised to look into the matter. He didn't mention that the Mohrs had been to see him a day earlier.

After Britton left his office, Schindler went back to contacting the insurance agents. It took less than an hour to find what he'd been looking for. His next move was to confer with Prosecutor Zellar.

"I think you'd better find out who this David Davis is," Zellar told the detective when Schindler had laid out all the facts he had gathered concerning the suspicious life insurance policies that Davis had accumulated on his wife, Shannon Davis. "We may have a homicide on our hands."

Dick had departed the sheriff's office at about ten in the morning. At noon, seated at his kitchen table having lunch, he tuned the radio to the Hillsdale station and was jolted by the announcement that County Prosecutor Ronald C. Zellar and Sheriff Edward O. Webb had decided to reopen the investigation into the sudden death of Shannon Mohr Davis.

"Boy, that was easy," Britton almost shouted, assuming that the decision to reopen the case was based solely on his visit to Schindler two hours earlier.

Realizing that word would eventually reach Toledo, Dick determined that he should break the news to Bob and Ceil first.

"What do you think, Dick?" Ceil asked when he told her the case had been reopened.

"You won't tell Dave what I say, will you?"

"Oh, no, we won't tell him."

"Well, I think something's awful fishy."

"Dick, so do we. Bob will be up to see you tonight."

That evening, Bob and Bobby arrived at the Brittons', where Dick and Ann conferred with the pair, exchanging suspicions and comparing recollections of events of the days just prior to Shannon's death. Bob told the Brittons of his and Lucille's meeting with Al Schindler and with Zellar.

"I think something's going to get done now," Dick predicted.

The next day, Britton returned to Hillsdale to see Schindler a second time. He had recalled David's interest in having the expected letter from the funeral home forwarded to him in Florida as soon as it arrived.

"There's only one thing he would be expecting to get from a funeral home, a death certificate," he told Schindler. "Everything is looking so suspicious, like he killed her but I don't know why he would."

"How about life insurance?" Schindler asked matter of factly.

"He doesn't have any. I heard the deputy and Bob Mohr both ask him. Dave doesn't have any life insurance on Shannon."

"Is that what he told you?"

Dick nodded, and Schindler opened a file folder he had been holding.

"How about $330,000 in life insurance?"

9

"You'd better find out who this David Davis is," Prosecutor Ronald Zellar had instructed Al Schindler. Neither man could have anticipated what "finding out who Davis is" would uncover.

Digging deeply into the various insurance policies held by David Davis, Schindler spent hours on the telephone and days roaming Wright Township, interviewing neighbors and nearby farmers, seizing each rumor like it was a wild rabbit and squeezing it until the life in it was gone or it magically transformed into something even more intriguing.

The detective was particularly attracted to the mysterious fires that had occurred on Davis's property.

On the night of September 7, 1976, while David was away and Howard Sensabaugh, a neighbor, looked after his farm, Davis's barn burned to the ground.

"There's nothing in the barn," Davis had told Sensabaugh just before leaving. "You won't have to bother with the barn."

He collected $6,000 for the barn, plus a quantity of hay and a combine he claimed had been destroyed in the fire.

The Sensabaugh house, on the farm Davis purchased in April 1979, that had been rented out by Davis and which had been vacated several weeks earlier, burned in the early-morning hours of March 10, 1980, within a week after Davis told Dick Britton how easy it would be to burn a house and make it appear to have been an accident. Davis collected $29,100 in insurance for the destroyed three-and-a-half bedroom farm-house.

"You make it look like you're redecorating, have paint thinner and other flammables around," David had said.

In his report, Waldron fire chief Michael Stuck listed the cause of the fire as "wood stove" igniting painting materials.

The neighbors, bound by their "mind-your-own-business" code, enjoyed a healthy skepticism about the fortuitous combustions but said nothing until Schindler prodded them.

"I don't know if anyone was suspicious about the barn burning, but the house was so obvious," Herbert Frank, a Lickley Road resident, commented.

It was the history of Davis's life insurance purchases that Schindler found most alarming.

On October 2, 1979, eight days after their wedding, Philip Rick met with David and Shannon at their farm and took their applications for two "Economatic term life insurance policies," both for $110,000 each, with a double indemnity rider that would net $220,000 if either died of accidental causes. The monthly payments on the two policies totaled $149.30.

Three days later, on October 5, they bought a new MGB convertible and took out a policy that would pay off the $10,227.38 purchase price, finance charges, and insurance costs if either of them died.

On November 1, Shannon cosigned for a $25,000 farm loan Davis had taken out on September 14, ten days before they were married. They also took out a policy with Mutual Service Insurance Co. to pay off the loan if either died.

Two weeks later, Davis was named beneficiary of the Hartford Life Insurance Company policy supplied to Shannon by her employer, Flower Memorial Hospital. The policy, which had named Bob Mohr as beneficiary, called for a payment of $26,644.80 if Shannon died of natural causes or $52,289.60 if her death were accidental.

A fifth insurance policy to pay off the $13,500 debt for the purchase of a new two-ton Chevrolet farm truck was issued in both David's and Shannon's names.

Shannon had yet another policy, taken out in 1976 with the New York Life Insurance Co., naming her father as beneficiary, and calling for the payment of $10,000 upon her death. Davis replaced Bob Mohr as beneficiary on April 28, 1980.

The six policies on Shannon's life totaled more than $330,000. An insurance research study in 1976 found that the median insurance owned by females in the U.S. was about $14,660 in households having a total income of $25,000 or more. Davis held more than *twenty times* that amount on Shannon's life.

Schindler discovered two other chilling bits of information as the result of his investigation: At the time of Shannon's death, the Hartford policy would have expired in just six more days, and the Mutual Service life policy, a 10-month term, nonrenewable insurance policy, was due to expire on September 1, 1980. These two policies totaled $78,289.60.

In addition, Rick advised Schindler that the double indemnity policy on Shannon was in its thirty-day grace period. Davis had not made the July payment which was due on the eighth.

"The bastard was so hungry he didn't want to waste the money on another payment," Schindler said.

10

What did they have? That was the question confronting Al Schindler. Before proceeding any further, it was necessary he assess the quality and quantity of the information he had gathered on David Richard Davis.

He knew that Davis was a psychopathic liar, a condition that, like puberty, had apparently crept up on him slowly and mysteriously at first and then continued in a full-blown rush that altered him forever.

Schindler knew that Davis was almost certainly an unprincipled arsonist and thief twice over; he had obtained moneys from insurance companies under the fraudulent and felonious claims of accidental fires. And he was a rapacious husband who before the honeymoon was over had insured his bride's life in amounts obscenely beyond all reason and decent propriety.

There was no question in Schindler's mind that Davis was all that. But was he a brutal, calculating killer?

"We have a possible homicide," he told Zellar in a meeting in which he laid before the prosecutor the information he had collected about Davis. "But there's no way we'll ever be certain without an autopsy."

"Then we'd better order one," Zellar replied.

However, it wasn't as simple as requesting an order of exhumation from a local judge; Shannon had been buried in Toledo, in another state, out of the jurisdiction of Michigan courts. It would require the cooperation and consent of officials in Lucas County, Ohio.

To strengthen his case for an Ohio exhumation,

Schindler first obtained a search warrant to seize the X-rays taken at Thorn Hospital of Shannon's head and neck on the night she died. He then sent the films to Dr. Lawrence R. Simson, Jr., a highly respected forensic pathologist at Edward Sparrow Hospital in Lansing, Michigan, for evaluation. Simson replied that the mysterious lines on the X-ray of Shannon's cervical spine were not fractures but flaws in the film. Now Schindler could argue that there was sufficient uncertainty about the actual cause of death to justify an autopsy.

But before that, there were still the territorial egos to be considered. Dr. Robert Harrison, medical examiner for Lenawee County, was contacted and advised that an autopsy on the body of Shannon Davis was now imperative. Dr. David Acus, the Hillsdale County medical examiner, received a like notification. The two county officials then proceeded to operate in opposite directions.

On August 14, 1980, Dr. Acus wrote to Dr. Simson, directing the pathologist to "accept the care and custody of the body of the decedent Shannon Davis, to conduct an autopsy and examination to determine the true cause of death pursuant to my powers under the statute. You are to accept the body from the Hillsdale County Sheriff's Department, maintain the body under your control during the examination period, and return the same to the care and custody of the Hillsdale County Sheriff's Department."

Dr. Simson was further directed to "forward the results to the Hillsdale County Medical Examiner and the Hillsdale County Prosecutor" when the autopsy had been completed.

On the same day, a similar letter was dispatched to Dr. Harry Mignerey, the Lucas County, Ohio, coroner, advising him that an order of exhumation had been signed.

Under Ohio law, the order of exhumation need not

be signed by a judge. The prosecutor or the coroner in the county where the body had been buried was empowered to sign the order. Neither Acus nor Harrison had any legal standing in the decision to disinter Shannon's body.

Al Schindler prepared the paperwork for the Lucas County prosecutor's office and took it to Toledo, where he met Prosecutor Anthony Pizza and Chief Prosecuting Attorney Curtis Posner. It was decided that Lucas County would assume charge of the autopsy. Posner obtained a written consent form from Bob and Lucille Mohr—an unnecessary but considerate act—signed the order of exhumation, and notified Coroner Mignerey that his office should direct the exhumation and autopsy. Mignerey replied that he was willing to assist but wanted Hillsdale authorities present during the examination. Such arrangements were made; the autopsy would be conducted within ten days.

Bob and Ceil felt nervous anticipation at the news that an autopsy would finally be performed. They tried not to think about the precise details of what was going to happen, concentrating instead on what would come out of this ghoulish procedure: They would now have proof that Shannon had been murdered and her killer would be brought to justice and made to pay for his terrible crime.

11

The bright early-morning sun cast long shadows through the trees, painting the gently rolling grounds in a patchwork of alternately vibrant and mutted greens and browns. Along Parkside Boulevard the traffic flow was increasing as the working population of Toledo began the arduous daily commute from home to work. Even to those viewing the burdensome trek as an unavoidable emotional assault, it promised to be a beautiful summer day.

The small group—less than a dozen people—gathered around Calvary Cemetery's lot 273, in section 37. They stepped back as the engine of the white backhoe sprang to life, belching a plume of dark smoke and diesel fumes, raised its mawlike jaws and positioned itself over the rectangle of newly sprouted grass before plunging into the earth for a savage bite of sod and earth.

It was shortly after seven on the morning of August 25, 1980, exactly thirty days since Shannon's grave had been sealed. Already it was being disturbed.

Among those gathered around the gravesite were Dr. Harry F. Mignerey, Lucas County coroner; Dr. Steven Fazekas, deputy coroner; his wife, Renata Fazekas, also a deputy coroner; Joseph Inman, chief investigator for the Lucas County coroner's office and his assistant, Timothy Fish; Detective Al Schindler of the Hillsdale County sheriff's department; Roberta Jasin Scherting and David R. Jasin, Jr., representatives of the David R. Jasin Funeral Home, Toledo.

The intact concrete vault cover was lifted at eight o'clock and the brown hardwood coffin removed. It was transported to the Lucas County coroner's office by a Jasin funeral home hearse. Accompanying the coffin in the hearse were Dr. Steven Fazekas and Roberta Scherting. They arrived at approximately 8:15 A.M.

The coffin was opened by David Jasin at 8:20 and the body inside was identified by Roberta Scherting as that of Shannon Mohr Davis.

Dr. Steven Fazekas, assigned to conduct the actual autopsy, with his wife Renata assisting, ordered the body removed from the casket and, after the clothing was removed, placed on the autopsy table. The others quietly witnessed the procedure. Photographs were taken throughout the autopsy procedure. These valuable pieces of evidence would later "disappear."

The official Lucas County autopsy report, number 312-80, reads:

> The body is dressed in a dark green nightdress and robe, black underslip, pantyhose and pink underpants. Heavy mold is on the face, some on the hands and feet.
>
> An embalming incision is in the right inguinal area, a trocart hole is in left midabdominal wall. The epidermis is slipping over the abdomen, thighs, back of the body and back of the head.
>
> The body is that of a 25 year-old female, measuring five feet-five inches in length and weighing 136 pounds. The scalp hair is brown, six inches long. The eyeballs are decomposed. There are no petechial hemorrhages in the palpebral bulbar conjunctive. The teeth are natural. The breasts symmetrical.

The initial portion of the autopsy report covered the gross pathology, or external examination of the body. It then moved on to a description of the injuries both external and internal as the surgery on the body continued.

The wound to the scalp was observed as a "three-and-one-half inch laceration in the left parietal scalp." The wound had been sutured at the funeral home and a "hardening compound placed in the wound," as noted in the report. The scalp was "reflected" or peeled back from the skull and hemorrhages in the left temporal muscle and hemorrhaging in the right and left parietal and entire occipital scalp were found. The skull bones were not fractured.

An orbital cut was made in the skull with an electric bone saw, allowing the skull cap to be hinged back to permit access to the brain. The brain was removed, weighed (1,300 grams), and visually examined.

> The brain is soft due to postmortem change. There are no epidural or subdural hemorrhages. No injuries are seen on the left side of the brain. Subarachnoid hemorrhage is present over the lateral aspect of the right frontal lobe and lateral aspect of the right temporal lobe, the area measuring four inches by two inches.
>
> The brain is swollen as evidenced by tonsillar herniation.

This portion of the report refers to the openings at the base of the skull where the spinal cord enters from the spinal column into the bottom of the brain. The swelling was believed to have resulted when the brain was forced down into the openings as it rebounded within the skull as the result of a severe blow sustained by the head.

The brain was placed in a formalin solution for fixation and later laboratory study.

A gray-colored bruise on the top and back of the left shoulder was examined and measured, as well as a small bruise on the upper back of the right arm. Incisions revealed hemorrhages in the subcutaneous tissue just below the skin. A small discoloring on the fourth finger of the right hand was noted.

Hemorrhages in the subcutaneous tissues of the upper back and trapezius muscles on the right and left side were observed. No hemorrhage in deep back muscles of the posterior neck and occiput. Spinal column is not fractured. No epidural or subarachnoid hemorrhages are seen in spinal canal and no contusion hemorrhages are seen in the spinal cord. There are no neck injuries.

A classic "Y" incision—beginning at the outer edges of each shoulder and meeting in the center of the chest and continuing in a single cut extending downward to a point immediately above the pubis— allowed access to the thoracic and abdominal cavities and the organs within.

The stomach was opened and the contents examined to reveal that shortly before her death Shannon had ingested a meal consisting of grayish-yellow, pasty food material (probably potatoes, corn, green beans, and meat).

Further inspection of the abdominal organs determined that Shannon had never been pregnant and that her left ovary contained a two-and-a-half centimeter "chocolate cyst."

Tissue samples of the liver, kidney, spleen, lung, and muscle were collected. Once these specimens had been studied and tested chemically and microscopically, this data and other information gained from the autopsy would be analyzed by the forensic pathologists, and the results would—hopefully—tell them what exactly had caused Shannon's death.

The grisly process now complete, the remaining organs were placed in a large plastic bag and reinserted into the abdominal cavity, the cranial cap, consisting of hair, scalp, and skull bone, was repositioned and hastily sutured in place.

The earthly remains of Shannon Mohr were then returned to the coffin, the lid closed and sealed, and returned to the cemetery where it was once again lowered into its grave and filled over with the still-damp earth. The entire process, from the first bite of green sod to the dropping of the last clump of dirt had taken approximately four hours. Only the ugly scarred rectangle over her grave remained as evidence that her slumber had rudely been disturbed.

In their Point Place home, Bob and Ceil waited for the results of the morning's efforts. It would be a painracked wait and the report, when it finally came just three days before Shannon's 26th birthday, would be unthinkable.

12

"As far as I'm concerned, this case is closed," Prosecutor Ronald Zellar announced in a press release on September 3, adding that there had been an "inordinate amount of publicity generated by this case."

Zellar had based his decision to drop the case on a verbal report from forensic pathologist Dr. Steven Fazekas. Zellar had telephoned Fazekas when his office still had not received a copy of the autopsy results a week after it had been performed and his office had been besieged by the press for information about the autopsy.

Zellar told the press that the autopsy showed a cut on the left side of Shannon's scalp, evidence of bleeding on the right side of the brain, upper back injuries and bruises on the left shoulder. There was no evidence that Shannon had been beaten.

"In short, the injuries were consistent with the initial information received . . . that she was thrown from her horse," Zellar said. "At this time, there is no evidence of foul play. Based on this information, I am recommending that the investigation by the Hillsdale County Sheriff's Department be discontinued unless new information is forthcoming. No one has been charged with a crime, and no one specifically is under investigation."

Zellar refused to answer further questions by reporters, telling them that no other information about the autopsy would be released. He admitted that Davis had not been questioned in connection with the investigation. "He's out of the state and unavailable."

As for the results of the autopsy, the Fazekases determined that "Shannon Mohr Davis died of a head injury. A large scalp laceration was in the left parietal scalp (and a) contracoup subarachnoid hemorrhage was on the right side of the brain, indicating that the injury was sustained in a fall. In addition, there were diffuse soft tissue hemorrhages on the left shoulder and upper back, which indicate forceful contact with a broad surface."

A "contracoup" hemorrhage results when the head strikes a hard surface, causing the brain—which essentially floats within the skull—to rebound against the inside of the skull on the side directly opposite to that striking the hard object. In the case where the head is struck with a heavy object, such as a rock or a blunt instrument, the injuries to the brain are directly below the point on the skull receiving the blow.

The autopsy findings were unequivocal: Shannon had been injured in a fall and the resultant injuries were of sufficient gravity to have caused her death.

Zellar's office refused to release the autopsy report to the press. His secretary commented: "I guess he doesn't want anyone to have the results. The investigation isn't totally, absolutely closed. It's going to be discontinued, unless new information surfaces."

It mattered little that an autopsy report was clearly public record and could not be suppressed by anyone, and that the prosecutor was exceeding his authority by refusing to release it.

Schindler and Sheriff Webb defended their actions by claiming that the press had created an hysterical climate that tainted the efforts and conclusions of their efforts.

Schindler emphasized that the purpose of the investigation was to determine whether a crime had actually been committed. It was not established that one had, he insisted.

"Before there was any evidence that there had been a crime committed, it had already been aired, publicly convicting a man of a crime," Schindler railed at the assembled reporters. "The fact had not been taken that this death might have been an act of God. The man's past was dug into and publicized; he was tried and convicted of this act.

"What many people failed to understand was that there must be a crime committed before a person can be charged. Then there must be evidence produced to prove beyond a shadow of a doubt that the subject committed the crime."

He said that with the ruling by the experts that this was an accidental death and not a criminal matter, "I had to withdraw from any additional investigation."

It was enough for Zellar and for Schindler that everything they were responsible for doing had been done. Case closed.

It was not enough for Lucille Mohr. It wasn't nearly enough!

Lucille hung up the phone, her face gone ashen, her knees weak, the words uttered by Al Schindler—*Case closed*—still ringing in her ears. How could it be? How could the autopsy have found that Shannon had fallen from her horse and struck her head as David had claimed? Something must have been overlooked, a mistake of some kind must have been made.

Two days earlier they had retained Sheldon Wittenberg, a combative Toledo lawyer who wasn't afraid of a challenge. Well, thought Ceil, he has a challenge now. We're not going to let this drop no matter what the damned autopsy says!

When a reporter from *The Blade,* Toledo's daily newspaper, contacted him a few hours later, Wittenberg echoed Ceil's sentiments: "This case will not die."

Wittenberg had already determined a course of action in the event that, for whatever reason, Davis was not indicted. Since the autopsy had failed to implicate him in Shannon's death, the first actions they should take would be to attempt to have the medical findings reviewed. Ceil would appeal to the forensic pathologists to reconsider their opinion.

In addition, since having the investigation canceled would now open the door for Davis to collect the insurance money, steps must be taken to close that door.

"He's probably been lying low until he sees what the investigation turns up. We need to get him out in the open; what we want to do is to smoke him out."

As a matter of fact, Davis was, at that very moment, at his mother's Lansing, Michigan home; he had returned from Florida the day before Shannon's body was exhumed. He did not go to Toledo, nor did he call the Mohrs to determine what the autopsy had revealed.

After the first week traveling around Florida, Davis sent Barbara Matthews back to Michigan to allow her to prepare for the reopening of school. He moved on to the home of Buddy and Cathy Brown, in Tavernier, a small town in the Florida keys. Buddy owned and operated a scuba diving school and had given Davis diving lessons during a previous trip to the keys with Shannon, and the two men had become close friends.

"He showed up totally unannounced. Presto, there's David," Buddy recalls.

"It was on a Monday, about the first part of August," Cathy remembered. "He walked up and it shocked me. I said, 'Hey, is Shannon with you?' He said no. And then he just broke down and cried. His grief seemed sincere."

Davis was invited to stay with them, sleeping on a sofa in their den. He remained in Florida for another two weeks where he "rested, read books, and went scuba diving."

On August 24 at about one in the morning the phone rang. It was a call for David. Buddy had the impression the call came from David's mother. Actually it was David's friend, Bob Burns; David had given him the Browns' number before he left Michigan, in case he had to be reached.

"Your neighbor, Dick Britton, was here today," Burns told Davis. "He said that there's talk that Shannon's death didn't look like an accident anymore, the newspapers and people are talking murder. You'd better get up here and clear things up."

David took the call in the kitchen, speaking in hushed tones. Two hours later there was another call for Dave, followed an hour after by a third. The next morning he announced that he had to go home. Buddy and Cathy did not press him for reasons. He flew back to Michigan, leaving his van with the Browns, saying he would return for it in about four to six weeks.

While they thought his departure was strange in its suddenness, the Browns didn't press him for an explanation.

Back in Michigan, Davis met with Burns on about August 27.

"I saw him socially in Ann Arbor. We met at the Village Bell for a beer. He was unaware that an autopsy had been done on Shannon. I told him I'd seen it on the news the night before."

Davis became upset and rushed to a telephone to call his attorney. The attorney said it was his opinion that they should have had their own pathologist in attendance at the autopsy.

Davis then sent word to Barbara through Burns, telling her that he wanted to talk to her before the sheriff questioned her, and asking her to call him.

"We drove to her place," Burns would later state. "But her parents were there and David didn't want to approach her while they were present. He asked me to go back and talk to her."

Burns thought that his friend's actions were, if nothing else, mysterious. But, like the Browns, he didn't ask for an explanation. It was the Davis magic that allowed him to act in a most bizarre fashion without being accountable to those who believed they understood him.

The cryptic message intensified the emotional anxiety the young schoolteacher had suffered during the last few weeks. Newspaper accounts of the possible poisoning of the woman identified as David's wife, and of exhumation and autopsy, had her mind swirling with fear and doubt. Now came this curious message, suggesting that somehow she was involved in all the apparent intrigue that surrounded David Richard Davis, the most remarkable man she had ever known.

What was behind it all; how did it all come about; how did she suddenly find herself in the middle?

It was in the spring of 1979. She had noticed him across the hall, in the chemistry lab. He was tall, blonde, blue-eyed, and ruggedly handsome. She asked around and several other teachers at Addison High School quickly let her know that he was serving as a student teacher, he was single, and his name was David Davis.

They had talked several times, chatting comfortably in the cafeteria or in the hall outside their classrooms. Barbara found him to be smooth, charming, glib, and entertaining. He was athletic and powerfully built and Barbara felt the tingle of excitement whenever she was near him. On April 4, they began dating, seeing each other socially almost every night.

He told her he had served in Vietnam as a major with the Marine Corps, that he had seen a great deal of combat action for which he'd received a number of medals, and that he'd been seriously wounded several times. She believed it all.

"He was very good with a gun. I'd seen him fire a gun; he taught me to fire a gun. He was exceptionally strong, very fearless. I'd never seen him afraid of anything at all."

Almost from the beginning of their relationship, Davis periodically brought up the subject of marriage, never coming straight out with a marriage proposal but dancing around the topic, mentioning casually that perhaps someday they should "just suddenly get up one weekend and run away to Las Vegas and get married there."

At one point, however, Davis was more direct regarding a potential marital union.

"On one occasion he told me he already had an engagement and wedding ring in the desk in his den. He said that he'd bought the rings for a girl named Karen who had died tragically and [he] was kind of broke up about the whole thing but still kept them."

Barbara was simply not ready, so early in their association, to make such a serious commitment. She managed to stall him with statements such as, "Let's see what develops in this relationship. Let's try this a little longer before we make any judgments."

Throughout the spring and summer of 1979, Davis continued to pressure the pretty schoolteacher, never excessively, never to the point that she considered breaking off the relationship.

From September 9 until September 17 she and Davis did not see each other, although they had several phone conversations. During one telephone call, Davis told Barbara that he had to go to Washington, D.C. the following day. He didn't explain the purpose of the trip, and Barbara didn't ask. At ten o'clock on the night of September 17, he appeared at her home and suddenly the whole relationship had changed.

"There's something I have to do," he told Barbara gravely. "It will appear that I'm married but don't believe that, just trust me."

He told her that what he had to do would not take longer than a year, that it was dangerous and could "kill both of us," and that the less she knew about what he was doing the better off she would be. He said that he wouldn't be able to see her during the year his "work" was going on but at the end of the year they would be able to resume contact and would be free to go away together.

"He told me that he would be getting about $250,000 for what he had to do and that there would be more money coming later. He talked about getting a sailboat and sailing the Caribbean or possibly going to Australia."

Although she was extremely confused and disappointed, Barbara assumed that, as a result of his trip to Washington, he had somehow been recruited into undercover work for the government, that perhaps he would be acting as a bodyguard for someone in the federal witness protection program. It was a natural assumption for her to make; she had from the start been impressed with his "fearlessness" and his physical strength. "Frankly, I would feel very protected if he was around."

She had barely adjusted to the unpleasant prospect of not seeing Davis for a year when, three weeks later, he suddenly appeared at her home.

"Is what you're doing over so soon?" she asked in surprise.

"No, but I couldn't stand not to see you, so here I am."

With the naiveté of an adolescent schoolgirl, Barbara accepted his incredible stories, never really questioning his outrageous claims. Such unbelievable gullibility would not have surprised Davis. He could fool anyone, anytime with the most flagrant Machiavellianism; almost no one had ever challenged him. And those who doubted his veracity had never been so rude as to openly dispute him.

About the middle of October 1979, Davis's affair with the willowy teacher settled down to a once-a-week schedule during which he visited her, usually on Wednesday night, telling her that it was his day off. He never talked about what he was doing and Barbara rarely asked. In March of 1980, he suddenly disappeared for a six-week period. When he showed up again in May, he made no mention of where he'd gone or what he'd been doing. And she didn't ask.

During part of the time he was gone, David and Shannon were in Fort Lauderdale, Florida, sailing and scuba diving. While there, they met Cheryl Hogan, who was on a college spring break, vacationing with several friends from Ohio and Michigan.

"When I was getting ready to fly back home, Shannon and David offered to drive me to the airport," Cheryl recalls. "They picked me up at the hotel and then we stopped in some little greasy spoon of a restaurant. And while we were sitting there, we began talking about how open the sale of narcotics was, that people would walk up to you on the street and offer to sell you anything you wanted. Suddenly, David proceeded to tell us that he had the opportunity to transport some drugs back to Michigan."

Both Shannon and Cheryl were stunned.

"David, you're kidding," Shannon insisted.

"No I'm not; you just put them in the back of the van and drive up I-75."

"You're nuts," Shannon all but shouted. "Don't you realize that if we got caught doing that, I could lose my nursing license? You've got to be out of your mind."

Davis dropped the subject instantly, acting as though the conversation had never taken place.

"He never talked about what he was doing," Barbara Matthews would later state, "or about—I hesitate to use the term—to call it a marriage, because I didn't think he was married."

What Davis did do was to instruct Barbara "not to come by the farm, not to call" him there.

Although obviously possessed with the patience of a saint and the trust of a puppy dog, even lovely Barbara Matthews began to grow anxious.

"In December of 1979 I asked him how much longer his business was going to take. He was very vague. In the spring—in May—I asked him again and he said, 'Not much longer.' "

His brief once-a-week visits and the enduring need for secrecy was fast becoming a chafing irritation to her; after nearly fifteen months the relationship had become mired, going nowhere. Barbara ached for more stability, for an end to the enigmatic commitment about which he would never speak and about which she could never ask.

"How much longer is this going to go on, David?" she asked in a final fit of desperation.

"A few weeks; it'll be over in a few weeks."

The question was asked and the answer given during the first week of July 1980. Shannon had at that point a "few weeks" left to live.

William Ransom, owner and proprietor of Bill's Barbershop in Hudson, knew David Davis from several past visits to his shop. He'd found him articulate, talkative and highly opinionated. Others who had been in the shop when Davis was holding court had a more succinct impression of the man. "I thought he was a real asshole," one regular patron of the shop says.

Apparently the magic of his persuasive powers found no fertile ground in Bill's Barbershop.

Ransom, who ran a small sideline supplying hairpieces, false beards, and moustaches, remembers that Davis came into his shop in July of 1980 to place an order for a beard and moustache. What made the transaction particularly memorable to the barber was the color of the two pieces.

"Normally, I place an order for a customer after color-matching the pieces to his natural hair."

Davis selected a set that was shades darker than his own blonde hair. "For what I'm going to use it for, it doesn't make any difference," he announced when the color disparity was brought to his attention.

By 1980 standards, a hundred dollars for the beard

and moustache, professionally made of all-natural hair, was not cheap.

"It didn't make sense to pay that kind of money and not want to have the color match exactly; it wouldn't have cost any more or taken any longer."

Later, when asked, Ransom would suggest one possible reason Davis didn't want the false hair on his chin to match the color of the natural hair on his head. "He may have been planning to dye his hair to match the whiskers."

Barbara Matthews had no contact with Davis after his statement that the "business" would be over in a "few weeks," until July 25 when he called her and told her that it was over. Barbara had seen the newspaper account of Shannon Davis's death in a riding accident and found nothing about which to be suspicious.

"I made a joke about his business being over. I assumed that she was not dead; she was being protected and that she was moved on to some other spot; protecting her was over and she was somewhere else. I did not think she was dead."

He came to see her soon after that phone call. He told her that what he had been engaged in was finished and that he was now free to see her. He mentioned that he was going to Florida but he did not invite her to accompany him.

"I kind of invited myself. He said he was going to leave and I was in the process of buying a house. And if I hadn't gone with him then I would not have been able to go at all since school was going to start in September and I had to have time to get ready. So I said, 'Well, listen, if you want me to go along I have to go now, I can't wait.' "

"Fine," he replied. "Come with me."

She returned to Michigan early in August, and had no further contact with Davis during that month. When Bob Burns stopped by to deliver his message, she was under the impression that David was still in Florida and was planning on returning right away. She would have been even more puzzled had she known that he had been in the state for almost two weeks.

On September 9, Lucille, accompanied by her attorney, Sheldon Wittenberg and her daughter Terri, met with the Fazekases at the Medical College of Ohio.

"We just don't believe that Shannon died in the manner the autopsy indicated," Lucille explained. "We think there are a lot of other questions that should have been asked. If she was killed in a fall, as you say, then we'd like to know how the fall occurred."

Renata Fazekas shook her head.

"We can't tell you how the fall happened; all we can say with any certainty is that the injuries to the brain are consistent with having been caused by the head striking a hard object."

The husband–wife scientist team were flooded with compassion for the tiny woman who sat before them. She looked as though she had been ambushed, pushed into a corner, and menaced by a ghostly antagonist; she appeared bewildered and frustrated.

Unable to bring comfort to the beleaguered lady, the Fazekases closed the meeting. As she was about to leave their office, Ceil turned, looked at the pair, and said, "No matter what you say, I'll never understand how she could have received an injury serious enough to kill her from just walking her horse."

Ceil's parting words, *just walking her horse*, jolted Renata.

Suddenly, a new twist had been introduced that caused the pathologists to have second thoughts. While their original findings were not, at this time, altered by what appeared to be new evidence, certainly additional study was warranted to determine if another element might have figured in Shannon's death.

Born and raised in Europe, she unconsciously translated English phrases into her native German. Lucille had said *walking her horse*. In German, to walk a horse meant to lead the animal from the ground. The brain injuries they had found could never have been caused by Shannon falling against a rock while walking on the ground.

A simple misunderstanding in language was about to send in motion a whole new set of forces that ultimately would affect and redirect the search for the cause of the strange death of Shannon Mohr Davis.

13

Robert Keller, an investigator for the Lucas County coroner's office, at the direction of Renata Fazekas, telephoned the Medical College of Ohio toxicology department to request that certain tissue samples from the autopsy on Shannon Davis be subjected to a screening test to determine whether "abused drugs" were present.

The toxicology lab, in addition to functioning within the college and the hospital, engaging in research projects and acting as a teaching arm for the medical students and medical residents, also performed services for the Lucas County coroner's office.

On September 10, the samples, which had been stored in a freezer at the college since the autopsy, were removed by Thomas Carroll, supervisor of laboratory technicians in the toxicology lab at MCO. He thawed and prepared tissue specimens from Shannon's liver, kidney, and spleen. Carroll, in readying the samples, was unaware that two separate screenings for drugs had earlier been done by the Michigan State Police crime lab. On July 25, 1980, the fifteen-milliliter blood sample taken from Shannon's body the night she died was tested for alcohol content. The results indicated that no alcohol was present in the blood specimen. On August 15, prior to the autopsy, the specimen was again tested, this time for toxic chemicals, particularly barbiturates, neutral, or basic drugs. The test report issued on August 27 was negative; no drugs were present in the blood sample.

Carroll, with more than twenty years experience at MCO in biochemistry and pharmacology, subjected the tissue samples to a "general screen," the procedure used when there has been no request to search for a particular agent. The "screen," composed of a series of different tests designed to identify the most commonly encountered substances, is divided by methodology. Some tests, called "spot tests," use a small portion of urine (this was available among the specimens from Shannon's autopsy), or an extract from tissue samples that are combined with a chemical reagent, to look for color changes that would provide an indication as to the substance being tested. Where no color change has taken place, further testing becomes necessary.

The next step—or more accurately, another type of analysis—is to chemically divide the agents, looking for essentially two different groups based on the chemical nature of the specimen; basic drugs or drugs that behave chemically as a base element, and all the other types of drugs—acid and neutral drugs.

If these initial procedures are unproductive, gas chromatography, a more complex and sensitive analytical tool involving chemical extraction, is routinely employed. In gas chromatography, the specimen to be analyzed is introduced by hypodermic syringe through an injection port into an oven that has been heated to five or six hundred degrees. When the specimen is injected it instantly vaporizes—turns to a gas—and is swept through a three- to four-foot glass column of the gas chromatograph, which contains a highly sophisticated packing material that is very sticky for certain types of chemicals and tends to slow them down. Each component of a specimen has a different time in which it is able to make its way through the packing material. This is called "retention time." The precise time it takes for a chemical to make its way through the glass column and go through a "detector" determines what the chemical is. The results of the test are recorded on a graph on which a line is inscribed, rising and falling in peaks at various points on the moving graph as each individual chemical comes off the glass column. The location on the graph determines the composition of that part of the specimen being tested and the height of the peak indicates the concentration of that element.

Carroll would later recall how surprisingly uncontaminated the embalmed tissue he was analyzing was, making his tests all the more accurate and free of "artifacts" that might complicate the testing procedures.

As the graph came off the printer, Carroll noted the presence of those elements he would expect to find in human tissue: amino acid, hydrogen, phosphorus, nitrogen—all in basically the concentrations expected. However, one line, near the end of the graph, caught his eye. The position on the scale did not conform with any compound with which he was familiar and it was coming off the column in a high concentration.

He puzzled over the strange tracing, attempting to identify the compound.

"At one point I thought it might be Demerol but had to rule that out."

Periodically, over the span of about one week, Carroll subjected the unknown compound to a battery of tests, trying to coax the material into giving up its identity, without success.

Finally, in desperation, Carroll went to his immediate superior, Dr. Robert B. Forney, Jr., a thirty-five-year-old Ph.D. and associate professor in the MCO department of pathology, who was also the director of the toxicology department.

"I have a compound I can't identify. I need help," Carroll announced.

Young Forney was a 1967 graduate of Indiana University in Bloomington. He received a doctorate in toxicology from the university in 1974. He did his postgraduate work on a fellowship with Case Western Reserve University School of Medicine in Cleveland,

Ohio. His training was in the school's department of pathology, with later experience in the Cuyahoga County coroner's office. He accepted a faculty position with MCO in 1976. He was also named a diplomate of the American Board of Forensic Toxicology, the highest level of certification within the field. Forney came by his expertise naturally. Robert Forney, Sr., who had established the department of toxicology at the University of Indiana, was known as one of the nation's top three experts in the field.

Toxicology is the science of poisons. Forney's practice was restricted to human poisoning, both clinically—in living persons—and postmortem—after death. The field embraces laboratory science in terms of analysis for the purpose of identifying and quantitating poisons in human tissues and fluids, and interpreting these findings as to their effect. He was very good at what he did.

Forney was aware that questions had arisen as to the cause of Shannon Davis's death and that an autopsy had been performed to obtain the tissue samples now in the lab, and that part of the investigation was to rule out the possibility of drugs or poisons being involved. But that was the sum total of his knowledge about the case; the lab had not been provided with an investigation report to help them know what to look for.

The toxicologist examined the graph and decided that the characteristics of the analysis performed indicated that the specimen had "forensic interest."

"It appeared to be in great quantity and appeared to be a drug, perhaps, a medicine of some sort."

He and Carroll made some initial guesses as to what the substance might be, but quickly ruled them out. He thought that the chemical characteristics indicated that it was alkaline and that it had a nitrogen atom within the substance at some point.

They began to consider substances that were alkaline and that had a nitrogen atom, trying to get a match.

Tests of other tissue samples from the autopsy uncovered the presence of the unknown compound in more than one sample, and in different concentrations.

In attempting to identify the mysterious substance, they had first to rule out the possibility of instrument error; they had to employ fresh reagents in the analysis to insure that the reading they were getting wasn't caused in the lab itself; they had to obtain samples of the actual embalming fluid used by the Jasin Funeral Home to use with tissue samples from other sources containing no foreign substance, to see if the fluid might react with the tissue to produce a substance such as had been found. They tried to identify the source of the substance, if not the substance itself.

Periodically, when there was time available from their other obligations, Forney and Carroll would perform experiments to rule out possibilities.

"We had a very large number of chemicals we were looking at," Forney says. "There are over 250,000 chemicals in common use and we had searched for and ruled out maybe a thousand."

He decided that tests run on a mass spectrometer, a piece of state-of-the-art testing equipment that was much more sophisticated and sensitive, might prove more successful. Unfortunately, the mass spectrometer was a relatively new and extremely expensive piece of electronic machinery. MCO did not have one; in 1980 few laboratories in the country had the resources to purchase this equipment. But Forney knew what institutions possessed it. He sent tissue specimens to laboratories in Michigan, Virginia, and Utah, asking for help in identifying the substance without significant results. "It might be fatty acid," the labs in Virginia and Utah suggested. The others were unable to give even a qualified estimate of what the compound in the tissue might be.

* * *

Dick Britton suffered his own frustrations. The news that the Hillsdale authorities were dropping the investigation into Shannon's death left him flabbergasted.

"After they found out about the insurance and the lies he told, how can they just drop it?" he demanded. "He killed her; how else could it have happened?"

He tried to talk to Al Schindler, the Hillsdale detective who had spearheaded the investigation, to determine why he couldn't continue looking into the matter. Schindler wouldn't take his phone calls. When Dick drove to Hillsdale to confront the policeman, the receptionist told him Schindler was "in Minnesota on vacation, fishing."

"On vacation?" Britton thundered. "What's he doing on vacation when we need him here?"

"Everyone is entitled to time off," he was curtly informed.

Back at his farm, Dick phoned Paul Manning Krawzak, a reporter with the *Hillsdale Daily News*.

"I don't understand why Schindler would leave town right now," he told the newsman.

"Let me check on it."

Later that day, Krawzak called back.

"Schindler isn't in Minnesota," Dick was told. "He's right there in his office. He just doesn't want to talk to you."

The word came like a two-by-four between the eyes. "Doesn't want to talk to me? Why not? A beautiful young woman was probably murdered, and he doesn't want to talk about it?"

Britton was not the only principal in Shannon's death who was being shunned by the detective. He was refusing calls from Bob and Lucille as well. They had acted "irate" with him, he said.

Britton's certainty that Davis had killed his lovely young wife was not unique in Wright Township; once word of six insurance policies totalling over a quarter of a million dollars began to circulate through the area, the consensus among these naturally suspicious farmers was that "Davis is guilty as sin."

"My husband doesn't have that much insurance on me," many women were saying. "I don't think he has *any* insurance on me."

14

At the *Detroit Free Press* a city editor read through a clip-file containing a few brief items from the *Free Press* and several small Michigan wire service reports concerning the obscure case of a suspected wife killer in Hillsdale County. Looking at the assignment board, she decided the story might warrant more in-depth treatment. For the assignment she selected Billy Bowles, a seasoned forty-nine-year-old reporter with almost a decade of service at the "Freep," to look into the matter.

Billy was an excellent choice for the assignment. A "good ol' boy" from Georgia, he had eighteen years journalistic experience at newspapers in Georgia and South Carolina. In 1967, he was recipient of the Ernie Pyle Award for his coverage of the war in Vietnam. He also won the University of Missouri-INGAA Award for business and economic reporting.

In 1971, Billy accepted a position with the *Free Press* as a general assignment reporter covering political and labor stories. At one time, he was chief of the paper's City-County Bureau.

He was born in the back of his father's tiny general store in Chattahoochee, Georgia, in February 1931.

In a nineteen-year period, his parents, Jim and Hatti Bowles, begat nine children, including one set of twins. Billy was the youngest. The eleven-member Bowles family lived in quarters no bigger than a good-sized modern living room.

Billy arrived as the country was in the early torments of the Great Depression. "I can't imagine how my parents made it through," Billy recalls.

By the end of his first year on earth, his father had closed the store, "when his customers could no longer pay," and moved his family to a nearby farm.

The Depression savaged the people in the North Georgia hills. But life on the farm had at least one advantage that the poor and destitute of the cities did not enjoy.

"Even in the depths of the Depression, we were never hungry. I remember eating a lot of milk gravy and biscuits for breakfast and cornbread and sweet milk for supper. Midday meal, or 'dinner'—nobody called it lunch—was the big meal of the day, with lots of fresh or home-canned vegetables that we grew ourselves. And because we had a cow, hogs, and chickens, there was always plenty of fatback, pork sausage, milk, eggs, and frying-sized pullets."

In about 1935, the family left the farm when Billy's father, Jim, went on the road with a medicine show, hawking patent medicines between acts by banjo pickers, contortionists, and comedians.

Billy's brother Doyel traveled during the summers with Jim, who set him up in a comedy act.

"Doyel wasn't any good at it though," Billy recalls his father remarking years later. "He laughed at his own jokes."

There was a lot of laughter in the Bowels family. But they had a very serious side as well.

"Daddy liked to sit with his cronies in front of Hershel Holloways' store, arguing politics and retelling ancient political stories."

Coursing through Billy's bloodstream were genes that had been passed down the generations of the Bowles and Waters clans; genes that bore an indelible imprint that read "commitment": a dedication to the belief in justice and honor and country. Both Billy's grandfathers had fought on the Confederate side in the Civil War; both had been captured and imprisoned in

Union prison camps—Bart Bowles in Elmira, New York, and Daniel Waters in Virginia. Both walked back home to Georgia after their release.

Billy's father enlisted in the U.S. Army during the Spanish-American War and served in Cuba. Billy's uncle Gene Bowles recalled that when Jim returned from the war, Bart "didn't like Jim to wear the Yankee uniform. He said he had shot at that uniform for four years."

Uncle John Waters had served with valor in World War II and was awarded the Silver Star during the 1944 Italian campaign.

After graduating from the University of Georgia with a journalism degree in 1953, Bowles worked as a reporter in Charleston, South Carolina, and Washington, D.C., for the Charleston *News and Courier,* and for the Associated Press in Nashville, Tennessee. He later became managing editor of the *Columbus Enquirer* in Columbus, Georgia.

Billy Bowles had an instinct for an important story, and once that instinct was prodded into action, he was a veritable ball of fire. No detail was unimportant, no piece of a complex puzzle was overlooked. Bowles was nothing if not thorough. In his nine years with the *Free Press* he had earned the reputation of being quiet and soft-spoken while at the same time a tireless, tenacious investigator. That reputation would be reinforced as he looked deeper into the Shannon Davis case.

On August 27, whirling like a cyclone, he plunged into an investigation of David Davis's background.

He called Al Schindler, who would say only that he had worked on the case and that there was "no warrant yet."

He next called Lucille Mohr to ask if she had heard from David since the autopsy report had been announced.

"Not a word," Ceil replied curtly, responding to

attorney Wittenberg's admonition to not talk about the case.

Did she know how he might reach David's mother? No, she knew his mother's first name was Martha and that David's stepfather was called James but she didn't have their last name.

Next, Billy drove to Wright Township, eventually locating Lickley Road. He stopped his car near the home at 1036 Lickley, writing a description of the property in a reporter's notebook:

> Yellohouse w/ slant porch, yello & red out bldgs, hammock, wood piled out [under] tin roof of 1 out bldg next to house. 2 chaise lounges, corn in 2 silos (wire), one full one nearly ½ full.
> Jeep Trk
> Chevy
> boat
> bicycle

From there, he drove down Lickley to the house next to the Davis farm. It was the home of eighty-four-year-old Oxley Fox and his sixty-four-year-old wife, Neva.

During the Niagara of speculation, rumors and gossip eddying around the tragic death of Shannon Davis, no one cared much about what Oxley and Neva thought. Now, this fellow from the city, who looked and spoke just like one of their own, had appeared and was *very* interested in what they thought.

"He claims he got hurt at Chrysler in '74. Want to know what I think he is?" Oxley thundered. "He's a parasite on society."

The Oxleys provided Billy with a great deal of background information about David and Shannon Davis. They also filled him in on David's previous marriage, as well as on how Davis had bought his original sixty-four acres, a house and outbuildings from a neighbor named Richard Britton and another forty acres and a house from Howard Sensabaugh. They told of the cruelty they saw in David.

He had ponies, and one day when one of the animals nuzzled up to him, he became furious and shot the pony as his wife Phyllis and his two young daughters watched in horror.

On another occasion one of the remaining ponies got into his bean field. Davis went out to the field and shot it, hooked his tractor to the carcass, and dragged it into the woods. "The Sensabaughs saw it."

Someone had turned him into the county animal control people during the winter of 1979 for not feeding his horses.

The Foxes also told Billy about Phyllis, a nice girl, and about the Davis's two daughters, "eight and five when they come here. They lived here more than they did at home," and how one day Phyllis "come over and said, 'I'm going to leave. My lawyer said to stay, but David said he was going to shoot me right between the eyes if I didn't leave.' She left him."

"Shannon was a nice, nice girl," Oxley said. She was so dependable that he could set his clock by her.

"She left for Toledo at five-thirty every morning to work. I'd say, 'It's five-thirty, there goes Shannon.' "

Davis didn't work, Billy was told, he stayed at home, pretending to be too ill to go out and get a decent job.

Using newspaper clippings and information they had gathered in the area, the elderly couple gave Bowles a thorough rundown on the events and participants in the most dramatic event to occur in Wright Township in decades. When they had finally exhausted their storehouse of local history, observed facts, second-hand utterances, and juicy tidbits of gossip, Billy had a list of thirty-two areas to research and double-check.

As he drove away from the Foxes', he carried with him a wispy mental picture of a troubled man who did not appear to be terribly popular in his community; a man who exhibited streaks of cruelty toward his wife, children, and helpless animals; a man who somehow had collected money for intentionally burned property and a faked occupational injury; a man who drove his first wife out of their home, only to marry again and have his second wife die under suspicious circumstances. Not an enviable character. Yet this single visit to one neighbor couple would never produce all that was necessary to know about David Davis, all that Billy Bowles needed before he would be satisfied.

Like County Prosecutor Ronald Zellar, almost a month earlier, Billy Bowles decided that he'd better find out who this David Richard Davis was.

15

Billy Bowles had taken on a study in the abstract, attempting to decipher the complexities of a most complex individual. David Davis, like everyone, was no single entity but rather a melange—a blend of the bits and pieces of his past experiences that colored his character and molded his personality.

To know who Davis was, Billy had to find, examine, and fit together the manifold fragments that combined to create the man. It would be a protracted exercise.

David Richard Davis was the product of the bellicose wartime union of Martha Jean Allen and David Ellsworth Davis, a linking that survived twelve tempestuous years. The marriage ended in ruins in 1954 leaving two children—David Richard, born in 1944, and Dayne Ann, born in 1947—emotionally wracked by the incessant wranglings of their hopelessly bitter parents.

After the divorce, young David and his sister moved with their mother to a small house in Flint, Michigan. The elder Davis saw his children on weekends.

"We never got close," Davis speaks of his son with obvious regret. "He was close to his mother and to her folks. But even so, he wasn't the type who showed affection. As far as giving you a hug, he just wouldn't do it."

Still, the father enjoyed a deep sense of pride in his son's achievements.

David, early on, demonstrated a superior intellectual grasp of mathematics, logic, and clever planning.

He also showed a strong determination to manage events, to manipulate situations to his advantage.

At eleven he was the youngest newspaper carrier in Linden, Michigan, a small hamlet not far from Flint. Deciding that the accepted practice of calling on each of his customers every week to collect his money was a foolish waste of his time and effort, he devised a method that allowed for payment on a monthly basis. It was a practice that apparently had never before been tried and was not viewed with enthusiasm by the newspaper's circulation manager. But since the subscribers on David's route found monthly payment less bothersome than paying by the week and indicated their approval, the new system was allowed to continue. It worked so well that soon other carriers had adopted the pay-by-month method.

Family members remember David as an intelligent and responsible youth who took pride and care in his appearance.

"He always had a 'butch' haircut, he wasn't a long hair, always slick as a button. If he even got his tennis shoes dirty, he would take them off. Never drank, never smoked. He was no troublemaker, wouldn't fight," recalls one relative.

"He was very good in school and never caused any problems," his father recalls. "He loved to fish and loved to go to the movies. You could send him fishing or to the show alone and never have to worry about him. He'd come home safe and on time."

David's father also enjoys describing his son's phenomenal mental recall.

"He had a pure photographic memory. He could read a book, put it down, and then tell you exactly what it said and tell you what page everything was on. I would test him sometimes by asking him on, say Friday, what the front page headline of the paper was on Monday. He could quote the headlines of every story on the front page. I would check it out and he was always absolutely correct."

Even as an adolescent, he was intellectually advanced for his age. The grandfather of one of his childhood friends taught David to play chess when the boy indicated an interest in the game, and he quickly became extremely competent at the challenging game.

Young David was enrolled in what is now the McKinley Middle School in Flint, where he completed his elementary and junior high school education. Friends from junior high remember him as an "ordinary kid who got better grades than most." In 1958, he entered Flint Southwestern High School, considered the best public high school in the city, where he blossomed academically, becoming a member of the student intelligentsia.

"Dave was a part of an elite group," says Elizabeth Calkins Enders, a teacher and faculty adviser to the literary society and the bridge club during David's years at the high school. "It was a group of the most alert, active, intelligent students who were around then. Southwestern was a very desirable high school in those days and it drew the best kids."

Michael Utt, a member of the class of '62, doesn't think of Davis as having been "brainy," although many of his teachers remember him that way. "When you say brainy, you think of the person as being passive and nonsocial. Dave was a very social individual. He was a very amiable individual from what I can remember. He appeared more mature than the average high school student. He was able to relate with a number of different types."

Another acquaintance at Southwestern High, John Gondol, now a Methodist minister in East Texas, remembers David as a "normal kid, a friendly teenager." He recalls that both he and David were "as my kids like to call me, a 'nerd.' There was a number of us who were. Egghead isn't really a fair description under the circumstances. The literary society in 1962 in Flint, Michigan, wasn't going to attract a large number of guys. But it did attract a large number of girls, which wasn't a bad deal."

David's friends were among the brightest in his class; most went on to highly regarded professional careers.

Not all of his former classmates, however, held him in high regard.

Donald McDonald, a high school acquaintance, remembers that Davis could talk his way out of most of the trouble in which he occasionally found himself, and that he was an intelligent overachiever, but someone who blithely lied and embellished facts about himself.

"He was a bullshitter; he was good at it . . . real good at it."

"He wanted to make himself more important," says Charles Oleszychi, a lawyer with the U.S. Department of Energy and one of David's best friends in high school. "Anything he told you, you would take with a real large grain of salt."

Oleszychi, with the vague hint of an admiring smile, recalls that others envied Davis because he used his time so efficiently, which permitted his involvement in many class activities while working after school at a local fast-food restaurant.

He also admits that Davis "was always conscientious, unlike me. He'd come home from school and sit right down and do his homework and be ready to go out and do something." He enjoyed touch football and going to a local "fun park."

He also tells of David's use of a very limited French vocabulary.

"He could barely speak French at all, but he would rattle off the few words he knew to try and impress people, even if what he said made no sense at all. But he was such a charming fellow, most people liked him."

David West, who knew Davis from the high school debate team, found him less than a "hale fellow, well met."

"He exhibited an arrogance and a contempt for people; he had a total disregard for any morality or rules and thought everybody else was really stupid. His theory was whatever you could get away with was okay.''

When Davis graduated in 1962—with a 3.72 grade point average and in the top three percent of his class of 511—he had been involved in such "brainy" organizations as the literary society, the debate team, and the bridge club. In his senior year, he was president of the French club. His picture is scattered throughout the 1962 edition of the Southwestern High School yearbook, peering out from group photos of a half-dozen social and intellectual organizations. His graduation picture displayed a smiling, clean-cut young man with an almost shy glint in his eyes.

In his senior year, Davis met Phyllis Webberly, an intelligent albeit somewhat naive girl, with a warm, sunny smile, and a very pretty face. Phyllis saw in David an encouraging potential. Someone not as brilliant as others believed him to be, but nonetheless a person who might in time achieve something worthwhile. She became attracted to him and they began to date regularly.

In the fall of 1962, David entered the University of Michigan at Ann Arbor on a tuition-only scholarship.

His academic successes in high school did not follow him to the university level. His four years at Michigan were unremarkable, his social contacts spotty and, for the most part, not long lasting. He continued his association with several friends from Flint's Southwestern High School. One of the friends, Charles Oleszychi, remembers that Davis, while a sophomore, ordered a U of M class ring with the designation "M.A. 1966," indicating that Davis was to be awarded a master's degree that year. "He said the M.A. ring was to add a few years to his age to impress girls," Oleszychi says. "He thought it was funny." In fact, Davis received the lesser bachelor degree in 1966. His major subject was psychology, with a minor in chemistry.

On November 7, 1964, in the middle of his junior year at U of M, he and Phyllis Webberly were married in Flint's Holy Redeemer Catholic Church. A nonbeliever, he refused to convert to Catholicism.

On April 24, 1965, Mary Beth Davis, the first of his two daughters was born, and three years later, on May 15, 1968, Donna Mae joined the small family. It was later rumored that Davis had a vasectomy following Donna's birth. If the rumor is true, Shannon, who had dreamed so intensely of having a family of her own, was unknowingly doomed from the outset to have her fervent wish denied her.

Most of his old friends lost touch with Davis following graduation. In 1976, he came to Oleszychis' wedding in Flint but did not come into the church. His presence was discovered later when Oleszychi spotted him in photos taken outside after the ceremony. At Christmastime 1979, Davis paid a surprise visit to his old friend, but left after a short time, claiming to have a date with a *Playboy* or *Penthouse* playmate. Although this visit came barely three months after his marriage to Shannon, he never mentioned her to the Oleszychis.

During the fall of 1966 and the winter of 1967, Davis took graduate courses in psychopharmacology, anatomy, physiology, and neuroanatomy. But he didn't do well in any of them, was put on academic probation after his first semester, and dropped out of the program completely halfway through the second.

"Not making it in grad school was a severe blow to him," Phyllis would later observe.

In 1978 he took a brief series of courses in education at Adrian College, a small institution in southeast Michigan, ostensibly to earn a teaching certificate. But he got only as far as the student teaching portion of the program.

He was never a member of the U.S. Marine Corps, was never in Vietnam. During the period from 1962 to 1966, while a student at the University of Michigan, he worked at various times in the university blood bank, drove an ambulance for the Staffan Funeral Home in Ann Arbor, managed two local apartment complexes, and sold encyclopedias.

From August 7, 1967 to January 1, 1974, he was employed by the King-Seeley Corp., maker of speedometers and other instruments for the auto industry. King-Seeley was bought out by the Chrysler Corp. and became the Introl plant of Chrysler. Davis stayed on after the takeover, becoming head of security at the plant. Among his duties at Introl was investigating employee disability claims.

On New Years Day 1974, Davis went to the plant even though he was not scheduled to work that day, spurning Phyllis's offer to accompany him. While there, he claimed he went into the deserted plant to investigate a suspected burglary. A short while later he was found by a security guard, lying on the floor, unconscious.

At Ann Arbor's St. Joseph Mercy Hospital, where he had been taken, he told doctors he could not remember details of what happened to him—only that there was an "explosion" in his head. He did not see anyone and could not be certain if he had been struck.

Doctors could find no external head injuries, and tests failed to establish any internal injuries or disease. Davis claimed to have a severe headache and difficulties with his vision.

Physicians and specialists at the hospital had to depend on what Davis told them in an attempt to diagnose his injuries. Their reports indicated that he had great difficulty in counting fingers held twelve inches from his face, that he had lost his sense of taste and smell, and could not recognize words or read.

He was placed on medical leave and began receiving disability payments from Chrysler, the Social Security Administration, and an accident policy he had with the State Farm Insurance Company. His benefits eventually totaled more than $20,000 a year.

Davis underwent periodic medical examinations to remain qualified for workmen's compensation benefits from Chrysler until February 27, 1979 when, at his request, he was given a lump-sum settlement from the corporation. In the five-year period, he had collected a total $62,190.35 from workmen's compensation, in addition to $455 a month from Social Security and $740 a month from State Farm Insurance Co.

Medical reports filed on Davis in 1974, 1975, and 1977 stated that he appeared to be suffering "word blindness," intense headaches, photophobia, and a difficulty in recognizing odors.

During examinations on March 21, 1974; May 30, 1974; November 18, 1974; and January 29, 1975, doctors reported that Davis was unable to tell time or recognize paper money and had expressed "*an interest in learning Braille*"; that he claimed he could make out printed words only by tracing each letter in the palm of his hand; that he could not see holes in the ground from the seat of his tractor; and that "large objects are seen but are not distinct, small objects are not seen at all . . . Prior to (the accident) he was able to read 100 pages an hour. But now he is unable to read at all."

A battery of tests were carried out on him, including one pancerebral angiography (a form of X-ray) and two electroencephalograms, none of which showed an abnormality of any description.

Dr. S.M. Farhat, M.D., a neurologist, in a letter to Dr. Wilbur Dolfin, dated January 16, 1974, stated that Davis was "a healthy appearing man who is alert and oriented. His occular fundi are normal. He does not have visual field defect on gross confrontation. The discs are normal. Extraocular motions are full and he has the ability to converge . . . He has no difficulty with the other cranial nerves . . . he has no aphasia. He has no anomia or any difficulty with calculation. His motor examination is normal. Sensation is normal. He has a good sense of coordination and no ataxia. Reflexes are 1 to 2+. He is able to walk in tandem without too much difficulty."

In spite of the inability of the medical world to find physical causes for his problems, Davis insisted that his headaches and vision difficulties improved only slightly over a two-year period and that he had blacked out twice while out in the barn on his farm, which prompted his doctors to decide that his condition was probably permanent, making it impossible for him to return to work.

He was sent to a counselor at the Vocational Rehabilitation Service, but after a few visits began failing to keep scheduled appointments and eventually stopped going altogether.

In February 1976, Davis underwent a laminectomy —a surgical fusing of several spinal discs—after complaining of low back pain that began, he said, after he had hurt his back while lifting a heavy object on his farm.

During the period when he was "unable" to see properly or to read at all, Davis went to Tennessee on a hunting trip, where he shot and killed a wild boar. The boar's head was later mounted and hung on a wall in the den at his farmhouse.

His neighbors recall that during the time he was drawing workmen's compensation because he could not see well enough to work or drive a car, he was hunting deer and pheasants, driving cars and trucks on the highways, reading newspapers and books—he was partial to mystery thrillers and science fiction—was attending classes at Adrian College, and playing paddleball at an area YMCA. He also continued to ride his horse and operate farm machinery, harvesting soybeans with a combine, which, farmers insist, is exacting work requiring excellent vision.

"The cutter has to be kept a few inches above the ground," neighbor Bob Godfrey says. "A guy with 20/20 vision can't hardly combine soybeans."

Dick Britton recalls how Davis would ask him to

read the farm auction ads in the newspaper aloud because he couldn't make out the small print.

"After a year or so, he quit faking it. He kind of let his guard down. You could only fake it for so long."

Britton says that Davis's supposed vision problems became a community joke. "It got so that when he'd drive by, the neighbor kids would yell, 'Ha, ha! There goes the blind man.' "

After his Chrysler "injury," Davis never again held regular employment but, instead, lived on settlements received from insurance policies. And, as Billy Bowles would discover, there were a number of those.

After his interview with Oxley and Neva Fox, Bowles's next stop was the Hillsdale County courthouse, where he began digging into the records. He found in the district court files Case Number 6-474, a decree of divorce granted on July 23, 1973 in the matter of: Phyllis Davis, defendant vs. David Richard Davis, plaintiff. David had divorced Phyllis exactly seven years to the day before Shannon's death.

Under the terms of the dissolution, David was to pay Phyllis $7,500 at $300 a month for her share of the Lickley Road farm; she was to keep their 1975 Dodge pickup truck, while David was to keep all the farm machinery, tools, and the 1971 Dodge van.

In addition, Phyllis was granted custody of the two girls with visitation allowed David, as long as he had a relative with him or a letter from his doctor stating that it was "safe for him to drive an automobile and that it is safe for the children to be with him." He was also to pay $38.75 per week per child, pay medical insurance for the children, pay $210 in Phyllis's attorney costs, and make alimony payments equal to his personal Social Security disability benefits.

On October 15, 1975, circuit court judge Kenneth G. Prettie issued a restraining order and temporary injunction against David on the basis of testimony by Phyllis, in which she said that she was in fear for herself and the children because of physical violence inflicted upon her and her daughters. Davis had, in the past, threatened her life, hit and kicked her, shoved her against the wall, hit her on the back of the head, and used other violence against her and the children.

The restraining order was granted "without notice (to Davis) because of the danger of bodily harm" to Phyllis and the children.

On July 15, 1976, the friend of the court's office recommended, because Davis was at that time alleged to be $7,621 in arrears on his child support payments, that he be required to turn over the $740 a month State Farm insurance benefits through January 1979, as well as $224.60 a month per child in Social Security payments, to be increased to $336 per month at a later date.

On December 21, 1976, the court issued an order for Davis to show cause why he should not be held in violation of the terms of the divorce decree. Although he had been ordered to pay Phyllis a total of $7,500 at $300 per month, as of December 21, 1976, he had paid a total of only $139; he had not visited the children; he had "structured his financial affairs so as to favor a lump-sum settlement of his disability workmen's compensation claim with Chrysler Corp"; and he planned to leave the state.

In 1977, Phyllis petitioned for a contempt citation against Davis, claiming that he had failed to fulfill his obligations under the decree of divorce, that he was $1,361 in arrears on his child support and other payments. At that time, Phyllis was working part time as a playground leader with a rural Michigan school system, for which she received $68 biweekly.

The court, in its findings, denied her petition for a contempt citation against Davis, but ordered Davis to pay $1,361 in arrear payments to be paid at $100 per month, plus the $300 a month, as per the divorce judgment.

* * *

Billy decided that there was definitely a story here. What he knew he had to do now was to begin knocking on doors, starting the long, tedious process of canvassing an area, hoping to find someone who would have special knowledge and who would be willing to cooperate. Usually, it is a frustrating, time-consuming, and quite often, fruitless process. Yet for the investigative journalist, as well as the law enforcement officer, it is an essential, irreplaceable function.

His next stop was the home of Richard Britton, the neighbor he'd been told knew Davis best.

"What can you tell me about David Davis and the death of his wife?" he asked casually, standing at Britton's door.

"Boy, am I glad to see someone who's interested. Come in here, I can tell you plenty," was the farmer's immediate response. "If everybody knew as much as I do and was sittin' on a jury, I don't know how they could do anything but convict him."

The intrepid reporter from the big-city newspaper was an answer to Dick's prayers. If the Hillsdale officials would no longer talk to him, he would talk to whomever would listen. Perhaps if this guy wrote a story about the case, it would get the sheriff off his behind and start doing something. What Britton didn't expect was the fervor with which Bowles would approach the story.

Sitting in Britton's kitchen, Bowles listened for several hours as Dick poured out his suspicions, his fears, his discoveries about the young man he said he had thought the world of. "If I could clear his name, I would," he insisted.

With Billy hurriedly taking notes, Britton, in a protracted monologue, traced his relationship with Davis from the day he first arrived at the Britton farm with the real estate agent handling the sale of his sixty-four acres, on through the years when the two men had grown as close as brothers. He described Phyllis as "a good woman. I liked Phyllis . . . She was kind'a on the heavy side, you know, and David had often complained about her, said he didn't like being married to a fat woman."

Dick spoke of the lies he discovered David was telling about his nonexistent military career. "He told me he was a captain in the Marines, and he told the Mohrs he was a major. I guess he got promoted on his way to Toledo." And he told of David's claim that he had six years of college and was studying to be a doctor; how he had been orphaned and had lived with his grandfather in Texas, where he shot birds from his granddad's airplane.

Billy learned from Britton of two of the other women in David's life; Barbara Matthews, "Dave's last girlfriend before Shannon," and Kay Kendall, a sophisticated and intelligent young woman who worked, he thought, as an interior decorator. Kay and Dave were engaged to be married, but she broke it off suddenly.

"He brought a lot of women around here, to show them off, I guess. He always brought them by to introduce to us."

When David told the Mohrs that he and Shannon were going to marry, Ceil had asked him if he had ever been married before. "He said he hadn't," Britton told Billy.

It would be shown later that he lied again about his marriage to Phyllis when he and Shannon were married in Las Vegas; on the wedding license application, he had answered "no" to the question, "Previously Married?"

"She found some papers in a drawer at their place; the divorce papers, I think," Britton remembers. "She asked Ann, one day, what Dave's first wife was like. She wanted to know what kind of person she was. But she never told her parents; they found out about it after Shannon died."

As he had countless times before, Dick recounted the events of July 23, 1980, reliving once again the horrible experience of viewing Shannon's motionless body in the weeds near the woods, recalling the ghastly color of her face and his certainty that she was dead. His narrative carried Billy through the trip to Hudson's Thorn Hospital, and recounted the conversations he overheard, first with the sheriff's deputies—*I don't have any insurance on her*—and with the Mohrs—*We talked about it and she said she wanted to be cremated . . . I don't have any insurance on her.* Britton also told Billy of Davis's inquiry the morning after Shannon's death—*Do you know if Ralph Wise still wants to sell his farm?*

Britton gave Billy names and some addresses to aid in his investigation: Phyllis, now remarried; Barbara Matthews, "may live at Round Lake"; Kay Kendall, used to work in Jackson; Bob Burns, a dentist, good friend of Dave's; Shannon's parents, Robert and Lucille Mohr, on 116th Street in Toledo; Dorothy and Howard Sensabaugh, former neighbors, now living in Lambertville, Michigan, just north of Toledo.

When he left, Billy Bowles had twenty-eight pages of notes, every one golden.

By 1980, Phyllis had remarried, returned to college to earn a teaching degree, and was putting her life back together. The sudden spotlight that was focused on her because of her past marriage to a man who may have murdered his second wife was uncomfortable, unwelcome, and unreasonable. She routinely refused interviews with the news media.

"I'm really not interested in contributing in any way."

But Billy Bowles was as persuasive as he was persistent, and Phyllis eventually agreed to talk to him about her life with David Davis.

"I feel so badly [about Shannon's death]. I identify with her family.

"It's unfortunate that people underestimate his cleverness and intelligence. I've been of the belief for many years that he is not mentally well. Being dropped from the graduate program was the turning point in his life.

"With David, everything and everybody is expendable. This isn't the end. It will continue. There will be another suspicious thing happening. You see, he doesn't fear death, or life imprisonment.

"When his grandfather died is the only time I've seen him express grief or anguish. To him, the strong live, the weak die.

"He tried to get in the CIA and his main ambition was to be an assassin. He took a test for the CIA one time, before the accident.''

She said David seemed to undergo a change after the incident at Introl.

"He wasn't at the farm the majority of the time after the accident. He would be gone for six weeks to four months. He couldn't renew his driver's license after the accident (because he supposedly couldn't see) but he drove anyway.''

Phyllis knew of his philanderings. He took out a separate post office box, "where he could receive mail from his girlfriends. I knew he went hunting in Tennessee with Kay Kendall.

"He was brutal to animals—always has been. He shot the girls' horse with a shotgun.

"I've told the children everything. They're afraid he might come back here.''

In one chilling statement to Billy, she said: "If anything happens to me, Mr. Bowles, please look into it. I'm sure he feels threatened right now.''

Billy had an instinct for an important story, but that instinct was wasted in this case. The dullest mind would have been stirred to life after listening to Dick Britton for three hours.

He plunged into his own investigation of Davis's background, interviewing neighbors suggested by Britton, members of Shannon's family, former employers, teachers, and university personnel. He tracked down Davis's father in Linden, Michigan. He contacted the defense department and learned that Davis had never served in the military in any capacity.

Most of the people Billy was able to reach confirmed much of what Dick Britton had said about the enigmatic Davis, occasionally adding an anecdote here and there. "We played cards with him once in a while when Kay Kendall was living with him," Howard Sensabaugh stated. "He taught us how to play Euchre and once I got to where I could beat him, he'd get mad. Once he said, 'This is enough of this shit,' and left Kay setting there. Later he came over and said, 'Let's play cards.' I said, 'No, Dave, we don't want to play cards any more.' We never played again."

Sensabaugh told Billy of one humorous eccentricity that David had. Still finding the recollection laughable, he told of how, "when David drove his tractor, he always wore earmuffs because he couldn't stand the noise." To a lifelong farmer, who had to endure a multitude of discomforts, the image of someone wearing earguards while operating an essential and regular piece of farm machinery was ludicrous.

Referring to his daughters, David "used to say, 'Those girls are going to be rich little girls when I die,' that's what he always said," Dorothy Sensabaugh recalls.

"Dave always said, 'I'll never live to be an old man,' " Howard remembered.

And Billy called Davis's mother, Martha Brandon who declined to talk on the advice of her lawyer.

"There are other people who are hurt by this," she said. "There are little girls. Dave isn't here. He's gone back to Hillsdale."

He attempted to interview Davis at his farm, but, as he had anticipated, got no cooperation.

"He came to the door and I told him who I was and that there had been suspicions raised by Shannon's mother that there was something afoot."

Davis stood with his back propped against the front door, his head lowered, his eyes on his shoes.

"If I have a statement, I'll call you," Davis said. "Nothing in my life was ever newsworthy and I don't think it's newsworthy now."

"He didn't just go inside and slam the door but he didn't really answer any of my questions," Billy remembers. "He kept referring me to his lawyer. I asked a number of questions, took maybe five or ten minutes asking questions, he kept referring me to his lawyer."

Exasperated, Billy finally asked Davis the one question he had come to have answered: "Did you kill your wife?"

Davis didn't deny that he had, he didn't admit that he had, he simply referred Billy to his lawyer.

"I have nothing to say right now."

Bowles attempted to interview Barbara Matthews by telephone, asking her if she had accompanied Davis to Florida after his wife's death.

"I prefer not to comment other than to say that he's a friend of mine."

On the night of September 23, Billy visited Barbara's home in Hudson, but she refused to let him in and declined to answer questions about her relationship with Davis. "I have company, and I've said all I have to say to you."

In the drive next to the house, Bowles noticed a yellow pickup truck. He had seen the vehicle before, when he had tried to talk with Davis at his farm.

In early October, Dick Britton received a phone call from Davis. He had just returned from Florida, he said, and was at his mother's home near Lansing. He'd actually been living there since the end of August.

"I've been reading some of the newspaper accounts about the sheriff's investigation," he told Dick. "I'm so sorry you've been dragged into this. Dick, I don't care what anyone else thinks about me, but I do care what you think. You've been like a brother to me."

"They've said some awful things here, Dave," Dick replied.

"This insurance thing, that's just a big mistake."

"You mean you don't have no insurance?"

"Dick, that's all just a big mistake."

"Boy, I'm glad to hear that. It makes me feel a lot better."

Several days later, David moved back to his farm. He called Dick almost as soon as he had returned.

"Dick, I'd like to explain to you what happened back in the woods."

"Dave, I would sure like to know."

"Can you come over?"

"I'll come right over."

A few minutes later, in Davis's kitchen, tears welling in their eyes, the two men expressed their feelings for each other, how much each meant to the other, what close friends they had been.

"You've heard about a number of insurance policies, Dick. I'd like to explain them to you."

Davis then launched into a long, rambling discourse dealing with his and Shannon's joint ownership of the farm and the cars and machinery and how he became worried, because of the difference in their ages, that something might happen to him and "she would be saddled with a lot of debt." He explained that they had agreed that there should be life insurance policies taken on each of them to protect the other—just in case. He insisted that it had always been his policy to insure possessions, that he believed very strongly in life insurance. He insisted that there had been no motive on his part to overinsure Shannon and that he would never consider doing anything to harm her.

"People are saying that I killed her. Why would I do that?" he demanded, tears again flooding his eyes and streaming down his cheeks. "Why on earth would I do that?"

Britton stood facing him, his face now drained of color, a coldness rising from deep inside him. He suddenly realized that, as much as he wished to, as much as he prayed he might, he simply did not, could not believe this man.

"Dave. Don't lie to me. You've already lied to me too much."

"How? When have I ever lied to you, Dick?"

"You told me your dad had died in World War II. I found out your dad is alive; he lives up in Fenton, Michigan." Britton had misunderstood where the elder Davis lived. Linden is a small town near the larger community of Fenton.

"That's not my biological father. My biological father was a boyfriend of my mother; he came home from the service on leave, got my mother pregnant, and went back. That's who I would consider my father."

"You told me you were a captain in the Marines. You told me those war stories about being injured, about how the Vietnamese shot you when you were hanging from a tree, and your mother says you were never in the service. How do you explain that?"

"Dick, all that was true. You know I was in the Marines, or else I wouldn't have all this firsthand knowledge. But, if you ask the government, they will deny it."

"Well, what was you in? Was you in the CIA or spying or something like that?"

"I just can't tell you more," Davis replied. "I can't tell you more, but I *was* in the Marines."

Dick shook his head and stood up to leave. Davis had lost one of his most loyal believers. His carefully crafted tale of a life he had never lived was beginning to crumble, questions he'd never before had to confront were being asked, and his answers were not satisfactory. He would not become opaque. His continued presence at the site of his young wife's tragic death was feeding a growing suspicion surrounding the circumstances of her death and increasing the pressure

Davis had been under since July 23. It was time to get out.

"Dick, I can't live here any longer, I want to sell you the farm. I want you to have it."

Britton was dumbfounded.

"I can't buy this farm. You can get a big price for this place. I can't afford it."

"Yes, you can. I want you to have it and I'll sell it to you cheap enough so you can afford it."

Dick was intrigued. How much? he asked Davis. The whole ball of wax for $130,000, was the reply—the buildings, the acreage, the machinery, and all crops in the barn and in the field.

"A hundred and thirty thousand dollars—in cash—and I'll just walk out the door. I've found an island in a river in Oregon. I'm moving there and no human being will ever see me again."

Britton said he'd think it over and get back to him.

The offer was tantalizing beyond belief; the acreage alone was worth $130,000. But there were other considerations that troubled Britton. What would Bob and Ceil think of him if he were to buy the farm?

That evening he called Toledo and talked to Bob Mohr.

"I thought too much of that girl to profit from her death. If you think it would be wrong, I won't buy it."

"Ceil and I would have no objection to that, Dick. If you don't buy it someone else will."

The deal was struck the following day and the paperwork to effect the transfer was begun. It would take four to six weeks for the deal to be processed. The final papers were signed and Davis now told Britton that he was going to Florida to buy a yacht with the approximately $65,000 he would net from the sale of the farm after all mortgages, loans, and other debts were liquidated. This time he was going without Barbara Matthews.

Billy had begun his investigation on August 27. Now, as his deadline for the story grew near, he sensed that there was still very much to learn about the dark and sinister man who seemed to have an almost Svengali-like ability to twist and manipulate everyone with whom he came in contact. This was not the end of the story. Hundreds of telephone calls and scores of visits to principals in this drama lay ahead; thousands of pages of tedious notes were still to be taken; hour after hour of poring through public records and legal papers still loomed in front of him. And even then, after all the effort, after all the questions and the digging and the probing, Billy had no idea how it would end—if, indeed, it would ever end.

16

Billy's exposé hit the newsstands in the Sunday, October 12, 1980, edition of the *Free Press,* occupying the top third of the front page and two full, uninterrupted pages in the front section. It contained an incredible 209 column inches of words, photos, and maps.

The story was a devastating portrait of the highly suspicious death of a twenty-five-year-old woman and the discovery by family and friends that the woman's husband, dearly loved and highly respected, had lived a life of absurd, deleterious untruths, and whose actions called his account of Shannon's injury and death into serious dispute.

The story detailed the insurance policies Davis had taken out and strongly hinted that the disability claims were fraudulent. It brought to light the falsity of his claims of being a Vietnam veteran and war hero, and recounted the events in the hayfield on the evening of July 23 and later at the hospital in Hudson. The story told of Davis's claim that he had no insurance and of his initial insistence that Shannon's body be cremated. The initial failure to have an autopsy performed was also mentioned.

The newspaper account did everything but declare that Davis had butchered his wife in the quiet rural grove. But there was little doubt left to the reader that he had more than a sufficient motive for doing so.

The sheriff's investigation, the publicity, the rumors, and the gossip about David had taken their toll on Barbara Matthews. She was wrapped in fearful doubt about the man to whom she had happily given herself. David's strange behavior since the death of the woman who Barbara believed he had been guarding for the federal government did little to reassure and comfort her. He had acted mysteriously in the past, but since his return from Florida he had seemed more evasive, more abstruse than ever before. Barbara had pretty much decided that her life would be less complicated, more balanced and secure if David Davis no longer had a place in it.

Shortly before Billy Bowles's unexpected visit on September 27, David, also unexpected, had arrived.

"He said he'd come to pick up a gun, the one he'd taught me to shoot with, and I was pretty much hysterical because by this time I'd figured that something was wrong. I really didn't want to talk to him. It was kind of 'take this and go away' and, you know, 'Don't bother me again.' He told me that he'd not done what everyone was whispering that he'd done, that he'd not killed anybody and that he would be proved innocent."

He told Barbara that Shannon had actually died just the way it had been reported in the newspapers, that she'd fallen from her horse and struck her head on a rock and died. Did she believe him?

"I kind of got to feeling guilty because I'd judged him without really knowing both sides of the story. I became more comfortable with him again and, yes, I did see him again."

On October 13, Davis telephoned Buddy and Cathy Brown to ask that they pick him up at Miami International Airport on the 15th.

The Browns by this time were well aware of what had been happening in Michigan since David's departure in August.

"We don't think it would be a good idea for you to come back here again, David," Buddy said coldly.

There was a long pause on the other end of the phone line, and then David's voice, sounding distant and weak, like it was being strained through an audio filter.

"Okay. I understand."

On the 16th he showed up unannounced at the Browns', explaining that he'd come to pick up his van. He made no attempt to try to discuss or explain the news accounts that had him suspected of killing his wife for more than a quarter million dollars in insurance money.

"Buddy told him that he didn't want him to go diving with us," Cathy recalls. "That he didn't want our family subjected to him. He was only here five minutes."

It was to be the last time they would see him.

On October 17, the Hillsdale County Board refused to honor a bill to pay for the autopsy performed on the body of Shannon Mohr Davis. The reason: Prosecutor Zellar said he hadn't requested the procedure and the county shouldn't have to pay for it.

The public interest in the Billy Bowles comprehensive study of David Davis and the mysterious death of Shannon Mohr Davis did not inspire a renewed interest in the case by the Hillsdale authorities, which surprised and infuriated Dick Britton. Why wouldn't somebody do something, why couldn't they determine exactly what had happened in the woods that night? Certainly something must be done to bring Davis to justice, and by God, if no one else would act, then Dick Britton would!

On October 20, Dick sat at his kitchen table and wrote a letter to Frank Kelley, the attorney general of the state of Michigan.

Sir:
My name is Dick Britton, I would like to talk to someone about the David Davis case that appeared in

the Detroit Free Press, Sunday October 12, 1980, where his wife was killed and he had $330,000 life insurance on her. I can't put it in this letter as it takes too long. I have tried to talk to the Hillsdale Co. Sheriff Department, and they don't seem interested at all. This man David Davis just lives off ins. co. I am sure he killed this girl and I can tell you how he did it. I just can't stand by and let him get away with it. Someone, somewhere must be interested in what happened to this nice girl that never hurt anyone in her life. If you can send someone down, come in the morning as it takes quite awhile to tell it all.

                                        Richard L. Britton

Quiet, unassuming Richard L. Britton, by the simple act of writing to a public official, was about to unleash the full powers of the sovereign state of Michigan to ascertain exactly what had happened to "this nice girl that never hurt anyone in her life."

On October 23, 1980, members of the staff of Flower Memorial Hospital planted a tree on hospital grounds in Shannon's memory.

17

Since the days when he was a high school junior, Donald Addison Brooks had wanted to be a Michigan State Police officer.

From the instant he decided what he would do with his life, he never wanted to be anything else; he hadn't longed to be a member of just any police department, it had to be the Michigan State Police.

"I took some kidding from friends," he admits. "But it never changed my mind."

Born on March 29, 1949 in Lansing, Michigan, he was the only son of Robert and June Brooks. He had a sister, Patricia, one year younger. In high school, his nonacademic interests were largely centered on football, baseball and basketball, and on a pretty coed named Kathy Russell.

Following graduation in 1967, Brooks enrolled at Lansing Community College, where he spent one year before transferring to the University of New Mexico on an athletic scholarship.

In 1971, Brooks applied for admission to the Michigan State Police Academy and was accepted in August of that year.

In February 1972, he married Kathy, his high school sweetheart.

His first posting after the academy was in the uniformed law enforcement branch of the department as a trooper in Benton Harbor on the southwestern side of the state. It was while there that he worked on his first homicide investigation.

''It was a smoking gun case. Two men worked together at a sawmill. They got into an argument over
money, one got a shotgun and killed the other. It
wasn't complicated and we closed it quickly.''

In 1975, he was transfered to the Lansing post and
then, in November 1976, to Detroit for a thirty-day
assignment before being given a highly dangerous undercover job with the state police's narcotics bureau.
He held this job for a long and nerve-racking two and
a half years.

In July 1979, Don was returned to Lansing to avoid
the possibility of his true role being uncovered and to
relieve him of the potential burnout that threatens undercover police.

In October 1980, he was promoted to the rank of
detective sergeant, and by virtue of his invaluable experience as an undercover officer, he was offered a
position in the newly created attorney general's intelligence and surveillance unit.

He was told that since there would be a short period
before the actual startup of the new unit would take
place, he would be assigned to the attorney general's
general criminal investigation division.

On November 4, about two weeks after reporting to
the attorney general, Brooks was directed to undertake
a preliminary investigation of a potential homicide in
Hillsdale County.

''I got the case through normal rotation; my case-
load was such that I had an opening and could take on
a new investigation. My superiors thought that it would
be cleared up in a week or so, and it would be all right
to give it to me.''

What was thought to be a simple matter, easily com-
pleted, would occupy the next nine years of his life.
By the luck of the draw, Detective Sergeant Donald
Addison Brooks had been given the Shannon Mohr
Davis case.

Michigan is one of the few states allowing their attorney general to intervene in criminal cases that

would, in other jurisdictions, be the exclusive property of county prosecutors. This seeming intrusion upon the purview of county government was specifically provided for by the state legislature and is not exercised frivolously but is employed in major criminal cases or in situations where the county prosecutors fail, for one reason or another, to press for indictment.

The first item on Brooks's agenda was to assure himself that Britton's complaint was not that of a crackpot, a constant problem for law enforcement. Reassurance came easily and soon. In addition to Britton's October 20 letter, a barrage of similar reports began coming into the attorney general's office from citizens in Michigan and Northwest Ohio.

On October 31, 1980, Lucille Mohr's mother wrote:

> I am writing in regards to my granddaughter's death who supposedly fell from a horse and was killed.
> We are not satisfied as to the cause Mr. Davis gave us of what happened to Shannon.
>
> Lucille Abrams

The same day, Jane Schenck, a longtime friend of Bob and Ceil, wrote, in part:

> The law department of Hillsdale County needs some cleaning up. Sounds to me like there are a lot of shady things going on.

On November 9, 1980, Maribeth Petro of Toledo wrote:

> I am . . . upset at the quality of police detection (in Hillsdale County) . . . Please help—Please care enough to seek justice (in) the Shannon Davis case.

The following day, Rev. Stephen Petro, Maribeth's husband, was moved to write that he was speaking up "in behalf of many people who are concerned that the case of the death of Shannon Davis was not properly handled.''

For the next two months the letters continued arriving in Lansing.

On November 13, 1980, Mrs. Walter Ray, who, following her signature added ''a concerned citizen,'' wrote:

> The hospitals and police departments are so lax . . . and leave the crime to be dismissed and the criminal to commit the same act again.

On December 2, 1980, this letter arrived:

> No man who was innocent would take off for Florida with a girl friend a week after his wife died. I just hope and pray he suffers for what he has done.
>
> Mrs. V. Cooper

Perhaps the most touching of the many letters received by the attorney general was one written on Christmas Day 1980 by Shannon's sister-in-law Judi, Bobby's wife:

> I miss her so much . . . knowing she will never be here with us again . . . Please do everything in your power to see that David Davis gets what he deserves.

There is no accurate count of how many letters concerning the Shannon Davis matter were received by the attorney general's office.

''We didn't keep all of them,'' Stanley Steinborn, chief assistant to Frank J. Kelley, Michigan's popular attorney general, stated. ''We read them all, forwarded them to the criminal division for disposition where some were routinely discarded.''

According to one estimate, a total of thirty-seven letters asking for a state investigation of Shannon's death were received over a six-week period.

As 1980 faded and prepared to give way to 1981, a general mood of pessimism clouded the air in the criminal division.

When a reporter asked Steinborn to predict the outcome of the Davis investigation, he replied rather grimly, ''I suspect our conclusions are going to be that there's no evidence. The cops haven't found anything. It's the old story; you need evidence.''

Don Brooks had virtually no facts dealing with the woman's death. ''I'm sure he killed this girl and I can tell you how he did it,'' Britton's letter had insisted. Brooks decided to visit the farmer, to hear firsthand exactly what the farmer knew. He telephoned Britton to make arrangements to come down the following day.

''I didn't think anybody really cared,'' the surprised Britton told Brooks.

''Somebody cares,'' the detective replied. ''*We* care.''

The next morning, sitting in the Brittons' kitchen, Don read Billy Bowles's newspaper story, shaking his head when he had finished.

''If this is even fifty percent accurate, we're on to something here.''

As the two men walked out to the field and the wooded grove where Shannon was supposed to have fallen, Britton filled the detective in on the events that had occurred since the Bowles account was published.

An hour later, Don was speeding back to Lansing, his head buzzing with one major question demanding an answer: Assuming Davis in fact killed his wife, precisely how did he do it?

18

By mid-November, attorney Sheldon Wittenberg was ready for the second stage of his attack on David Davis.

"The Mohrs weren't interested in having the insurance money. What they wanted was to have their son-in-law charged with their daughter's murder. All I could do for them was to buy enough time where law enforcement could accumulate enough evidence to indict him. That's how I could help these wonderful people; delay Davis in getting his hands on the money and then disappearing."

On behalf of the Mohrs, Wittenberg filed a civil suit in U.S. District Court in Detroit asking the court to deny Davis the proceeds from any of the insurance policies on Shannon's life in which he was named as beneficiary, claiming that he was not entitled to the monies "because he feloniously and intentionally killed" her.

The suit also accused Davis of failing to seek proper medical assistance for Shannon.

"Instead," the pleadings went on, "he dragged his injured wife to the edge of the wooded area and later transported her to a hospital in a private vehicle."

The Mohrs also retained James Hayne, a Hillsdale attorney, to petition the Hillsdale County Probate Court to set up an estate fund into which any insurance money should be paid until the civil matter was settled.

The actions were taken in response to a suit filed in

October by The Prudential Insurance Company asking that the court decide who was entitled to proceeds of the insurance policy on Shannon's life. Once they had been alerted to the Hillsdale County sheriff's reopening of the investigation into Shannon's death, all insurance companies carrying the $300,000 in insurance on her life withheld payment of the funds. Now, Wittenberg was acting to permanently deny Davis those monies.

And, in a move that Davis must have felt added insult to injury, the Mohrs also filed a $150,000 "wrongful death" suit against Davis.

But Davis was not to be intimidated by the legal thrusts of the Mohrs. On November 21 he filed his own suit in U.S. District Court demanding $62,000 from three of the insurance policies he held on Shannon. The suit, filed by James Cmejrek, an Ann Arbor attorney retained by Davis, claimed that failure to pay the insurance money amounted to a "bad faith" breach on the part of the insurance companies and demanded full payment plus interest and $25,000 in damages from each of the companies.

The policies were written by the New York Life Insurance Company of New York, for $10,000; Mutual Service Life Insurance Company of Arden Hills, Minnesota, for $25,000; and the Hartford Life and Accident Insurance Company of Hartford, Connecticut, for $27,000.

The same day, Davis's attorney filed yet another suit in District Court demanding payment of the $220,000 on the Prudential double indemnity policy, and also asked the court to dismiss the Prudential suit that argued that Davis might not be entitled to the money if the "beneficiary intentionally kill[ed] the insured."

In his suit, Davis argued that there was no evidence that he was in any way responsible for the death of his wife and called attention to the findings of the Hillsdale prosecutor's and sheriff's investigation and the subsequent autopsy results, which upheld the original determination of accidental death caused by a fall.

If nothing else, Davis was demonstrating that he would not be put off.

Detective sergeant Don Brooks buried himself in his investigation of Davis and the events surrounding Shannon's death, carefully sifting through the evidence developed in the Hillsdale County sheriff's investigation and Billy Bowles's incredible probe of the Davis case, constantly looking for new clues, fresh leads, and a better understanding of what may have motivated Davis to take his wife's life. But equally important, Brooks was still obsessed with the question of how it might have been done.

Don was under the supervision of John Wilson, a crusty, impatient assistant attorney general who demanded the very best from his subordinates. Wilson did not willingly suffer incompetence or ignorance and was not especially inclined to civility toward those who he believed to be wasting his time. He frequently terminated unsatisfying or unproductive telephone conversations by simply hanging up the phone—no matter who was on the other end of the line. Don Brooks appreciated and admired Wilson's toughness and wanted to demonstrate that he could be as tireless, as persistent, and as efficient as his boss.

One of the first calls Brooks made was on the toxicology lab at the Medical College of Ohio in Toledo. There he met for the first time the young, intense toxicology scientist, Dr. Robert B. Forney, Jr.

During the meeting Forney remarked that in screening tissue samples from the autopsy on Shannon they had discovered a compound that had defied identification.

He produced the graph with the tracings of the chemical analysis of Shannon's tissue and pointed to the vertical line near the end of the strip of paper.

"This is the peak right here. See how clean it is?

Because it's so clean, that means that I think that it's a drug. This is important to the case; it's got to be if we can identify what that is.

"You could be a great help to me," Forney told Brooks, explaining that determining what types of toxic compounds were readily available to residents of Hillsdale County could give them a speedy clue to what the mysterious chemical found in Shannon's tissue might be.

Forney asked Brooks about Davis's background and Brooks mentioned, among other things, that Davis was a "dirt farmer" and that he had some large animals on the farm.

The two men discussed the possibility of contacting area veterinarians who may have serviced Davis's animals.

As Don began his survey through Hillsdale County, a theory about Shannon's death began developing. He reasoned that if Davis had indeed murdered his wife, he had to accomplish it in a manner that would defy detection by medical experts; if his claim that Shannon had accidentally fallen from her horse was to be accepted, the injuries that would be seen by medical and forensic pathology experts would have to be consistent with his story. Brooks knew from the Bowles story that Davis had taken courses at the University of Michigan in psychopharmacology—which, he learned, dealt with the effects of drugs on behavior—physiology, and neuroanatomy. He would, therefore, have a good understanding of the manifestation produced by a brain injury and the difference between having a skull strike a hard object and a solid, or blunt, object being used to bash a person's head. Given that understanding, Davis would, if he did slay his wife, have realized that he would have a single opportunity to inflict the injury. He would not be able to repeatedly smash Shannon's head against a rock until sufficient damage was done to cause her death and then convince medical authorities that the injury was caused by a fall from her horse.

If all of this were true, Don realized, it would require that Davis be able to accomplish his end with minimal resistance from his victim. If Shannon were to put up an aggressive struggle to save her life, the lingering physical evidence would give the lie to his claim; if he bound his wife with a rope or strap, marks might remain that would generate questions; if he struck her with a fist—to knock her out—that bruise would certainly remain. Brooks knew that a killer as intelligent as Davis seemed to be would have considered his plan carefully and would have taken pains to conceal his act. It therefore seemed to the police officer only reasonable that Davis would have taken precautions to immobilize his victim to insure that he had the opportunity to cause an injury to her skull that would be sufficiently traumatic to end her life and still bear all the physical corroboration of a dreadful but blameless accident.

An immobilizing agent meant one thing to Don—an incapacitating drug, perhaps one of the type that the toxicologists at MCO had found but were unable to identify.

Drugs of many varieties were used by farmers on their livestock to perform minor animal medical and surgical procedures; everything from foaling horses to castrating steers to euthanizing sick or injured beasts. As he and Dr. Forney had agreed, Don began calling on veterinarians in the Wright Township area. At a stop in Camden, he was told by veterinarian Larry M. Granger that there was a compound available that was widely used in the castration of horses. The drug was called "sucostrin" and was a muscle relaxant that was related to curare, used by Amazon natives to poison the tips of their arrows.

The chemical was considered a prescription drug but not a "controlled substance" by the Federal Food and Drug Administration, and could be obtained by farmers without too much difficulty.

Brooks, his nerve ends tingling in anticipation, contacted Dr. Forney. He had a list of chemicals he had been informed were in frequent use by farmers in the area—pesticides, herbicides, and various "critter" poisons. But his excitement was centered mainly on sucostrin. He felt that he probably had what he had been looking for—a "smoking gun."

19

Dr. Robert Forney took the call from Don Brooks, listening earnestly as the detective read an inventory of chemicals readily available to anyone in Hillsdale County, silently canceling out one compound after another as failing to have the basic properties of the unidentified substance.

"Sucostrin," he repeated when Brooks offered the chemical as one possibility. That was a brand name; the generic was chemically known as succinylcholine chloride, a potent muscle relaxant.

The drug was a compound used in both human and animal surgery and in electroshock therapy; it almost instantly paralyzes every muscle in the body except the heart. Although the effects of the drug are relatively short in duration, if proper precautions are not taken to provide oxygen to the lungs, the patient could suffocate and die within a few minutes. Forney smiled. They could quickly rule succinylcholine out of their search, he decided. Even a first-year pharmacology student could tell you that succinylcholine could not be traced in human tissue.

Succinylcholine chloride is a depolarizing neuromuscular blocking agent used in surgery as a muscle relaxant, frequently used in abdominal surgery, in aligning fractured bones, and in assisting in the intubation of devices to inspect the larynx, bronchial tubes, and esophagus, as well as in relaxing throat muscles prior to inserting tubes used in administering anesthesia. It has also been used in controlling seizures associated with electroshock therapy. A powerful, quick-acting drug, succinylcholine, when injected directly into the bloodstream, starts affecting the body's muscle system in a uniform pattern almost immediately, beginning with the head and continuing with the neck, shoulders, limbs, abdomen, and then the critical muscles that control breathing.

The *Physician's Desk Reference* carries a warning about the drug:

> *CAUTION, Succinylcholine should be used only when apparatus for assisted or controlled respiration with oxygen is available, and should be administered only by persons well versed in the use of such apparatus.*

The drug is a chemical relative to curare, the highly potent poison used by South American Indians to tip their arrows. It is said to have been first introduced to the Western world in the early 1600s by Sir Walter Raleigh, the English navigator and historian, who supposedly brought the drug back with him after an expedition to the New World.

A typical medical dose by injection into the bloodstream will cause complete paralysis within sixty seconds, which will persist for about another sixty seconds and then slowly moderate over the next four to ten minutes as it breaks down into its component elements, succinic acid and choline—both of which are found naturally in the body. Because of this rapid decomposition, succinylcholine was considered untraceable when used to suffocate an unfortunate victim. It has frequently been used in fiction as the means of committing a "perfect crime," as any lover of mystery novels—such as David Davis—could attest. It was, according to no less an authority than the noted criminal lawyer F. Lee Bailey, "an ideal murder weapon."

In July 1966, a pair of grand juries—one in Monmouth County, New Jersey, the other in Sarasota

County, Florida—indicted for murder thirty-four-year-old Dr. Carl Coppolino.

Coppolino was accused of murdering his wife Carmela, herself a physician, and his lover's husband, William Farber, fifty-four. In both cases the prosecution contended that Coppolino had used succinylcholine chloride.

Marjorie Cullen Farber, fifty-two, testified at Coppolino's murder trials that she and Coppolino plotted to kill her husband when the Coppolinos and Farbers were neighbors in Middletown Township, New Jersey; that on July 30, 1963, Coppolino gave her a hypodermic syringe and a vial of a deadly drug that he said could not be identified.

Marjorie told the jury that she mixed the drug according to Coppolino's instructions, filled the syringe with it, and attempted to inject her husband's leg while he slept.

But Farber awoke suddenly, complaining of a cramp in his leg, and Marjorie had to withdraw the needle after only a small amount had been injected. Farber went to the bathroom where be became ill and fell gasping to the floor.

She said that Coppolino arrived and gave Farber a sedative to put him to sleep and then attempted to suffocate him by putting a plastic bag over his head. But Farber began vomiting and Coppolino gave up the attempt.

The following day, according to Marjorie, Coppolino returned and said that he was going to give Farber another sedative. The two men argued and Marjorie claimed that Coppolino stormed out of the bedroom raging, "That bastard's got to go."

Later, he gave Farber an injection and waited, complaining, "He is a hard one to kill. He is taking a long time to die."

Finally, she testified, Coppolino placed a pillow over Farber's face and leaned on it with his full weight until Farber was dead.

Coppolino had, months earlier, resigned his job as a staff anesthesiologist at a Riverbank, New Jersey, hospital and could not legally sign the death certificate. Instead, he had his wife, Carmela, a physician with a pharmaceutical company, sign the document, listing coronary artery disease as the cause of death. The health department accepted the certificate and no autopsy was performed. Farber, an insurance agent and retired Army lieutenant colonel, was buried with appropriate honors at Arlington National Cemetery.

The affair between Marjorie and Carl eventually broke up and the Coppolinos moved to Florida in April 1965. Marjorie followed them there and bought property next to their home on fashionable Longboat Key.

In August 1965, Carmela, thirty-two, apparently in good health, died suddenly in her bed. Although Florida required an autopsy in death cases where the deceased had not been under a doctor's care, local authorities ruled that Carmela had suffered a heart attack. Carl had $65,000 in life insurance on his wife.

Forty days after Carmela's death, Carl married Mary Gibson, his bridge partner.

In November 1965, Marjorie, perhaps in a fit of contrition, walked into the office of Sheriff Ross Boyer in Sarasota, Florida, and shocked him with the confession that she had conspired to kill her husband in New Jersey two years earlier; that a doctor, now living near Sarasota had been the one to actually murder her husband with a drug that couldn't be found in the body after its use. She said that she suspected the doctor later killed his wife in Sarasota County.

Marjorie had brought her attorney with her but did not ask for immunity from criminal prosecution.

Coppolino hired F. Lee Bailey to defend him.

The first trial was held in Freehold, New Jersey, in December 1966, where the prosecution argued that Coppolino had obtained succinylcholine from a doctor friend shortly before each victim died.

The bodies of William Farber and Carmela Coppolino were disinterred and autopsies performed. Dr. Milton Helpern, chief medical examiner for the City of New York and the nation's best-known forensic pathologist, testified that toxicologists were unable to find succinylcholine intact in Farber's body, and that the cause of death was a double fracture of the cricoid cartilage of the throat, a common injury in cases of manual strangulation. He said that Farber's heart was healthy, and that while the arteries of the heart were diseased, it was not far enough advanced to have caused his death.

Bailey responded with two medical experts who testified that coronary disease had killed Farber and that the neck injury had occurred after his death.

The jury deliberated for four and a half hours before returning an acquittal of first-degree murder.

Four months later, Coppolino went on trial in Naples, Florida, for the murder of his wife, Carmela. Helpern, again testifying for the prosecution, said that Carmela's heart and other vital organs were healthy. He said that the cause of death was an injection of succinylcholine.

The pathologist said he based his finding on chemical tests that turned up excessive levels of succinic acid and choline, the products, he claimed, of succinylcholine.

One of the toxicologists testified that there was a concentration of choline around a needle track found on the dead woman's right buttock. While they did not find succinylcholine chloride intact in the body, they explained that the chemical breaks down too quickly in the body to be isolated in tissue samples.

On April 28, 1967, following a twenty-five-day trial and sixteen hours of deliberations, the jury convicted Coppolino of second-degree murder in the death of his wife. He was the only person to that date to have been convicted in the United States of murdering someone with succinylcholine. Judge Lynn Silvertooth sentenced him to life imprisonment.

WANTED for MURDER

DAVID RICHARD DAVIS

Wanted for the murder of his wife, SHANNON DAVIS on 7-23-80. Victim was killed by succinylcholine poisoning, a strong muscle relaxer. Suspect has formerly lived in Flint, Michigan, Ann Arbor, Michigan and Pittsford, Michigan. Suspect has recently spent time in southern Florida and the Carribean. Suspect was last seen in Port-au-Prince, Haiti on December 24, 1981. Suspect is an experienced recreational diver and sailor. Suspect often talks about Viet Nam War experiences. <u>SUSPECT SHOULD BE CONSIDERED ARMED AND DANGEROUS.</u> A reward is offered by a private donor to the first person that provides information leading to the arrest of David Davis.

Buscado por el asesinato de su esposa, SHANNON DAVIS, ocurrido el día 23 de julio de 1980. La víctima murió a causa de envenenamiento con succinylcholina, un fuerte relajante muscular. El sospechoso ha vivido previamente en Flint, Michigan, Ann Arbor, Michigan y Pittsford, Michigan. El sospechoso también ha vivido un tiempo en el sur de Florida y en el Caribe. El sospechoso fue visto por última vez en Port-au-Prince, Haití, el 24 de diciembre de 1981. El sospechoso es un buzo aficionado y un marinero aficionado con destreza. Frecuentemente habla de sus experiencias en la guerra de Vietnam. <u>SE CREE QUE EL SOSPECHOSO PORTA ARMAS Y ES UN INDIVIDUO PELIGROSO.</u> Un donante particular ofrece una recompensa a la primera persona que provea informacion conducente al arresto de David Davis.

Recherché pour le meurtre de sa femme, SHANNON DAVIS, le 23 juillet 1980. La victime a été empoisonnée par de la succinylcholine, un puissant médicament provoquant la relaxation des muscles. Le suspect a anté-rieurement vécu à Flint, Ann Arbor, et Pittsford dans l'état du Michigan. Le suspect a récemment passé quelque temps dans le Sud de la Floride et dans les Caraïbes. Le suspect a été vu pour la dernière fois à Port-au-Prince, Haïti, le 24 décembre 1981. Le suspect est devenu expert en plongée sous-marine et en navigation pendant ses loisirs. Le suspect parle souvent de ses expériences personnelles de la guerre du Viet Nam. <u>LE SUSPECT DOIT ETRE CONSIDERE COMME ARME ET DANGEREUX.</u> Une récompense est offerte par un particulier à la première personne qui fournira des renseignements aboutissant à l'arrestation de David Davis.

If seen, please call collect:
Michigan State Police
517 - 373 - 1120 (8a.m. to 5 p.m.)
or 517 - 332 - 2621, ext. 105 (after 5 p.m, or on weekends)

Sept. 1979

Jan. 1981

AGE: 9-27-44 (37 years of age)
HT: 6' - 0''
WT: 190 lbs.
HAIR: Blond
EYES: Blue

3 - 82

Thousands of posters were distributed throughout the Caribbean and as far as Australia, but it was a television show that finally led to Davis' arrest.

Shannon graduated at the top of her nursing school class.

Shannon Mohr Davis.

Shannon Mohr and David Davis.

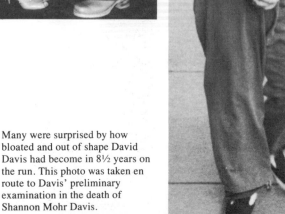

Many were surprised by how bloated and out of shape David Davis had become in 8½ years on the run. This photo was taken en route to Davis' preliminary examination in the death of Shannon Mohr Davis.

John Skrzynski, David Davis, and Thomas Bleakley. The change in Davis' appearance had been so drastic that when witnesses were asked if Davis was in the courtroom, they responded in the negative.

Kay Kendall. She believed Davis when he told her he worked for the C.I.A. She was Davis' first candidate for murder, but backed out of the wedding plans.

Barbara Matthews. She also believed Davis was working for the government, even after reading of Shannon Mohr's death.

Tori Abrams. Shannon Mohr's cousin was practically the only member of the family not enthralled by David Davis. She remembered seeing drug vials in the freezer.

Cheryl Nicholaidis. "You're the most beautiful woman in my life now," Davis would tell her after Shannon's funeral.

ACCIDENT
1. PHOTOGRAPHS OF
SCENE OF ACCIDENT
TAKEN BY POLICE OFFI
2. PHOTOS TAKEN BY
RICHARD BRITTON
3. CLOTHING WORN BY
SHANNON DAVIS
4. PHOTOS OF FIRST
AUTOPSY

Defense attorney Tom Bleakley. Eminently knowledgeable in biochemistry, he determined to put both toxicologist Robert Forney and his methods on trial.

Prosecution witness Robert Forney, Jr. He endured cross-examination so confidently that many spectators commented that he reminded them of actor/comedian Chevy Chase.

Prosecution witness Thomas Carroll. His testimony gave jurors a basic understanding of what led up to the discovery of succinylcholine in Shannon Mohr's body.

Prosecutor Mark Blumer. Winning a conviction became more than a professional obligation for him.

Donald Brooks. Shortly after being promoted to detective sergeant of the Michigan State Police, he began work on the Davis case, which would occupy the next 9 years of his life.

Circuit Court Judge Harvey Moes. Gentle and considerate off the bench, he could be a tyrant in the courtroom.

Bearded again, and sporting more pounds than during his trial, David Davis is led away after receiving his sentence of life without the possibility of parole.

Bob and Lucille Mohr. They vowed not to rest until David Davis had paid for murdering their daughter.

Martin Blumer and Lucille Mohr, after the verdict.

The Florida Parole and Probation Commission granted Coppolino parole on September 26, 1979, on condition that he not practice medicine in Florida. He has tried unsuccessfully to win a pardon from the governor.

In 1980, he published a book, *The Crime that Never Was*.

Nine years earlier, F. Lee Bailey wrote about the case in his own book, *The Defense Never Rests:*

> The story was tailored to the public fancy. A young wife, a deadly drug . . . a darkly sinister husband . . . Succinylcholine chloride possesses a property that makes it an ideal murder weapon . . . it breaks down in separate components normally present in the body, becoming virtually undetectable.

If Coppolino was the first to be convicted for using the deadly drug in a murder, he was not the only one to be tried for the charge.

Another medical doctor, Arsenio Favor, twice stood trial on charges that he murdered his wife, physician Nenita Favor, in Harlem Hospital, New York City in 1977. A family friend testified that he had found a nearly empty vial of succinylcholine chloride in the Favors' medicine cabinet after Nenita's death. Favor said he had no idea how the drug got there. The prosecutor claimed that Favor had injected his wife with the drug while she was a patient at the hospital receiving intravenous medication for an infection after minor breast surgery. Medical examiners were unable to find a cause of death.

The first trial ended in a mistrial on June 8, 1978. In the second, the jury found him not guilty.

Over a ten-month period in 1965 and 1966, more than twenty unexplained deaths occurred at a small osteopathic hospital in Oradell, New Jersey. The mysterious deaths became known as the ''Doctor X'' case.

Dr. Mario Enrique Jascalevich became the focus of

an investigation by the Bergen County, New Jersey, prosecutor when a colleague of Dr. Jascalevich reportedly found eighteen vials of curare, most empty or near empty, in Jascalevich's hospital locker.

After a two-week investigation the case was dropped for lack of evidence.

Ten years later, a *New York Times* reporter, Myron Farber, reinvestigated the deaths and wrote two articles about a "Doctor X." A grand jury reopened the matter and quickly issued an indictment against Dr. Jascalevish, charging him with five counts of murder.

After a thirty-three week trial, during which two of the five murder counts were dropped for lack of evidence and the *Times* reporter was jailed for refusing to surrender his notes to the court, the jury acquitted Jascalevich.

In the summer of 1975, fifty-six patients at the Veterans Administration Hospital in Ann Arbor, Michigan, suffered unexpected breathing failures, twenty-three of them in one night. Eleven died of what was later found to involve a curarelike drug, Pavulon, a muscle relaxant used in surgery.

The FBI later arrested two nurses: Filipina Narciso and Leonora Perez, charging them with murdering five of the patients and poisoning ten others who survived.

On July 13, 1977, after several of the charges had been dismissed, the jury found the two women guilty of five poisonings.

Judge Philip Pratt overturned the verdict five months later on grounds that misconduct by the U.S. attorney's office had denied the women a fair trial. Pratt ordered them retried, but the U.S. attorney dropped the charges on February 1, 1978.

Dr. Forney thought for a moment. It was a waste of time checking out succinylcholine as the possible unidentified compound found in the tissue samples taken from Shannon Davis. It was all but written in stone that succinylcholine couldn't be extracted in tact from human tissue. Still, what could it hurt?

He suggested that lab director Tom Carroll go to the pharmacy and obtain some succinylcholine and run it through the gas chromatograph to "quickly rule it out" as the mystery substance.

A short while later Forney happened by the lab and saw Carroll at the chemical extractor.

"Where you able to get the succinylcholine?" he asked. "Do I need to make a phone call?"

"No, I obtained it."

"Have you had time to begin looking yet?"

"Oh, yeah, I got right on it."

"Well, what happened? Did it . . . it didn't . . . we didn't get any results, did we?"

"I'm still extracting it."

Forney was puzzled. It would be much simpler to rule out succinylcholine by running it through the chromatograph to demonstrate that it would not peak as the unknown substance had. Instead, Carroll was running the succinyl through the same screening process that had been used on the tissue samples during the initial stages of testing.

"Why are you extracting it?" Forney inquired.

"I thought that's what you wanted me to do."

"Tom, you *know* it won't extract, why bother going to the effort?"

So certain was Forney that the drug could not be traced that he bristled at unnecessary procedures that would only prove what they already knew.

"I didn't believe that it would either extract or chromatograph."

Carroll left the extractor and moved to the chromatograph, where he injected a sample of succinylcholine into the machine.

The two men watched as the machine whirred and chugged, waiting for the graph paper to begin feeding out of the printer. Slowly the narrow strip inched out, a single ink tracing running along the bottom of the graph. Suddenly the tracing pen shot upward.

"To my surprise," Forney says, "there was a response."

Forney and Carroll looked at each other and then back at the graph.

"The relative retention times are the same," Forney said at last. The vertical line was in the exact same place on the chart as the mystery substance. It was a match, an exact match.

"Bingo," Carroll shouted. "It's succinyl!"

Forney couldn't believe his eyes. Everyone knew that succinylcholine didn't extract. The mystery compound couldn't be succinylcholine, it just couldn't be!

"I was astonished. I was completely befuddled."

20

Bob Forney was intrigued. What was causing the mysterious peak on the gas chromatograph?

He and Carroll had run the tissue samples through five separate gas chromatographs, each with different column configurations, to determine whether they could get similar peaks. From each of the five chromatographs they observed retention times—peaks— that were identical to their original test and identical to the test on succinylcholine.

Tom Carroll was euphoric. The big man with the snow-white hair felt like dancing around the lab, bridling the impulse when he observed a grim scowl on Forney's face.

The toxicologist was not satisfied by half with the puzzling results of his high-tech marvels of electronic wizardry; there had to be another explanation for the peak they were getting.

Finally, he concluded that whatever the unknown compound was, it was definitely *not* succinylcholine. He decided that what was being extracted from the tissue samples was a succinylcholine metabolite that may have reacted with the embalming fluid to produce de-methylated succinyl-mono-choline methyl ester—a false succinylcholine.

The basis for his implacable insistence that they were dealing with some chemical other than succinylcholine was the simple fact that succinylcholine was highly water soluble—its molecules literally glued themselves to molecules of water—making extraction by known methods impossible. Suddenly his focus was shifting, moving from attempts to determine what the unknown compound was to proving that it was not succinylcholine.

Obtaining an uncontaminated tissue sample from sources other than those taken from Shannon's body, Forney mixed succinylcholine with the pure tissue and then subjected the mixture to the extraction process, attempting to pull the succinylcholine out of the mixture, to isolate it as had seemingly been done with the unknown compound. As he had expected, the succinylcholine wouldn't extract.

"I need to know more about that peak," he concluded when he and Carroll had exhausted all resources within the laboratory to identify the abstruse chemical.

Where Forney was resolute, his lab assistant was glum. He was reminded of how he'd felt as a child when told there was no Santa Claus.

Forney thought that testing with the mass spectrometer offered the best hope of determining what the mystery compound might be.

Where the gas chromatograph vaporized and analyzed a substance to determine its component parts, mass spectography bombarded the specimen with an electronic beam to fragment the substance into its individual elements. The pieces resulting from the bombardment formed a molecular fingerprint of the various segments that could positively identify what the elements where.

Without a mass spectrometer in his own lab, Forney's only hope was to perhaps be allowed by an institution owning the instrument to run tests on the unidentified compound in Shannon's tissue. He began calling labs that had the equipment. His search ultimately led him to Chicago, to the Hewlett-Packard Company, manufacturers of "mass spec" machines. The company was willing to make available the instrument they used to train those who purchased the machines. But Forney and Carroll were given only one day—when there were no training classes—to perform their tests, and it took the entire day just to set the machine for the tests they wanted to run; when the day was finished they had yet to perform a single procedure. The company representatives were sympathetic but said there was nothing they could do. "It will be another month before we have more time available for you."

The next stop was Wright Patterson Air Force Base near Dayton, Ohio, where they were given access to a combination gas chromatograph-mass spectrometer, a more sophisticated testing apparatus. However the results achieved were still not to Dr. Forney's satisfaction.

"I had some confirmation, but I had some questions. The mass spectra contained many of the elements that were present in succinylcholine, but it contained a number of other elements that were not. At this point I believed that it was possible that [the unknown chemical] might be related to succinylcholine, but the mass spectra at this point indicated to me that we had more than just succinylcholine."

The problem with the tests, Forney decided, was that the Wright Patterson instrument was routinely used to analyze jet fuels at very high concentrations; residue from previous testing was contaminating the Forney tests.

"What I really needed was an instrument that was used in medicine rather than in aerospace."

Forney knew of an instrument that was particularly set up and tuned for analysis of drugs in the same family as succinylcholine. The instrument was in the laboratory of Professor Bo Holmstedt, a longtime friend of Forney's father. Holmstedt was engaged in nerve-gas poisoning research with a particular interest in neuromuscular blocking agents such as acetylcholine. This was of special interest to Forney, for when two acetylcholine molecules are linked together they form diacetylcholine—also known as succinylcholine.

But Bob Forney had a problem—actually he had two problems: He wasn't certain that Professor Holmstedt would be interested in his investigation and, even if he should be, Holmstedt's laboratory was located at the Karolinska Institute in Stockholm, Sweden.

Early in 1981, Forney attended an international meeting of toxicologists in San Diego, California. Looking through the meeting's registration list, Forney was pleasantly surprised to see Professor Holmstedt's name as one of the attendees.

Before the conference had concluded, Forney approached the professor to discuss his research difficulties. Holmstedt was instantly interested and immediately offered his laboratory to Forney for testing to isolate and determine whether succinylcholine was actually present in Shannon Davis's body. It would be a joint effort.

But there was still the problem of distance. Forney had no way of knowing if the Medical College of Ohio would allow him a leave of absence for whatever time would be necessary to complete the research and, if so, if they would allow him to take Tom Carroll along to supervise the extraction process that he and Forney had devised. And then there was the problem of expense. Neither Forney nor Carroll were financially able to shoulder the cost of travel, housing, and other expenses for a possibly protracted stay in Sweden.

Shortly after his return from the San Diego convention, Forney was contacted by Don Brooks, who was curious about the toxicologist's progress in identifying the strange chemical in the tissue samples. Forney explained that his research had indicated the possible presence of a succinylcholine-related substance, but that there were still too many questions to be answered before he could say with certainty that Shannon had died from an injection of the muscle relaxant. He mentioned the Holmstedt offer but said that because of cost and other problems, it was impractical, at present, for him to consider it.

Brooks, ebullient at the thought that the toxicologist might be narrowing the search for the cause of Shannon's death, didn't think a trip to Sweden was necessarily so impractical. He discussed the results of his conversation with Bob Forney with his superior, John Wilson, and asked if there might be a way, should the medical college agree to let Forney have the time, that the state of Michigan could send the scientist to Sweden. Wilson believed there was; a federal grant, which would pay all the costs of such a trip, was available, but it would be up to Frank Kelley, the attorney general, as to whether an application for the funds could be made.

Frank Kelley is something of a conundrum in Michigan politics. A lifelong Democrat, the son of a Democrat leader in Michigan politics, he was appointed to office as attorney general in 1962 by Governor John Swainson, a Democrat, to fill an unexpired term. Kelley was elected to a full term eleven months later and has since been reelected to eight consecutive four-year terms—six terms under Republican administrations.

A wiry little Irish Catholic, born, raised, and educated in Detroit, he received his baccalaureate and juris doctor degrees from the University of Detroit. He was admitted to the Michigan Bar in 1951.

The only Michigan attorney general to be elected president of the National Association of Attorneys General, he has earned the respect and admiration of both political parties in Michigan and of judicial and law enforcement officials throughout the United States.

In twenty-nine years as Michigan's top lawyer, Kelley developed an aggressive consumer protection program, fought polluters, worked hard for civil rights and civil liberties.

His only political foray beyond the office of attorney general was in 1972, when he attempted to unseat an incumbent U.S. senator. Kelley lost in a landslide.

It has been said that he once remarked that he was the youngest attorney general in the history of the office and, when he was eventually carried out, he would be the oldest.

Kelley studied the proposal to send Robert Forney to Sweden to attempt to isolate and extract succinylcholine from Shannon Davis's tissue specimens.

The attorney general understood that there was a substantial risk that he could be approving a costly trip to a foreign country for a scientist to test a highly experimental procedure that might prove totally unreliable. But Kelley was no stranger to risks.

"Go for it," he told Stan Steinborn. "The worst that can happen is I'll be accused of sending someone on a junket."

21

While the paperwork for the grant to send Forney to Sweden was being prepared and the criminal division of the attorney general's office continued its investigation of David Davis, the civil lawsuits filed by the insurance companies, Bob and Lucille Mohr, and Davis himself wound their ponderous way through the court system.

In December, Bob Mohr, on his petition to the Hillsdale County Probate Court, was named administrator of Shannon's estate.

The suits initially filed in November 1980 were beginning to appear in formal hearings in U.S. District Court in Detroit in January 1981.

The process opened with pleadings, complaints, counterclaims, cross complaints, and notices of taking depositions. Case numbers were assigned and the long, tiresome ritual plodded along.

Notice of summons and complaint were served on New York Life Insurance Company, Mutual Service Life Insurance Company, and Hartford Life and Accident Insurance Company on Davis's behalf, naming them as defendants and arguing that the companies' "refusal to make payment to plaintiff amounts to a bad faith refusal to pay a legitimate claim upon the mere allegation, which is without foundation and unsupported by any evidence, that the plaintiff intentionally caused the death of the insured." For this "bad faith," Davis was seeking a total of $75,000 in exemplary damages—$25,000 from each of the three companies—plus $62,000 in insurance benefits, plus interest, costs, and attorney's fees.

In a second suit, Prudential Insurance Company of America was named as defendant for "refusing on the mere allegation, which is without foundation and unsupported by any evidence, that David R. Davis intentionally caused the death of the insured Shannon Lou Davis," and seeking the "policy proceeds plus interest plus an unspecified amount in exemplary damages."

In their answer to the complaint, The Hartford Life and Accident Insurance Company cited Michigan law, which "prohibits the paying of life insurance benefits to a beneficiary who intentionally kills or aids in the killing of the insured."

Through their attorneys, the insurance company acknowledged that "Davis may be entitled to the $27,000 benefit as the designated beneficiary under the policy." On the other hand, the company said, Bob Mohr "may be entitled to the amount of the insurance under the policy because under Michigan law MCLA 700.251 the benefits may be payable to the estate."

Hartford admitted its liability in the amount of $27,000 and asked to pay "the total proceeds" of the policy to the court and let the court decide who gets it.

The other insurance carriers involved eventually followed suit and petitioned the court to take the money and award it to whomever it decided should receive it.

Perhaps the most provocative episode to come out of the clutter swirling around the legal process occurred on January 20, 1981, when David Davis, sullen and defiant, presented himself in the Ann Arbor offices of James R. Cmejrek, his attorney, to submit to a mandatory deposition in the Mohrs' suit against him.

The proceeding was to be a *de bene esse* deposition, which is legalese for testimony or evidence taken *ex parte,* or from a one-sided or partisan point of view, and allowed to be admitted by the courts at a later time provisionally, subject to future challenge. The *de bene esse* deposition is allowed to be taken outside the normal course of a trial in order to prevent evidence being lost "by the death or absence of the witness where the witness cannot be examined in the regular way" during normal court proceedings.

Sheldon S. Wittenberg, the Mohrs' attorney, objected at the outset to this form of deposition taking because it allowed Davis to leave the jurisdiction and to return to Florida—or wherever else he chose to run. The objection, however, would go into the record and decided later by the court—when it might be too late.

The deposition was taken in a small office, with the participants seated at a rectangular conference table. By chance, Lucille Mohr took a chair directly across from where Davis would sit to give his testimony, forcing her to look upon the face of this hated man for the more than three hours it would take to question him.

"I was scared to death," Ceil recalls. "I noticed he had on the leather boots that he used to wear on the farm and I knew he always carried a small knife in one of the boots. I was afraid he might go berserk and try to kill us. I thought I'd have a heart attack."

Once, during the taking of testimony, Davis looked straight into Ceil's eyes, "as though he was trying to say to me that he couldn't have harmed Shannon." But Ceil says she shot back a frigid glare, "letting him know that 'you won't fool me again, you son-of-a-bitch.' "

Throughout the proceedings he attempted to make eye contact with Bob Mohr, but Bob sat with his head down, refusing to look upon the man he now knew in his heart had murdered his beloved Shannon.

In 177 pages of sworn testimony, Davis proved to be evasive, forgetful, unresponsive, deceitful, and at times hostile and contentious.

The deposition would prove to be particularly meaningful since, in all the proceedings to follow involving

Shannon's death, this would be Davis's solitary experience as a witness under oath.

Present during the taking of the deposition, in addition to Davis and his attorney James R. Cmejrek, were Wittenberg; Gary Miesle, Wittenberg's law clerk; Bob and Lucille Mohr; and Susan A. Simpson, the shorthand reporter who would record the testimony.

The deposition began at about 9:40 A.M. and continued well into the afternoon.

Under direct examination by Cmejrek, Davis testified to his background before meeting and marrying Shannon Mohr.

Among the first questions Cmejrek asked was if Davis had been married prior to his marriage to Shannon. Davis admitted that he had and when asked how that marriage had ended, he replied with a single word: "Divorce."

He was next asked when the divorce had occurred.

"I don't remember. Do you know?"

"I believe it was 1975. Does that sound correct?"

"Could be. I honestly don't remember."

He was then asked to explain why his employment with the Chrysler Corporation had ended.

"I was injured and unable to continue working there."

"Could you just briefly tell us how you were injured, what occurred?"

"I was in the plant. Security was part of my responsibility. I was struck in the head by vandals, unknown, apparently."

During all previous questioning by doctors, representatives of Chrysler, state workmen's compensation and insurance company officials, Davis had consistently indicated that he didn't known exactly how he had been injured, only that he'd had an "explosion" in his head. There had never been any evidence of any sort to indicate that "vandals" had attacked him.

Under direct examination he testified that he had a

continuing vision problem and intense headaches for which he was taking medications.

"Where you able to do your farming operation with the problems that you had?" Cmejrek asked.

"For the most part, yes."

This, too, was contrary to claims made in order to maintain his disability payments.

Davis insisted that the only insurance policy he was aware of, other than the $110,000 life insurance taken out with Prudential, was "some group insurance through the hospital." He stated that it was his understanding that Bob Mohr was the named beneficiary on that policy and that he learned after Shannon's death that Bob's name had been removed and his name put in its place.

"All right," Cmejrek went on. "Now, did you subsequently learn of a life insurance contract insuring her life with the New York Life Insurance Company?"

"Some people have contacted me. I don't know their names or positions. I've been told by them that Shannon had a New York Life policy that was in effect and that sometime after that she had—it used to be in Bob's name and that she had changed it to my name. I didn't—that's what they told me. I didn't know that."

According to a representative of New York Life, Davis made formal application for payment on the policy the same day Philip Rick filed with his company, Prudential.

He said he had no knowledge of the beneficiary change before her death, that he and Shannon had never discussed the change.

He acknowledged that there were other insurance policies but that they had been credit life insurance taken out when he and Shannon purchased the yellow MGB that Shannon drove, the farm truck he used to haul grain, and a combine. Davis said that it was just a routine matter to take out the insurance when such items were purchased to protect the bank or finance company's interest in the event of the death of either him or Shannon.

"All right, and what was your understanding as to what would happen if something happened to either you or to Shannon in terms of—if death occurred?"

"The vehicle would be paid off."

Davis said that the amount of the Prudential policy was determined on the basis of the amount of their combined debts at the time the policy was taken out. *"We were never insured for more than the amount of our debts."*

"Did you ever meet with any other life insurance agents?" Cmejrek inquired.

"No."

Cmejrek then took Davis through the events of July 23, 1980, the day Shannon was killed. His description was essentially the same as that given to Hillsdale County sheriff's deputy Tino Gimenez at Thorn Hospital. However, Davis made an important departure from his previous descriptions to the deputy, to Dick Britton, and to the Mohrs, when he testified that Shannon had never regained consciousness from the moment she fell from her horse.

"For a short time, as in only a few seconds, I thought she may have been conscious but as it—she was not conscious. I waited a few minutes there hoping that she would recover consciousness . . . When it became apparent to me that she was not going to become conscious, I carried her to the edge of the woods where we had just ridden in."

He also testified that when he and Britton returned to the field where he had left Shannon, she "had no respiration." He said that he administered mouth-to-mouth respiration all the way to the hospital and that upon arriving at Thorn, "she was not breathing on her own, but she did have a pulse."

Cmejrek asked about Davis's trip to Florida after the funeral.

"How did you get to Florida?"

"In a truck, in the van we bought."

"Did you drive?"

"I had a friend who helped me drive."

Next, Cmejrek asked about the amount of insurance on Shannon's life.

"The allegation has been made that there's something around $330,000 in life insurance policies in this matter, involved in this matter. Were you aware of that amount of proceeds of life insurance prior to her death?"

"It may seem strange, but I just never paid any attention. I never expected anything. Again, my only comment about that is, from the time Shannon and I were married, we never incurred any insurance more than the amount of our debts. The only exception to that is that policy that had the accidental part of it."

In a final series of questions by Cmejrek, the attorney asked:

"There's also an allegation in the answer filed in this matter that you dragged your wife from the point at which she fell off her horse to the edge of the wooded area. Is that true?"

"Dragged her?"

"Yes."

"I carried her. I used an approved technique for transporting an unconscious person as taught to me by the American Red Cross."

"It is also alleged that she was dead on arrival at the time she arrived at the hospital. Again, when you arrived at the hospital, did she have a pulse?"

"She did."

"Her respiration at that point was nonexistent?"

"That's correct."

"Were you at that point, administering mouth-to-mouth resuscitation?"

"I was."

Now it was Sheldon Wittenberg's turn to question Davis, and he approached the cross-examination as a professional fighter would in the opening round of a championship boxing match, feeling out his opponent with flicking jabs, waiting and watching for an opening. In a chain of twenty-seven benign questions the wily lawyer led Davis through a recounting of his childhood years, with inquiries about the date and place of his birth, the names of his parents, the city he'd grown up in, the schools he'd attended, the people he'd lived with in his childhood, and his post-high school education.

"Where did you go to school after that?"

"University of Michigan."

Davis had watched Wittenberg with the look of a lamb staked out as prey for a tiger. In the opening stages of cross-examination, his answers to the attorney's questions were economical—one word and even one syllable when possible.

"Okay, when did you enroll?"

"Sixty-two."

"You enrolled in 1962?"

"Yes."

"How many years did you go to Michigan?"

"Full time, five years."

"What was your major?"

"Undergraduate major was in psychology."

"Did you have any such thing as a minor at that time?"

"Chemistry."

"You received a degree in what year?"

"Sixty-six."

"Okay, what type of degree was that?"

"A bachelor's degree."

"Bachelor of Arts, Bachelor of Science?"

"B.A."

"Did you have any schooling after that?"

"Yes."

Either Davis knew, or his lawyer had instructed him carefully to not volunteer any information and to just answer the question asked. But Wittenberg was becoming frustrated with the abbreviated response he was getting to simple background questions.

"Could you please tell me what it was?" Wittenberg asked, a razor edge showing in his voice.

Whether he sensed Wittenberg's annoyance or had become relaxed and more confident, Davis seemed to loosen up and become more responsive and forthcoming in his answers.

"I was enrolled full time as a graduate student in the year sixty-six, sixty-seven."

"Where?"

"University of Michigan, then from then on I was in—I took part-time graduate courses, not leading to a degree, ever."

"You never received another degree?"

"No."

"What were some of these courses that you took? Do you recall?"

"Sure. Neuroanatomy, physiology, two different physicologies, kinesiology. I guess that's all I can remember."

"Where you ever a medical student?"

"The graduate program there in pharmacology is part of the medical school."

"Where you ever considered a medical student?"

"Yes."

"According to whom, the University of Michigan?"

"Yes."

"Were you in their medical college?"

"Leading to a Ph.D., not an M.D., but it's all part of the same school."

"Now, are both your natural parents still living?"

"So far as I know," Davis replied, now growing flippant.

"Well, do you have contact with your father and your mother?"

"No."

"None?"

"None with my father."

"But you do have contact with your mother?"

"My mother was alive this morning."

"One time, Mr. Davis, did you tell Mr. and Mrs. Mohr that your father was killed in World War II?"

"Yes."

"And that you were raised by Dominican nuns?"

"I told—I had some experience with Dominican nuns."

"Well, did you tell Mr. and Mrs. Mohr that your father was killed in World War II?"

"Yes."

"Was he killed in World War II?"

"Not to the best of my knowledge."

"Did you ever play intercollegiate sports in college?'

"Intramural I played. I started on the freshman team in 1962."

"Did you tell anybody that you played football for Bo Schembechler at the University of Michigan?"

"No."

"You never told the Mohrs that?"

"That I played for Bo Schembechler?"

"That's right."

"No."

"Did you ever tell Jack Abrams that?"

"No."

"So if they said that, they're mistaken?"

"If they said I played for Bo Schembechler?"

"No, I said if they said you told them you played for Bo Schembechler—"

"They would be mistaken."

Wittenberg was on the scent now and he began to press Davis heavily.

"Were you ever in the armed forces?"

"No."

"Never in the armed forces?"

"Never."

"Did you ever tell anyone you were in the Marines?"

"Yes."

"Okay, and who did you tell that you were in the Marines?"

"I don't—more than one person."

"Did you tell Shannon that you were in the Marines?"

"Shannon knew everything about me."

"Did you tell Shannon you were in the Marines?"

"I also told her I wasn't, yes."

"Please be responsive to my questions."

"Yes."

"Did you tell Mr. and Mrs. Mohr that you were in the Marines?"

"Yes."

"Did you tell Tom and Regina Davis that you were in the Marines?"

"Yes."

"Did you tell Richard Britton that you were a major in the Marines and wounded in Vietnam?"

"Yes."

"That you stepped on a land mine there and were nearly blinded?"

"I did not say that."

"You never told Richard Britton that?"

"That's correct."

"Did you ever tell Richard Britton that you spent one year in the Ann Arbor Hospital blinded by a land mine in Vietnam?"

"I have never said that."

"How about a rocket blast or a burst? Did you ever tell Richard Britton that, that you were wounded in Vietnam?"

"I have told him I was injured there, yes."

Davis admitted under questioning that he had spoken to several of Tom Davis's high school classes and during those appearances he had spoken about his experiences in Vietnam.

"Okay, all right. Mr. Davis, you just told us that you were never in the services. You were never in

Vietnam. Why would you do this? Why would you lecture a class about your war experience of Vietnam if you were never there?''

''I have no answer.''

''Pardon?''

''I have no answer.''

''So you didn't tell the truth then?''

''Apparently.''

Wittenberg now eased up on the choke chain he had been tightening around Davis's neck, taking him back again to recite some of his past history, during which Wittenberg elicited an admission that Davis had once worked as an assistant in a chemistry lab, that he knew how to prepare chemical solutions, knew the combination of chemicals that would be needed to make certain items in the lab.

''If I was told to do it, I could do it.''

Davis also testified that he had worked in the University of Michigan Hospital blood bank and that part of his job was using hypodermic needles to extract blood for testing.

Davis's experience in processing disability claims while an employee of the Chrysler Corporation was also brought out in cross-examination.

Wittenberg began to bear down again, asking Davis about his purchase of the Lickley Road farm. For no apparent reason, Davis became obstinate, refusing to respond to questions about the purchase price of the farm.

''Who did you purchase the farm from?''

''Richard Britton.''

''What amount?''

''I don't recall.''

''Well, was it over $10,000?''

''I don't recall the purchase price.''

''Well, was it over $10,000?''

''I believe it must have been.''

''Was it over $25,000?''

''I don't recall.''

"You don't know if it was over $25,000?"

"I don't recall the purchase price of the farm."

Several questions later, Davis was asked:

"Do you know what you sold the farm for?"

"Yes."

"Well, what was that amount?"

"Well, I sold the farm and the equipment and the crops all together."

"Okay."

"For a total of, I believe it was, $130,000."

About his previous marriage to Phyllis, Wittenberg asked, "What was the reason for the divorce?"

"I don't know that we gave one," Davis replied. "We just weren't—we were incompatible."

"Is it correct that on October 14, 1975, a restraining order was issued from the Hillsdale Circuit Court restraining you because of threat of bodily harm to your wife, that you hit her in the back of her head and shoved her against the wall and threatened her life?"

"It is not true that I struck her at any time."

"Is it true that a restraining order was issued from that court on that date?"

"Oh, I don't know."

"Never struck your wife?"

"Never."

"Never threatened her life?"

"No."

"Never hit her in the back of her head?"

"No."

"And if she made these statements, they were lies?"

"They were."

"Who was given custody of the children?"

"She was."

"Did Shannon know of your previous marriage?"

"Yes."

"When did you tell her?"

"Before we were married."

"Where were you married to Shannon?"

"In Las Vegas, Nevada."

"Okay. On your marriage application, where it stated, have you been previously married, what did you put?"

"I think it says, have you been previously married or divorced in Nevada, and I put no."

"If the question said, were you previously married, what did you put?"

At this point, for one of the rare times during the entire taking of the deposition, Jim Cmejrek voiced an objection, stating that Davis understood that the application asked if he had been previously married or divorced in Nevada. When Wittenberg insisted that he was posing a different question and attempted to ask it again, Cmejrek continued his objection. Wittenberg tried again to get Davis to admit that he had lied on the application.

"If in fact the form said, were you previously married—"

Davis interrupted the question, replying: "I have been previously married."

Wittenberg knew it was pointless to continue to press that point and shifted back to whether Davis had informed Shannon of his previous marriage.

"Okay. Did you tell Shannon, however, that you were never previously married?"

"No."

"Did you tell Mr. and Mrs. Mohr that you had never been married?"

"I don't discuss my marriage. I asked Shannon, at one point, when she was going to tell her parents and her response to me was, 'I'll know when the time is right,' and I trusted her on that."

"I'll repeat my question. Please try to be responsive. Did you tell Mr. and Mrs. Mohr that you had never been married previously?"

"Not to my knowledge, no. I don't recall having any discussion with them about a previous marriage."

The exchanges between the crafty lawyer and the cunning witness became most heated when Wittenberg inquired about the other women in Davis's life during the period between his divorce from Phyllis and his marriage to Shannon.

"Did you have any girlfriends between these two marriages?"

"Yes."

"Could you give me their names?"

"Is that a proper question?" Davis asked Cmejrek.

"If you recall them, you may be responsive. If you don't, just simply tell the counselor that you don't recall."

"Yes, I had girlfriends and, no, I will not name them."

"You're under oath, Mr. Davis," Wittenberg admonished. "You're required to answer all questions truthfully and please be responsive to my question. What are the names of some of your girlfriends you had between your marriage to Phyllis Webberly and Shannon Mohr?"

"Sir, the judge can damn me if he will, but it has no bearing and I'll not answer that question."

"That's not up to you," Wittenberg persisted.

Cmejrek attempted to come to his client's rescue, insisting, "Well, I'll object for the record that it is not relevant to this lawsuit. As I understand the question, it is what prior girlfriends he had between the time of his divorce and his marriage to Shannon Davis. I don't believe it's relevant and the witness has indicated that he cannot answer the question."

"No, he has not indicated that he cannot answer," Wittenberg shot back. "He has indicated he *will not*, which is improper in a deposition."

"And my instruction to him is not to answer a question and, Counselor, if you wish an answer to the question, we'll take that up with Judge Feikens. I believe it's totally irrelevant."

Now the opposing attorneys were growing testy, their tempers nearing the flash point.

"Well, again, note your objection and I'm asking the question," Wittenberg thundered.

"I've instructed him not answer, Counselor. We can take it up with Judge Feikens."

"No, that's not the way to conduct a deposition."

"You don't have to tell me how to conduct a deposition, Counselor."

Wittenberg backed off; there would be other opportunities to get what he wanted. He knew the names of the women, he didn't need Davis to tell him who they were. It was a complex and calculated trap that he was setting. He would spring it later in the proceedings.

Instead, he inquired about such less-important matters as whether Tom and Regina Davis were married at the time David first met Shannon; when he had proposed marriage; and if he told her of his previous marriage at the time of their Las Vegas wedding.

He then questioned Davis on the matter of exactly what his debts had been immediately after the marriage and whether Shannon had actually been listed as a principal on the various land contracts, mortgages, and loans. He asked again about the insurance policies.

"Okay, you stated, as I understand it, Mr. Davis, that you took out the policy to cover your debts?"

"Yes."

"Could you tell me, at the time you took out the Prudential policy, what your debts were, specifically?"

"Specifically?"

"Yes."

"Okay. A Federal Land Bank mortgage."

"In the amount of?"

"I don't recall. I don't know what it was."

"Well, Mr. Davis, you said that you took out the policy to cover your debts?"

"Yes."

"And you said that was the reason you took out that amount?"

"Yes. At the time I knew. I don't remember that number now."

"Okay, go ahead. What was your next debt?"

"A land contract."

"Land contract for what?"

"Forty acres of land."

"Where?"

"Lickley Road, okay."

"The Federal Land Bank was for what?"

"Sixty-four acres of land."

"Where?"

"Lickley Road."

"Whose name is the property in?"

"Mine."

"Was Shannon's name ever put on the property?"

"She was at the Federal Land Bank; not, to the best of my knowledge, on the other one."

It was determined that, in contradiction to his claim that no insurance was carried on his and Shannon's life above what was owing in the various debts they carried, the amount of insurance held in her name alone far exceeded what was owing at the time of her death.

It was also brought out in cross-examination that after Shannon's death Davis called Flower Hospital to ask if the policy on Shannon was still in effect. When told there was such a policy, Davis asked the name of the beneficiary and was told that he was so named. Davis claimed that he asked if the beneficiary could be changed back to Bob Mohr and was told that it could not.

He claimed that he received a call from a New York Life Insurance Company representative concerning an insurance policy Shannon had taken out several years earlier, which was paid up and in effect. He said that he asked her if the beneficiary could be changed to name Bob Mohr and was asked by the representative if that was what he wished, to which Davis said he replied, "Not at this time. . . . I just wanted to know if it can be done."

Under questioning, Davis claimed he couldn't recall the amount of the lump-sum settlement with Chrysler, and at first said that he thought the State Farm policy might have been taken out by Chrysler but, under prodding by Wittenberg, indicated that he may have taken out the policy himself. He at first said that the State Farm policy was a major medical insurance and then admitted that it also carried disability coverage. He said that he no longer had a copy of the policy and couldn't remember the full amount of the coverage.

Davis admitted that, at the time he supposedly suffered serious visual problems, he went on a boar hunt in Tennessee and, in fact, shot and killed one of the wild pigs.

"Did you have any trouble seeing when you hunt[ed] them?"

"Did I have any trouble seeing? Yes. I did shoot a boar at point-blank range, six inches off the muzzle of the gun."

"The boar was six inches from you?"

"Yes, point-blank range, from you to me."

Wittenberg, in another sudden change of direction, went back to questions about insurance benefits.

"You're still receiving Social Security, isn't that correct?"

"Yes."

"How much is that?"

"I don't know."

"You receive a Social Security check every month?"

"I don't receive a check. It's deposited in the bank. I don't ever see it."

"Do you keep track of your personal finances?"

"No."

"Who does?"

"Right now, no one."

Under continued questioning, Davis admitted that there were dollar limits imposed on the amount of other income he could legally receive while maintaining his Social Security benefits, and that he had sold grain grown on his farm. However, he argued that his farming venture did not show a net profit and, therefore, he was in compliance with the letter of the law.

He testified that in 1976 he had visited several Central American countries while on a teacher exchange program offered through Michigan State University, that among the countries he visited was Mexico, Guatemala, El Salvador, Honduras, Nicaragua, Costa Rica, and Belize. He said he also visited the Bahamas that same year.

He admitted that marijuana was grown on his property, but insisted that some friend had thrown the seeds on the ground and that Davis had mowed the plants down.

He was questioned again about the fires in his barn and farmhouse and about the money he had collected on two fire insurance policies he held. But he insisted that the fires were purely accidental and that no evidence had been found to suggest foul play in connection with the fires.

Under Wittenberg's rapid-fire questioning, Davis testified that Shannon was not a good horsewoman and that she had fallen from the black mare on at least two other occasions. He said that after her death he asked Dick Britton or another neighbor to take the horses and sell them at auction.

"The last I saw of the horses, they were wandering around the field and he, Dick, gathered them up and said, what did I want to do with them, and I said, I'm not interested in seeing them again."

Wittenberg led Davis through yet another recitation of the events that occurred the evening Shannon died; how they had left their farm, had ridden to the Brittons', spending about a half hour there before starting on the return trip, this time electing to ride through the wood lot; how he had gone first along the trail into the grove because his horse was "more spirited" and the black mare would always follow the large white horse; how he had heard Shannon scream, had turned in time to see her on the ground under her mount.

"What position was Shannon in when you went to her?"

"She was lying on the ground."

"Face up, face down?"

"She was moving as in—not as in walking but as in random movements."

"Was she face up or down?"

"Face up."

"Sprawled out or curled?"

"I don't know."

"Well, you went to her. You saw her, right?"

"I did."

"She was face up?"

"Yes."

"But you don't know—you say she was moving. What type of movement, hands, legs?"

"Random movements, yes, hands and legs."

"Was she conscious?"

"At first I thought she may have been for a very brief period. I thought perhaps she was trying to say something, but nothing was intelligible to me."

"Did you later that evening tell Dick Britton that she told you, I'm okay, go get help?"

"I thought she was trying to say something. I don't know what it was."

"Did she have her shoes on or off after the fall?"

"I wasn't concerned about her shoes and, as I recall, one or both of them fell off as I was carrying her back. They may have been on, they may have been off. I don't remember. I had too many things to be concerned about."

"Well, but you said one or two of them may have fallen off as you were carrying her."

"At least one of them fell off as I was carrying her to the edge of the woods. I don't know whether the second one was on or off at that time."

"Did you tell Dick Britton that you dragged her through the woods?"

"Dragged her? I can't imagine that I would have used that word. I used the technique by which I was taught to carry an unconscious person."

The day was wearing on; the combatants were showing the effects of the long, grueling ordeal; tempers were short, patience was exhausted. There was much Wittenberg had not covered, much territory that he still wished to explore. Still, his time was limited and he sought to develop as much information as time would allow. He was painfully mindful of the strong possibility that this would be his only opportunity to question this witness.

The suit he'd filed on behalf of the Mohrs asserted that David Richard Davis should not benefit from the insurance proceeds resulting from the death of Shannon Mohr Davis because he had, in fact, caused that death. As he glanced at the notes in front of him, the outline he had prepared for this cross-examination, he felt a sudden sense of panic, a terror flooded through him that he may not have accomplished all he had set out to do. He was certain he had proven Davis to be an unrepentant liar; he was certain he had proven that Davis lied when he testified that he hadn't told others that Shannon was conscious after the fall and had told him to go for help; he had proven that Davis had lied when he claimed that he hadn't been aware of the amount of insurance he had on Shannon's life; that he had lied repeatedly about his alleged military service; that he had lied when he insisted he had not told the Mohrs that he hadn't been previously married; that he had lied when he claimed to have carried Shannon out of the woods and that her shoes, which were found with the laces untied, had dropped off; that he had lied when he claimed that Shannon had a pulse right up to the moment Dick had driven into the hospital parking lot. There was no fear in Wittenberg that he had not shown Davis up for the liar he was. But how much weight would his examination of this witness bring to bear in convincing a court that the liar was a ruthless killer as well?

Sagging in his chair from the terrible strain the day had pressed down upon him, Sheldon Wittenberg wondered, *Have I done enough?*

Shaking off this fleeting caress of doubt, he moved again to the attack, probing again into what he'd told others about life insurance on Shannon.

"Now, that evening did you tell anyone that there was no life insurance on Shannon?"

"No."

"Didn't say that to the sheriff's deputy?"

"No."

"Funeral home employee?"

"No."

"The Mohrs?"

"I don't recall any discussion of insurance. Bob told me that there was some insurance through the hospital and I told him that as far as I knew, he was the beneficiary of that. I don't recall any other discussion about insurance. I did not volunteer any information."

"You had no discussion of insurance with Dick Britton, is that correct, that evening?"

"That evening?"

"Yes."

"I don't recall any."

"Did you request that Shannon's body be cremated?"

"We had a discussion and she said that if anything happened, she would prefer cremation. I related that conversation to Bob and Lucille. They responded vehemently against it and I said, fine, whatever is best for the family. That's the only time I mentioned it."

Wittenberg was now ready to return to the subject of Davis's girl friends.

"Did you go to Florida two days after the funeral?"

"Yes."

"Who did you go with?"

"A friend helped me drive."

"What was the friend's name?"

The trap had been sprung and Davis was caught in it. Once he'd admitted that he'd gone to Florida after the funeral and that someone had accompanied him, he couldn't refuse to give the name; the damage had been done, he had taken a woman on a trip two days after burying his wife, and withholding her name would only make it look worse.

Still, Davis attempted to pull his feet from the fire by offering as little information as possible—he answered with a last name.

"Matthews."

"First name?"

"Barbara."

"Barbara Matthews?"

"Yes."

Davis was beginning to sweat now. Lucille remembers that he had kept his arms folded across his chest throughout the examination and that once when he lowered them, the sides of his shirt under the arms "were soaked with sweat."

"Okay, and how long have you been friends with Barbara Matthews?"

"I think I met her two years before."

"Okay, and you were seeing—were you seeing Barbara Matthews during the course of your marriage to Shannon?"

"I had seen her . . . I had no romantic contact with her in any sense of the word."

"How frequently did you see her?"

"I don't know . . . I saw her from time to time."

"Did you visit her at her home?"

"I did stop by her house one day."

"How often did you visit her at her home?"

"I don't recall."

"Did you ever take a trip with her before the trip to Florida?"

"Yes."

"When was that?"

"I don't recall. Before I was married."

"Was it out of the country?"

"No."

"Was it to Florida?"

"No. I recall going to Detroit and going to Ohio and that's all."

"Did you share the same room with her?"

"When? What are you talking about?"

"Your first trip with her, before you were married?"

"Yes."

"Did you stay in a hotel, motel?"

"I believe so. I don't remember where."

"Do you remember how you registered?"

"I assume with my name. I don't remember."

"Mr. and Mrs.?"

"No."

"Did you have an affair with Barbara Matthews while you were married to Shannon Mohr?"

"No."

"Did you ever take her out while you were married to Shannon?"

"No."

"What was your relationship with Cheryl Hogan?"

"Shannon's cousin, relative. That's all."

"Did you ever take her out after Shannon died?"

"Did I take her out?"

"Yes."

"No."

"Did you have dinner with her at Loma Linda's after Shannon died?"

"I visited a friend, Tom and Regina Davis. They invited me to go out to dinner with them. I accepted and before we left, Cheryl Hogan drove up and she, too, went with us. The four of us went to dinner."

"Did you tell the Davises and Cheryl Hogan that night that you're going to have to sell the farm because of inheritance taxes?"

"What I told them was I didn't know what the outcome was going to be and I didn't know what the taxes were going to be on the farm."

"Did you tell them that there was a possibility you'd have to sell the farm because of inheritance taxes?"

"No."

"Do you know Kay Kendall?"

"Yes."

"How?"

"She's a former friend."

"What period of time?"

"During the time I was divorced and before I met Shannon. I would have to say seventy-six, somewhere in there."

"Nineteen seventy-six to what time was she a friend?"

"I don't know. We had several dates on and off."

"Did you ever tell Kay Kendall that you struck your ex-wife?"

"No."

"If she said that, she'd be mistaken or lying?"

"I can't make any comments about other people, I guess."

"Do you own any other property besides the farm?"

"Real property?"

"Yes."

"No."

"Any other farms?"

"No."

"Did you tell Shannon and other people that you own farms all over the country?"

"No."

"How long have you had your beard?"

"I don't think I shaved since Shannon's funeral."

"Ever had a beard before?"

"Oh, yes, several times."

"During the time you knew Shannon?"

"No."

"Who is Buddy Brown?"

"Buddy Brown is a resident of the state of Florida. He taught Shannon and I scuba diving."

"Did you ever go scuba diving with Shannon?"

"Yes."

"Ever go sailing with Shannon?"

"Yes."

"Did you tell Dick Britton that taking a wife sailing is a good way to get rid of her?"

"No."

"Never told Dick Britton that?"

"No."

"Did you visit Buddy Brown when you were in Florida after—"

"Yes."

"Did you stay with him?"

"Yes."

"Anyone else?"

"No."

"Well, Barbara Matthews stayed with you, did she not?"

"She flew back."

"She flew back immediately?"

"Yes."

"She did not stay overnight in Florida?"

"Oh, I think she did."

"Where did she stay?"

"Pardon?"

"Where did she stay overnight in Florida?"

"I don't know."

"You're telling me she didn't stay with you?"

"No, I'm not saying that. I said I don't know where. I don't recall the name."

"She did stay with you overnight in Florida, did she not?"

"Yes."

"This was approximately two or three days after the funeral, is that correct?"

"I don't recall. I don't recall how long it took to drive down there. Something like that, yes."

"Now, Mr. Davis, you've made certain statements concerning Vietnam, concerning the fact that you served there, the fact that you served in the Marines, the fact that you told Mr. Britton certain things that you acknowledge weren't true, is that correct?"

"Yes."

"Okay, why, then, should we believe you now when you have acknowledged lying in the past?"

"I didn't kill my wife. That's why you should believe me, because I didn't do it."

"But you have lied in the past."

"Not about anything having to do with my wife."

There were a host of things having to do with Shannon about which Davis had brazenly lied. But Sheldon Wittenberg knew that he had done all the damage he could hope to do at this stage. He would have to wait and hope for another day.

"I have no further questions."

Davis left the office quickly, dashing to the elevator and out of the building.

Bob and Lucille remained, conferring with Wittenberg in the corridor, shaking their heads over what they'd heard in the past several hours.

"There had been times when he was sitting there lying when I wanted to shout at him that he was a bullshitter," Lucille said later. "But Shelly had told us that we weren't to say anything aloud. I couldn't believe that he could just sit there and say those things that he knew were untrue, knowing that we knew they weren't true."

Davis went straight to Detroit's Metropolitan Airport, preparing to fly back to Florida. He had a thirty-three-foot sailboat—the *Butterfly*—and a new girlfriend waiting for him in Fort Lauderdale.

While his attorney was clearing away the legal impediments that currently prevented him from getting the insurance monies, he would use the funds he had managed to accumulate from the sale of the farm and his autos to cruise the Caribbean. When Jim Cmejrek straightened it all out, he could send him what was left after the legal fees were deducted. In any event, he had no plans to return to Michigan.

Before he left, however, there was one loose end he decided to tie up.

Going to a public telephone at the airport, he dialed Barbara Matthews's number.

"He wanted to know who I was dating, and if I'd talked to the police and what I'd told the police," Barbara would later state. "I said I talked to them a couple of times."

She had the impression that Davis was asking her not to tell the police anything about their relationship.

"The hint for me was to follow what he'd said about not seeing him or having any relationship with him. You know, 'For your own protection, don't say anything.' "

Before he ended the conversation, Davis added yet another untruth to the mountain of deceit he'd erected that day.

"Where are you?" she'd asked him.

"I'm in Detroit—at the airport. I came in for a deposition concerning my suit against the Mohrs and the insurance companies. It was real funny. They have a half-assed attorney representing them; I had to laugh at him. I want you to know that *I didn't mention you or anything about you.* It isn't anybody's business except yours and mine, and *I made certain that you were protected.*"

22

All through the dreary winter months, Don Brooks pursued his investigation of Davis, looking for information that would link him to some kind of drug that could be demonstrated as part and parcel of a plan to murder his wife. He was learning a great deal about Davis but had developed little that could positively tie the man to the drug suspected of causing Shannon's death.

Since being assigned the case the previous year, Don had devoted about ninety-five percent of his time to the investigation; he was logging as much as fifteen hundred miles a month, ranging as far as Ohio and Florida to seek out and interview anyone who might be able to contribute valuable information. He estimated interrogating as many as sixty individuals.

Tall, blond, and ruggedly handsome—with a moustache that didn't quite fit his face and would later be discarded—the thirty-two-year-old detective more than made up for a lack of experience in homicide investigation with an intense obstinance that would, as the weeks stretched into months and then to years, mutate to dedication. Some perceived his dedication as arrogance and his interest in the case as full-blown obsession. When a superior ordered him to close down the investigation because the case was "going nowhere," Don came dangerously close to insubordination by intemperately refusing and threatening to work on his own time if necessary.

He had established himself as a competent, loyal

police officer during his nine years with the department. He'd twice been given commendations for his work and had demonstrated that he could be relentless in his pursuit of lawbreakers. But at the same time, he was compassionate and humane even to the criminals he had sworn to apprehend and bring to justice. One young man Don had twice arrested and later sent to prison, had when he had served his time and been released, asked Don to be in his wedding party.

Don had begun his investigation of the Davis case by visiting Hillsdale, requesting the cooperation of the Hillsdale County prosecutor's office.

"They were very cooperative, opened their files and had no qualms whatsoever," he says. "They were very receptive."

Zellar had been voted out of office in the previous fall elections and his successor as county prosecutor immediately pledged himself to help "in whatever way I can" to clear the case. The same was true with Al Schindler, who would soon leave his post.

After calling on Dick Britton, the Mohrs, and Bob Forney, Brooks managed to interview Barbara Matthews who—now convinced that Davis was not what she had once believed him to be—quickly became very cooperative, so much so that she had telephoned him on January 20 to tell him of Davis's call from the airport.

Don had also met with Kay Kendall, now living in Cadillac, a small community in northwestern Michigan.

Tall and sophisticated-looking with reddish-brown hair and warm, liquid brown eyes, Kay had begun dating Davis just before his divorce from Phyllis. She and Davis had traveled extensively to San Francisco, Florida, Memphis, Tennessee, and the state of Washington.

They had dated rather continuously from 1974 until the spring of 1979. They had begun dating in 1972, but Davis suddenly disappeared for nearly two years, telling her later that "he went to Tokyo on a CIA assignment."

Asked later if she believed what Davis had told her, Kay replied, matter of factly, "Of course. I believed everything he ever said."

It was said that Kay was the real love of David's life, the woman he most had hoped to marry.

"He had proposed several times," Kay recalls. "But I just felt I wasn't ready for a big step like that."

Early in 1978, Davis talked her into going to a jewelry store in Jackson, where they selected matching golden wedding rings. But something about him bothered Kay and, although she lived with him on his farm beginning in 1974, she could never agree to marry him. She managed to put him off for a time. Finally, however, she agreed to fly to Las Vegas to be married.

"Then, just a few hours before our flight, I decided that it just wasn't right; I told him I couldn't go through with it."

David's close friend, Bob Burns, would later recall how depressed Davis had become after being spurned in his plans to marry the lovely Kay Kendall; how he sulked and even cried at the failure of his bid to have her as his bride, to be married in "one of those cute little wedding chapels in Las Vegas."

He didn't discard the wedding rings, however, he kept the woman's ring in his desk at home. In 1979, in Las Vegas, he placed that ring on the fourth finger of the left hand of Shannon Lou Mohr.

In addition to his CIA fabrication, Davis had committed essentially the same perjury with Kay as he had with the others who had come in contact with him since his appearance in Hillsdale County, repeating the stories of his courage and valor on the battlefields of Vietnam, of being wounded and almost blinded, of being within a few months of graduating as a medical doctor. And he had been as successful in charming her as he had with the others.

It was becoming a painfully familiar litany to Don

Brooks; he'd heard it from the lips of almost everyone he'd interviewed.

While everything Don had learned about the ubiquitous David Davis led him to believe that Davis could never hope to be selected as man of the year, Don had been utterly unable to develop evidence that was so damning that he could be brought to trial for Shannon's murder.

The detective would have been far more encouraged had Kay thought to recount an incident that had occurred at Davis's farm near the end of 1978.

He had been reading a newspaper article when he suddenly became very excited. He showed Kay the article and told her that it concerned a method by which a murder could be committed without fear of detection. The newspaper account dealt with the Carl Coppolinio case and the use of succinylcholine.

In February 1981, Don interviewed a number of Shannon's relatives. Among those was seventeen-year-old Tori Abrams, Shannon's first cousin.

Tori was one of the rare relatives who was not terribly impressed with David.

"I didn't like him," she recalls. "There was nothing specific; I felt guilty about it. Shannon had told me that David had been engaged once before and that his wife-to-be was killed in an automobile accident on the way to the church, and he had vowed that he would never get married. Then he met Shannon at the wedding reception. It was very romantic. I wanted to like him but I couldn't; he made me feel uncomfortable."

Still, she had to admit that the newlyweds appeared happy. "They seemed to relate well to each other."

Tori had visited the Davis farm on five or six occasions and had spent the night there three separate times. During one of the visits, she saw something that would later be of supreme interest to Don Brooks and would play a vital role in future events.

In the butter compartment, located in the refrigerator door, Tori noticed ten or twelve hypodermic needle syringes, and in the freezer compartment, grouped in bunches, were twelve to fourteen medicine vials containing four different types of drugs.

"I asked Shannon about them and she said that Dave used them for the animals. They had some puppies and he was going to use the medicine to inoculate them; that's what he told her."

She remembered that there were chemical symbols on the vials and there were brand names but none of it made any sense to her. She couldn't tell Don what the chemicals were.

Still for Brooks, the possible connection to succinylcholine was becoming stronger although not yet certain; there were missing links in the chain. In an attempt to establish a direct connection between Davis and the paralyzing drug, Don spoke to three veterinarians in the area, asking if any had supplied the drug to Davis. All said they had not.

Next, he sent letters to thirty companies that supplied various chemicals by mail, inquiring whether David Richard Davis had ever placed an order for chemicals. None reported he had.

But *could* he have received the drug through mail order, Don wondered, perhaps using an alias? Was it possible for someone to obtain succinylcholine through the mail? Don decided on a method to determine just how easy it would be to lay one's hands on this deadly drug using the mails. He discovered that, while succinylcholine was not a "controlled substance" in the strict definition of the term, it could not be purchased over the counter. However, lab technicians could order it through the mail, and science teachers on the high school level could, with the written approval of their principals and on school stationery, order and receive shipments of the potentially lethal chemical.

With the knowledge and support of his superiors in the attorney general's office, Don sent letters to mail-order chemical companies on the stationery of a ficti-

tious high school. Using his real name but claiming to
be a chemistry teacher, he was able to purchase a substantial quantity of succinylcholine from three or four
chemical supply houses without difficulty.

The case against Davis was building slowly, the
pieces were beginning to come together.

When the last of the winter snows had cleared, Don
went back into the woods where Shannon had died,
bringing with him an electronic metal detector. He
swept the woods from one end to the other, hoping to
find a hypodermic needle, without success.

If his search of the woods did not yield worthwhile
results, an item of grave importance would soon surface.

Near the end of April, Tori, while visiting at her
Aunt Lucille's home, noticed a medical journal on the
dinner table. Leafing through the publication, she came
upon an article concerning muscle-relaxing drugs that
was illustrated with several photographs of drug vials.
A bottle in one of the photos attracted Tori's attention.
"That's what I saw at the farm," she told Ceil. The
vial was labeled "Anectin."

"Aunt Ceil didn't let on that there was anything important at the time."

But, after Tori left, Ceil called Don, ablaze with
enthusiasm.

"Something happened tonight that you should know
about."

A day or two later, Don telephoned the Abrams and
asked if he might come by for a second interview with
Tori.

"He brought several bottles like the ones in the
magazine and asked me if I could pick out the one I'd
seen. I pointed to one that had the Anectin label."

Don reacted phlegmatically, thanked Tori, and left.
It would be years later that she would learn the true
importance of her identification.

If Don had appeared unaffected as the young woman

pointed to the Anectin vial, inside he was seething with exhilaration. At last! He now had one indispensable piece of evidence, he had a major segment of the foundation upon which a viable case against Davis for the murder of Shannon could be built. Anectin was a brand name for the drug succinylcholine.

23

Bob Forney and Tom Carroll arrived in Stockholm in early May. They brought along tissue samples taken from the kidney, liver, and spleen during Shannon's August 1980 autopsy.

They also carried with them the obstinate conviction within the scientific community in general and the toxicological, pharmacological, and biochemical branches in particular that succinylcholine could not be extracted intact from human tissue.

This intractable posture was due to a simple chemical given: An enzyme in the body known as acetylcholinesterase attacks succinylcholine and begins breaking it down into succinic acid and choline, its basic constituents, almost immediately upon entering the bloodstream, a process that is virtually complete within a few minutes.

In the Carl Coppolino case, the prosecution depended on the testimony of forensic pathologists who claimed they had found "unusually high concentrations of succinic acid" in the tissue of the two murder victims, thereby leading to the feeble conclusion that the muscle relaxant must have been employed.

Forney believed this to be an unreliable test to determine whether succinylcholine had been administered because there is *always* a high concentration of the acid in the body.

Bo Holmstedt was of the opinion that succinylcholine persisted in the system longer than medical science had previously believed.

Forney believed that the unidentified compound found in Shannon's tissue was possibly some byproduct of succinylcholine, which gave him hope that if Dr. Holmstedt was correct it might be possible to find succinylcholine itself. The problem was in the extraction process.

Succinylcholine is difficult to identify for two fundamental reasons: The drug is so potent that extremely small concentrations will cause death—with so little of it in the system, finding it is exceptionally challenging. Secondly it is extremely water soluble.

Bo Holmstedt, sixty-three, was a member of the faculty of the prestigious Karolinska Institute in Stockholm. It is from this institute that the Nobel Prize originates; members of the faculty, who also belong to the Royal Academy of Sciences at Karolinska, select the Prize winners.

Dr. Holmstedt—he is affectionately called "The Professor" by other members of the Swedish scientific facility—had been conducting research studies on acetylcholine as it applied to chemical warfare. His gas chromatography and mass spectrometry equipment was set up to analyze the family of drugs to which acetylcholine and succinylcholine belong. It was the perfect spot for Forney to continue his research.

As the result of a series of conferences with Dr. Holmstedt, Dr. Forney, Carroll, Dr. Ingrid Nordgren, an associate of Holmstedt in toxicology who was spearheading the research on acetylcholine, and Britt-Mari Petterson, a chemist in Holmstedt's lab, it was agreed that the most likely method of isolating the drug would be through the use of what is called "ion-pair extraction," a procedure that neutralizes the negative charge on the succinlycholine molecule. By eliminating the electrical charge, the compound loses its affinity for water and can then be extracted into an organic compound that is then capable of being analyzed.

Over a period of approximately two weeks, the scientists worked on the extraction problem, ultimately settling on a multiphase procedure that required the making of certain reagents that would be employed in the ion-pair extraction process to guarantee a potent sampling of the compound. Creating the reagents in the lab as opposed to using commercial products, which were available but were not sufficiently pure, was but one example of the care and caution Forney demanded.

Using the combined gas chromatograph-mass spectrograph equipment, they were able to identify succinylcholine in high concentration in the tissue samples brought from Toledo.

As the graph came off the machine they found that not only did they have the original unknown compound but they also had what they'd come to find: succinylcholine. The peaks of the unknown compound and the succinylcholine were so close together that, on the much shorter column of the gas chromatograph, the two peaks overlapped. But the longer, seventy-five meter column of the mass spectrograph was able to separate the two elements, placing succinylcholine in the exact spot, with the exact retention time succinylcholine should have.

Not satisfied, the scientists sought to verify their experiments with other tissue samples taken from hospital patients on whom the muscle relaxant had been used. Even Holmstedt was able to contribute some of his own tissue samples.

"He coincidentally had an attack of appendicitis," Forney recalled with a wry smile. "And moaning and groaning as he was going into the surgery, he was heard to exclaim, 'Use succinylcholine, and get me some specimens.' "

Now convinced that their research had successfully extracted and isolated the drug, Forney and Carroll prepared to return to Toledo. They did not bring back with them the identity of the unknown compound; what that chemical was has yet to be discovered.

* * *

John Wilson was notified by Forney of the results in Stockholm; he was ebullient.

"These people are ecstatic," he announced after the call had been completed. "This is a first ever in the medical field; they're doing handsprings; Forney said they found succinylcholine intact for the first time. They found pure succinylcholine; they found the pure form over there."

As bits and pieces of information began to accumulate, as his venal past slowly became exposed, as evidence gathered began to point more and more in a single direction, the case against David Richard Davis acquired its own momentum and it began to move inexorably to overwhelm and consume him.

24

Tom Carroll flew back from Stockholm on May 27, and Bob Forney followed three days later. The euphoria surrounding their discoveries would continue for months among everyone connected with the Shannon Mohr Davis affair.

While the two scientists were out of the country, John Wilson and his staff were busy building their case, hoping to accumulate enough evidence to justify an arrest warrant against Davis. Wilson and Brooks were refining possible tactics that might be employed.

"There are two ways we might go," Wilson told an acquaintance. "We could send Don down to Hillsdale County to file a complaint with the Second District Court. In this state the prosecutor can issue a warrant on the basis of a complaint. The other possibility is to request a one-man grand jury look into the case."

As part of the investigation they went to the Mitchell Public Library in Hillsdale asking to see their circulation records, hoping that Davis may have checked out books dealing with drugs or with cases where succinylcholine was used in the commission of murder. They were particularly interested in F. Lee Bailey's book, *The Defense Never Rests,* which chronicled the Carl Coppolino case. They were told that circulation records were confidential and would not be released, citing "Constitutional protections." Then they asked whether or not Davis had a library card. They learned that he did not then, nor had he ever had a card. That tack was abandoned.

It was next discovered that after selling the farm, Davis had rented a storage locker at a moving and storage facility in Adrian, where he left some personal possessions.

Wilson decided that a request for a search warrant to inspect the contents of the locker would be made. But not just yet; he was unwilling to telegraph his intentions to Davis too soon.

In the meantime, Forney was asking for a second autopsy in order to obtain tissue samples to try to locate possible injection sites. However, a tentative approach to Lucas County prosecutor Anthony Pizza had not been met with enthusiasm.

"He said that he might not want to go along with it," Wilson muttered.

A call was made to Lucas County coroner Dr. Harry Mignerey, who said that he had no objections to ordering a second exhumation. But, whether the doctor was also political or perhaps simply obstructionist, he backed down on his original "no problem" position and began hedging whenever the subject of ordering the exhumation was brought up, stalling for an unknown reason.

A few days after Memorial Day distressing news came from the Mohr family. Bob, who had never accepted his daughter's death effortlessly, buckled under the strain.

"Bob Mohr is in the hospital," Don was told as he came into the office. "It isn't a heart attack, they don't know what it is, maybe the strain, going out to the grave and all."

Don was sent to Florida, to "tail Davis for a while," while work on getting authorization for a search warrant and the exhumation ordered continued.

It was June 29 when the search warrant was signed by second District Court judge James E. Sheridan. The warrant called for a search of the rented area at the Frank Hunter and Sons Moving and Storage property in Adrian, Michigan, and authorized the seizing and searching of boxes of personal effects. Specifically, the warrant authorized the search for "certain check ledgers, records of correspondence or financial transactions with or literature from companies that sell or distribute succinylcholine or other nerve blocking agents; chemistry, pharmacology or biochemistry textbooks or handwritten notes or publications or literature relating to succinylcholine, its usage, method of action and contraindications, syringes, vials or other containers or paraphernalia re storage or administration of succinylcholine, books concerning animal medicine containing descriptions of animal gelding, records or correspondence about insurance on the life or property of Shannon Mohr Davis."

Their search of the Adrian locker would prove essentially unproductive.

At about the same time, information was being released indicating that the tests developed by Dr. Robert Forney had shown that Shannon had been administered a lethal dose of succinylcholine shortly before her death.

The sum and total of the case thus far developed by the Michigan Attorney General's office and the efforts of Don Brooks was that David Davis had sufficient training and education to know and understand the use, effects, and forensic traceability of succinylcholine; had the knowledge and opportunity to obtain the drug; possessed a derivative of succinylcholine as well as syringes and needles; had insured, or permitted to be insured his wife Shannon to an extraordinary amount; had a history of untruths, lying about his previous marriage and fraudulently and falsely indicating on the application for a marriage license in Las Vegas that he had not been previously married; and had probably courted several women, possibly with the intent of finding someone to marry, conceivably to insure their lives and then kill them.

But of all the circumstantial evidence that had thus far been developed by the persistent efforts of people such as Don Brooks, Billy Bowles, and the Mohrs, the scientific findings of Bob Forney and Tom Carroll and those others in Stockholm offered the most impressive argument that Davis was the cold-blooded killer of his young, vulnerable, and unsuspecting wife.

If Forney's "technique" could be sustained it posed a damning question that Davis would be hard pressed to answer: If he didn't introduce the powerful muscle relaxant into Shannon's body, then *how did it get there?*

Although the toxicologist may well have perfected a laboratory method by which the elusive chemical could be isolated and extracted, and while his tests in Sweden had supposedly found the drug in tissue samples taken from Shannon's body, there was still the problem of locating the site of introduction—the location of the needle punctures.

It would be of invaluable assistance in supporting Forney's claim that the woman had died from a lethal injection of the muscle relaxant if further forensic tests could be conducted—another autopsy should be performed.

Since Wilson and Brooks had already made overtures to officials in Lucas County, urging that a second exhumation and autopsy be authorized, there was reason to believe that the procedure would ultimately be approved.

The most distasteful constituent of the decision to unearth Shannon's body for a second time was the emotional devastation that might be visited on Bob and Lucille, who had already sustained more than their share of emotional torment.

Don met with the couple, explaining the importance of gathering additional tissue samples to validate the accuracy of the newly christened "Forney Technique" and to attempt to locate needle punctures that would prove exactly how and where the drug had been administered.

"It isn't going to be a full autopsy," Don tenderly

assured them. "They want to take a few samples from some of the bruised areas, Dr. Forney believes he can find where David injected her."

"I have to know," Ceil insisted. "I have to know exactly what happened; I think Shannon would want us to press on, to answer all the questions."

At about 7:30 A.M.—a warm, sunny day—on July 1, 1981 a backhoe, for the second time in less than a year, slashed into the green sod over Shannon's grave. For the second time the dark wooden casket containing her mortal remains was dragged from what was supposed to have been its final resting place and loaded into a hearse to be transported to the Lucas County coroner's office.

With Drs. Steven and Renata Fazekas, the Lucas County deputy coroners, Dr. Robert Forney and Tom Carroll, Don Brooks and Detective Lawrence G. House of the Michigan State Police, representatives of the Jasin Funeral Home, and about a dozen other observers in attendance, the coffin was once again opened to reveal the corpse inside.

The exposure to the light and the air and the autopsy surgeon's knife of the previous August had ravaged the body within.

"There had been extensive postmortem decomposition since the prior autopsy," the report would state.

Gross discolorization had occurred over some parts of the body, seemingly manifesting itself as bruises that had not been apparent during the earlier examination. A plastic bag containing some internal organs was trailing from the autopsy incision on the frontal torso.

"I was interested in the state of decomposition of the body at that point," Forney would later state. "I was interested in the way the coffin looked. I was interested in the state of the organs which had been returned to the body from the first autopsy. And specifically I was interested in obtaining some specimens for study.''

Forney supervised the collection of the specimens, striding around the body, pointing out to Renata Fazekas those portions he wanted excised.

Needle marks are difficult to locate on a fresh corpse; on a body deceased for eleven months, they are all but impossible to locate. For that reason Forney searched the areas of bruising, which he felt would be the most likely injection sites.

In laboratory experiments on rats injected with succinylcholine, Forney had observed a surprising phenomenon. Where the drug had been introduced into muscle structure, a cyst had formed around the chemical as the body reacted to the irritating quality of the drug, walling off that part of the body to prevent further intrusion of the irritant. Forney reasoned that if the succinylcholine had not gotten into a vein but into subcutaneous or muscle tissue, an observable cyst might have been formed. A question Forney believed might be answered in a second exhumation was: Was a cyst present in Shannon's body?

He directed the pathologist to what appeared to be a deep bruise on the upper right lateral arm near the shoulder, which was discolored. A deep section approximately six inches in length and two to three inches across was cut out of the arm.

On either side of the excised bruise on the right arm, the imprints of four human fingers toward the front, near the shoulder, and a single thumb imprint at the rear were clearly visible, appearing as if a hand had gripped the shoulder with great force, causing the skin to be lacerated. Identical, but less obvious impressions were found in the same general location on Shannon's left arm.

Another area that interested Forney was a darkened spot on the dorsal aspect of the right wrist, in front and high up where the arm and the hand join. A section of this part of the body was cut away.

There was a bruise on the right thigh that, upon being cut open, appeared to have been a superficial injury that probably occurred before death. A specimen of this bruise was taken for examination.

Specimens were cut out of what appeared to be bruises on the face, and others were taken from the left and right breasts and from an area over the sternum that looked to Forney like a puncture mark that he thought might be a needle wound. Actually it was the spot where the blood sample had been taken by Dr. Dickman at Thorn Hospital the night Shannon was killed.

Tissue specimens were taken from the upper left arm, the left wrist, and the left thigh. Forney wanted these specimens as control samples by which he could compare any deviation between the bruised specimens and those that were unblemished.

The brain was horizontally sectioned into slabs about the thickness of bread slices. The upper and lower teeth and jaws were removed for testing.

The specimens were taken by Forney immediately after the autopsy and placed in a secure freezer at the Medical College laboratory.

Later he prepared and examined the tissue samples histologically—under the microscope. In the sample taken from the upper right arm, Forney noted that about one centimeter beneath the surface of the skin was what he had expected to find: a cyst. It was not, however, in muscle structure but rather in the subcutaneous fat layer between the overlying skin tissue and the underlying muscle. Just as he'd noted in the rat experiment, the body had attempted to seal off the irritant to prevent it from pervading other parts of the body. This physiological reaction would have materially slowed the effect of the muscle relaxant.

To adequately determine whether succinylcholine residue remained in the tissue samples, Forney would have to make yet another trip to Sweden.

* * *

Shannon's body was returned to the casket and transported back to the cemetery where, for the third time, it was lowered into the ground and covered over. Bob and Ceil, aware of what had been occurring that day, sat in the quiet shadows of their home and silently prayed that this would bring a merciful end to the savage interruption of what was supposed to be the peaceful and eternal sleep of their cherished daughter.

25

Forney, this time alone, returned to Stockholm. His stay there would be brief. The tissue samples he brought with him yielded significant quantities of succinylcholine; not as pronounced as were found in the earlier samples—the chemical was slowly disintegrating—but still in concentrations great enough to leave no doubt in his mind that succinylcholine had been the instrument that caused Shannon's death.

In Lansing, Wilson conferred with Attorney General Frank Kelley about the case and the evidence thus far accumulated. It was decided that a one-man grand jury should be appointed to hear the evidence.

The option of having Don Brooks file a complaint with the Hillsdale authorities was ruled out for the simple reason that it might give Davis's attorney a clue as to the scientific evidence Forney had developed.

On September 10, a formal announcement was issued by the State Court administrative office in Lansing, naming Lenawee County Circuit Court judge Kenneth B. Glaser, Jr., to act as a one-man grand juror to weigh the evidence and determine whether anyone should be charged with killing Shannon Davis.

"I was appointed to investigate, I think it's called the Davis case," Glaser, a crusty, intense, nononsense judge told the press. "I don't know the details of it, because I don't read the crime news. My only purpose is to investigate and determine whether there is any reason to indict anyone."

Judge Glaser began taking testimony shortly after eight in the morning on September 10 with a seven and one-half hour parade of witnesses, including Al Schindler and Ceil Mohr.

Testimony was closed to the public with only the judge, John Wilson, Don Brooks, and a court stenographer allowed in the hearing room located in the basement of the Hillsdale County courthouse. The witnesses called were permitted to have an attorney present if they wished. Most did not.

Members of the press were allowed no closer than the lobby of the juvenile division, where the hearing was conducted, and were unable to find anyone who would admit that the grand jury was in session. Even courthouse custodians, reporting for work at seven that morning, were barred from the basement area.

Among those called were men who had known Davis from a Michigan hunting camp where he had discussed bow-and-arrow hunting with poisoned-tipped arrows.

Glaser held a second session the following day and then postponed further sessions indefinitely, pulling a cloak of secrecy around the entire proceedings. There would be numerous delays and then the grand jury would quietly disband without any further hearings. Glaser, apparently, had heard enough.

On September 25, with Cmejrek pressing hard for depositions from both Forney and Carroll, assistant attorney general Mark E. Blumer visited U.S. District Court judge John Feikens in Detroit, seeking to postpone the taking of the depositions.

The thirty-two-year-old lawyer had been in the attorney general's criminal division about three years and was fast making a name for himself as a reliable, competent attorney who had a taste for the most difficult criminal cases.

"I knew the Davis case was in the office," Blumer says. "But I didn't know much about what was happening. John Wilson operated on a strict need-to-know basis and I guess he decided that I didn't need to know much about the case at that point.''

The State of Michigan was not a party to the Davis civil suit and Blumer was sent to Detroit first to file a motion to formally intervene as a ''party in interest'' because the state might indict Davis on a criminal complaint.

Wilson was still introducing evidence with the grand jury but was not yet ready to arrest Davis. Cmejrek had learned of Forney's involvement in the criminal investigation and wanted to depose the two scientists to get information about their findings. But Wilson didn't want Davis to know at that time exactly how much they knew about the drug found in Shannon's system.

Blumer's second mission in Detroit was to get Judge Feikens to hold off on the federal case until the state was ready to indict, and to get an order blocking the depositions of Forney and Carroll.

''The problem with this was that Wilson never fully explained why this was all necessary. All he said was, 'Go tell the judge to hold off.' This was typical Wilson—'Go do it. I don't have to tell you anything, just do it.' ''

Adding to Blumer's problem with lack of understanding of his superior's tactics was the fact that Judge Feikens was notoriously cranky, a bellicose jurist who ate young lawyers alive.

''There I was telling the judge to please not go forward with this case because it will screw up our murder case and he's asking why. How the hell was I supposed to know; I was just down there asking him not to do it.''

In desperation Blumer suggested that Feikens call Judge Glaser. Feikens took the suggestion and, following a judge-to-judge conversation during which Glaser apparently told Feikens that the grand jury was very near to a murder indictment, Feikens went along with the delay.

In the meantime, Don Brooks and the state police assigned to the attorney general's office lost track of Davis. Martha Brandon, David's mother, told the press in mid-September that she had last heard from her son about ten days earlier when he telephoned her from the Bahamas. She said he wasn't expected back in Michigan.

Attorney Cmejrek was telling all who asked that he had no idea where Davis was. "I can't reach him, I have to wait until he phones me. He phones when he feels like it."

Davis was using his boat, the *Butterfly,* as his head-quarters, sailing the Caribbean, returning periodically to Fort Lauderdale for provisions and to call his mother and his attorney. He would frequently stop at private residences on the water with their own docking facilities and ask to use the dock for a day or two, making it difficult to be located by law enforcement or Coast Guard personnel, both of which had been requested by Don Brooks to keep an eye out for him.

The previous November, in a Fort Lauderdale bar, he met a young woman named Yvonne Munroe, a fun-loving, do-your-own-thing individual who found the idea of making love under the star-encrusted skies of a Caribbean night and dozing under the warm Gulf of Mexico sun the ultimate in living the good life. She immediately accepted Davis's invitation to sail away with him.

He told her that he had his own company back in Michigan, a glitzy private security operation that provided bodyguards to wealthy and influential people. He had to make periodic trips to Michigan to "take care of business affairs," but he always returned to the *Butterfly* and to Yvonne.

Physically, she was not what Davis was usually attracted to; she tended to be somewhat stocky, reminiscent of his first wife, Phyllis, who, as he complained to Dick Britton, was "too fat." And she had an irresistible penchant for filling the pages of her diary with extravagant descriptions of the times, places, and conditions of their lovemaking.

But if Yvonne was lacking in the alluring qualities of his most recent conquests, she was loyal, a virtue Davis most needed at this time.

Days turned to weeks in Lansing and Toledo, and then to months with no activity. The press lost interest in the story, confining themselves to small items, buried inside the paper or reported in a sentence or two on the six and eleven o'clock news, recounting that yet another delay had been granted in the federal civil suit. By the end of September, the story had no interest for anyone save the principals in the drama.

Bob and Ceil waited, relying on an occasional call from Don Brooks, advising them that the word was out in Florida to watch for Davis. For Don, the frustrations were mounting. "We're in the hands of the federal government now," he told a friend. He felt impotent, having to depend on someone else to get results. For the young, zealous police officer, depending on someone else was not something he accepted easily. He wanted action and he was determined to see results. He wanted David Richard Davis. He wanted, foremost, to be the one to bring him back to Michigan in chains. He wouldn't get his wish.

In October, Judge Glaser issued his decision: There was sufficient evidence to believe that David Davis had murdered his wife and a true bill of indictment should be issued. However, the decision was kept from the public with the hope that Davis would surface long enough to be apprehended and returned to Michigan to stand trial.

Months later, Glaser would praise the efforts of John Wilson and Don Brooks.

"They did just a great job of putting the evidence together," he was quoted as saying. "I just can't say enough for them."

Finally, on December 24, word was leaked to the

press that a federal warrant had been issued, charging Davis with unlawful flight to avoid prosecution.

Those among the public interested in the case assumed that the full resources of the Federal Bureau of Investigation would be put in play to find and arrest Davis, now a fugitive from justice. Just the significance of a federal warrant gave many cause to believe that Davis's days of freedom would be brief; many believed that within days, weeks at the most, he would be once again in the Wolverine State, preparing to answer to the charge that he had murdered his wife for money.

The same day the newspapers announced the issuance of the fugitive warrant, Davis called his lawyer from a hotel in Cape Haiten, on the northern coast of Haiti. Cmejrek advised his client that this was no longer a civil matter; his position was now critical, he could not delay in returning to Michigan to answer the murder charge. Davis gave the attorney his assurance that he was returning immediately to turn himself in.

"He told me there was some trouble in Michigan," Yvonne says. "He said he was being sued for negligence in the death of his first wife. He said these were just 'scare tactics' to get him back in the state."

He then advised Yvonne to return to Baltimore, where her parents lived, to spend the Christmas holidays with them and then to return to Florida and get a job. He told her he would come back to get her when he had cleared up his legal problems. But first, he asked her to telephone her sister in Fort Lauderdale to inquire whether police or reporters had contacted her asking questions.

He put her on a plane the next day, again assuring her that he would return to her. His next step was to telephone his mother in Lansing, Michigan, to tell her where his sailboat was and ask her and Jim to fly down and retrieve it. He said he was sending her the title and that she should sell it as soon as possible.

And then he simply vanished.

26

The U.S. Coast Guard had twice boarded Davis's boat in the weeks just prior to his disappearance, and although the felony warrant against him had been issued almost two months before—earlier than the formal announcement indicated—no action was taken by the Coast Guard to detain him during the encounters in the Caribbean. In addition, Davis was reportedly spotted on a Caribbean island in mid-December but was gone before authorities could find him.

The *Butterfly* was found docked at a Haitian marina on December 29, but again, Davis had left before police could nab him. The boat was seized but later released to Martha Brandon who, with her husband, sailed it to Providenciale Island in the Turks and Caicos Islands near the Bahamas, where it was sold to a local hotel owner.

Less than three weeks later, Davis was back in the news. In a grotesque incident, Dr. Robert A. Burns, Jr., Davis's close friend, was run over and killed by an automobile while jogging near his home early on the morning of January 21.

While the immediate speculation centered around Burns's close relationship to Davis and the possibility that the dentist's death was somehow connected to the fugitive, evidence quickly proved that the fatality was purely accidental. It had been dark and the road was snow covered and icy. Burns apparently darted in the path of the approaching auto, which skidded on the slippery road, striking and dragging the unfortunate runner several dozen yards. He was pronounced dead at the scene and no charges were filed by the police against the driver of the car.

On February 11, Judge Feikens awarded $65,247 in death benefits from three of the insurance policies on Shannon's life to the Mohrs.

Two other policies—credit life policies securing chattel loans—had been liquidated shortly before Davis left the country.

Payment on the largest insurance policy, the Prudential one worth $220,000, was delayed in an action by the company, which now claimed that the money should be awarded to no one since there was reason to believe that Davis had purchased the insurance with the intention of killing his wife.

In awarding the money from the three policies to Bob and Ceil, Feikens noted that Davis had not appeared in court and was apparently not interested in pursuing his claim to the money.

During this hearing, James Cmejrek was granted his request for permission to withdraw as Davis's attorney.

Cmejrek told Judge Feikens that he had last talked to his client on December 24, when Davis reached him by telephone at his Ann Arbor home. During that conversation, Cmejrek said, he advised Davis of the warrant for his arrest. He quoted Davis as saying he would return immediately to Michigan to turn himself in. But Davis broke his pledge, the attorney said, which left him no choice but to withdraw from the case.

In April, the Michigan state police issued a wanted poster that was circulated through the Caribbean area—particularly in places Davis was known to have visited in the past—offering a $3,000 reward for information leading to the arrest of David Davis. Three thousand copies of the poster, printed in French, English, and Spanish, warned that Davis should be considered armed and dangerous, and contained photos of Davis both with and without a beard. The poster further indicated that the reward had been posted by a private donor. Don Brooks later identified the Mohrs as the "private donor."

Nineteen eighty-two labored through its remaining months, painfully overtaking the second anniversary of Shannon's death, inching by what would have been her twenty-seventh birthday, lingering agonizingly at the third Christmas without her.

In an out-of-court settlement in March 1983 between the company and the Mohrs, Prudential agreed to give them approximately $200,000 in benefits, with $20,000 plus interest amounting to more than $10,000 being returned to the company.

Sheldon Wittenberg told the press he had approved the settlement in order to avoid a civil trial, which would have made public evidence that could have prejudiced a future criminal trial.

The settlement marked the conclusion of the legal warfare that had been initiated almost as soon as Bob and Ceil discovered that Davis had cruelly lied to them about the insurance.

The shrewd attorney had accomplished exactly what he had set out to do in the very beginning.

"The Mohrs were never interested in the money," he would insist years later. "What they wanted to do was to keep Davis from getting it; they wanted to delay him, hoping that evidence could be found to show that he had killed Shannon, evidence that would lead to a charge of murder."

He had succeeded admirably in delaying and ultimately preventing Davis from getting what Wittenberg and the others closely involved with the case believed that Davis had killed Shannon for—the money.

Wittenberg counted himself among the others who became convinced that Davis had gotten away, that he might never be found. But at least, the attorney felt, he's running without $300,000 to make his flight more comfortable.

"I'm a criminal lawyer; much of what I do is connected with defending those who the public consider the bad guys," Wittenberg says. "It was a very good feeling to do something to help the Mohrs. There's no question in anyone's mind that they are the 'good guys.' "

Don continued spending as much of his time as he could spare keeping track of the efforts to locate Davis. He periodically contacted the FBI offices in Miami to determine if any leads had been developed and, hopefully, to keep them interested in the case. And he regularly checked with Interpol, the world law enforcement and information network, hoping for some word on the fugitive.

Rumors began circulating that Davis had become involved in drug smuggling or gun running and had been murdered by rival smugglers. Brooks discounted the gossip; Davis *couldn't* be dead, he *must* be alive. How else would Don be able to bring him back in manacles to stand before the bar?

While Bob seemed, now, to have come to terms with the tragic loss he and Ceil had suffered, had conditioned himself to the understanding that his daughter was gone and he could never get her back no matter how much he grieved, no matter how much he hated, Lucille was totally unwilling to forget. Nor would she hear of Davis being dead; that would be much too easy for him and it would deny her the chance to watch him squirm as he suffered the humiliation of a trial. It would rob her of the satisfaction of knowing that he was imprisoned—caged like the wild animal he was— made to spend the rest of his life in a pen, never again to be free to hunt and fish and sail and scuba dive, and to do those other things civilized, decent individuals can do, those things he most enjoyed.

Ceil and Don Brooks were willing to wait as long

as it took, but they would not relinquish the certainty in their hearts that Davis was still out there, somewhere, and that eventually he would be caught. This conviction was all they had; for Ceil it was what kept her alive.

27

No one seemed much interested in the Shannon Mohr Davis case any longer.

The newspapers and the radio and television stations, whose reporters for months had hammered on the Mohrs' front door, elbowing and jostling each other in an effort to get their cameras, lights, and microphones, or their notebooks and felt pens, as close to the wide-eyed and threatened couple as possible, were now gone. The blinding TV lights were dark, the poking and thrusting microphones no longer intimidated or presented the danger of facial and dental injury. The shouted questions were stilled, the constantly ringing telephone was silenced. Bob and Lucille had been mercifully left alone with their memories and their pain.

Even Billy Bowles, the man most credited with bringing Shannon's death and her husband's possible culpability to the attention of a stunned and troubled public, had been assigned to other stories.

For the relatives and friends of Bob and Lucille, the magnitude of what had happened July 23, 1980, had not diminished. But the passage of time had a dulling effect. And the emotional torment that had at first attended the horrifying realization that a sweet, gentle, loving young woman had been savagely slaughtered by a man almost everyone trusted and admired began to dwindle as their shock and outrage softened.

To some, there was continuing dismay at having been so thoroughly taken in by this cunning, depraved man whose hateful corruption had left them forever tarnished. They would find it difficult to ever again have faith in a stranger.

"How could he have been able to fool us so?" was a common grievance voiced among the Mohrs' inner circle.

A very few, who might have said, "I told you so," kept their silent counsel.

Jack Abrams had made statements to both Bob and Ceil before Shannon's death that called to question the image many had of David.

"I never liked him," Jack recalls. "My niece invited me up to the farm to go hunting with him once. He climbed a tree with a .3006 rifle with a scope. You can't hunt with a high-powered rifle in southern Michigan, it's against the law. And he went out at night to hunt with a spotlight, and 'shining' deer is against the law. He was cruel to animals, he didn't treat them like I thought a sportsman would. Once I saw him throw a wine bottle at a couple of kittens."

When he related the hunting incidents to Bob, his brother-in-law simply shrugged and said, "It's his property, he can do anything he wants."

"I don't think the game warden would feel that way," Jack replied.

Yet Jack had occasion to feel somewhat guilty about his dislike for Shannon's husband.

"Ceil once told me, 'David really thinks a lot of you,' and I felt bad because I didn't like him."

But even Jack could be fooled by a bold and skillful liar. When he was telling everyone he had been a U.S. Marine, Davis was daring enough to tell Jack he had been in the *Army*.

"He knew I had been in the Army and he told me he'd been in the Army in Vietnam. He talked about different kinds of weapons they'd had there and about shells that exploded at different levels; he was so sharp, I never caught him in any lies. I bought it."

Jack recalls an incident after Shannon's death that,

in retrospect, makes him think he might have put a scare into Davis, that for an instant made him feel that Jack knew something Davis didn't want anyone to know.

"David came into the house from the funeral home. He looked like he was crying; he came up to me and put his arms around me and hugged me. Then I said, 'I got to talk to you; I want to talk to you outside.' When I said that, the color just drained from his face."

All Jack wanted was to ask if his niece had suffered. Davis told him, "No, she went quick."

Jack and his wife Sandy and daughter Tori were among other relatives and friends of Bob and Ceil who, as the months crept slowly along with no word of Davis, observed the awesome effect his continued freedom was having on both of them, but particularly on Ceil.

"Whenever there was a family get-together, a birthday party or whatever, the subject of David would always come up. It was a continuing thing," Tori says. "It was apparent to us that he had gotten away, that they would never find him again. We got worried about Aunt Ceil and Uncle Bob, it was not doing them any good, we wished they could just put it behind them and get on with their lives. It was just eating them up."

Jack saw the impact as being greater on his sister. Bob, he thought, had managed to get his feelings under control. "But for Ceil, the subject of David came up most of the time; it was a never-ending conversation."

Jack, like his daughter, wanted Ceil to put the tragedy behind her. "I tried to talk to her, to tell her that she shouldn't dwell on it."

But Ceil's response was, "If you've never lost someone, you can't understand."

Earlier, Jack had been most worried about Bob. "Ceil was so strong; the real strong one. She was like a bulldog, she just hung right on. Bob showed his hurt more than Ceil."

Ceil was hemorrhaging emotionally; her former son-in-law's continued freedom was an egregious wound that festered, that would not heal.

"I want him caught," Ceil insisted. "I won't be able to rest until they catch him and put him behind bars—forever."

Sandy Abrams, like most of the others in the family, had been totally taken in by Davis.

"Tori and Jack must have sensed something I missed," she says. "Whenever I was around him, he seemed very attentive, he seemed very kind, considerate, and hospitable. I was charmed by what I saw. Shannon seemed so happy on the farm. It was as though she was saying, 'This is my *home* and I want my family here.'"

Today, Sandy feels that if Shannon had not had the disastrous experience of having been engaged to a married man who apparently hadn't planned to divorce his present wife, she probably wouldn't have been so quick to marry David. And, if she had second thoughts about the marriage afterward, she probably wouldn't have told anyone in the family.

"It would have been very hard for her to say that she had been involved with one rotten apple, and now, here she was with another one."

One of Sandy's great fears was that many might consider Shannon as having been hopelessly gullible. "She was naive, but she wasn't stupid," Sandy insists. "She was very intelligent."

Rumors about Davis continued: He was in Mexico City for the Pan American Games, or in the Bahamas, or in Florida, or in the jungles of Central and South America. Reports had him back in Michigan and remarried. But for the most part, the general concensus was that he had been killed.

The simple truth was that no one knew where he was or what had happened to him. He had dropped from the face of the earth. His mother claimed not to have heard from her son since December 1981.

In Lansing, it appeared that Don Brooks was all but alone in his belief that Davis was still alive, and in his determination that he would be found. At the Michigan attorney general's criminal division, the Davis case was "dumped."

28

A major reorganization within the criminal division of the Michigan attorney general's office occurred in 1984 in which two distinct units were created—the criminal division and the tort defense division, which was responsible for defending state employees in damage and negligence actions.

John Wilson was transfered out and Robert Ianni, an intense veteran of Frank Kelley's administration, was told to take over the criminal division.

One of the attorneys remaining in the division was thirty-four-year-old Mark Blumer, the assistant attorney general who had been sent to Detroit to stall the civil action in federal court without knowing exactly why the delay was so important.

Blumer, in his six years with the criminal division, had impressed his superiors with his competent trial work; he was winning about two-thirds of his cases, a very respectable record considering the fact that he seemed to find himself prosecuting the most challenging cases. His vigorous pursuit of the accused earned him the affectionate title ''the office pit bull'' among his fellow workers, an appellation that his wife of nineteen years has seriously objected to.

''I don't think he's a pit bull. He's more like a Saint Bernard; big and strong and lovable,'' she says, and then, with a bubbly giggle in her voice, she adds, ''and he barks and drools.''

Still, she has never been surprised at the characterization of her husband as a determined, aggressive lawyer.

"He's compulsive," she says. "He wants to excel. I'm always asking him, 'Tell me, what's the obsession du jour?' "

Mark enjoys an excellent reputation, not only with other members of the criminal division's staff but with opposing attorneys as well. On more than one occasion, a defense attorney has called Blumer and said, in effect: "My client has told me his side of the story, now you tell me the truth."

He is also the butt of some good-natured joking by those who know him well.

Ron Emery, who once worked in the criminal division with Mark before transfering to the newly created tort defense division, gave Blumer the nickname, the "Jewish Cowboy," because of Mark's fascination with firearms and because Mark once returned from vacation wearing cowboy boots and carrying a comic photograph of himself, his wife, and their two children dressed in costumes of the Wild West.

Ron took one look at Mark swaggering around the office in the cowboy boots, shook his head, and muttered, "No way, Mark. No way."

On the wall of his office, Mark has a photograph of movie star Charles Bronson aiming a huge six-shooter. Below the photo are the words, "Here is my Counteroffer."

Once, when Emery received a death threat from a murder defendant, Blumer took him to a gun shop and helped him select a shotgun.

"Then he and a friend took me to a rifle range to practice. It took them a half-hour to forty-five minutes to unload all their shooting equipment," Emery recalls. "It looked like they were going to war."

After that, whenever Emery called Mark's home and Susan told him that Mark wasn't at home, his standard reply became, "Out on maneuvers, eh?"

Emery praises Mark on his courtroom work.

"He's a quick study, smooth in the courtroom," Emery says. He adds, "I think that he may be sometimes less strong in the law, but he gets results."

He recalls the old legal saw: "If the facts are against you, resort to the law."

"Mark never had to worry about the law, the facts always took care of things."

Emery says that a lawyer has to have confidence in himself and in his case. "Mark has it in spades."

Bob Ianni, Mark's immediate superior, admires his "mastery in the courtroom," and calls him "most capable."

Diane Vander Moere, Blumer's secretary from 1983 until 1989, describes him as "very intense on all his cases," but not demanding in the office.

"He doesn't brood about his losses—just a quick blowup and then he gets on with the next case. He's very easy to work for."

Born Mark Edward Blumer, in Detroit on September 19, 1949, he was the firstborn of Abraham, a physician, and Joyce Dashow Blumer, a schoolteacher and distant relative of Sam Dash, the attorney who gained national prominence during the Watergate hearings.

A precocious child, Mark began talking at a very early age and was speaking complete sentences before eighteen months of age.

"People would stop in the street and listen to him," his mother recalls with undisguised pride.

She also remembers that Mark, in elementary and junior high school, was unable to tolerate the wrong child being accused of something. "He would speak up no matter whether it was a teacher who did it or another student. He felt he had to speak up for the person wrongfully accused."

An insatiable reader as a child, his preferences ran to mysteries, Sherlock Holmes, and anything about the Federal Bureau of Investigation.

As early as he can remember, his treasured ambition was to someday become an FBI agent. In the third grade his class was assigned to chose and develope a year-end project. Where his classmates built birdhouses, wrote poetry, or confined themselves to other childish arts and crafts, Mark fingerprinted everyone in the class, and then went on to categorize the entire collection of print cards.

A child of many fascinations, he developed an interest in amateur radio and, at the age of twelve and a half, became the youngest "ham" operator in his license classification.

"He would stay up all night reading or talking to people all over the world," Joyce Blumer says. "He developed an interest in foreign languages. He spoke Spanish fluently. He studied German for a while."

And Mark had talents that surprised even his mother.

"When he was in high school he was in a musical production. I remember women coming up to me and congratulating me on my son being the star of the show."

What they referred to was Mark's ringing tenor voice in a vocal trio and again in a barbershop quartet number.

"He used to sing around the house, but he never sounded the way he did on stage."

Today, his creative and artistic passions are directed to woodworking. Equipped with a sophisticated workshop of power tools, Mark unwinds by making furniture and cabinets.

"A lot of people in the office have 'Blumer originals,'" a staff member comments.

Overweight as a child, he was the prey of merciless taunting from his contemporaries. At the age of eleven, a young girl compared him to a cartoon elephant. Mark decided he'd had enough; he wouldn't be put upon and he wouldn't be ridiculed. He stopped eating lunches and commenced a grim regimen of exercise and weightlifting. He dropped the flabby pounds and replaced them with hard muscle. He never went back to his early obesity.

"He jogs and belonged to a rowing club," Bob Ianni notes. "He keeps himself in excellent shape."

Mark's fascination with the FBI survived high school.

"I'd heard that the two fastest methods to get into the bureau was as an M.P. in the military, or with a law degree."

He opted for the law.

He enrolled in a special program at Michigan State University in the liberal arts-oriented Justin Morrill College, specializing in international relations and intensive language studies.

"The school doesn't exist anymore," Blumer says. "It was a product of the sixties, JFK, and the Peace Corps."

As was true in high school, Mark was a good student in college—but not a brilliant one.

"My brother Robin is the truly brilliant one in the family. He is the smartest person I've ever known. He went straight from high school to med school. He was a National Merit Scholar and was invited to attend Harvard. He went, instead, to the University of Michigan."

Mark speaks with equal admiration and affection for his brother Gary, the Blumer's second son, a teacher of music at Detroit's Wayne State University and an accomplished jazz pianist.

Mark was something of a loner during his university days, shunning fraternity membership—"I felt no need for one"—and confining his friendships to a relatively small circle.

"Morrill College was a notorious center for marijuana in the late sixties. I never touched it and became somewhat of an outcast. Some thought that I was a narc; there were some there at that time."

He dated several girls, never seriously until his dormitory's residence adviser, Herbert Peter Sorg suggested that he might like to meet a friend of his girlfriend.

He agreed to a blind date with nineteen-year-old Susan Nathan, an alluring, brown-eyed speech therapy major who possessed an exquisite sense of humor, a happy bubbly laugh, and a perky figure.

For her part, Susan found Mark appealing for several "important" reasons: "He had a very big head—that's what we have physically in common. Neither of us can buy a hat that fits. He wore his hair short and it appeared that he washed his feet regularly. We were both just nineteen years old and not very deep."

The couple quickly found themselves at ease, and Mark, whose sense of humor matched Susan's, was able to rub away any residual tension she may have felt.

"He started joking right away. We went through the usual small talk like, 'What does your father do?' and he said, 'My father's and obstetrician,' and I said, 'Oh, really?' and then he said, 'Yeah, he told me to go out and knock up some business.' I had only known him about an hour and I thought, I like this guy."

The feeling was mutual. Mark never again dated anyone else. The couple were married soon after graduation.

Mark's university grades were too low for admission to the University of Michigan law school, but he scored well on the Law School Admission Test and was accepted by the University of Detroit Law School. He graduated and was admitted to the Michigan Bar in 1974.

His enthusiasm for an FBI career had not paled; he had applied to the bureau immediately upon graduation from the University of Detroit, took the test, and passed. But the bureau had a policy of not informing an applicant where they stood on their waiting list. Mark couldn't afford the luxury of waiting for them to make up their minds to admit him to the academy; he took a job with a small law firm in the Detroit area, embarking on what was to be a brief, albeit dour and unsatisfactory career in the private practice of law. After an abbreviated tenure, Mark quit the firm without another job to go to.

"I actually considered giving up the law and becoming a newspaper reporter, in legal reporting."

Shortly after graduation from law school, he had, at the urging of a classmate, made application for a position with the office of the Michigan attorney general. The day after he quit his job with the private law firm, he got a call from the secretary of state's office. They used the same list as the attorney general's office and they were in need of a lawyer for their license appeal board; they said that his name had come up. Would he be interested?

"I've always been lucky enough to be in the right place at the right time."

He started work at the secretary of state's Detroit office three days later.

But the license appeal board was a dead-end job for the young and promising attorney. On a day off, Mark got a call from Tom Phillips, a friend working with the attorney general. There was an opening in the Detroit office that Mark would be perfect for.

"I was afraid I might acquire the reputation as a 'jumper,' going from one job to another. I talked to some people at the secretary of state and they all convinced me I'd be crazy not to take the offer with the attorney general."

But the Detroit job evaporated in a budget cut. There was, however, a position available with the attorney general—in Lansing. It was another quandary for Mark. He very much wanted to join the attorney general's staff but had recently purchased a home in the Detroit suburb of Oak Park, his parents lived in nearby Southfield, and he was not terribly thrilled with the prospect of making such a move. To add to his frustration and uncertainty, Susan was pregnant with their first child.

With a timorous uncertainty, he accepted the Lansing

posting and was assigned to the education division writing legal opinions.

It was a terribly boring job but, since all of the opinions went through Sol Bienenfeld, the chairman of the attorney general's opinion review board, Mark's labors attracted important attention.

One day, Sol stuck his head into Mark's office—an abandoned closet—and asked bluntly: "Wanna go to work for me?"

"I thought he was joking," Mark remembers. "Everyone loved Sol. I was honored that he just talked to me."

Sol, a fatherly looking man with gray hair who seemed never to be without an outrageous cigar stuck in his mouth, was considered one of *the* legal scholars in the state of Michigan.

"When I first went with him, it was just great; I had my choice of the cases that didn't fit in other divisions."

But a top official returned from a leave of absence and took over the most interesting cases, leaving Mark to return to writing opinions. After two years, he went to the deputy attorney general and asked for reassignment. He was transferred to the criminal division, a move that would have a profound effect on his career.

In his new position, he found himself in the "pit" of the courtroom arena, trying criminal cases. He loved it from the start.

"I never feel so alive as when I'm in a courtroom fighting a battle of wits."

According to Susan, "He can be thinking about a case while he has his feet up in his recliner. He doesn't pace," she says. "He likes to work out his aggressions on the vacuum cleaner."

She describes how he will vigorously run the sweeper back and forth across the carpet while considering some legal problem, only to stop suddenly and rush to a legal pad where he furiously scribbles notes concerning a "brainstorm he'd just had of something he wanted to say in a trial." Then, after writing a long paragraph, he dashes back and continues the vacuuming.

He talks to Susan about his cases, which she admits are "interesting, like crime novels." She says that if he were into banking law it would "bore me to death."

Susan, coming from a family background that was not built on solid relationships among the members, was decidedly impressed with how close the Blumer family was.

"He was always telling me these cute little stories about things that happened in the family during his childhood. I'd stop him and kiddingly say, 'Oh, oh, here comes another *Leave It to Beaver* story.'"

His close relationship with his parents and brothers has transferred to his own family. He and Susan have a small circle of friends, but do not go out much, preferring to spend most of their time at home or doing things with their two children, Justin, fourteen, and Melissa, eleven.

Ianni and his wife are among the small social circle in which Mark and Susan sometimes circulate. Though they occasionally have dinner together, it has not interfered with their professional relationship. Ianni finds that they can work well together in a superior–subordinate role and still enjoy each other's social company.

Ianni obviously has tremendous respect for Mark's abilities, allowing him to select the cases he will try and reject those he believes have no merit. "He's pretty much on his own," the head of the criminal division states.

Beginning in 1978, Mark found himself deeply entangled in a series of fascinating criminal cases. Two in particular stand out in his mind as his favorites.

In 1984, he took over a murder case from Ronald Emery, who was being transferred to the tort defense division.

Douglas Loyer, of Tawas, Michigan, was accused of

killing his wife by tying her spread-eagle to their bed and then suffocating her with a pillow. He then went to work. When he returned, he called the police and tried to convince them that a motorcycle gang had murdered his wife.

The only time Mark would lose his control in court occurred during the Loyer trial. In the midst of the trial, the judge approved a motion by the defense attorney to reduce the charge from murder one to second degree.

"The judge had removed the jury to hear the defense motion and then granted it. It was Friday, noontime, and I asked him to give me the rest of the day to go to the Michigan Court of Appeals to request an emergency appeal before he told the jury about the reduction in the charge."

Instead, the judge gave him the lunch hour. Trying to find an appeals court judge at lunchtime on a Friday was a study in foolishness.

When the court reconvened, the judge noted that since there was no order from the court of appeals to stop him, ordered the jury brought back in and informed them that he had reduced the charge from first-degree murder to murder in the second degree. He then told the defense to go ahead with its case. But the defense attorney said that his witnesses were not ready and asked for an adjournment for the balance of the weekend. The request was granted and the jury taken out. Mark was stunned.

"I just lost it, I blew up for the first time in a courtroom," he recalls.

"Wait a minute," he blustered at the judge. "Before we leave this courtroom, I want the record to reflect that you have just prevented me from getting a first-degree murder conviction because you wouldn't give me the rest of the day to go to the court of appeals, and now you're letting the defense attorney off because he doesn't have his witnesses ready. I want to make sure that the record is real clear about what just happened here.''

It was as close as he would ever come to going to jail for contempt. The trial continued and Mark won a conviction on the second-degree murder charge.

The Garza case would be a career gamble for Mark because initially he would urge the attorney general to allow him to proceed to bring the suspect to trial on a murder charge when there was no body to sustain the allegation that a homicide had been committed.

In the mid-1970s, Robin Adams was reported missing from her home in rural Caro, a village in Michigan's thumb area, where she had been employed as a babysitter. The local police assumed that Robin had left town on her own, perhaps to escape from a love affair that had turned disagreeable.

The case, while not closed by the area state police post, was left latent in the files.

In 1985, Dan Miller, then a detective sergeant with the state police, was assigned to the post. The first task given him by the post commander was to go through the dormant files and to either close them or reinvestigate them until they could be resolved one way or another.

Miller came across the file detailing the unexplained disappearance of Robin Adams and instantly became totally immersed in the case. There were a number of elements to the mystery that intrigued Miller and would not be put to rest.

''He investigated the hell out of it,'' Blumer would say years later.

What Miller found was that Robin had dated Melvin Garza, a mercuric roughneck with a black and brooding nature, during her senior year in high school. She had tried to break off the relationship, but Garza was having none of it.

One afternoon, soon after Robin sought to free herself from his covetous grip, Garza broke into her home and gave the young woman a frightful beating.

The following day, when Robin's mother came to visit, she was so appalled at her daughter's condition that she immediately marched the girl to the Caro police to file an assault and battery charge against Garza. But the philosophy of the local constabulary was that most of these cases were generally settled between the parties without going through the time and expense of court action. Consequently, they routinely recommended a cooling-off period.

"If you still want to press charges in two weeks, come back then," Robin and her mother were told.

Two weeks minus one day later, Robin Adams disappeared. The police investigated and concluded that she had probably run away, either out of fear of Garza or to simply go somewhere else.

During the investigation, Garza voluntarily came to the police with a letter on Robin's stationery, and in a handwriting identified as hers stating that, since *Garza* had broken off the relationship and there was no longer a reason to stay in Caro, she had gone with friends who had decided to start a new life in California. The letter was postmarked St. Joseph, Missouri on a day when Garza had an unbreakable alibi.

The police believed there was no cause to question the authenticity of the letter, and Robin was written off as a runaway.

But eight years later, when Dan Miller came across the case, he saw, beneath the veneer of an unhappy young woman fleeing to a more promising life, a more sinister explanation for her disappearance.

He took his suspicions and the evidence he had accumulated to the county prosecutor. But there was no body.

"No body, no crime," he was told.

However, Dan Miller was not a police officer to have his instincts ignored. When a new prosecutor was elected to the office a short time later, Miller took the case to him. Again he was confronted with the same bureaucratic recalcitrance.

No body, no crime.

Finally, he contacted the attorney general's criminal division.

"Who is the craziest assistant attorney general in your office; one who will take an impossible case?" he wanted to know.

The answer was brief and instantaneous. "Mark Blumer!"

Then Mark Blumer was the man Dan Miller wanted. A minor conspiracy was arranged whereby Mark would be the only attorney in the office when the case was officially presented, assuring that he would be the one to whom it was assigned.

Miller's information was not faulty; Blumer was the "craziest assistant attorney general" in the division, and he proved it by leaping to the case.

Building on the information already marshalled by Dan Miller, Mark was able to uncover two salient facts concerning the letter supposedly from Robin.

Earlier, Dan Miller had turned the letter over to a handwriting expert who found that, while the penmanship bore a remarkable similarity to documented exemplars of Robin's hand, the letter was, nonetheless, a forgery. Furthermore, the expert was prepared to testify that Garza had created the forgery.

In addition, Blumer learned that there are people whose great passion is to collect postmarks from various U.S. cities, and among the cities favored are those with "saint" in their designations. St. Joseph, Missouri is one of them. Postal employees in such communities have become accustomed to receiving letters addressed to the post office and containing a stamped, self-addressed envelope. These letters are routinely postmarked and mailed back to the sender without ever knowing what the envelope contains.

Mark reasoned that Garza was aware of this and had set up an alibi for himself using this quaint philatelic custom.

He took what he had thus far accumulated to Frank Kelley.

"We don't have a body," he told the attorney general. "But I think we have a strong enough case, one we can win."

There was, certainly, the potential danger for embarrassment for the attorney general's office and, for that matter, for Kelley himself, in authorizing the prosecution of a murder charge with no tangible evidence of a dead body. But Kelley's Irish daring was stirred. He told Blumer to go ahead with the case.

The legal term *corpus delicti* is Latin for "the body of the crime" and not, as many assume, the corpse itself. The prosecution must present to the court sufficient evidence—the corpus delicti—to cause the court to believe that a crime has been committed and that the individual, or individuals named in the charge probably committed it.

Working very closely with Dan Miller over many months, Mark constructed his case based on evidence suggesting that: Robin Adams's family and friends had not seen nor heard from her in eight years; Garza had used correspondence he had received from Robin to forge a letter designed to give the appearance that Robin was safe and many miles away; Garza had a history of violence against Robin and had viciously beaten her on at least one occasion; and her disappearance had come just one day before she was scheduled to press criminal charges against him in connection with the beating. There was sufficient reason to believe that Robin Adams had been murdered and that Melvin Garza was the most probable person to have committed the murder.

Taking the case to a one-man grand jury, Mark succeeded in obtaining an indictment against Garza for the murder of Robin. From there they proceeded through the preliminary examination, at which probable cause to believe that Robin Adams had been murdered and that Melvin Garza had killed her was established to the satisfaction of the district court judge. In addition, Garza's sister was indicted as an accessory to Robin's murder.

"We were all ready to go to trial and I was confident that we had enough to get a conviction," Mark remembers.

Then, just two weeks before the trial was scheduled to begin, the body of Robin Adams was found.

An informant contacted the police and stated that he knew something about Robin's disappearance. Assured that his identity would remain secret, he led Dan Miller to a wooded area behind the Garza farm, where the girl's body was supposedly buried.

However the topography had changed so much in the eight years since the killing that he was unable to locate the exact spot where the grave was located.

Detective Miller spent three days in an unsuccessful attempt to find, with the advice of archaeologists, the grave of Robin Adams. Finally, the state police district commander authorized a major search team to look for the spot where the body had been buried. Using a skirmish line, the officers began patrolling the woods, using metal probes to test suspicious spots.

The state police commander, Leonard Miller, watching the operation, for an unknown reason wandered off in the opposite direction to the search. Suddenly he called out to Dan Miller, instructing him to bring his probe to a depression he had noticed in the ground. The probe slid easily into the earth; the grave had been found.

The area around the suspected gravesite was sealed and Mark was notified. He contacted the Michigan State University School of Archaeology and arranged for a team of archaeologists and anthropologists to come to the site. Using trowels and brushes, they excavated the ground as they would a thousand-year-old archaeological dig.

Over an eleven-hour period the body was slowly, meticulously unearthed. This unusual method of recovering a dead body yielded valuable evidence that proved the exact dimensions of the grave and what type of implement had been used to dig it.

Blumer knew approximately what time of day Robin had disappeared. Fitting that against an alibi Garza had established for that day, he took one of the archaeologists back to the site armed with the identical type of garden spade the scientists had determined had been used to dig the hole into which Robin's body had been placed, and had the identical size grave dug about five feet distant from the spot where Robin's body had been found. Blumer timed the procedure with a stopwatch. Duplicating as closely as possible the exact conditions under which Garza would have dug the grave, they were able to prove that the grave had to have been dug before Robin was killed, thereby establishing premeditation.

The case was held up by the FBI as an excellent example of homicide investigation and, as a result of what the bureau considered a landmark case, Mark has been frequently invited to address Federal Bureau of Investigation classes in investigative procedures in using scientific evidence—fulfilling, to a small degree, his lifelong ambition to be a member of this elite investigative body.

With the discovery of Robin's body, Garza's defense attorney, Michael Callahan—who was a practicing Catholic priest in addition to being a lawyer—quickly contacted Blumer to offer to plea bargain for his client, suggesting that Garza might be willing to plead guilty to the lesser charge of second-degree murder. Blumer went back to Frank Kelley with the offer. Kelley, not one to easily move in the direction of least resistance, told Blumer, "I'm willing to lose the case but I wouldn't sell it. No deal."

The trial went ahead, with the state asking for a

conviction for murder one. Garza was found guilty of that charge and was sentenced to life in prison.

Perhaps the greatest irony connected with the Garza case was the fact the very day Robin's body was discovered would have been her twenty-fifth birthday.

29

On September 17, 1982, fifteen-month-old Chelsea Ann McClellan was rushed by emergency ambulance from a small clinic to a San Antonio, Texas, hospital when she began experiencing respiratory problems following a pair of inoculations. The little girl died two and a half hours later. The shots had been administered by Genene Ann Jones, a licensed practical nurse at the Kerrville (Texas) Pediatric Clinic, who had been instructed to give the little girl inoculations for DPT and measles-mumps-rubella.

Since Chelsea's sudden death could not be attributed to any known medical or physical cause, an autopsy was ordered.

It was later discovered that as many as 120 deaths had occurred in a four-year period in the pediatrics intensive-care unit at the Bexar County Medical Center in San Antonio. An unusual number had been the result of sudden, unexplained respiratory distress and almost all of them had occurred on the three-to-eleven evening shift. It was also learned that Genene Jones had been on duty during each of these baffling fatalities.

After conducting its own internal investigation, the hospital, to eliminate a potentially serious problem, and without notifying police or openly admitting that a baby-killer was on the staff, got rid of Genene by releasing all licensed practical nurses under the ruse of "upgrading" the nursing staff. The sudden deaths stopped.

On August 24, 1982, Genene went to work for Dr. Kathleen Holland, owner of the Kerrville pediatric clinic. Dr. Holland, who had known and worked with Genene in San Antonio and considered her a capable, competent nurse, was delighted to have her on her tiny staff.

On the clinic's second day of operation, Petti McClellan arrived with fourteen-month-old Chelsea for a 1 o'clock appointment to have Dr. Holland examine the little girl's "bad cold."

While the doctor took Chelsea's medical history, Genene was down the hall with the toddler, keeping her occupied and out of mischief.

After about five minutes, Dr. Holland heard the nurse tell Chelsea: "Don't go to sleep, baby. Chelsea, wake up!" Shortly thereafter, Genene called, "Dr. Holland, would you come here?" The doctor went down the hall to the examining room and found Chelsea unconscious on the examining table with Genene fitting an oxygen mask over her face. Genene later claimed that she had been playing with the child when suddenly Chelsea slumped over, not breathing.

The Kerr County Emergency Medical Service was summoned and Chelsea was rushed to nearby Sid Peterson Hospital in Kerrville, arriving in just two minutes.

By then, Chelsea was breathing on her own. She was kept in the hospital's ICU for ten days, during which a battery of tests were administered in an attempt to locate the cause of the seizure and respiratory arrest. No explanation was found.

Three days later, another episode of respiratory arrest at the clinic, this time involving a one-month-old girl who suddenly stopped breathing after being left alone with Genene for a short time. After another emergency run to the hospital, the baby's condition dramatically improved and no cause for the breathing problem could be found.

On August 30, two incidents of arrested breathing

in infants occurred under Genene's care; both recovered after emergency transport to hospitals.

The number of children to the hospital in Santa Rosa from Dr. Holland's clinic—there had been three in three days—began to generate questions among those who remembered the whispers concerning Genene Jones in San Antonio. One staff member told Kathy Holland that she would not accept any further admissions from the Kerrville clinic if Genene accompanied the patient.

There was some small sense of relief among the medical personnel in the fact that at least all of the children had recovered; there had been no deaths. Then came Chelsea McClellan's second visit to Kerrville clinic.

Petti McClellan had come to the clinic to have Dr. Holland look at her son, Cameron, who had the flu. But, because of the emotional trauma of her first visit three weeks earlier, the doctor asked to examine Chelsea, even though her mother reported that the girl had exhibited no respiratory difficulties since that time.

While Petti met with Dr. Holland in her office, Genene took Chelsea into the examining room. A few minutes later, Dr. Holland came into the room where she briefly examined the girl and ordered two inoculations.

Petti held Chelsea on her lap as Genene injected a hypodermic into the child's thigh. Within seconds, Chelsea began having trouble breathing. Genene calmed the panicked mother, telling her that her daughter was simply reacting to the pain of the shot. She then administered the second inoculation, this one in the other thigh. By this time, Chelsea wasn't breathing at all.

She was taken first to Sid Peterson Hospital and, when she was able to breathe on her own and her condition appeared stabilized, was then transferred to a hospital in Santa Rosa. But on the way, Chelsea's condition once again deteriorated and her heart suddenly stopped beating. In spite of the dedicated efforts of the emergency room staff, the girl died.

Three hours later, Genene Jones was back in the Kerrville clinic when nineteen-year-old Lydia Evans arrived with her five-month-old son Jacob. She had come to see Dr. Holland about Jacob's crying spells, which had been going on for a month; Lydia feared something serious might be wrong with the little boy.

Dr. Holland was still at the hospital, arranging for the autopsy on Chelsea, but had called the clinic to tell Genene that she wanted Jacob brought directly to the hospital because she wanted to examine him there.

Jones told the boy's mother that she would have to draw some blood for tests and would have to start an IV on the boy. When the mother asked why, she was told that if Jacob went into seizure while conducting the tests, they would be able to administer medication without delay.

"Jacob has never had any seizures," Lydia said.

Genene asked the mother to leave the examining room because she might be upset at seeing the blood drawn from her tiny son.

A few minutes later, Lydia heard Jacob scream six or seven times and then suddenly stop in mid-scream. The receptionist, who had gone into the room, burst out and dialed the hospital asking that Dr. Holland be paged *immediately*. Jacob had stopped breathing.

Jacob was rushed to the hospital where he was stabilized and later released. There was no explanation for his respiratory distress.

Dr. Holland and Genene Jones were considered heroes by the parents of the children who had come so close to death and then survived. Even the McClellans believed that Kathy and Genene had done everything humanly possible to save little Chelsea. They went so far as to take out a two-column advertisement in the local newspaper, thanking everyone who had shown such tender compassion in their time of pain and especially acknowledging the help given by Dr. Holland

and Nurse Jones, who had extended "Chelsea's stay by their caring in such a sensitive way. A care which extended beyond our loss and helped us more than anyone could ever know."

But the small medical community in Kerrsville was beginning to wonder what was going on; the number of children being admitted to intensive care with respiratory distress was soaring and there was no rational explanation. One physician was prompted to comment that in his forty-three years of medical practice he had never had a single breathing failure in one of his pediatric patients. "To the best of my knowledge, we've never had one in Kerrville," he said. Something had to be wrong.

There were two more incidents at the clinic following the death of Chelsea McClellan. During the second, a girl suffering respiratory arrest was rushed to the hospital, where an anesthesiologist in the emergency room observed a reaction from the child as she fought Dr. Holland's attempt to insert a breathing tube in her throat. She was struggling to raise her right arm to grasp the tube. The doctor had seen this phenomenon before.

"It just reminded me of what I'd seen in the operating room," the doctor said. "The child appeared to be trying to reach up, but didn't seem to be able to get its hand up. It was jerky, uncontrolled movements with a purpose, but an inability to accomplish that purpose."

The child was coming out from under Anectine.

The doctor took his observations to another staff physician and the decision was made to call an emergency meeting of the staff's executive committee later that afternoon.

At the same time, yet another crisis was being played out in the hospital's emergency room.

During the upheaval at the clinic, another patient had been waiting to see the doctor. His mother was told to bring the boy to the hospital emergency room.

While seated in the hospital waiting room, Genene came out and took the boy back into the emergency room. A few minutes later, she called out that the boy had arrested.

Dr. Holland raced down from the ICU and was told that the boy had a throat clogged with mucus and was having trouble breathing. The doctor ordered a pair of drugs to ease his distress. On the boy's bed, a half-filled syringe was found. No one knew what it was or where it had come from. Dr. Holland squirted the clear liquid out and disposed of the needle. The boy's condition improved and he was declared out of danger.

Everyone breathed a sigh of relief; there had been enough crisis in the small hospital that day to last a lifetime.

Meanwhile, the hospital administrators had come to the conclusion that the children entering the emergency room suffering respiratory distress had been given Anectine—the brand name for succinylcholine—but were not yet certain how they were getting it. There was little doubt that someone at the Kerrville clinic was administering the powerful muscle relaxant, and many believed that it was Genene Jones.

Succinylcholine was kept at the clinic. Dr. Holland had ordered it to have on hand in the event she had to intubate a child who was fighting it off with clenched teeth. But she had never used it or ordered its use on a patient in the time the clinic had been in operation. However, Genene was aware of its presence.

The police were brought into the case and the suspicions and the circumstantial evidence available was presented.

A full-scale investigation was launched and by late 1983 a grand jury had been convened to look into the charges that Genene Jones had caused the death of Chelsea McClellan and the nonfatal poisoning of seven other children, allegedly with succinylcholine.

Kerr County district attorney Ron Sutton, who was in charge of the case, had a familiar problem: How do you prove that succinylcholine was used when everyone knew that the compound could not be isolated in human tissue?

Dr. James Garriott, a San Antonio toxicologist and friend of Ron Sutton, had recently learned of a test to extract the drug from human tissue. The test had been perfected by a colleague in Toledo named Robert Forney. Garriott called Forney and asked if he would agree to help the prosecution in a case involving succinylcholine. But Forney was under a secrecy order by the Hillsdale County one-man grand juror and didn't believe he would be permitted to assist in such a fashion. Instead, he suggested that Bo Holmstedt be contacted.

Holmstedt agreed to conduct the new test and Chelsea's body was exhumed for the purpose of obtaining tissue samples. The specimens were then taken by Dr. Fredric Rieders of Philadelphia—who had previously worked with Bo Holmstedt—to Stockholm for analysis. The tissue, removed from two injection sites on Chelsea's thighs, proved to contain significant quantities of the paralyzing drug.

Next would be the problem of getting the court to allow the results of the tests as evidence in the trial of Genene Jones.

The standard for determining admissibility of scientific evidence was established in the early 1920s in the case of *Frye v. Unites States,* which held that such evidence is permitted if it is generally accepted within its scientific discipline. A hearing—known commonly within legal circles as a "Frye hearing"—was held to determine whether this unique procedure adequately met the test of "general acceptance."

The court held that it did, and what would later become known as "Forney's Technique" was introduced. Bo Helmstedt testified about the procedure at the trial. The jury was convinced.

On February 15, 1984, a jury of seven women and five men, in the 277th District Court of Williamson

County, Texas, found Genene Jones guilty of the murder of Chelsea McClellan. In the penalty phase of the trial, the same jurors failed to recommend mercy.

She was later convicted of attempting to poison the seven other children. Including her murder conviction, Genene was sentenced to a total of 159 years in prison. She is appealing her convictions.

''Forney's Technique'' had withstood its first court test. There would be others.

30

Early in 1987, a unique new television production, *Unsolved Mysteries,* made its appearance on the NBC network. A ''docudrama'' dealing with unsolved crimes or missing persons and using, as much as possible, actual participants in the events depicted, *Unsolved Mysteries* was the forerunner of a new brand of television that would quickly generate a host of similar programs dealing with real-life situations.

The show created a great deal of interest among the viewing public, including the personnel of the Michigan attorney general's criminal division.

''When I came in the office the morning after the show, everyone was talking about it,'' Mark Blumer recalls. ''I said something like, 'We ought to get them on the Davis case.' ''

Agreement was unanimous and a few days later, Detective Sergeant Doug Barrett, now assigned to the division to work on the Davis case, contacted the show's production company.

''We have a case here that you might be interested in,'' he told Mike Mathis, one of the producers.

Indeed they were. Within weeks, representatives of the production company were contacting principals in the story to determine if they would cooperate in the filming of a segment on the mystery of Shannon's death.

One major problem immediately surfaced. Judge Kenneth Glaser, the one-man grand juror, had admonished all the witnesses called before him that they were forbidden by law to discuss the case with anyone. Could people such as Dick Britton, Bob and Lucille Mohr, Robert Forney, and Don Brooks participate in the show's production without violating the judge's order?

The attorney general's office, recognizing how important the national exposure of the case could be in locating the fleeing David Davis, went to the judge to request a waiver of his secrecy order to enable the television show to be filmed.

The judge, not wanting to stand in the way of anyone's potential television career, however brief, was quoted as saying, "I can't give you my permission to do this, but I won't tell you not to."

That was enough.

With the assurances that they would not be subjecting themselves to a possible contempt citation, those who had appeared before the grand jury agreed to take part in the production of the show's segment.

In mid-September, the production crew arrived to begin filming. In Toledo, they shot footage of Bob and Lucille talking about Shannon and how much they had thought of their new son-in-law and of their suspicions after Shannon's death. It was very emotional for the distraught couple, having to deal all over again with the pain and bitterness they had relived so many times before. But they understood the importance of having such wide public exposure to the horror they had suffered, and their fervent hunger to have Davis located and brought back to face justice made the agony bearable.

The film crew visited the Medical College of Ohio to shoot footage of Bob Forney and Don Brooks, recreating their meeting during which Forney illustrated the mysterious peak on the gas chromatograph.

Two days were spent in Hillsdale County at Dick Britton's farm and the farm on Lickley Road, with professional actors portraying Shannon and David.

"Man, I wouldn't want to do that again," Dick

complained after two days of shooting. "That's hard work; we had to keep doing it over and over again."

Scenes at Thorn Hospital involving Dick, Bob and Lucille, and medical hospital personnel were shot.

In one scene, Bob was supposed to recreate his argument with David over Davis's intention to have Shannon's body cremated. He couldn't do it; there was just so much he could allow himself to relive. The slowly healing wounds in his soul were reopened easily. Ceil's wounds were not scarring over; her hatred for Davis continued to fester and would not be cured until he had been made to pay for what he had done. Ceil played the scene.

Finally, scenes at Calvary Cemetery were shot to depict Shannon's funeral and later exhumation, with the cooperation of the cemetery officials, using a freshly dug grave and a coffin supplied by Jasin's Funeral Home. The emotional drain finally became too much for even Ceil to withstand. She and Bob did not participate in this part of the filming.

The editing and final production was rushed through, and on Sunday night, November 29, 1987, the Davis segment of *Unsolved Mysteries* aired on prime-time TV.

The show drew an audience estimated at more than thirty million viewers, capturing top ratings for its time period that night and figuring in the top ten ratings leaders for the week. Even more important, it created a much wider interest in the Shannon Davis case.

This show was credited with winning the series a permanent, prime-time spot on the network's schedule. Later, the host of *Unsolved Mysteries,* actor Robert Stack, in an appearance on *The Tonight Show,* was asked to choose the most memorable of all the unsolved mysteries presented on the series. Without hesitation, Stack replied, "No question; the David Davis case."

Optimism was running high in Toledo, in Hillsdale County, and in Lansing. Telephone tips began coming into the show's producers, the FBI, the Michigan state police, and the state's attorney general's office almost immediately from individuals who had seen the show and believed they knew where Davis was. But, as the days and then weeks wore on and all the leads were chased down and found unproductive, the earlier torpor resettled over those whose lives had been so thoroughly shackled to the events that had destroyed one life and permanently scarred so many others.

For Don Brooks, the disappointment at the failure of the television show to locate Davis was not assuaged by his current distance from the Davis case.

The policy of the Michigan state police is to periodically rotate assignments and Don had been in the attorney general's office much longer than usual.

"My time for a new assignment was coming up," Don says. "Gary Peterson at the Lansing Post was looking to make a move and was interested in working in the criminal division, and I wanted to work in the investigative division, so we made the switch."

Don looked upon the transfer with a degree of relief. "The case seemed to be getting nowhere and I felt the change would be good for me psychologically. I knew that if Davis ever was caught, I'd be right back in it."

While Don's ability and dedication to the case had never been questioned, Mark Blumer had become troubled with the emotional attachment Don and the Mohrs had developed, which might cause problems should Davis be found and brought back for trial.

"The Mohrs were thoroughly likeable people and Don had become extremely close to them, and they to him," Blumer says. "I was concerned that they had grown to depend too much on Don, and I didn't want to have the problem of Don having to hold their hand, so to speak, throughout a difficult trial, where they would be called upon to get up on the stand and testify."

Meanwhile, the efforts continued. Doug Barrett, as

the detective responsible for the Davis case following Lieutenant Gary Peterson, went through the routine of running down every lead, no matter how unlikely, that came in; checking with the FBI and Interpol on a regular basis.

In February 1987, the Americas' Cup yacht races were being held in Melbourne, Australia. There was some reason to believe that, because of Davis's interest in boating, he might travel to Australia to attend this major yachting event.

A popular Detroit radio personality, J.P. McCarthy of WJR, and Frank McBride, a Detroit yachtsman, would be broadcasting daily from Melbourne during the event. A representative from Frank Kelley's office phoned McBride and requested that he and McCarthy take with them a quantity of the ''wanted'' posters that had been circulated through the Caribbean, for delivery to Australian police and distribution during the yacht races. Both men readily agreed to transport and deliver the posters.

To learn more about the introduction and use of the scientific evidence identifying succinlycholine employed in the Genene Jones trial, Mark and Doug Barrett traveled to San Antonio to confer with Ron Sutton and his staff and to interview witnesses testifying about the Forney Technique.

Mark continued to be pessimistic about the chances of Davis someday being apprehended and brought to trial. Bob Ianni had, from the day the criminal division began working on the investigation, told Mark, ''One of these days they're going to locate that son-of-a-bitch. It will be your case, so you'd better study the files on it.''

Mark read some of the newspaper clippings dealing with the case, and then largely ignored the growing files on it.

The 1962 graduating class from Southwestern High School held its twenty-five-year class reunion in the summer of 1987. Davis, a member of that class, had turned out to be a celebrity of sorts, prompting the organizers of the reunion to mail an invitation to Miami—where they heard he was last seen—and to decorate the reunion hall with the "wanted" posters and newspaper clippings of his exploits.

"Actually, we were afraid he *might* show up," one of the class members said.

On December 28, 1988, a rerun of *Unsolved Mysteries* containing the Davis segment was broadcast. While those involved in the case were openly pleased that there would be yet another attempt to find someone who recognized Davis and could pinpoint his exact location, privately many—such as Mark Blumer— found it difficult to generate a great deal of enthusiasm for the possibility that this rerun would do what the premiere showing had not. The suspicion that Davis was dead had taken a firm hold in the hearts and minds of many closest to Bob and Lucille.

The flurry of press activity surrounding the initial presentation of the David Davis segment on *Unsolved Mysteries* was largely absent this time. For Bob and Lucille, the phone had ceased its insistent ringing and the steady parade of journalists had disappeared from the front door.

Because the memory of Shannon's death was so strong and so closely associated with their home in Point Place, Bob and Ceil had moved from the area, hoping that a change in surroundings might somehow mask the chronic reminders of their painful loss. But after several years and a pair of relocations, Ceil knew that distance would have no effect on remembrance. If anything, the agony seemed to increase with the miles. They found a home just two blocks from the place where their youngest child had been born and raised.

Meanwhile, in Hawaii, a woman watched the television rerun, unable to believe what she had seen. Picking up the telephone, she dialed the Honolulu police. "I know where David Davis is," she told the officer answering her call.

PART THREE

The Judgment

31

American Samoa, a group of five volcanic islands and two coral atolls, is an unincorporated, unorganized territory of the United States located some twenty-six hundred miles southwest of Hawaii in the South Pacific Ocean. The only American territory south of the equator, it has a combined land area of seventy-seven square miles and a population of just over thirty-two thousand people.

Although much of the island group receives American television through a satellite hookup, no one saw the December 28 rebroadcast of *Unsolved Mysteries;* a typhoon raging through the South Pacific had made television reception all but impossible that day. However, the program was shown in the islands a few days later.

Rip Bell was not available for television watching on either day; he was busy as chief pilot for Samoa Aviation, a small commuter airline serving the seven islands, flying mercy missions to the storm-ravaged out-islands, bringing food and other supplies in and flying the sick and injured out.

Rip was looked on as an authentic hero among many of the natives living on the smaller islands. And he was considered an excellent pilot by his employer, Connie Porter, vice president and co-owner of Samoa Aviation.

"He was great to work with," Mrs. Porter says. "He's the best chief pilot I've ever worked with."

He'd come to American Samoa in 1985 from Bethel,

Alaska, where he'd been a bush pilot, and was hired by Arthur Dalton of Manu'a Air, who considered Rip "a hell of a pilot. He was highly egocentric, but he was the best pilot we had."

But after making him chief pilot and flight director, Dalton fired Rip in 1987 for causing dissension among other pilots.

Many of the pilots in the islands claimed that he was a showboater and a cowboy who took unnecessary risks.

After being let go by Dalton, Rip moved over to South Pacific Island Airways, where he eventually became chief pilot and director of operations. In December 1988, SPIA was taken over by Samoa Aviation and Rip continued with the new owners as their number-one pilot.

Tall and burley with shaggy blonde hair and a full beard, Rip had a habit of always wearing a floppy "rag" hat and mirror sunglasses. Once, when his boss at Manu'a complained about the appearance of his hat and ordered him to stop wearing it, Rip refused. "That's my trademark," he insisted.

On October 30, 1986, Rip had married Maria Koleti' Sua, a Western Samoa native whom he met when she was a ticket-taker at the Pago Pago airport. He called her "Sam."

Rip had shunned the more lavish lifestyle his $2,800 a month salary could have afforded him to live in a small shack in the tiny village of Tafuna, about two miles from the airport. He and Sam planned to save their money to build a more conventional house for themselves, their dog Churchill, and the children they talked about having.

Rip was considered an easygoing individual by many of the island residents—low key, polite, and considerate. Some thought him to be generous to a fault, helping to support Sam's large family in Western Samoa.

But Rip Bell, respected and admired by many as a

"great guy," carried a terrible secret around with him. He had spent eight years living a monstrous lie. The name on his pilot's license, on his driver's license, and on his paychecks, the name on his marriage license, David Myer Bell, was a phony. His real name was *David Richard Davis*.

32

On January 3, 1989, Detective Sergeant Doug Barrett was in his office at the attorney general's criminal division.

His thoughts were not on the possible whereabouts of David Davis. He was aware that the *Unsolved Mysteries* episode on the Davis case had been rerun the previous week; he'd already gotten more than ten calls from viewers who claimed to have seen Davis in a number of locations around the United States.

None of these tips panned out any more than the seventy-one phone calls he'd received from all over the United States—and even a few from outside the country—following the first presentation of the TV show. One caller from Alaska claimed, "I'd swear I saw that guy in a bar in Fairbanks two years ago."

Since assuming responsibility for the Davis case in 1987, Barrett had made periodic checks with the FBI and Interpol; he'd made contact with eight skindiving organizations worldwide, and in one case had arranged for photos of Davis to be published in the group's magazine. He'd also traveled to Cincinnati to speak to the International Association of Special Investigations, an organization of insurance company investigators, about the Davis case.

"We considered that there was a possibility that Davis might try to use the same operation with other insurance companies and thought that we should alert them to be on the lookout for this," Barrett says.

Doug had little continuing enthusiasm for the chance

that Davis would be located as a result of this second showing of the television program. He was therefore jolted out of his chair when he received a call from Don Brooks.

"Hey Doug, I just talked to a woman who says she knows where Davis is. I think this is the one."

Barrett rushed to Don's office at the Lansing state police post to sit in while Brooks called the woman again to obtain additional information.

While Don no longer had an active role in the Davis case, because of his high visibility during the early years of the investigation, he continued getting telephone calls and letters in connection with the search for David Davis.

"Whenever something about the case came in to Don, he would send it on to me or call and tell me what he had and to ask if I would handle it."

It was just such a call that Brooks received on January 3. A woman in Hawaii had watched the *Unsolved Mysteries* rerun, had recognized Davis, and had called the Honolulu police department. But according to the woman, the officer taking her call didn't seem to know what she was talking about. She called back the next day and talked to a different policeman. This time, the officer understood exactly what she was trying to tell him and referred her to the producers of the TV show in Los Angeles. From there, she was referred to Don Brooks.

After being reassured that her identity would never be revealed, the woman began providing information that sent the hairs at the back of Don's neck tingling.

"She told us what name he was using and exactly where he was; even gave us an address and phone number," Barrett recalls. "She had written him letters; he had even visited her in Hawaii the weekend before, during the holidays. She knew he was married, she described the scars he had, and related conversations she'd had with him. She also told us he'd been a bush pilot in Alaska."

The two detectives agreed that this tip looked very promising indeed.

Their next step was to contact Alaska and ask that the bureau of motor vehicles fax them a photo of David Myer Bell's driver's license.

The tension grew as the fax began coming off their machine. Would this really be the lead they had been praying for?

"We took one look at the picture and knew we had our man," Barrett remembers.

Back at the criminal division offices, Mark Blumer strolled in and someone shouted, "We've located David Davis."

Mark looked skeptical; there was always a glut of good-natured kidding and practical jokes circulating among the staff. This had the imprint of another practical joke.

"Oh, really," he replied without amusement. "Where?"

"Pago Pago."

"*Sure!*" he said, stomping into his office and closing the door.

The FBI in Honolulu was notified that the object of their search had been definitely located in American Samoa. Now there would be the agonizing wait for the federal agents to act, to get to the islands and arrest David Davis.

"This guy is a planner," Don told Barrett, apprehension obvious in his voice. "If he gets the least bit hinkey, he'll cut out. They've got to move, now. This cat is not in the bag."

Don wanted desperately to let Bob and Ceil know what they had learned. But he was terrified that something might go wrong and Davis would escape yet another time. It would savage the hapless couple. He finally called Ceil and told her that they had a promising lead to Davis's whereabouts and that he would keep them advised. He made the same call to Dick Britton.

"Don told us that they had some real good leads," Ceil would say later. "But they'd had good leads before that didn't turn out, so we had no reason to think that they'd found him this time. Still, we certainly hoped they had, which made the waiting all the more unbearable."

In Hawaii, FBI special agent Robert Heafner contacted Michael Sala, chief of the Samona police, advising him that a wanted fugitive was in his jurisdiction, and that Heafner was flying in to make the arrest and requesting the help of Sala's special police agents.

The FBI agent arrived in Pago Pago on the afternoon of January 5 and immediately rejected the suggestion that they attempt Davis's arrest at his home in Tafuna. The area was thick with vegetation that might make escape possible. Instead, a watch was placed on the airport and outgoing planes were checked to insure that Davis hadn't gotten wind of the FBI's presence. Even cars in the parking lot were checked.

Heafner knew that Davis was scheduled to pilot an early-morning flight that was to depart at 7:15. To insure that Davis would not make a run for it in another plane, all outgoing flights were held up and the airport sealed to departing aircraft.

At about 6:50, the officers watching the airport observed Davis walking toward the terminal. They watched as he entered and went to the coffee shop and purchased a soft drink. As he moved back into the terminal lobby, Heafner and one other officer approached him.

"David Richard Davis?" Heafner asked.

"I don't think I know such a person," Davis replied, looking surprised.

"Are you David Myer Bell?"

"Yes."

Heafner then showed the man a copy of the "wanted" poster and said, "I have a federal warrant for your arrest for unlawful flight to avoid prosecution.''

Davis was frisked and handcuffed and led to a police car. At the police station he was advised of his rights and informed that if he gave false information about his identity he would be subject to local charges.

Asked again if he was David Richard Davis, he shrugged and replied softly, ''What can I say? It's me.''

He also confirmed his true date of birth, and was then whisked to a maximum-security cell in the Tafuna Correctional Facility.

Davis was allowed to telephone his wife, Maria. ''Don't be alarmed,'' he told her. ''I'm in jail. I'm being accused of murder; they're going to take me back to Michigan. Don't cry, and don't listen to anybody. I'm going to clear this all up.''

He asked her to bring him some books.

In Lansing, it had been an eternal wait for the phone to ring and the word flashed that the man they had been seeking for eight years was finally in custody.

A shout rang through the office shortly after one in the afternoon when the call from the FBI finally came.

''They got him, they got him, he's in custody.''

Don Brooks grabbed the phone and dialed Toledo.

''Ceil,'' he said, almost softly. ''We got him; David's in custody.''

''My heart was pounding out of my chest,'' Ceil remembers, tears once again flowing with the memory of the relief she'd felt at long last, hearing the words she had prayed for through the long, pain-wracked years.

''I couldn't believe it,'' was Dick Britton's response to Don's call. ''I'd about given up any hope that he would really be caught. It was a celebration.''

In Atlanta, Georgia, Billy Bowles was called by the *Detroit Free Press* and told to get on a plane and head for American Samoa. He was back on the Davis case.

For Mark Blumer, the news came as a definite surprise. It also came as somewhat of a rude awakening.

"One of these days they're going to locate that son-of-a-bitch," Bob Ianni, Mark's boss, had told him years earlier. "It will be your case, so you'd better study the files on it."

Mark had largely ignored those urgings. Now Ianni's words echoed in Blumer's head. It would be his case; he would have to know everything there was to know about David Davis and Bob Forney and his unique method of extracting the deadly drug that had been used to kill Shannon—especially he had to know about the "Forney Technique."

There was the distinct possibility that he would have to be prepared to go into a preliminary hearing on the murder charge against Davis in as little as twelve days, ready to explain to the court enough about the method used by Forney to convince the judge that Davis probably killed his wife.

To do this, Blumer, in effect, became a student of Dr. Robert Forney, spending hours listening as Forney gave him a crash course in toxicology, chemistry, and associated sciences.

In addition, the assistant state attorney general had the psychological, criminal, and legal background of the case to thoroughly absorb.

Benefiting from the information supplied by their informant in Hawaii, Blumer and his staff knew that Davis had worked as a bush pilot in Alaska. They were thereby able to trace his movements backward, eventually enabling them to answer the question that was on the minds of those familiar with the Davis case: How did Davis end up halfway around the world as an airline pilot in American Samoa?

When Davis fled Haiti, he still had a fair amount of cash left from the sale of his farm and other possessions in Michigan. He flew to Florida and from there to southern California.

Knowing that he was now a hunted man, Davis,

highly intelligent, reasoned that it would be necessary to fashion a totally new identity to go with the name change he had given himself March 13, 1978, when he had applied for and received a Florida driver's license in the name of David Myer Bell.

While living in Michigan, Davis had accompanied Dick Britton—a licensed private pilot—on a number of occasions when Dick would rent a light plane to fly to farming conventions, auctions, and the like.

"I let him handle the controls once in a while, you know, when we were flying level. He never took off or landed; he didn't seem all that interested in flying. He wasn't very good."

But Davis was more interested than Britton knew. He had purchased an ultralight while he and Shannon were on their honeymoon, had put it together, but probably never actually flew it. He later had his friend Bob Burns sell it for him after moving to Florida.

Davis knew that the police would be looking for him in areas and occupations with which he'd been most familiar. No one, he believed, would think to look for him in aviation.

Early in January 1982, Davis—now using the name David Myer Bell—appeared in the Los Angeles suburb of Santa Monica, sporting a full beard. He enrolled at the Claire Walters Flight Academy, seeking a private pilot's license, the lowest FAA-ranked pilot rating.

"He showed up here with some money, but not a lot. He was able to buy his flying time," Claire Walters, owner-operator of the flying school for twenty-seven years, recalled.

Flying at least two hours a day, Bell—who urged people to call him "Rip"—was able by early February to pass his FAA check ride and was awarded his private pilot's ticket.

In June he was awarded an instrument rating, and a month later upgraded his ranking to "commercial pilot."

He had so impressed Claire Walters with his ability

to so quickly master the art of flying, that she hired him as a flight instructor.

"He was a good student and when he became an instructor, he showed up regularly and did his job," Walters says. "He said his father and mother were both doctors, and that his grandfather had been extremely wealthy and had left him with a trust fund."

Rip told Walters's daughter that he had been married just three weeks when his wife drowned.

Claire eventually rented him a one-room apartment in a converted garage next to her Santa Monica hillside home. The only furniture he wanted was a bed, Walters says.

"I looked in one time and there were clothes scattered all over the place. He lived like a bum. I couldn't understand why women would want to come there."

She had other reasons to question why females would want to see him.

He had begun putting on a great deal of weight. "He was such a big whale; there was no good reason for a woman to look at him twice." But, the indications are, many did.

As a flight instructor, Rip enjoyed his female students—especially the young and pretty ones.

"The only time I saw him really mad was when I transferred a pretty blonde from his ground school to another instructor," Walters said. "He went out of his mind."

He apparently made a number of romantic conquests among the women he taught to fly. "They all wanted to fly with Rip," according to Claire. "Sometimes he had eight or ten students in his ground school class, all of them women."

She recalls one occasion when Rip left with a pretty female student for what was scheduled to be a one-hour instructional flight. He returned three hours later with the front of his trousers unzipped. One of the other pilots, glancing down at the open fly, asked, "What are you doing, advertising?"

There were so many women visiting Rip's spartan living quarters that Claire once joked that he should install a revolving door. She also recalled that one of his students "shacked up with him" in his garage apartment and told wild stories about what they did in the shower. She didn't explain how she knew what was going on in the shower, however.

Among the women Rip became close to during his stay in California included a Beverly Hills dentist and a real estate saleswoman who both thought Rip had a "death wish" because of his daredevil antics—flying close to mountain peaks or down dangerous canyons.

One of Rip's students, a thirty-five-year-old woman named Lori Sellers, dated him over several years and took a three-week trip to Alaska with him in 1983. She called him "an adventurer," and said it was "one of the things she liked about him."

Johnette Slavey, Lori's roommate, recalls that Lori had told her that Rip was a Vietnam veteran who had been terribly wounded. "She felt sorry for him. He'd been through so much."

Lori was a very independent person. She'd lost both her parents in the span of a single year, and had lived in Venice, California, an area noted for a "different" type of people.

"But Rip had this control thing," Johnette remembers. "He hated that she smoked. He would snatch the cigarettes out of her mouth as she was trying to light them up."

In mid-1984, for reasons she never explained, Lori suddenly became suspicious of Rip's background. She did some checking on her own and discovered that he "wasn't what he said he was."

Whatever Lori uncovered appears to have caused her grave concern. When her roommate Johnette got married in late August, Lori moved out of the apartment they had shared and began to drift. She would not provide a forwarding address to keep Rip from finding her, according to Johnette's husband, Gene.

By November of that year she had left the Los Angeles area, telling Claire Walters that she would return to use up the flying time she had already paid for. Years later she had not returned for her flying lessons or the money.

She was found late one night by the Maui, Hawaii police severely beaten and left for dead. Many people who knew her and Rip immediately suspected that he had finally caught up to her and silenced her. However, on August 14, 1986—the night of the beating—Rip was twenty-six hundred miles away in American Samoa.

It is doubtful that he was particularly worried about having whatever Lori knew made public. He frequently dared the fates to unmask him. On at least one occasion he discussed, with one of his romantic interests, his former wife, Shannon, who had died in an "auto accident." Later he said that Shannon had perished in a drowning accident. And one night Rip was in a group of acquaintances and the men were boasting about the worst things they had done in their lives. When Rip's turn came, he said, "I'm wanted for murder." Everyone laughed, and went on to other topics.

Following his return from the Alaskan trip, he went to Claire Walters with the demand for a higher hourly rate for his flight instruction services.

"He had an expanded view of his worth," she recalled.

Claire agreed to the higher rate, but then effectively froze him out by assigning new students to other instructors.

In the fall of 1984, Rip quit his job and moved to Bethel, a small fishing village on the southwest coast of Alaska. He had heard that there was an opening for a bush pilot.

The almost total absence of a road system in that part of the state made air travel the only practical means of moving about.

"He called us when he heard that we needed someone for a few months. I hired him over the tele-phone,'' said Ron Peltola, owner of Bush Air, a charter service which flew into small, isolated settlements, transporting fishermen, schoolteachers, and public health nurses. ''When he walked in here he was wear-ing *shorts*.''

Peltola considered Rip a hard worker. ''He was al-ways willing to fly, although I could tell he hadn't had a lot of experience when he came here.''

Rip left Alaska in November and went to Hawaii. Dick Britton used to refer to David Davis as a ''snow bird,'' one who hated cold weather. ''If they ever find him it will be in a place that's warm.''

In Hawaii, he met Barbara Wilcox, a petite beauty who ran a scuba equipment shop and diving school. Rip moved in with her for the winter, sometimes teaching tourists to dive.

The following summer, he was back in Alaska, this time obtaining a float plane rating that allowed him to fly the seaplanes that operated off rivers and lakes in the region, making him more versatile and supposedly more valuable to Bush Air.

But after attempting a crosswind takeoff from a river—a violation of company rules—badly bending a wingtip and leaving his passengers while he flew the damaged aircraft to Anchorage—another violation— Rip was fired.

During his brief stay he had added to the number of friends he had made during his first summer in the north. He had been almost universally accepted by the people he met, most believing everything he'd told them—that he was the son of two very wealthy doctors and the great-grandson of a man who made a fortune running guns during the Civil War; that he'd sailed his own boat around the world; that he'd been a college professor; and that he'd been married once to a woman who died in a tragic accident.

While flying in Alaska, wanted by the FBI, it was rumored that he not only routinely transported prisoners for the Alaskan state police and other law enforcement units, he also gave flying lessons to Bethel's chief of police.

After a stopover in Hawaii, he headed for the most distant and most secluded of American possessions—the place he'd be most unlikely to run into someone from his Michigan past, the place he felt most certain Don Brooks would never think of looking, the place where *no one* would think of looking.

American Samoa.

33

The news of the arrest of David Myer Bell—gentle, generous Rip Bell—came with the jolting numbness of an electric shock to those in the American Samoa archipelago who knew, loved, and respected him.

"He's not the kind of person to do such a thing," Maria Koleti' Sua Bell, twenty-three, insisted. "He's not a violent person. We were the happiest couple on the island."

A beautiful Samoan woman with an excellent figure, Maria attracted Rip's attention when he first met her. "I like a woman with knockers," he'd told a pilot friend.

He told her that he had trouble pronouncing the name "Koleti' " and decided instead to call her "Sam."

They were married about a year after their first meeting. He had no insurance on her life, only on the old Isuzu pickup truck.

"Rip said insurance was a waste of money," his wife explained.

They rented living quarters for a while and then bought a quarter-acre piece of property in Tafuna for fifteen thousand dollars, paying one thousand a month for the land.

"Rip hired some people to help him build our house. It cost fifteen hundred dollars. He had no money when he came here. We used my personal savings."

It was a pitifully small, one-room shack made of aluminum and plywood that had its bath and toilet facilities located in back, fifty yards from the house. The inside was furnished with a couch and a wooden bed, a refrigerator, and an old television set. They had no stove for cooking.

"We never cook. We eat sandwiches and salmon."

Maria and Rip had a very frugal lifestyle in spite of the more than two thousand dollars a month he made as a pilot and the four hundred Maria brought home as a secretary with the local department of public works. Maria said they were trying to save to build a better house but that a lot of their money went to aid her large family in Western Samoa. Other than playing a round of golf at a nearby course each night, the couple rarely went out and almost never entertained.

Maria said Rip preferred staying at home where he drank a couple of beers a night and read. He enjoyed science fiction and books by Stephen King. "We have all Stephen King's books."

Maria insists that Rip is very mild mannered, incapable of hurting anyone. "I still believe he didn't do it," she says. "I take his word for it. I don't turn my TV on, I don't listen to the radio, I don't listen to people because I'm afraid they'll say something bad about Rip."

She said that about all she knew of his past was that he had grown up on a Florida farm and that his parents were both dead. "He never talked about his past."

But he was not so secretive about his fabricated life with other acquaintances, giving them variations on the old theme of wealthy physician parents, a gun- (or on occasion, a rum-) running ancestor, a stint as a teacher (sometimes a physics teacher in high school, sometimes in college, and sometimes in Central America). He continued telling his tale of having served in the Marine Corps in Vietnam and having been wounded (sometimes by a grenade, sometimes by a rocket, and sometimes by a land mine) and blinded in the war. His stories were invariably accepted, with a few minor exceptions.

Kevin Kahauolupua, a copilot with Samoa Air, says that there were a few times when he had questioned Rip's veracity. "Every once in a while I would have my doubts because he'd come up with some amazing stories. But I never did catch him in an out-and-out lie. I liked him a lot."

Carl Trinkle, another airline employee, considered Rip a "model citizen" who flew to the islands in the middle of the night to help those injured in the storms. Trinkle points to the many good things he claims Rip did in helping young pilots get a start in aviation.

"These kids—their careers are off the ground because of him; they're now candidates for the major airlines because of Rip."

Sarei Schwenke, a neighbor, found Rip to be a kind, considerate neighbor. "I like the man because he's good to my parents and my children," she says. "He comes and cleans all my lower windows."

Rip had brought Maria's brother-in-law, John Harrison, to the island when Harrison was in Hawaii, looking for work.

"I answered an ad for a mechanic with Hawaiian Airlines but failed the physical exam—bad back. I talked to Rip on the phone a couple of times and he sent me a ticket to Pago Pago."

Rip, then general manager for Manu'a Air, hired him and paid for half the cost of shipping his household goods to Samoa.

Pisita, Maria's sister and John Harrison's wife, claimed that Rip would get Maria "everything she wanted. She's happy, and I like him a lot."

On January 9, 1989, after several days of stormy weather that grounded the flights to Hawaii, a brief hearing took place before the territorial court, where Davis announced that he was willingly returning to the United States to prove his innocence. Then Davis, in handcuffs, was placed aboard a Hawaiian Air jet. Seated in the last row and accompanied by FBI agent Robert Heafner, Davis bid goodbye to a half dozen airport workers. John Harrison was one of those coming aboard to say his farewells.

"He told me to take care of things here until he could straighten out the matter in the states. He thanked me. He had tears in his eyes."

Earlier Maria Koleti' had been allowed a five-minute visit with her husband at the jail. He told her not to follow him to Michigan, but to stay in Samoa and to keep her job.

"He doesn't want me to go to America because people will never leave me alone," Maria says. "I'm going to stay here and wait for him to come back, no matter how long it takes. I know he will come back for me. When he gets back he will tell me all."

With his friends waving tearfully, Rip's plane lifted off and headed for Hawaii.

After more than eight years, David Richard Davis was returning to Michigan and David Myer Bell was gone forever. Rip was no more.

34

Ceil Mohr saw the newspaper and television photos of David, handcuffed, arriving in Honolulu. Bearded and bloated—he now weighed in excess of 240 pounds. He was wearing a bright Hawaiian print shirt and grinning as if he thought it all a monstrous joke.

"I'm not guilty of anything I'm charged with," he told reporters as he was hustled through the airport terminal. "I'm going back to Michigan as soon as possible. I want to get it resolved."

He still thinks he can fool people, Ceil thought. *He thinks everybody is stupid and he can talk his way out of anything.* She despised her former son-in-law. She wished she could reach out and slap the grin from his piggish face. "You rotten bastard," she muttered in a deep, trembling voice.

The news media was once again in a feeding frenzy, hammering on the door, asking for interviews, wanting to film the couple yet another time.

Bob and Ceil sat together on the couch and politely answered the insistent questions.

"I'm elated, I'm elated. I want that son-of-a-bitch locked up so bad," Ceil said. "I've waited eight years for that and I hope he's suffering right now."

"There were many times we felt like giving up hope," Bob responded. "But we knew that someday the right lead would come through. We just hoped it would be in our lifetime."

"We just can't say enough kind words about the

attorney general's office and Don Brooks and Doug Barrett. Don has held us together," Ceil added.

As for Don, who also watched the news reports, his jaw muscles tensing, he wanted desperately to fly to Hawaii to bring Davis back; it had been the one image that had haunted him for more than eight years. Now he wanted it even more. But he knew it was not to be; there were several considerations that ruled out his being allowed to go and get Davis, not the least of which was financial. It was simply cheaper to have the U.S. marshall's office, which maintained a transportation service, bring him back to Michigan.

In Honolulu, a federal magistrate, at the request of the FBI, dismissed the fugitive warrant and ordered Davis held until transportation arrangements could be made between the marshalls and the attorney general in Michigan. It would be weeks before Davis would arrive in Michigan. It was time Mark Blumer would find extremely valuable.

Davis had waived extradition. This allowed the ponderous legal apparatus to crunch into gear and begin its laborious business.

Once the accused was back in Michigan there would be a formal arraignment during which the state would make its charge against Davis and he would respond with his plea. The court would then decide whether there was sufficient cause to bind the defendant over and to schedule a more detailed examination to determine if there was probable cause to believe that a crime had been committed and that Davis was likely to have committed it.

In the "preliminary examination," the state would be responsible for supplying enough of the evidence it had collected and introducing some of the witnesses it would wish to have testify—if a trial were ordered—to convince the court that a trial on the charges should be held. The process would take months and delays and postponements were inevitable.

But, to begin with, Mark had to be prepared for a

battle with Davis's defense attorney—whoever that might turn out to be—over the introduction of the scientific evidence developed by Robert Forney. Proving that Shannon had been murdered by the use of succinylcholine was crucial to the state's case and the defense would certainly attempt to have it excluded in a "Frye hearing."

Next, Mark had to construct a pattern of behavior by Davis that would demonstrate that he had meticulously planned and plotted Shannon's death.

Using the fruits of Don Brooks's investigation of Davis, Mark drew up a chart establishing the series of romantic alliances Davis had with Kay Kendall, Barbara Matthews, and Shannon Mohr, detailing when he had first encountered the women, illustrating how long the affairs had each lasted, and showing when he had abandoned one for the next.

It became immediately apparent to Mark that Davis would meet a woman, and very soon thereafter would propose marriage. When he was turned down he quickly dropped that woman and began a search for the next. The pattern was obvious. Davis was looking for a woman who would marry him—someone he could insure and then murder. Kay and Barbara had wisely spurned his marriage proposals and had lived. Shannon had accepted and had died. Davis's plan was to murder his wife; it really didn't matter to Davis who she might be.

As Mark looked at the six-foot-long chart he'd had drawn up that, in graph form, traced Davis's activities since the 1970s, something caught his eye. It was the notation indicating when Davis had obtained a Florida driver's license under the name David Myer Bell. Mark was stunned.

"Look at that," he almost shouted to members of his staff seated in his office. "He got the phony driver's license just a couple weeks before he proposed to Kay Kendall. He was already planning a getaway!"

Doug Barrett smiled. "We wondered how long it would take you to notice that," he said.

Everything fell neatly in place for the young assistant attorney general; his opening remarks to the jury were already beginning to form in his mind.

Davis had sufficient knowledge about poisons, he knew about the effects of muscle relaxants, he knew about succinylcholine, he had several vials of the drug in his refrigerator along with the needles and syringes to inject the compound, he had a large life insurance policy on Shannon's life, and he had the occasion to use the drug on his wife. He had motive and opportunity. His wife had died under questionable circumstances and an autopsy had eventually proved that succinylcholine was present in her body. There was no other explanation for the drug being there except that Davis had injected it into her during their ride in the woods. But how did he accomplish it?

A routine interview with Tom Davis, one of David's Michigan friends, provided an important link in the chain of events occurring on July 23, 1980, that helped to explain exactly how and why Davis and Shannon were in the woods at the back of their farm.

"David told me that his sex life with Shannon was terrific," Tom had said. "He mentioned that they made love in all kinds of places; once they even made love out on their front lawn."

Recalling the untied tennis shoes found in the woods, Shannon's unbuttoned blouse, and the evidence of horses having been tethered in the small clearing near the rock on which Shannon supposedly hit her head, Mark believed he understood exactly what had taken place that evening. He knew he had a case he could successfully prosecute.

35

On February 1, 1989, U.S. marshalls delivered David Davis to the Federal Building in Lansing. There to meet him were Doug Barrett and Donald Brooks.

"We'd had about twenty minutes warning that the marshalls were bringing him from the airport," Brooks recalled. "It was a tense time while we waited for them to arrive, and when the car drove up and I saw him through the window, it became very emotional for me. Here was the son-of-a-bitch I had been hunting for more than eight years, and I found myself looking at him like he was a son I had never expected to see again; like a father seeing his son come back from Vietnam. I had to turn around and walk away until I could compose myself."

Don wanted to interview Davis, and Davis readily agreed. They spent an hour together, with Doug Barrett seated in the room with them.

"We chatted about what he'd been doing all this time," Brooks says. "But he never gave me anything more than bullshit statements, like 'I can't believe this is happening. I didn't kill Shannon, I loved her,' and 'The Mohrs were harassing me and I became afraid I'd be accused of Shannon's death, so I just ran.' "

When Brooks asked pointed questions of Davis, he would respond, "I don't think I should answer at this point."

Don rode in the state police car with Davis when he was transported to the Hillsdale County jail, where he would stay until his trial was over. But again Davis had nothing important to say and their conversation became forced, finally dropping into silence.

He was housed in a maximum-security cell that was monitored on TV.

"Mr. Davis is in a cell by himself," Sheriff Gerald Hicks told the press later. "He is being treated like any other person who has been arrested for such an offense."

The sheriff said that Davis was allowed library privileges and read a good deal, but he wouldn't reveal what Davis was reading. He also said that Davis was not allowed to watch television. He added that the prisoner had visitation privileges.

On February 2, 1989, with a cold driving sleet pelting the large group of newspeople gathered on the sidewalk in front of the district court annex, across the street from the Hillsdale County Courthouse, Davis, dressed in drab green jail coveralls, was escorted by sheriff's deputies inside. He ignored the shouted questions: "Did you kill her?" "Can you get a fair trial here?"

Fifty reporters and the curious crowded into the small courtroom of district court judge Donald Sanderson.

During the ten-minute arraignment, charging that "on July 23, 1980, he did kill and murder his wife Shannon Mohr Davis," he allowed as how he couldn't afford legal representation in spite of the three thousand dollar a month salary he had earned during his years in American Samoa, and asked for a court-appointed attorney. "How do you account for the money you were making?" Judge Sanderson wanted to know.

"My wife has a large family and we were making payments on a pickup truck."

Sanderson appointed Terry Trott, a Hillsdale attorney, to act as Davis's attorney. But Trott disqualified himself on the grounds that he and his partner, Jim Whitehouse, had done legal work in the past for Dick

Britton, who would be a material witness in Davis's trial.

David Grassi, thirty-one, of Hillsdale was called in and agreed to act on Davis's behalf. In exchange for his services, Hillsdale County would reimburse him $1,525 a month, plus $100 a day if the trial lasted longer than two days.

Judge Sanderson ordered that Davis be held without bond and set February 14, at 9:30 A.M., as the date of the preliminary hearing. The date would be changed.

Just before Davis was ushered out of the courtroom, the judge asked him if he had anything to say.

"No, sir," he replied softly.

Seated in the audience, glaring at him as he was led away, were Bob and Lucille Mohr. Davis seemed to consciously avoid making eye contact with his former in-laws.

The preliminary hearing was held on February 28, in the same crowded courtroom, with Judge Sanderson again presiding.

At the defendant's counsel table, in addition to Davis, again dressed in coveralls and still unshaven, was David Grassi, his court-appointed attorney, and two other men who were introduced to the court as Thomas Bleakley, forty-nine, of the Detroit law firm of Bleakley and McKeen, and his associate, thirty-eight-year-old John Skrzynski.

Bleakley, an expert on pharmacology and biochemistry, had tried many medical malpractice and product liability cases, but had never defended in a murder trial. Skrzynski was a former prosecutor in Oakland County, Michigan.

Tall and thin with flowing dark brown hair and a neatly trimmed beard that ran closely cropped along his jaw line, and a fluid moustache that he stroked frequently, Skrzynski had cold, piercing eyes and a thin mouth that never—in court, at least—arced in a warm, pleasant grin. The press quickly dubbed him "the assassin" and "the pit bull."

While Skrzynski slashed at prosecution witnesses, Bleakley, graying and dignified, looking more like a Methodist preacher than a lawyer, tended to be gentle, almost courtly when examining those testifying for the other side, often smiling through clenched teeth while attempting to get the answer he wanted.

The Detroit lawyers came into the case, they told reporters later, at the request of Grassi, a friend of Bleakley.

"We are volunteering our services," Skrzynski said.

Grassi, shorter than the other two and appearing a bit more portly, had an unpretentious, almost docile expression that gave the impression that he was somewhat uncertain about what he should be doing and really wished to be somewhere else. It became apparent before too long, however, that he knew exactly what he was doing. But the impression that he wanted to be elsewhere persisted.

Mark Blumer, exuding confidence, paraded more than a half-dozen witnesses before the court establishing that Davis had taken out a large insurance policy on Shannon's life shortly after their marriage; that he had denied it to Bob Mohr and to a sheriff's deputy; that he had scratches on his face at the hospital where Shannon was pronounced dead and later at the funeral home. Blumer's witnesses also testified that a drug was found in Shannon's body that later turned out to be succinylcholine chloride, the powerful muscle relaxant that had been thought to be untraceable.

It was enough for Judge Sanderson. He bound Davis over to the Hillsdale circuit court.

The defense petitioned for a Frye-Davis hearing to settle the question of the validity of the scientific evidence the prosecution intended to introduce.

The process dragged on through the spring and summer with hearings conducted before circuit court judge Harvey Moes, a sometimes contrary jurist who brooked no nonsense from lawyers practicing in his courtroom.

In addition to Bob Forney, Blumer introduced several other witnesses for the prosecution: Dr. James Garriott, the chief toxicologist in the office of the medical examiner of Bexar County, Texas; Emmett Braselton, a toxicologist with Michigan State University; and Bert La Du, professor of pharmacology in the University of Michigan medical school.

The three expert witnesses testified that Forney's technique for extracting succinylcholine from human tissue was widely accepted in the field, was "state of the art" and, that there was "no better or any other method with the sensitivity of this test."

The defense was able to marshall but two witnesses in an attempt to refute the validity of the test. They were Dr. Nancy Lord, M.D., who, in a deposition, testified that a survey she conducted had failed to find acceptance of the Forney test among other scientists; and Roger Wabeke, an environmental toxicologist, who claimed that Forney's test had not been independently verified.

Moes ruled that the test met the necessary criteria for admissibility and the results of the tests on Shannon's tissue would be allowed in.

His rationale in allowing the test was not made public to avoid the possibility of bias in the trial. In his rationale, Moes stated that "scientists, although small in number, have accepted the method." He also held that Dr. Lord's testimony, "is of less than any value. Her survey was rank hearsay."

The judge found that Mr. Wabeke, "even though well-intentioned, has absolutely no expertise in the area with which this court is concerned."

The trial of David Davis for the first-degree murder of his wife Shannon could now go forward.

36

The Hillsdale County Courthouse sits on a tree-lined square in the center of town surrounded by small shops and a couple of restaurants. In summer, colorful flowers surround the well-kept lawn. The ninety-two-year-old yellow stone building towers above the two-story buildings circling it.

Inside, a wide stone-tiled lobby occupies most of the first floor, with court offices fronting on two sides. A wide staircase, rising to the second floor, dominates one of the other sides, its well-polished banisters and treads worn by nearly a century of footsteps. A circular balcony rings the center, overlooking the main level.

To one side, double doors with frosted glass open onto the lone courtroom, a high-ceilinged vault with a tiered spectator area rising up perhaps a dozen rows accommodating two hundred people. A waist-high wooden barrier separates the audience from the tall, imposing judge's bench, the attorney's tables, witness and jury boxes. It is a picturesque old courtroom, in a picturesque old courthouse, in an picturesque old town. It looks like a plaster-covered structure that might have once occupied the backlots of movie studios in Hollywood.

Into this quaint setting, on the cold, raw morning of November 28, 1989, came the principals in a drama that had stretched over nearly a decade. They were there to decide the fate of a forty-four-year-old man accused of the cold-blooded murder of his young wife.

Packed into the courtroom were more than a hundred prospective jurors—the first segment of 225 notified to be available to serve—who were summoned to determine upon whose shoulders would rest the responsibility for determining the guilt or innocence of the accused.

Also, pushing and shoving into the courtroom, scrambling for unoccupied seats—preferably in the front row—were more than a dozen members of the press, representing newspapers in Detroit, Lansing, Jackson, Toledo, and Hillsdale, as well as the Associated Press and United Press International.

Television and radio stations had personnel present from Detroit, Toledo, Jackson, Kalamazoo, and Lansing. But their cameras and tape recorders were excluded from the courtroom during the selection of the jury. After that, under a newly enacted state law, they would be permitted inside, their numbers left to the discretion of the judge.

Mark Blumer, accompanied by Doug Barrett and Don Brooks, carrying boxes of exhibits, arrived and took their places at the prosecutor's table. Thomas Bleakley, John Skrzynski, and David Grassi—and a fourth man, who most in the room did not recognize—strode into the courtroom, nodded to Blumer, and then took their places at the defense table.

Everyone's eyes turned to the door at the left front of the courtroom, through which the lead character in the drama about to be played out was expected to enter.

Judge Harvey Moes came in from the door on the opposite side and climbed the bench as the bailiff called for everyone to rise, announcing that the court was now in session.

There was a low muttering as many looked quizzically at one another and wondered when they would bring in David Davis. The murmur faded as many suddenly recognized the fourth man at the defendant's table.

Dressed in gray slacks and a navy blue blazer, a white shirt and tie, his hair trimmed short, his face clean shaven, sat Davis. A shadow of his former self, he looked ten to fifteen years older and had lost—it would be stated later—seventy pounds in the ten months since his arraignment.

Before the trial opened, the judge and the attorneys estimated that the full trial would continue for no less than two full weeks and might last as many as three.

But to everyone's surprise, after examining just forty-three prospective jurors, the jury was sworn and seated in two and a half hours. The panel consisted of twelve men and two women. Two alternate jurors would be excused at the conclusion of the trial, prior to the deliberations. Their names would be chosen by a random draw performed by a tall, extremely attractive deputy court clerk named Marney Kast. Among the fourteen was one college graduate—a school teacher—an insurance salesman, two farmers, a housewife, two retirees, a computer salesman, a city employee, a former savings and loan executive, a truck driver, a construction worker, and two factory workers.

Blumer was delighted with the panel. "I don't like an overeducated jury; they tend to try and second guess your witnesses. I was certain that Bob Forney would be able to explain the complexities of his technique to these people and have them understand it."

After a short address to the jury by Judge Moes, explaining what their duties would be and admonishing them not discuss the case among themselves or with anyone else, not to read newspaper accounts dealing with the case or listen to radio or television reports of the trial, the judge recessed the court until one o'clock in the afternoon. He told the jury to "take your time getting back, enjoy your lunch, do a little shopping if you want."

When the court reconvened, Mark Blumer rose to

give his opening address to the jury, outlining what the state would attempt to prove.

"David Davis knew for a year before he met Shannon that his wife would die a violent death," he began.

Using the large multicolored graph he'd had prepared, he demonstrated to the jury Davis's pattern of looking for a young, professional, and vulnerable woman, dating her for a short time, and then proposing marriage "in a tiny Las Vegas chapel." Blumer showed that when the first woman refused him, he quickly found the next, and when she turned his proposal down, he immediately began looking for another.

He pointed to the fact that Davis had obtained a Florida driver's license using the alias David Myer Bell in 1978, just two weeks before he'd proposed to Kay Kendall.

"He had already created a new identity."

He detailed Davis's pattern of lies: the secret bodyguard assignment; the CIA trips to Japan; the statement to Barbara Matthews, "It may look like I'm married but I'm not."

Next he outlined David's first meeting with Shannon, his marriage to her, and his reappearance at Barbara's home to continue his affair with the pretty schoolteacher after he'd married Shannon.

Slowly, systematically, Blumer narrated the events of July 23, 1980, after Davis had told Matthews that "It's almost over." Mark described to the jury how Davis and Shannon had gone for their usual horseback ride, had stopped for a few minutes at the Brittons', and then had ridden off into the woods. Mark explained how, shortly thereafter, Davis had returned in a seeming panic, telling Britton that Shannon had been "hurt bad."

For nearly an hour, in a soft voice that was almost a monotone, Mark led the fourteen-member panel through the major elements of his case, showing them the marriage license on which Davis had lied about

being previously married, an aerial photograph showing the area around the Davis and the Britton farms
and the wood lot where Shannon died, and a photo—
at ground level—of the clearing in the woods and the
rock on which had been her blood.

When Mark had concluded his opening remarks,
Bleakley rose and approached the jury box.

He began with the story of a nine-year-old boy who
was found by his mother, hurrying away from their
home, carrying a few personal possessions. When
asked where he was going, the boy tearfully replied
that he was running away to live with his grandpar-
ents.

"I can't stay with dad," Bleakley claimed the boy
had replied.

The little boy, Bleakley said, was David Richard
Davis.

Bleakley went on to draw the comparison between
the pain Davis's father had caused him, prompting him
to run away in 1947, and the "anger and hostility" he
experienced from the Mohrs, which caused him to run
away in 1981. "His habit and tradition was to run
away," Bleakley said.

He told the jury that the death of Davis's wife was
the "most painful thing that ever occurred to him in
his life."

Dealing with his client's many amorous liaisons, the
suave lawyer suggested that Davis could be convicted
of adultery or of having girlfriends, but not of murder.

Then, using an easel and a large pad of drawing
paper, he inked with a marking pen a list of pieces of
evidence he said had "mysteriously disappeared":
photos of the scene in the woods taken by both Dick
Britton and the sheriff's deputy, the clothing Shannon
had been wearing that evening, the photos of the first
autopsy, all were missing.

He suggested that the state's case was built on un-
supportable conjecture that would become totally
transparent as the trial went on.

The opening arguments were concluded at 2:39 P.M. The People called their first witness, Shannon's mother, Lucille Mohr.

Blumer began his direct examination by asking Lucille, "Do you see David Davis in the courtroom?"

Ceil glanced around, looked puzzled, and shook her head."No, I don't," she replied. Blumer remained silent as Ceil continued to look at everyone at the two tables. Finally, recognition flashed across her face, her eyes widened in surprise. "Yes, I do see him."

Ceil's reaction would be consistently repeated throughout the trial as witness after witness would fail to recognize Davis at first glance; his appearance had altered to such a degree.

Under Mark's direct examination, Ceil recounted how Shannon had met and then married David, how she had felt that her daughter's marriage had "been made in heaven." She spoke about the evening of July 23, when she had helped her daughter on her horse, remembering that the white tennis shoes she wore—which were later found untied by the deputies—were tied. She also described the scratches she had observed on David's face.

Several days before the trial began, she had said that the two things she feared most about testifying were that she would break down and cry and that she would become angry and swear. She succumbed to one of her fears. Under direct examination by Mark Blumer, she suddenly broke down when describing the phone call summoning her and Bob to the hospital where Shannon died.

Davis glanced only infrequently at Ceil during her time in the witness box. For the most part, he rested his forehead in his hand as he wrote on a yellow legal pad.

Philip Rick, the Prudential Insurance salesman who had sold Davis the $110,000 double-indemnity life insurance policy on Shannon, explained the circumstances under which the policy had been drafted.

Blumer had decided early that he would introduce only the Prudential policy into evidence, reasoning that the jury might consider the other five an attempt by the prosecution at overkill. After all, he concluded, several of the policies were credit life, which almost everyone took out when making a sizable purchase. He believed the one huge policy, which Davis had taken out just days after returning from their honeymoon, would be sufficiently impressive to the jury to prove the prosecution's point of a calculated plan to murder his wife for money.

Dick Britton spent almost three-quarters of an hour repeating the testimony he had given at the grand jury and the preliminary examination.

Both Dick and Ceil had to undergo a more rigorous cross-examination than did Rick, who agreed with Bleakley that the amount of insurance Davis had purchased was not excessive for a farmer.

Bleakley prodded and poked at Ceil's testimony, attempting to have her admit that what she had said this time and what she had testified to at the preliminary exam differed from that given in a February 1981 deposition taken by Davis's first attorney, James Cmejrek.

"That man [Cmejrek] had me just as messed up as I am right now," she explained.

In a thirty-minute combative cross-exam by Skrzynski, Dick maintained his composure throughout, insisting that he was only interested in having the truth come out.

Skrzynski hammered at what he considered inconsistencies between what Britton had testified to in previous appearances and what he was saying now.

"Did you feel you had to help the Mohrs prove that David Davis had killed their daughter?" he asked.

"I'm just telling the truth," Britton replied in a soft, almost matter-of-fact voice.

The long first day of trial concluded with Britton's testimony, and the court was recessed at 6:17 P.M.

The second day began at 9:07 A.M. on November 29.

While all witnesses were sequestered prior to their testimony, once they had been excused they were permitted to remain in the courtroom to watch the balance of the trial.

Mark was aware that Ceil wanted to observe the rest of the trial. He knew, too, that there would be testimony that she might find hard to listen to. Bob was not scheduled to take the stand until the very end of the state's case and wouldn't be exposed to the more grizzly aspects of his daughter's death. But if Ceil insisted on hearing all of the testimony, Mark felt that she should hear some of what would be coming out from him—in private.

Before court opened, Mark led Ceil into a small office just outside the courtroom. "With everything we've been able to piece together, from the evidence, and everything people have told us, we believe we know exactly what took place in the woods the day Shannon died," he began. "I know you have some idea of what happened, but the reality is that it may be much worse than what you imagine. Some of it will be coming out today and I thought that perhaps I should tell you about it now, if you really want to know."

Ceil nodded. "I want to know."

"We're certain that David had been making preparations to kill Shannon from the day she agreed to marry him. He was able to obtain some succinylcholine and hypodermic needles. Two of the insurance policies he had on her life were due to run out soon; he knew he had to kill her before that happened. Having come up with the idea of the horseback riding accident at some point earlier that summer, we think he planned to do it sometime during the week before they left on their Florida vacation. But you created problems for him by showing up. Which explains the cool welcome you and Bob received when you arrived.

"Because time was critical now, he decided to go ahead with his plan whether you were there or not. He took the succinylcholine and a syringe out to the woods, probably during that day, hid them in the small clearing he'd found that had a large rock embedded in the ground.

"That evening, when they prepared for their usual ride, he insisted that you stay at the house with the dogs. He did this for two reasons: He couldn't have you along as a witness to what he was going to do, and he didn't want the dogs along either; they were both fond of Shannon and might have attempted to protect her. He didn't allow Dick's son to accompany them back for the same reason he couldn't have you along—there must be no eyewitnesses.

"We know from Tom Davis that David and Shannon had an active sex life, one that had them making love in unusual places, and it's quite likely that he had suggested that, since you were at the farm and they wouldn't have complete privacy, perhaps they should use the opportunity to make love in the quiet of the cool woods.

"When they left Dick Britton's, David vetoed Dick's suggestion that they take the route through the downed electric fence because it wouldn't put them at the spot that led to where he had concealed the drug and needle.

"Once they were in the clearing, out of sight of everyone, they dismounted and Shannon playfully kicked off her shoes and began removing her blouse. David tied up the horses and removed the drug and the syringe from the hiding place. Then, approaching her from the rear, he grabbed her and struck the needle in her right shoulder.

"But he had failed to get the needle to a vein and the poison was injected into the fatty layer between the surface skin and the underlying muscle. The drug didn't work as fast as it was supposed to, which probably surprised and upset him.

"Shannon must have realized what was happening; we're sure she put up a terrific fight for her life because of the bruises and because her feet were very dirty and because of the scratches on his face you saw at the hospital, and because Dick Britton noticed that the weeds around the clearing were matted down.

"Desperate now, David grabbed her by the arms and threw her down. We know this by the fingerprint bruising on both her arms. By now, the first injection was beginning to have some effect, she was growing weak and could no longer struggle with the same energy. He then gave her a second injection, this time in a vein in her right wrist. The drug took effect almost immediately, paralyzing every muscle. She was probably conscious, able to see and hear what was going on, understanding what was happening to her but unable to do a thing to prevent it.

"David, an extremely powerful man, then smashed her head against the rock with a tremendous blow. He waited, making sure she was dead before dragging her body out to the field and then riding back to the Britton farm."

There was a long silence as Ceil swallowed hard, choking back a flood of tears.

"Thank you, Mark," she said finally, her voice strained. "No one has ever explained to me exactly what happened. I wanted to know . . . I had to know."

Mark had tried to protect Ceil from hearing in court what had happened to her daughter, but his good intentions were unnecessary. As he walked into the courtroom, he was informed by Doug Barrett that Bleakley was asking the judge to keep Ceil out because he might want to recall her as a witness when the defense put on its case. Mark was furious. He believed that Bleakley was deliberately trying to keep Ceil out to prevent the jury from being influenced by her presence. It was not a unique ploy.

Ceil entered the courtroom assuming she would be allowed to observe the remainder of the trial.

"I'm sorry," Mark said, as he led her back into the

hall, telling her what he'd just learned. "If this is just a stunt to keep you out of the courtroom, I'm going to blow my top."

Joy Earl, Mary Emma Merillat, and Melanie Wheeler, nurses, and Kenneth Arnold, a physician's assistant, all personnel at Thorn Hospital, testified as to Shannon's condition at the time she was brought in. Their consensus was that Shannon had been dead on arrival—her pupils were fixed and dilated and unresponsive, that there was no heartbeat, no blood pressure, no respiration, and the E.K.G. monitor traced a flat line.

In his cross-examination of charge nurse Merillat, Skrzynski sparked Judge Moes's wrath for the first time in the trial. When the defense attorney persisted in thrusting his face in that of the witness and pointing his finger, Moes interrupted.

"Get back away from the witness," he ordered. "We'll have no dramatics." This would not be the only time in the trial that Judge Moes would reprimand the young attorney.

The defense attempted to suggest for the benefit of the jury that succinylcholine might have gotten into Shannon's body at the hospital, and that the emergency room personnel failed to use appropriate cardiopulmonary resuscitation methods.

Hillsdale County sheriff's deputy Roger Boardman detailed his visit to the hospital the night of July 23, 1980, and his visit the following day to the scene of the "accident."

Deputy Charles Gutowski followed with his account of the visit to the wood lot.

Dr. Harry Dickman was next, explaining that Shannon had obviously expired prior to her arrival at the hospital and that there was nothing medical science could have done to save her life. He also described Davis's behavior, which he found disgusting. It was the doctor's opinion that night, he said, that the patient may have broken her neck in the fall.

Tom Davis took the stand to say that he had recommended the breed of horse Shannon had ridden the night of her death because of its innate gentleness.

Under cross-examination by Skrzynski, Tom admitted that Shannon had fallen from her horse on at least one previous occasion.

Regina Davis, Tom's wife, testified about the scratches she observed on David's face the night after Shannon's death. She also recounted Davis's claim that he couldn't pay the funeral expenses because he had no insurance on Shannon.

Representatives from funeral homes in Hudson, Michigan, and Toledo, Ohio, gave information concerning the handling and disposition of Shannon's body. One of the representatives, Roberta Scherting, a relative of the Mohrs, testified about the scratches on David's face and about his claim that he had no insurance on Shannon.

Drs. Steven and Renata Fazekas, Lucas County, Ohio, deputy coroners, took the stand to describe their findings in the first autopsy. And Robert Keller, of the Lucas County coroner's office, stated that Shannon's internal organs were accidentally placed in a bath of formaldehyde for approximately ninety minutes, an admission the defense used to suggest that the preservative might have caused the mystery peak on the chromatograph.

The third day of the trial brought the two witnesses who followers of the case had waited to hear—Thomas Carroll and Dr. Robert Forney, Jr. It was the belief of many that the scientists' testimony would be pivotal in the trial. If what they said was believed by the jury, Davis would be found guilty. If it was not believed or, as they felt was more likely, not understood, Davis stood a good chance at exoneration.

Carroll carefully outlined the procedures he had followed in testing the tissue samples taken from Shannon's body following the request by Renata Fazekas to conduct a drug-toxicology screen after Lucille's visit with the pathologists. In an easygoing, unassuming narrative, he dealt with the technical aspects of chemical testing for drugs and the puzzling results he had obtained, only occasionally lapsing into incomprehensible scientific jargon.

Bleakley did minimal damage on cross-examination, managing to do little more than bring out the fact that Carroll was not licensed to practice medicine.

Bob Forney's stay on the stand would be longer and more comprehensive than was his colleague's. Forney appeared at ease and comfortable on the stand, with a conversational style and demeanor that reminded many observers of actor-comedian Chevy Chase. He used a number of color slides and simple metaphors to illustrate his testimony, introducing the jury to the abstract world of toxicology, pharmacology, chemistry, and molecular science.

Just as Mark Blumer thought they would, the jury remained attentive, interested, and apparently comprehending throughout the difficult two and a half hour presentation.

Bleakley spent the next fifty minutes attacking Forney's technique, attempting, largely without impact on the jury, to have him admit that his methods were unproven and that other techniques had been available for the detection of succinylcholine prior to Forney's newly developed test.

At one point, the adroit lawyer seemed to be trying to lead the toxicologist into a trap, endeavoring to have Forney admit that one of his principal interests in the Davis case was the prospect of enriching himself.

"Is it true you received almost $9,000 from the attorney general for going to Sweden and carrying the materials over there?" Bleakley asked.

"No. It was entirely paid in travel. I—in terms of cash, I did not," Forney replied.

"The total was almost $9,000?"

"Tickets bought and given to me."

"The total was almost $9,000?" Bleakley persisted.

"I would have thought it was a little higher than that."

Several jurors smiled at Forney's candor.

"What would be your best estimate as to the amount of money that the attorney general of the state of Michigan has given for the purpose of you conducting these tests?"

"Well, the travel reimbursement, I believe the tickets for both trips and the hotel rooms, and so forth. I thought it was closer to $13,000, but I—again, it's been a long time since I've—"

Bleakley, who was scoring no points with this line, interrupted with a new tack.

"And isn't it true that you have personally made money yourself off of this by testifying at a probate hearing, and to the tune of $1,500?"

"Yes."

"At one hundred dollars an hour?"

"That's correct."

"One hundred dollars an hour, in your opinion, would be a usual and customary and justifiable fee for the kind of work you've done?" Bleakley inquired, with just a hint of pompous indignation.

"Well," Forney responded, "my fee now is $125 an hour, so—and I think maybe $150 is more what I'd like, but you have to find somebody who is willing to pay it." Looking straight at Bleakley with an amused gleam in his eyes, he added. "I'm sure *you* understand that."

The courtroom exploded with laughter. Bleakley, realizing he'd been had, reddened and with his hands stretched at his side in an apologetic gesture, grinned broadly and responded, "What can I say?"

For all practical purposes the defense had lost its best opportunity to create serious doubt as to the validity of Forney's test.

After a few more questions, Robert Forney was excused with the thanks of the court, and Mark Blumer breathed a huge sigh of relief. His decision to select jurors with modest educational backgrounds had been affirmed.

Dr. Peter Goldblatt, a board-certified anatomic pathologist, described the specimens that were taken during the second exhumation of Shannon's body. Dr. James Harris, a board-certified neuropathologist, who testified that he had examined twenty-five hundred to three thousand human brains, claimed that the small contra coupe hemorrhage in the right frontal lobe of Shannon's brain was not sufficiently serious to have caused her death. Dr. Robert Hendrix, a forensic pathologist and professor at the University of Michigan medical school, agreed with Dr. Harris. Using color slides of Shannon's brain, he pointed to the small hemorrhage on the right frontal lobe, explaining that the actual damage was minimal and narrowly confined. He stated further that even when death occurred as a result of such head injuries, the patient frequently regained consciousness and usually lived for extended periods before the onset of severe symptoms culminating in death.

Don Brooks was called to testify about his involvement in the case, as well as his discovery that succinylcholine was a powerful drug that could kill without leaving a trace and that Davis may have had access to the drug. Brooks told the jury how, posing as a high school chemistry teacher, he'd been able to acquire a large quantity of the drug.

On cross-examination, Skrzynski suggested that Brooks had perpetrated a fraud, had lied by posing as a teacher in order to get succinylcholine.

"It was my intention to demonstrate how easy it was to get the chemical," Brooks replied.

The defense attorney also charged Brooks with having decided on Davis's guilt at the outset and having taken steps to support his bias. Brooks denied the charge.

He also denied Skrzynski's accusation that he had felt obligated, because of his close personal friendship with the Mohrs, to help them prove that Davis had murdered their daughter.

The prosecution was winding down. Mark had orchestrated his case well, neatly separating it into three basic movements. He had given the jury a full understanding of Shannon's death and the circumstances surrounding it; he had acquainted them with the medical and scientific aspects of her death and of the discovery of a method of extracting succinylcholine intact from human tissue, that everyone had believed could not be done; and he had shown that the drug had been found in high concentrations in the tissue of Shannon's body. Now he was about to probe into the character and the morals of the accused to demonstrate that Davis was sufficiently evil to have committed the crime with which he was charged.

Tori Abrams told the jury how she had seen medicine vials and hypodermic syringes in Davis's refrigerator. She explained how she had seen an article in a medical journal at the Mohrs' that was illustrated with photos of various chemicals, one of which was Anectin, the name she remembered seeing on the vials in the refrigerator. She had told her Aunt Lucille, who then notified Don Brooks. She had not understood the importance of her discovery until just prior to her appearance at the trial.

Bob Mohr was next to take the stand, where he was questioned about his son-in-law. He told the court of Davis's last visit to their home, when David said he was heading west, to "the desert." He also testified as to the events at Thorn Hospital on the night of July 23, speaking of Davis's claim to have no insurance at all on Shannon's life.

Cheryl Hogan Nicolaidis recounted the incident at the restaurant, a few days after Shannon's funeral, when Davis had proposed what to Cheryl was an offensive toast to his late wife, and had later accosted her in the parking lot, placing his hands on her buttocks, telling her that she was now the "most beautiful woman in my life."

The last of the prosecution's witnesses were probably of the greatest interest to the spectators who had packed the courtroom throughout the trial. Blumer had brought to the courthouse the three women with whom Davis had affairs since his divorce from Phyllis: Kay Kendall, Barbara Matthews, and Yvonne Munroe. But if any of the audience had expectation of sexually lurid testimony, they were cruelly disappointed.

What the women did disclose was a pattern of deception and outrageous lies by Davis, all of which they had totally accepted.

Kay Kendall told the jury about Davis's claims that he was working for the CIA and making secret trips to Japan, and she told of the newspaper article Davis had shown her that dealt with a muscle relaxant that couldn't be traced, and his statement that this chemical could be used to commit the "perfect crime."

The experience of being a witness was especially humiliating for Barbara Matthews. Now married, she left the stand after testifying to her association with David, her acceptance of his claim that he was not really married, and her trip to Florida following Shannon's death, collapsing into her husband's arms, sobbing uncontrollably.

The final witness for the state was William Ransom, a Hudson, Michigan, barber who had sold Davis a fake moustache and beard during the summer of 1980. The false facial hair was darker than Davis's natural hair, Ransom said, but Davis refused to have a careful color matching, saying that he was buying it as a joke and that it would be good enough for his purpose.

At 10:45 A.M. on December 4—the fifth day of the trial—having introduced the testimony of thirty-six witnesses, the People rested their case. It was now the defense's turn.

The consensus around the courthouse, as the trial

had progressed and the prosecution piled point on point, was that Davis's only hope lay in his taking the stand in his own defense. But, having said that, the amateur lawyers—and a number of professionals—conceded that he probably wouldn't. The danger posed in exposing himself to Mark Blumer's cross-examination was simply too great.

What then was the strategy of the defense to be? Unlike the prosecution, the defense had not released a list of prospective witnesses, although the rumor was that they intended to call about seventeen.

Tom Bleakley called, as the first witness for the defense, Dr. Robert Donald Laird, a clinical pharmacologist who had served on the faculty of Wayne State University of Michigan medical school. The doctor's major contention was that Shannon's death was most likely caused by a fall from a horse—this "expert" forensic testimony from a clinical pharmacologist.

Under cross-examination by Blumer, Laird admitted that he had never attempted to duplicate the Forney Technique.

Bleakley then brought back Roger Wabeke, who Judge Moes had characterized after the Frye-Davis hearing as having "absolutely no expertise in the area with which this court is concerned."

Wabeke claimed that the Forney Technique was fatally flawed because it "does not meet the scientific benchmark of replication."

Wabeke's total direct testimony lasted just five minutes.

Mark had little of importance to ask the defense witness; he had said nothing that materially damaged the case. He quickly waved the pharmacologist aside. He would save his energies for the "big guns" he felt Bleakley had waiting in the wings.

Mark was wrong; the wings were empty.

At 1:33 P.M., just one hour and three minutes after opening their case, Bleakley announced to a shocked and surprised court, "The defense rests."

"Are you ready for summation?" Judge Moes asked Blumer.

Mark was jolted by the brevity of the case for the accused. He jumped to his feet, buttoning his suit coat, and turned to Bleakley, bewilderment evident on his face.

"Frankly, Your Honor, I'm surprised at the sudden end of the defense case."

Bleakley immediately moved for a mistrial, arguing that the assistant attorney general's statement in front of the jury was prejudicial to the defendant's case.

Moes denied the motion, commenting: "To tell you the truth, I was surprised myself."

Bleakley then moved for a directed verdict on the grounds that the people had not proved their case. It is standard procedure to make such a motion. It is rarely granted. Moes denied the motion. Summations would begin the following morning, December 5, 1989.

37

"Ladies and gentlemen, these are the closing arguments of this trial," Mark Blumer began, shortly after nine on the morning of December 5, just six court days after the trial of David Richard Davis had begun.

As had been the case on all the other days, the courtroom was packed; people were standing out in the hall, hoping for a chance to get in later, if and when the high school civics class—the second of two such groups to visit the court during the trial—filed out.

"This is the time when the attorneys will tell you what we think has been proven by the various pieces of evidence and testimony that came into the trial," Blumer continued.

"Now, you will notice that as the case continues to the very end, that I'll have two chances to talk to you and the defendant's attorney will have only one. The reason is, traditionally, and as part of our system of government, the prosecution carries the full burden of proving each and every element that is necessary to make out a case, and because of that, the court recognizes that we have to have the opportunity to have the last say to make sure that all of the points we have to make are driven home."

Blumer interrupted his remarks at this point to thank the jury for their attention and to commend them for their ability to absorb, in barely a week and a half, very technical information that he said had taken him over a year to understand.

He also told them that he was responsible for their presence on the panel.

"You may be wondering why you. If you're wondering . . . why are you here, instead of somebody else . . . it's because I chose you. And I mean that, quite literally, I chose you."

He explained that he looked for jurors with "the God-given common sense to put all of the different pieces of evidence together and see the whole picture.

"I simply want people of community standing, and intelligence, and goodwill, who can listen . . . and see what is happening before their eyes, and understand that once in a while smoke drifts through the courtroom, but when you clear the smoke out of the way, you see exactly what happened in this case . . . and that's what you people all have, and that's why you're here . . . I was satisfied that you had what I was looking for.

"Now, the People have charged David Davis with committing the crime of premeditated, deliberate, first-degree murder on his wife Shannon. We have the burden of proving each and every element of that crime, and the evidence that we have brought into this courtroom has done that."

For the next hour, he systematically summarized the People's case, pointing out that he believed that, even without the toxicology evidence and the testimony of Tom Carroll and Robert Forney, the other elements of the case were sufficient to convict Davis of first-degree murder. He cited the Florida driver's license Davis had obtained using an alias, his excited reaction to the newspaper article about succinylcholine, his university courses in pharmacology, his relationship with two women that quickly cooled when they showed reluctance to marry him, his false statement of no previous marriage on the license he and Shannon took out in Las Vegas, the huge insurance policy on his wife so soon after the wedding, and his repeated lies to friends and neighbors.

He called attention to Davis's lack of remorse at the death of his wife of ten months, recalling the incident in the restaurant and the parking lot outside that had been testified to by Cheryl Hogan Nicolaidis, and his trip to Florida with Barbara Matthews less than a week after Shannon's death.

He then—just as he had with Lucille Mohr—took the jury through the events of the evening of July 23.

Next he discussed the scientific contribution of Bob Forney and the validity of the test he had developed.

In countering the defense's case, he brought up the testimony of Dr. Robert Laird, the pharmacologist.

"I got the impression that you people will understand from listening to his testimony that Dr. Laird was an expert in whatever he was talking about at that moment. He was admitted by the court as an expert in research pharmacology. But that didn't stop him from expressing an opinion about pathology, or about the cause of death."

He then compared Laird's professional credentials with those of Dr. James Harris. "I almost wanted to joke with Dr. Harris that he couldn't hold down a job, because we're talking about a man certified in neuro-pathology, he's certified as a general pathologist, and if that's not enough, ladies and gentlemen, he's also a Ph.D. in neuroanatomy. We're talking about a guy who may be one of the world's experts in the structure of the brain and the nerves that attach to it."

Blumer, as he had during the defense's case, dismissed what Roger Wabeke had to say.

Blumer talked about Davis and how he meticulously planned the murder of his wife. He closed his first summation with, "Ladies and gentlemen, you all heard the phrase, he gets away with murder . . . In the face of this evidence, and this testimony, if you do not find David Davis guilty of murder, first degree, premeditated, deliberate murder, he got away with murder.

"With this evidence here, we have proven to you,

beyond a reasonable doubt, that David Davis committed premeditated first-degree murder on his wife of ten months.''

After a fifty-minute recess, Tom Bleakley rose to have his turn at convincing the jury that his side should prevail.

To make a point he would stress throughout his seventy-minute summation, Bleakley uncovered a large poster that he set up on an easel in front of the jury. The poster—in yellow and black—was a promotional tool used to advertise the movie *Batman*, which was currently setting box office records throughout the country. The poster contained a circle with the Batman symbol inside. It had attracted widespread attention because it was an optical illusion. To some people it was what it was supposed to represent, a stylized bat with outstretched wings. To others it appeared to be an open mouth showing several teeth with wide gaps in between.

Bleakley began by telling the jury that the phrase, ''You'll believe it when you see it,'' had been turned around by the witnesses in the case, that the People's case was based on the presumption, ''When you believe it, you'll see it.'' He would repeat the phrase more than a dozen times during his presentation.

He cautioned the jury that in their deliberations they must strive to be totally fair, that they must ''function from the presumption of innocence,'' that it was the duty of the prosecution to prove, beyond a reasonable doubt, the guilt of the accused. Bleakley claimed that the state had failed to do so.

He challenged Blumer's claim that Davis had been playing mind games throughout most of his adult life, taking a perverted pleasure in being able to deceive others. ''There were mind games played,'' Bleakley said, ''but it was on the mind of some of these witnesses.

''I'm not accusing the fine people of being liars. I believe their thinking process was affected. The mind can play a little trick on you, and that's what some of these witnesses experienced.

''These people are seeing what they want to believe. When you believe it, you'll see it.''

He pointed to the poster and said, ''The power of suggestion is a wonderful thing as long as it has a noble purpose.''

He then went through the list of witnesses for the prosecution, pointing to what he claimed were glaring innaccuracies or inconsistencies in their testimony. He cited Cheryl Hogan's insistance that Davis's toast at the restaurant, two nights after Shannon's funeral, was in bad taste. ''There were two others at the restaurant. They didn't find the toast offensive.''

He said that Lucille Mohr was inconsistent in her testimony; that Dick Britton was inconsistent about the length of time David and Shannon were back in the woods; inconsistent about the shoes and whether they were tied or untied; inconsistent about how often his son Norman had stayed overnight at the Davis's farm.

Bleakley stated that Roberta Scherting had been inconsistent about which side of David's face had the scratches, and pointed out that while Regina Davis testified that she had seen the scratches, her husband Tom said he had not. And the attorney also questioned how Shannon could have caused the scratches if Davis had attacked her from the rear.

He said that Tori Abrams was acting under the ''power of suggestion'' when she claimed to have seen Anectin in Davis's refrigerator. He claimed that Don Brooks had become biased at the outset of his investigation.

The matter of Davis's insistence on having Shannon's body cremated was brought up. Bleakley drew the jury's attention to the fact that Davis did not insist, once the Mohrs had voiced their objection to it. He also reminded the panel that he offered no protest to the possibility of an autopsy being performed on his wife. This was not the act of a guilty man, Bleakley suggested.

Why did not the Fazekases find evidence of suffocation when they performed the first autopsy? Bleakley asked.

He completed his summation by again asking that the jury remember that to convict his client they must find guilt "beyond a reasonable doubt to a moral certainty."

A short, six-minute recess was taken, after which Mark Blumer gave his second summation. He spent the bulk of the forty-eight-minute address rebutting the statements made by Bleakley in his closing argument, accusing the counselor of having neither facts nor law on his side and of merely launching a "long list of attacks" on the state's witnesses.

"Did you get the impression from that closing argument that every single person who testified in this case was wrong about what was testified about, because if you did, then Mr. Bleakley was successful. He wants you to believe that every single person who came into this courtroom either intentionally lied or was misled . . . Do you think thirty-six witnesses were all wrong, and all wrong in the same direction for the same reason?"

Responding to Bleakley's claim that Davis would not have sacrificed his plan to have Shannon's body cremated so easily if he'd been guilty of her murder, Blumer reasoned that to have continued to insist on cremation would surely have created suspicion. As far as his willingness to have an autopsy performed, Blumer stated, "Mr. Davis, don't forget, went to the school of pharmacology. He knew that succinylcholine was believed at the time to be undetectable."

As to the Fazekases' failure to find evidence of suffocation, he stated that it is difficult enough to find such evidence in a fresh body and near to impossible in one that has been buried for nearly a year.

"Mr. Bleakley knows full well when he wonders

why the Fazekases didn't observe the characteristic bluish color of the skin in a person who has suffocated, because in the process of embalming a dye is injected to make the body appear pink and fresh.''

Referring to the defense attorney's "When you believe it, you'll see it" slogan, Blumer attempted to turn it around to use it on his opponent.

"Dr. Forney laughed at the suggestion that it was succinylcholine. Why? Because he knows you can't find succinylcholine in the human body after it did its work. Ladies and gentlemen, they believed they could not find it. So why did they see it? Take Mr. Bleakley at his best, at his word. If you believe it, you'll see it, right? They believed they *wouldn't* see it.

"So why *did* they see it? They saw it because it was unavoidably there. They ran it through the machine and they saw a peak they couldn't figure out, so they spent the next eighteen months of their scientific lives trying to figure out why it was there. They didn't believe it until they saw it.''

After defending the professionalism of the medical personnel at Thorn Hospital who, Blumer insisted, had done everything humanly possible to bring Shannon back to life, the assistant attorney general concluded his summation with:

"There is no question in this case that David Davis carried out a nearly perfect plan of premeditated, deliberate murder by poisoning his wife with a very subtle, very exotic chemical that caused her to die a rather horrible death. Because the drug did not kill any pain, it did not put her to sleep, it didn't alter her mind. It simply paralyzed her so she couldn't fight for her life. She couldn't even scream for help after the drug took effect. Imagine that, when you think about fairness. You want fairness, ladies and gentlemen? It's not fair that Shannon Davis isn't here today. I ask you to go back in the jury room, consider the evidence we have presented, and in light of this overwhelming evidence

I ask you to find that David Davis is guilty as charged of first-degree murder.''

Their part was over, these lawyers. They had no further control over what was to happen in the balance of these proceedings.

Judge Moes recessed for lunch, telling the jury to, ''without breaking a leg and trying to get back here in an hour, let's try to get back at about quarter to two. If you're in the middle of a sandwich, finish it. If you hit a store, and are in the middle of buying a present, buy it.''

When court resumed just before two-thirty, Moes began his charge to the jury, instructing them that ''sympathy or prejudice must not influence you in this case. Your duty is to determine the facts and you alone can determine what the facts are.''

He cautioned them that, because the accused is presumed to be innocent, he is not required to testify in his own behalf and that no weight was to be given his failure to take the stand.

He explained that they could make one of three findings: that Davis was guilty of first-degree murder, that he was guilty of murder in the second degree, or that he was not guilty.

At the judge's direction, deputy court clerk Marney Kast drew two names from a box on her desk. They were names of the two who were to be excused. Both were men—Randy Sanders and Donald Holmes. The jury now consisted of ten men and two women.

At 2:55 P.M., the panel was led out of the courtroom door, across the second-floor lobby, and down a narrow hall to the jury room. Two sheriff's deputies stood guard outside.

The judge explained that if the jury was unable to reach a verdict by six or seven that evening, they would be taken out to dinner and could then return for further deliberations. If a verdict was not reached by ten or eleven that night, they would be released and allowed to return home for the night and to resume their consideration the following day.

There were no bet takers among the spectators as to how long they would be out, but several reporters scurried away to find motel accommodations in the event that no decision was reached that night. So uncertain were the journalists in the crowd as to when the jury would return, that one half-hearted attempt to get a pool going to wager on how long they would be out—a traditional practice among newspeople at murder trials—found no takers.

There wasn't much doubt, however, as to what the verdict—when it was finally reached—would be.

Lucille Mohr, sitting in the lobby, nervously chain-smoking, would be allowed in the courtroom when the jury returned. She looked nervous and uncertain, her face pale and expressionless.

"Watch the jury when they come in; if they don't look at David, then it's guilty," someone told her, whispering the old wives tale that was rarely true.

At 4:43, less than two hours after the jury began its deliberations, there was a sudden flurry outside the courtroom as deputy Dale Schulte, acting as court bailiff, answered a knock from inside the jury room and was handed a note for Judge Moes.

After a hasty conference with the opposing attorneys, the judge announced that the jury was being brought back in.

Once back in their seats, Moes explained to the audience that the panel had requested to have read back the testimony of Dr. Peter Goldblatt, the anatomic pathologist who had examined the tissue specimens taken during the second exhumation, and also that of Dr. Robert Forney.

Judge Moes explained to the jurors that the court reporter, and the stenographic notes of the testimony they requested, were in Kalamazoo, some seventy miles distant. It would be a couple of hours before the reporter and the notes could be brought to Hillsdale.

Dr. Goldblatt's testimony took twenty-four minutes to give and Dr. Forney was on the stand for two hours and twenty minutes; it would take at least that much time to read back the testimony.

When the jury indicated that it wanted the testimony typed up to take back into the jury room with them, Moes advised them that it might take as much as a week to have a transcript of that portion of the trial prepared. Although this was not articulated to the jury, such a lengthy delay would pose extreme problems for the court—maintaining the purity of the jury; keeping them uninfluenced by publicity and possible intrusion of opinion by family, friends, and neighbors; avoiding the threat of tainting their deliberations.

The judge asked the jury to return to the jury room and decide whether they truely wished to have the printed transcript to use in their deliberations or just have it read to them in open court.

Mark Blumer huddled with Doug Barrett, Don Brooks, and the head of the attorney general's criminal division, Bob Ianni, who had come to Hillsdale to witness the closing argument. Blumer recalled that he was confident that he had done a good job, but was nonetheless more nervous about the outcome than he would normally be.

"For a long time, as I grew much closer to the Mohrs, I had been haunted by the thought, What if I lose? What would I say to these incredibly nice people who depended on me?"

Blumer, like Don Brooks, had fallen under the charming spell of Bob and Lucille. Mark's wife Susan said later that she somewhat resented Lucille. "I wished that I could make pea soup as good as she can," she said.

Pea soup was one of Mark's great favorites. "After tasting her soup the first time, I told Lucille, 'If my mother dies, you've got the job,' " Mark joked.

At five o'clock, another message was delivered to Judge Moes. The jury wouldn't need to read or hear the testimony they had earlier requested; they'd reached a verdict.

Lucille and Bob sat in the second row of the spectator's section. As the panel filed slowly back into the courtroom, Ceil watched their faces. A few glanced at Davis, a few glanced at her and Bob, but most kept their eyes diverted to the floor. She felt a sudden chill. "Please God," she prayed, "they aren't going to let him go." Then, as the next-to-last juror passed her, he glanced into her eyes—and smiled, ever so slightly.

Davis sat stoically at the defense table, as he had throughout the trial. But now he looked ashen, his jaw muscles clenched and relaxed rhythmically, with not even a hint of the cynical half-smile he wore much of the time. Bleakley's right hand rested on Davis's shoulder, as if he were trying to impart some additional strength to help his client face what was about to come.

There was activity near the judge's bench as the jury took their seats, and there was some residual murmuring throughout the courtroom, waiting for the bailiff to call the court to order. But Moes didn't wait, he abruptly announced, "The jury has arrived at a verdict, *murder one.*"

It came so suddenly and unexpectedly that for a second there was a stunned silence in the huge room before loud cheers and squeals of delight erupted from the audience, effectively drowning out the exclamations that burst from the throats of Bob and Lucille.

"Oh, God," Bob uttered, tears of relief flooding his cheeks. Ceil's response was quite a bit more direct. "Now, I hope they lock that godamsonofabitch in a cage for the rest of his life."

Jane Schenck, a lifelong friend, embraced Ceil, her face distorted and swamped with her tears.

The judge polled the jury. "Was that and is that your verdict?" It was, and they were allowed to leave the courtroom, Moes ordering no one else to leave until the jury had made its exit.

Television cameras focused on the Mohrs, Blumer, and the two state police detectives, on Davis and his defense team, looking glum and funereal as deputies reattached the handcuffs and leg irons Davis was forced to wear coming and going between the court and the county jail, and on Richard Britton, who was wiping away his own tears. Reporters shouted questions at anyone who could be found who had the slightest role in the nine-year-plus drama that was now grinding down.

"I made up my mind he would pay for my daughter's death," Ceil told a group of reporters crowded around her. "This gives me a little sense of peace. The thing that's hit me is it doesn't bring her back."

"That was a nice girl that died in those woods," Britton told the journalists who had sought his reaction to the verdict. "She didn't deserve that."

It was quite dark as Bob and Lucille drove back to Toledo. They felt weak and drained. The long wait had finally ended and there was a bittersweet residue that lingered. The revenge was almost complete, but it didn't bring the full elation that they had hoped would accompany the much-prayed-for word, "Guilty."

As on another late-night ride through the same rural areas more than nine years earlier, neither had much to say.

38

On Tuesday, January 16, the participants in the earlier trial—attorneys, defendant, Bob and Lucille and their supporters, and, of course, the press—gathered again in the old courtroom in Hillsdale. They had come to be present at the formal sentencing of David Davis. Davis, clad in the prison green coveralls over a blue sweat shirt, bound in ankle chains, sat expressionless.

During the weeks between the verdict and today, a presentencing report had been prepared. It was a mere formality since, under Michigan law, conviction of first-degree murder carried an automatic mandatory sentence of life in prison without possibility of parole.

However, the contents of the report could be a factor in the subsequent appeals Davis's attorneys had already announced were forthcoming.

Before sentence was passed, Thomas Bleakley took strong exception to the report due to what he characterized as "numerous infactual heresay."

"Anything particular in mind, besides the whole report is no good?" the judge inquired.

"The report is filled with numerous, numerous inaccurate facts, heresay from newspapers. It's simply a compilation of what this person (the official authoring the report) may have read in newspapers over several years," Bleakley said, adding that he was voicing a "general objection to the entire report."

The judge noted Bleakley's objection and then asked Mark Blumer if the state had any objections to the report.

"The state has no additions or objections," Blumer responded.

Prior to issuing the official sentence, Moes commented on the tremendous potential Davis had exhibited early in his life. He called Davis "educated, very smooth, very articulate, very clever." The judge pointed out that the murder had taken place after months or even years of planning. He stated that the type of act perpetrated upon society and especially upon his wife was one that prisons are made for.

Moes called Davis a "master of deception" who plotted and carried out a "murder for money." He then passed sentence: Life in prison without the possibility of parole.

Under the state's victim's rights law, the Mohrs had the opportunity to make a statement to the court before sentence was passed. However, they declined to do so.

In the confusion, Moes adjourned the court and Davis was led away.

Joe Swickard, reporter for the *Detroit Free Press,* was puzzled. Something had been overlooked.

"Isn't the judge supposed to give the defendant a chance to make a statement?" he asked Blumer.

Oh, Christ, Blumer thought. If Davis was not given the chance to make a statement, the sentencing would have to be repeated at some later time, and Mark didn't relish the idea of having to return to Hillsdale to correct this oversight. He rushed to the judge's chambers.

Davis was quickly returned and offered the chance to say something in his own behalf.

"Your Honor," Davis said in a barely audible voice. "I would say only very briefly that I have committed no crime."

Moes waved him away and the deputies ushered him out of the courtroom. He would spend this night within the walls of a full penitentiary—the first night of many.

Just prior to being led away, the deputies, for the first time in the trial, moved Davis outside the low rail separating the well of the courtroom from the spectators section. Never before had Davis been beyond the fence where he was all but mingling with the audience. The two deputies appeared not to notice that Bob Mohr was standing there. Davis appeared not to notice, either. The two men—the father of the murdered girl and the man now convicted of having murdered her—were inches apart, almost touching. Bob stood there, glaring at Davis, who never looked upon the face of his father-in-law. Within seconds the deputies led the prisoner away.

"What were you thinking just then?" a bystander asked Mohr.

"I was thinking how easy it would be to grab him around the throat and break his neck before anyone could do anything," Bob replied. That was the difference, he said, between a civilized human being and an animal.

"I would prefer the electric chair, but I'll take this," Ceil told the press, commenting on the sentence. "I feel like he gave us a death sentence, I'd like to give it to him."

"I've said right along that being in a cage the rest of his life would be worse than death for him," Bob said.

"I'd like to put a big picture of her in his cell and see what he thinks," Ceil added.

Several weeks earlier, the Mohrs, the Brittons, Mark Blumer and his wife, and a number of others connected with the seemingly endless attempt to put Davis behind bars, had gathered for a "hanging party" at Don Brooks's home in Lansing. It was a party to celebrate the successful conclusion of the Davis case.

A toast was raised to Davis during the party, a toast of hope that his every day in prison, for the rest of his life, would be agonizing beyond his endurance. The wine used in offering the toast was particularly enjoyable to those gathered. It had been found by Dick Britton when he took possession of the Lickely Road farm-house he'd bought back from David. Those gathered had raised their glasses in the hope of perpetual un-pleasantness for Davis, *using his own wine.*

Epilogue

Two days after Davis was sentenced to life in prison, Attorney General Frank J. Kelley wrote Robert Brown, director of the Michigan Department of Corrections. The letter read, in part:

> The reason for this letter is to advise you that based upon our experience in the long investigation and preparation of this case, we believe it is appropriate to consider and treat Mr. Davis as an extreme flight risk. He is very intelligent and manipulative. He has demonstrated an ability for long-range planning of his crime and escape routes. He will use disguises and alter his appearance where necessary (he lost 70 lbs. between arrest and trial). In addition, Mr. Davis is an experienced sailor and a highly qualified pilot.
>
> Because of these various factors, it took 8½ years and substantial good luck to capture Davis in Pago Pago, on the other side of the world.
>
> Whatever precautions you have at your disposal to prevent giving Mr. Davis an opportunity to disappear again would be well utilized in this case, in the interests of justice and the safety of the people of Michigan.

Originally housed in the Southern Michigan Prison in Jackson, Davis was moved—about two weeks after Kelley wrote his letter—to Marquette Prison in Michigan's Upper Peninsula.

Davis, who so hated Michigan winters, was committed to one of the coldest parts of the state. Marquette is situated on the shore of Lake Superior and is ubiquitously recognized for the icy blasts howling in winter off the frozen lake. Marquette Prison looks like a medieval fortress and is not known for its creature comforts. Its population consists of the toughest, most dangerous criminals in the state.

"He is considered an extreme escape risk and this is one of the most secure prisons in Michigan," George Pennell, administrative assistant at Marquette, told the Associated Press. "No one has escaped from here in the last twenty years."

Davis is kept locked in his cell except for a one-hour daily visit to the prison yard, meals in the dining room, and approved visits to the law library or exercise facility.

David Grassi says he has had some contact with his client since the transfer and that Davis is "not happy with his surroundings."

In the dark hours of the cold winter nights, with the wind whistling through the cracks in cell block windows and the terrible cries and curses of his fellow convicts jolting him from a mournful, cheerless slumber, Davis may well let his thoughts drift back in time and wonder if he hadn't made a single, pathetic error in an otherwise errorless scheme.

"If he had said that he had all kinds of insurance on Shannon, we would never have been suspicious of him," Ceil says. "We would have probably thought that he had been very smart to have done that. We probably would have been ashamed to have even brought the subject up."

If Davis is distressed at the dreadful consequence of his life, he seems to be alone.

In his home in Linden, Michigan, David Ellsworth Davis sits, a lonely, bitter man. He has had no contact with his son in more than fifteen years. He does not intend to have any.

"He got just what he deserves," he says sadly. "I

feel so very sorry for the family of that poor girl; I think I know how much they've suffered.''

Then, almost spontaneously, he utters a statement that the listener realizes cannot be that impulsive; he's thought long and hard about it. "It's too bad Michigan doesn't have the death penalty.''

Davis's mother tearfully acknowledges that "the happiest day in all of this tragedy was the day I heard David had been captured. I'd lived in fear during the years he was in hiding that he might do it again.''

Bob and Lucille continue to visit the small grave in the beautiful rolling, tree-shaded cemetery. There seems to be a greater feeling of peace surrounding them now.

"I feel certain Shannon was always near us, telling us to go and get him, to not give up,'' Lucille says. "Now, I think she's saying for us to get on with our lives.''

But they know there will never be a turning away from the painful realization that something irreplaceable was taken from them, a chance to live out their lives with a family that is whole, to have and enjoy the additional grandchildren they know now they will never have. There will always be a ghastly void, the greatest loss a parent can experience. They must travel through the years stretching before them, always just out of reach of the gentle touch they miss so much, forever just beyond the hearing of the loving voice and happy laugh that brightened so many years behind them.

Their hatred for the man who robbed them of a loving, giving daughter remains almost palpable. It is embodied in the stone set at the head of her grave. In a desperate act of contempt for their former son-in-law, the Mohrs battled for a year with cemetery officials to insure that their beloved daughter not spend eternity branded with his hated name. The small carved stone reads simply:

OUR DAUGHTER
SHANNON L. MOHR R.N.

Acknowledgments

I cannot publically thank all of those whose patient generosity and understanding made this book possible. However, I could not fail to acknowledge the assistance of some of those without whom this work could never have been completed.

Because of the priceless help provided me by Bob and Lucille Mohr, I gained a better understanding of what strength and faith and determination truely is. This incredible couple is a magnificent example of the best in parents, in citizens, and in human beings. I feel I am better for having known them.

Richard and Ann Britton, with typical country hospitality, welcomed me into their home and suffered my intrusions with good nature and total cooperation. Their help could not have been replaced.

To the many friends and relatives of Bob and Lucille, whose contribution was vital to this project, I express my heartfelt appreciation.

I owe a particular debt of gratitude to a pair of journalists. Billy Bowles, the former *Detroit Free Press* reporter who must be credited with creating a climate of interest and concern in what happened to Shannon Davis, made available his total collection of notes taken over a nine-year period and travels halfway around the world. The notebooks were a priceless contribution to my efforts, and they were given freely and without urging. I felt particularly proud to have been shown such magnanimity from the one person I felt was most qualified to have written this story. And

Debbie Myers, formerly with the *Hillsdale Daily News*, took much of her own valuable time to gather needed news clips that made my research so very much easier.

To the publisher and staff of the *Hillsdale Daily News*, who made many of the photographs appearing herein available to me on short notice, I express my deep appreciation.

To Cecil "Woody" Woodbury, Don and Dolores Woodbury, Sheryl Myers, Kelley Zahn, Darrell Staples, and Judy Williams, the owners and staff of Active Business Machines in Toledo, who made available the word processing system on which this work was written, who kept the equipment in constant working order, and saw to it that I had the necessary supplies with which to use it, I owe a great deal.

To Frank J. Kelley, the durable, tireless attorney general of the state of Michigan, I would like to express my thanks for his willingness to open his files on the David Davis case and to spend his valuable time with me, assisting me in understanding some of the complexities of his office and the workings of his staff. He has added to my already great pride in my own Irish heritage.

Bob Ianni, chief of the criminal division of the attorney general's office, must be commended for his quiet forbearance and good humor while enduring my disruption of normal routine.

Mark Blumer was a constant, invaluable reservoir of information and assistance for me in the preparation of this book. He was always available to answer questions and provide materials to me, and he consistently did so with a pleasant enthusiasm that made my frequent visits to his offices over many months not only incredibly fruitful but an exciting, gratifying experience, one I shall deeply miss now that there is no longer an excuse for my visits.

Don Brooks was the first principal in the drama surrounding the David Davis case who offered to assist me in my preparations to write this book. His contribution not only to my efforts but to the successful res-olution of the case cannot be overstated. It is my hope that he prospers and continues to achieve.

Mark Blumer once said of Doug Barrett that he "has absolutely no ego; he has no interest in applause, pub-licity, or credit. He is unaffected by publicity or media attention." Mark, as I discovered, could not have been more correct. Doug cooperated with me whenever I called on him, and did it in a quiet unassuming man-ner that I found refreshing and impressive. Unfortu-nately, because of his desire to stay in the background, I fear that much of the contribution he made to the Davis case will forever remain unheralded.

Marney Kast, the delightful deputy court clerk for Hillsdale County's circuit court, wins my respect and appreciation for her willingness to help obtain infor-mation I needed whenever she was able to do so, and to commiserate when court rules or legal roadblocks made it impossible for her to provide documents and other materials I sought.

I wish to thank the citizens of Hillsdale for the gen-tle kindness they extended to we outsiders who in-vaded and disrupted their beautiful, quiet community over the long process of seeing that justice was done. They made me feel welcome.

It is a sad truth that the completion of a project such as this brings with it a depressing melancholy. It fre-quently means that friendships developed over the long process required to produce a book of this type slowly fade and eventually disappear, as the necessity to move on to other things and other places makes protecting and nurturing these associations difficult and some-times impossible. I hope such will not be the case here.

Toledo attorney Jack Callahan deserves a word of thanks. A close, faithful friend, Jack was always avail-able to answer puzzling legal questions, acting as a handy, helpful source of information no matter what hour I needed it.

And finally, I owe a monumental expression of appreciation to my wife, Ann, and my children, John, Matthew, William, and Meredith. They have been a neverending fountain of inspiration and support for me during the long, lonely hours required in preparing this work. It would have been impossible for me to have accomplished whatever I have without their dedication.